THE GILTY PARTY

The Alchemist's Agent No. 1

E. M. BURNHAM

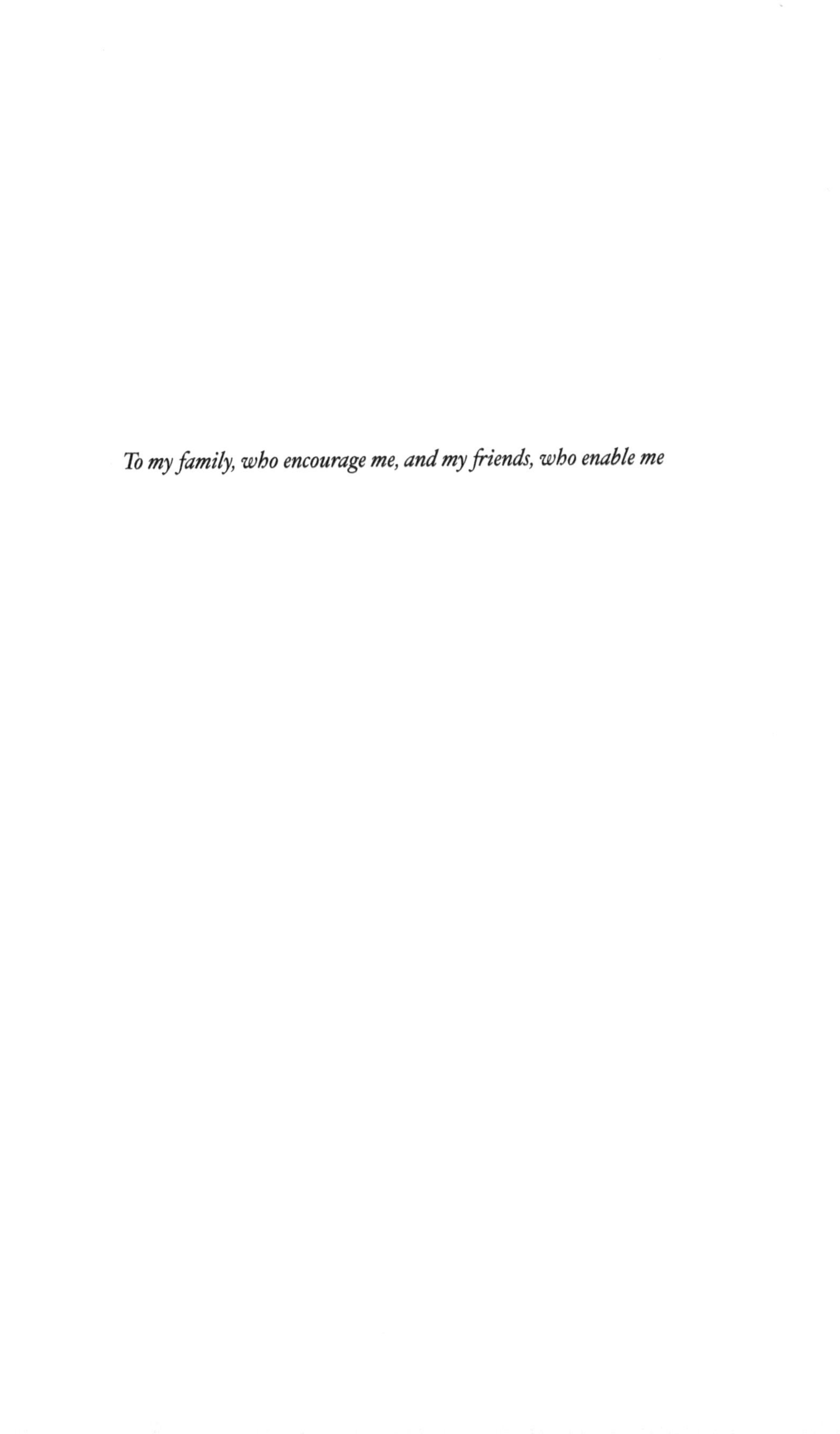

To my family, who encourage me, and my friends, who enable me

CONTENTS

❀ I ❀

Ibram Ucalegon rubbed the back of his neck as the swaying aerial gondola he traveled in rolled down its thick wire hauling rope. Their carriage shuddered to a halt on the track line at the relay station. A platform conductor held her hand up to the window while the gondola was redirected to the next line, and Ibram nodded, though he doubted she could see him. Beside him, Ahksell Solari, childhood friend and all-around fussbudget, leaned closer to the window and waved to the burly servants pushing their gondola from one section of the station to the next. He had to hunch down to do so, but Ahksell was both huge and friendly, and so never seemed to mind contorting into the oddest positions in order to fit in a courtesy.

"If you'd wanted breakfast, *Attendant* Solari," Ibram continued as he shuffled to the window screen next to the door to give Ahksell a little more breathing room. "You could have just eaten in your dormitory with the rest of your compatriots."

Ahksell grinned and shrugged. "But no one sets out a breakfast like your mother!"

Ibram rolled his eyes. They were alone in the carriage, which suited him well since that meant they could speak normally rather than whisper in order to spare the ears of their fellow passengers. Like many folk in the surrounding villages, Ibram's daily journey up the living mountain to the Sect of Seven Fires involved a carriage, two perpetual wheels, and a diversion from the imperial road through the deeply disturbing lift system which acted as the mountain's central transportation. It was rare that he had any space to breathe at all.

The aerial gondola rocked into its tracks as two different burly servants attached the spring-loaded grip to the hauling rope which rose up the mountain. Ibram swallowed heavily. Not that the air was doing him any good, regardless of personal space.

Ahksell waved at them as well, and then grabbed Ibram's shoulder for balance as they began to sway upwards. Ibram braced his feet; they both wobbled but soon found their footing again. The relay station dropped away from view.

"Besides," Ahksell protested, and Ibram tore his attention from the window. "Mentor Hobon wanted to speak with you, and I had no other plans."

"Which I would have learned when I went up the mountain without you needing to fetch me," Ibram pointed out. "Since I do that every morning. For my work."

Ahksell shrugged; it looked rather like a mountain range resettling itself. At all reports, Ahksell's growth spurt had begun soon after Ibram gone away and Ibram saw no evidence that it had stopped since his return. Ibram sniffed and turned back to the wire screen window. Deep green treetops waved beneath him; he grit his teeth. What a horrible way to travel.

Surely cutting a swath of roads up from the base of the mountain range had to be better than this—this lugging back and forth, like they were in the lunch pail of a giant walker. Simply because Ibram had never seen a better system in all his travels didn't make the relays the best. Other kingdoms doubtless had their own methods. He glanced about himself while Ahksell began to hum a tune Ibram didn't recognize. Their carriage featured four large square wire screened windows —an amazing expense if they hadn't been made by the alchemists themselves. It provided Ibram an excellent view of the world and his little place within it.

If he could manage to maneuver himself around Ahksell to face the back he might see the village of Lityen, where he'd been born and raised. To his left—upwards of course—perched the Preceptory of Yseult, seventh domicile of the Sect of Seven Fires, pride of the Vissilian Empire, nestled within the Emerald Mountains on the most western edge of the province of Vanima, a haven for alchemists and academics, and the sort of folk who enjoyed setting fires to find out what might burn. Ibram, for his sins, was employed there in a more-or-less unofficial family tradition.

"You come down the living mountain and eat my ama's cooking, but you won't tell me what Ladyship wants, even though you expressly came to the house to tell me she wants me to come to work," Ibram said. "This was your plan."

Ahksell grinned. "You know the mentor," he said. "I didn't want to prejudice you about the Monbriths."

Mentor Hobon—or Lady Azadiya Hobon, as Ibram knew her—operated out of her tower in Yseult as its Fourth Mentor. The preceptory believed in the refinement of the physical body, which seemed to mean they drank a plethora of oddly colored, often smoking, infusions and then gained the ability to jump very high and float boulders out of farmer's fields. If they were very good at it, they might gain enough control to not require their potions and pills; Ibram didn't want to know how they achieved that. Ahksell might have told him, but Ibram had firmly decided never to inquire.

"The Monbriths?" Ibram repeated. He furrowed his eyebrows. "What about them? I sent in that report two months ago."

"I don't think I was supposed to say that," Ahksell winced. He looked out the window, squinting. "Let's talk about the view instead."

Ibram poked him in the arm; Ahksell poked him back. The aerial gondola swayed upwards.

"You have to be the worst Attendant Yseult's ever produced," Ibram declared. "Not only have you never been in a fight in your life, you're also the least discreet man I've ever known."

Alchemists were supposed to be like cooks, hoarding their secret recipes and only releasing their by-products for a neat profit. Being the seventh preceptory, Yseult should have been more anxious than most to protect its secrets, yet its members were far more likely to play down their alchemical craft and stress their emphasis on physical education. Ibram had once heard Lady Azadiya declare that all anyone needed to join Yseult was the ability to dance.

It was just a smokescreen, really, to make them seem as approachable as an alchemist could be. Yseult tended to act as a kind of catch-all for the day-to-day affairs of the villages and farms that lay within the Imperial boundary which separated the Sect of Seven Fires from its more commonplace neighbors. Non-specific requests for mediation between angry competitors or a local investigation that no one wanted to bother a warder over always made their way to Lady Azadiya's desk somehow. That was where Ibram and the rest of Ladyship's agents came in, supplying discreet and professional service of whatever type might be needed.

"Oh now, that's not fair," Ahksell said. "I've been in a fight."

He reached up and touched the blocky black embroidery which covered the closure of his standing collared gambeson at the side of his neck, marking his association with the Preceptory of Yseult. The little stylized mongoose jumped when he swallowed.

Ibram snorted. "Running around the apple orchard being chased by bees is not a fight."

Ahksell shrugged. "Anything you can walk away from."

Ibram frowned down at his feet. What could Ladyship want to know about the Monbriths that he hadn't written in his report? It had been a very cut and dried case, if he recalled correctly. An old man—an itinerant blacksmith—had died, and Ibram had been sent out as a courtesy to the headwoman of the village to make sure everything was above board. The Monbriths had owned the draughtshop where the body had been found. It had all seemed rather mundane, to be sure.

He rubbed his thumb against his eyebrow. The thought that Lady Azadiya might be displeased with him made the back of his neck tighten in stress. Officially, he was employed by the Sect and merely attached to this particular preceptory, but in practice he was...well, in a way he was an illegal legacy hire. His mother had been an agent for the Preceptory of Yseult as he was now, and his father and sister were artisans who mostly took commissions from the Sect of Seven Fires.

Alchemists were forbidden by imperial law from having personal retainers; Ibram preferred to think of it as a grey area.

The swaying gondola swung to a gently rolling stop at the clearing station outside the preceptory. Two workers caught each side of the carriage and then pulled it along the short track to the disembarking platform before the next arriving gondola could smash into them. The platform conductor raised both hands and came up to the door to unhook the lock. Ibram lunged for freedom first and stood on the thick wooden beams, breathing the crisp mountain air. It smelled like hot metal and tree sap; he sneezed.

"It's the same air in the gondola, you know," Ahksell said.

"I don't believe you," Ibram muttered. He continued to breathe deeply.

The workers ignored them, already towing the empty gondola out of the way of the next one approaching. Ibram jerked his head, and then he and Ahksell stepped off the platform and down the broad stone stairway that lead to the compound proper. Ahead of them lay the huge metal and granite gates of the preceptory, opened to all visitors, but guarded by gigantic sparking lodestones set into the walls in a diamond pattern. Ama had told him once, when Ibram was a child, that the lodestones were infused with lightning, in such great amounts as to put the security locks folk put on their valuables to shame. She claimed invaders laying siege to Yseult would find a very lively welcome, but now that he was older Ibram didn't put much stock into it. No one had laid siege to so much as a rebellious hamlet in centuries, after all.

Ahksell fell into step with him once they passed through into Yseult, a courtesy which Ibram silently appreciated in deference to his own shorter legs. The Preceptory of Yseult resided in the lowest section of the sect's complex, for which placement, Ibram thanked Yilka the Green daily. A man still had to conquer the steep gradient of the lower sect courtyard to gain access to the interior, but at least Ibram had never gotten a nosebleed out of it. A few other agents of the sect greeted him as Ibram walked through, and bowed to Ahksell in passing. The sun was out, but not yet powerful enough to make its heat felt. Ibram tugged on his high collar and brushed a hand down the sect badge on his chest. His stomach gurgled.

"Here," Ahksell said. He dug into his belt pouch and then held out a wax paper bag full of crystalized ginger.

Stiff breezes ruffled Ibram's hair as he walked; he tucked the loose strands behind both ears. Ibram swallowed heavily. The trip up the living mountain always sent his stomach writhing, and only time had managed to reduce his queasiness to a level where he could mostly ignore it. Ahksell held the bag out and shook the contents. With a groan, Ibram grabbed the biggest piece of ginger he could feel from the bag, and then popped it into his mouth. They veered right down one of the smaller alleys that branched off from the main stone courtyard.

Yseult was conservative for a preceptory, no strange odors or mysterious outbreaks of dancing fever, and only the occasional unexpected explosion. It sprawled with training fields and wooden pavilions, stone dormitories and work buildings, and several garden manors responsible for feeding the mentors, attendants, learners and support staff who lived there. He glanced up at the First Mentor's manor house as they passed by and sucked on his ginger meditatively. A honeycomb manor was probably meant to make visitors from below feel at home when they arrived, but an entire palace raised out of the mountain, whole-cloth, without seam or joint? It just didn't seem altogether friendly.

He bit into the ginger and chewed the fibers, swallowing down the burn. His stomach grumbled to itself. Ibram nodded at the soldier standing guard outside the miniscule Scribes' Bureau tucked into the shadow of the other buildings. All the preceptories had them, a small nod to the empire's continuing interest. The guard nodded back, and then Ahksell had taken the corner and disappeared, which forced Ibram into a walk that could have been called a run in order to catch up.

"Why does Ladyship want the Monbrith report again?" he asked.

Ahksell's head wobbled left and then right. "She didn't say," he replied finally. "But I would wager it has something to do with the runners they sent up late last night."

Ibram paused until he remembered the name of the village. "Runners from Fontis?"

Ahksell guided them down the tree-lined path that led away from the main buildings. "One of them came up around the evening meal," he said, and then lowered his voice. "But the other had an Imperial badge worked in silver on his chest. He went straight to the Preceptory of Salacia."

Ibram glanced up at that, and caught Ahksell looking just as grim as he felt. The Imperial falcon in silver meant the Bureau of Justice and its Cohorts of Peace and Vigilance. Not the typical visitor up the living mountain at all. The sect was officially a loyal Vissilian guild, of course, but no one wanted an Imperial embarrassment on their back terrace. They walked past the training grounds in silence.

"Has Lady Sebbina requested a visit?" Ibram asked as they turned down the little courtyard outside the Attendants dormitories.

"Her Gracious Majesty's most cherished representative has not come up," Ahksell said. He leaned in closer, which was a bit like being loomed over by a boulder. "But Salacia's Second Mentor has been down the mountain since the first runner came to see Mentor Hobon and *she* has been in her office—oh, shh!"

Ahksell straightened and nodded sternly to a group of learners rushing up the path with their practice gars in hand. They had to be no more than ten in number, but more than made up for it in noise. The children parted to either side of them on the pathway, and Ibram batted one of the thick ash wood sticks out of his face. He glanced over his shoulder as the little ones clattered up the hill in a swirl of chatter. He raised his eyebrows at Ahksell, who shook his head; they walked on.

Lady Azadiya Hobon lived off by the inner curtain wall. As the Fourth Mentor, it was Ladyship's right to live wherever she well pleased, but Ibram was always struck by how odd the place looked amidst its surroundings, even here with its impossible lacy stone architecture. The middle of the empire—what they called the garden provinces—built their homes into equal, elegant sections, with shared walls mimicking honeycombs to capitalize on space. Lady Azadiya's tower squatted in seclusion, with its own kitchen garden and laboratory.

There was even a small stables for a palfrey and an old grey destrier of fourteen hands. From the outside, it looked like it had drifted off from some Western fortified castle with thick, smooth stone walls that stretched up for three stories and a tiled roof, and the windows set high up from the ground. The white plaster was always crumbling into the Spiny Orange bushes growing along the base of her home, and the huge stone slabs used as doors looked like they could withstand a siege.

Ahksell pulled the braided bell rope attached to a lodestone riveted to the outer wall, and then pushed open the doors and disappeared inside. Ibram followed, but rested his hand on the door as he passed over the threshold. Each eight foot tall rock was weighted by charms to swing lightly as a cloud, despite being more than two hands wide, but just walking past them made him want to shiver.

The tower's inhabitants were at work, as usual, with servants and learners scampering underfoot, and Attendants in green tunics carrying supplies and gigantic paper scrolls from one room into another. It often seemed like the whole of Vissilia swirled in the ranks of the Sect of Seven Fires, the muddled masses of a sprawling empire from the sea peoples to the mountain dwellers, the plainsmen and the denizens of the valleys. Ibram even knew of a few Eastern horsemen up in the Preceptory of Baran, explaining how their wind demons were actually gods. Yseult seemed to attract mostly folk from the garden provinces and the rivers, but these days a few pale Northerners had made their home there as well.

The lodestone bell tolled loudly as they walked underneath the wooden balcony. Somehow—no one had ever explained—the tiled ceiling was transparent inside the tower, and filled the stories below with daylight, directed by polished reflecting mirrors. Ibram paused to allow a flock of learners herded by their teacher out of the doors, and found himself staring down into the sunken main area.

The large intricate metal and stone fountain burbled in the center of the room, crowded by low couches piled high in cushions. On each couch sprawled Lady Azadiya's agents, seconded to her from the pool of arms-for-hire employed by the Sect. Ibram's avowed 'amitai,' his uncles and aunts, made up the bulk of them. They were no relation to his mother at all, but Merrilians behaved like Merrilians, no matter where they lived. They wore dark wool robes with ribs of silver embroidery down the front and worn stiff wool breeches, and their fur-topped boots came up to their knees. None of them wore a house badge or even an obvious clan bracelet, but each bore the hammered silver torch buckle connecting a leather strap to their wide belts. Ibram wore the same buckle against his chest. Technically, he was of an even rank as well, though no one ever acted like it.

Someone shouted for a song. In two seconds, one of them would have a gittern out, and then it was a fond farewell to good sense. Ibram walked along the row of potted plants, and smacked a stinging euphorbia when it tried to bite him. He craned his neck up and saw Lady Azadiya out on the second floor landing, throwing a glowing rock across the tower to one of her attendants. She kept her hand extended, conducting it to the other side of the building as it dipped and swirled like a bird in flight.

Ibram shouted, "What do you mean 'you want the Monbrith report'?"

The horde in the tower barely registered the new noise. High above him, Lady Azadiya leaned over with one hand gripping the ladder attached to the second and third floor railing. Her oval face, sharp-chinned and tan, looked down at him in the sort of fondness Ibram often imagined cats felt for smaller cats who did whatever they were told. Her dark hair, softly braided into one mass, fell down her shoulder and swung idly in the air. She had golden pins holding the rest of it off her face in a half-circle, and Ibram's father's best filigree work dripped from her ears and neck.

"I mean what I say!" she yelled down at him. Well, called strenuously. Nobles never yelled, that would admit inconvenience. "Come up, come up!"

She waved her hand like she was scooping air to the vaulted ceiling, and then disappeared. Ibram took a moment to brush down his clothing and make sure the hilt of his sica was tied securely at his waist. A complicated chord stuttered its way out from the crowd in the center of the ground floor, and Ibram launched himself up the wide stairway that curved around the entire interior of the tower with Ahksell close behind.

"You got any more of that ginger?" Ibram asked, glancing over his shoulder. He turned back just in time to dodge a maid carrying her bodyweight in expensive linen.

The wax paper bag appeared over his shoulder. He grabbed it, and rooted inside. Below, the amitai were threatening to sing.

"Still with the stomach?" Ahksell asked.

Ibram dug out another chunk of sugared ginger, and popped it in his mouth. He licked his fingers clean. "You still live sideways off a gigantic mountain, to be sure."

"It's not sideways," Ahksell said. "We're perfectly safe."

He scooted left to avoid an Attendant about to make the fatal mistake of reading a pamphlet while walking; Ahksell snagged her elbow and rerouted her into an empty room. Ibram wiped his fingers off on the sleeve of his green and brown leather gambeson. "There are 114 steps just to get to the lower courtyard, and a sheer drop with absolutely no handrail."

"Ah, but that's why we have the relays!" Ahksell laughed at him, but by then they were on the second floor outside Ladyship's office, and Ibram couldn't respond appropriately. He tossed the bag over his shoulder, and then straightened his collar as he entered with a short knock on the door lintel. Doors were never closed in the tower unless someone needed a great deal more privacy than Lady Azadiya normally tolerated. Ama said it was just that alchemists grew peculiar as they aged, but Ibram thought that was one of the half-truths they both favored in place of outright lying. He was pretty sure at whatever age Ladyship had escaped from the nursery into the world the doors had been flung wide in a matter of seconds.

The noise outside lowered to a murmur as Ibram walked further into the room on account of the pumice and bluestone tiles fixed to the lintels and floor. Lady Azadiya sat at her desk, writing something into one of her wooden ledgers with a green engraving pen that smoked as she sketched. He bowed with his hands on his stomach, and straightened almost immediately. It was an airy room, with large windows pouring down light from the loft on the third level, which had no stairs, nor ladder, nor even rope access, but could only be reached through alchemy.

Ahksell clapped him on the back as he went past to poke the bubbling glass cylinder Lady Azadiya held suspended by three thin steel chains from the ceiling; it sloshed and released a green smoke. Ahksell seemed delighted.

While Lady Azadiya finished her writing, Ibram glanced at the walls draped in white and red patterned tapestries. A long, curved wooden set of shelves lurked in the back, and the floor was dense with layered black-worked rugs. Plants and light globes hung from the beams in the ceiling. He eyed the back of one of the heavily carved chairs near Ladyship's desk, padded with thick pillows and tightly woven blankets. He remained standing.

Lady Azadiya set her engraving pen back into its portable furnace. She sat back in her wide, comfortable chair behind her enormous dark wood desk, and raised one eyebrow. Ibram sucked his ginger.

"You know, if you would stop closing your eyes every time you take the relay, you wouldn't have these episodes," she said. When she was at home, her Western accent lilted like burbling water.

"I don't close my eyes anymore," he said, but his weight shifted from one foot to the other without his permission. Ibram crunched down on the sugar coating and swallowed, and then cleared his throat.

"It does move very quickly, Mentor," Ahksell said, before Ibram could speak.

She shrugged, but nodded. She stood up to lean across the desk and tapped a small stack of loose sheets of paper. With one quick wave of her fingers, she spread them out in a fan. Ibram frowned.

"Those are my notes," he said, "and that's the paperwork the head-woman Mistress Denrind sent with me for you."

"And do you recognize the last bit of handwriting?" Ladyship asked.

He shook his head, and took a step closer to the desk. It didn't sit well with him that she'd taken the trouble to bring out the entire bundle from her archives to speak about the Monbriths, who hadn't really been involved except in a small legal capacity. He'd never seen her need to consult a single page after she had read it before.

"What prompted you sending for me, Ladyship?" he asked. "I woke late in the belief that peace had broken out in Vissilia."

"Ibram," she gasped and put one hand to her collarbones. "The grand Vissilian Empire is a bastion of peace from the Ice Sea to the Gulf of Summer!"

He felt the left corner of his mouth curl up. "And every subject free from strife."

"*Ibram*," Ahksell whispered in embarrassment.

"From the blessing of her gracious Imperial Majesty, may her sandals never touch dirt," she said, and then snorted. "Can I help when I am called upon, Ib-la?"

"You know that makes me sound like a children's sweet drink," he pointed out.

She ignored this. "Now, I have called upon you, and what do you do? Do you ask me what the matter is?"

"I just did." He waved his hand at Ahksell. "I have a witness."

"I see nothing but through my Mentor's eyes," Ahksell said.

"This is why you—"

"Enough, thank you." Ladyship pinched her ring finger and thumb together, and Ibram felt a distinct tug on his right ear. He shut his mouth.

Lady Azadiya came around the other side of her desk. The soft outer layers of her dress floated as she moved. She was out of uniform, but then Mentors were allowed a great deal more freedom than the lower ranks. For herself, she was dressed down. Her teal silk dress, high-necked and painted with purple and gold tennic birds, moved easily with all those layers, and her reinforced boots made the smallest sound on the polished wooden floor. She grinned, and flashed too many even white teeth for polite society.

"The Monbriths," she prompted. "I notice they appear in your notes, but do not feature."

Oh hang, something had really gone wrong in Fontis since Ibram had visited. "Small householders out past Fontis," Ibram said, going back over the facts as he recalled them. "They keep a draughtshop that doubles as an inn at the edges of their land, and grow marrows. Two sons, the oldest not very bright, and a daughter wasting her potential. The father died four years ago, and the mother never remarried. They have no idea how the body of Harken Tolk got to their syah berry patch, and they doubtless preferred that he'd found a nice timoleon bog to drown in, instead."

"Alas, two hundred miles off," Lady Azadiya said.

"One of the sons was the First Finder, wasn't he?" Ahksell asked. "The...younger one, I think."

"No, it was the oldest boy," Ibram said. "The middle child."

"Very well remembered though, Ahk-la," she said. "I fear we have reached the salient point."

"The salient... Oh, *hang*," Ibram groaned. "Ladyship, do not say it."

"I fear I must," she said. Her dark eyes tilted dangerously upwards in amusement.

"He had every moment in the world to screw up his courage!"

"Alas his courage remains quite loose," she said, and tapped the stack of papers. "I am informed by several letters that the second Monbrith child has not only failed to appear in court to explain his finding of the body, but he has himself gone off...probably to find his own timoleon bog, if he's smart enough."

Ibram groaned again. "He isn't."

"To be certain," Lady Azadiya agreed. She crossed her arms and walked to the back of her room. She pulled a stack of bound wooden slats and held it open in two hands, and then returned to her desk to set the stack down. Ibram could see the symbols burned into the wood as a set of formulae. He frowned and glanced at Ahksell, who shook his head.

"Have the warders been sent out?" Ibram asked.

Lady Azadiya nodded. "The circuit judge sent from the Court Civil was unamused."

"Also, you're wrong," Ahksell said.

"I beg your pardon?" Ibram twisted to stare at him.

Ahksell shrugged and lifted his hands. "They're not past Fontis."

"Yes, they are, that's why they sell rooms above their draughtshop. There's no other place large enough."

"*Yes*, but they're still within Imperial limits," he said. "So they count."

Ibram scrubbed his eyebrow. "Which means it's not the Monbriths alone who will be fined for not appearing in court."

"Fontis will also be punished accordingly," Ladyship said with a sigh. She tapped the wooden slat in front of her and then pulled the papers on top of her bundle. "And if this announcement I've received from Salacia runs true, then if the First Finder is not discovered, the village will be interdicted for the full fifty years, rather than a nicely manageable oppressive fine."

"Interdicted?" Ibram asked. The back of his head tightened.

She lifted one shoulder. "Sanctioned."

"But no one gets sanctioned anymore," Ahksell protested. "Not since…I don't even remember when!"

"The third year of Empress Soliya II's reign," Lady Azadiya said. She held up a piece of paper, frowned at it, and then set it down again.

"Isn't the usual response just a heavy fine?" Ibram asked.

She nodded. "Which says to me there must be something going on down there to prompt such a harsh prospective ruling."

"A prospective ruling?" Ahksell repeated. "So the judge might change their mind."

"To be sure," Ladyship said, though she didn't sound it.

Ibram's stomach grew heavy. Any kind of ruling that disrupted trade in Fontis impacted not just the village, but their entire corner of the province. A raising of the rates to pay off a court fine might slow trade for a while, but sanctioning sounded much worse. He tried to think what that meant, and could only stir a feeling of revulsion in his memory.

"Ladyship, how is a sanctioning even accomplished?" Ibram asked.

She shook her head and braced herself on her desk with both hands. "I would have you focus on the matter at hand," she said. "We can expand your education at a more convenient date, but the impact of this must be assessed immediately." She huffed in amusement. "You have been requested personally, you know."

"Me? Personally?" Ibram straightened up, and then tilted his head. "So to avoid their own work, the judge asks us to intervene?"

She shook her head. The morning light made her already youthful face seem even younger, but Ibram discarded the thought. She had looked the same age since they had been formally introduced when he was ten years of age. Alchemists were all like that.

"The Monbrith heir sent you a message addressed to the sect, after which I requested the viewing of these court documents from Mentor Armida," she said, and waved her hand at the stack of papers again. The mongoose signet ring on her first finger gleamed, and Ibram could just see the beaded end of her clan bracelet. He stepped up to the desk and looked down at the pile.

"You liked her, didn't you?" she asked suddenly.

"The younger Mistress Monbrith knows her mind," he said, and picked up the top paper. It was addressed to him in cheap brown ink but written in a firm hand, almost elegant. "Her name is Satya."

He glanced over the letter. Satya's request for aid sounded urgent, but the tone of her writing was also bewildered. Events seemed to have progressed quickly after he'd left Fontis. A dim—a very dim—memory of a classroom lesson wafted upward in Ibram's mind. A sanctioning was a municipal shunning, a holdover from ancient days when alchemists served in the royal courts of kingdoms long since absorbed into the empire. Some of them had even ruled those lost dominions. He rubbed his thumb over his eyebrow. In the firetale his teacher had told the class, even five years sanctioned could be the death of a village. No trade, no leaving, and no doubt, Satya Monbrith knew who her neighbors would punish first when tempers flared.

He set the paper down. "Ladyship, how can the judge do it? The whole village is bisected by an imperial road—an important one at that."

Ibram frowned. It was illegal to block an imperial road; the Judge's proclamation would invoke one law by outraging another. Lady Azadiya tugged on the end of her braid.

"That is none of your concern as of yet," Ladyship reminded him. "Mistress Monbrith the younger would like us to find her brother in the hope that his return would intercede with the court's displeasure."

"Do we agree?" Ibram asked, and looked up.

"No, the warders know how to search and it's best to leave them to their business." She twirled the fingers of her right hand. "I think there is nothing you as my agent can do that the Cohort of Peace already searching the area are not in the process of accomplishing."

Ibram brought up his hand without thought and just stopped

himself from rubbing his eyebrow. He'd been trying to break himself of the habit. The Imperial Ministry of Order had two main bureaus: Justice and Administration. The Bureau of Justice contained the Cohort of Peace for all Her Gracious Majesty's judicial needs and the Cohort of Vigilance in case anything Soliya IV owned caught on fire. Ibram much preferred working with the latter, but society was structured differently in the lands immediately surrounding an alchemical sect.

"No one could run far this near the living mountain," he said. "Even a day's ride out would place them in grabbing distance of a warder patrol."

In addition to the main garrison at Delbrite, the Cohort of Peace had warders stationed in strategic points all around the villages that relied upon the patronage of the Sect of Seven Fires. Ibram sometimes thought that their little corner of Vanima was more accurately described as a series of imperial waystations dotted by the occasional village. He often tripped over them in the course of his duties for Lady Azadiya.

"Who has been assigned the case?" he asked. "Vainamonien? Ilme?"

Lady Azadiya shook her head. "Commander Osthanes himself," she said. "Brought specially from Delbrite."

Ibram whistled lowly. "How did that come about?"

"I believe he was requested personally by the judge." Ladyship sighed and tugged on the end of her braid. "Something caused Rustam Monbrith to run when it was absolutely not in his best interests. Something has been overlooked, Ib-la. When you are searching for a man, you must investigate him as well."

He swallowed, and glanced at Ahksell, who winced. "You mean, I missed something."

She nodded.

"And now the village is paying the price." The back of Ibram's head throbbed. "I tell you, Ladyship, I don't know what else I could have done. Master Harken Tolk was dead when I arrived and nothing about his death, nor his corpse or belongings struck me as odd."

"And yet," she said.

Ibram sighed. "And yet," he repeated. "Do I tell Satya—I mean, the young Mistress Monbrith that I am investigating her brother and not looking for him?"

"No," Ladyship said after a moment of consideration. "I think we shall keep that between ourselves for now. And, if you hear something to indicate Monbrith's whereabouts, more to the good. Regardless, the request must be answered."

"I'll read through my notes again, and be at Fontis tomorrow," he said.

Ladyship resettled her sleeve, and rubbed her fingers over the trimstone bead of her clan bracelet. "Take Ahksell with you this time."

Ibram frowned. "What? Why should he come?"

"I want a closer look into the body," she said. "They left it under a sealing charm, of course. Let us see what Ahk-la can make of it."

"The man was in his seventies," Ibram protested. "His corpse was immaculate. I can tell the difference between a murdered man and a merely dead one."

"And yet this young Monbrith has run away from all his life's responsibilities, and there was no reading of the body based on my own agent's report," she said. "Kivan the Red will have answers."

Ibram did not groan aloud at that assertion, but it was a close run thing. It was typical that Lady Azadiya brought in Kivan the Red rather than the magistrate's looming wrath. Ladyship didn't give the filip for the Imperial presence within Vanima.

"You aren't even dedicated to him," he said. "How could this be any concern of his?"

She raised her eyebrows and Ibram settled back on his heels. He cleared his throat. "Not that Catha the Grey is uninterested in justice," he muttered.

"Twins naturally share interests," Lady Azadiya agreed. "But perhaps we should concentrate on the matter at hand."

Ibram had never put the question to her, but it was odd for Ladyship to be dedicated to the Western goddess of death and recompense, while most of her agents had been dedicated at birth to the Western god of fair justice and mercy. Ibram often wondered why Ama had given him to Yilka the Green, the three-faced goddess of skillful hands, but she was certainly an easier divine being to do proud.

"It is strange." Ibram swallowed. "But, Ladyship, I investigated the body and the site where it was found. Rustam—he was shaken, but nothing was out of the ordinary concerning Tolk's body, nor his room at the Monbriths' draughtshop."

Ladyship looked to her right. "Who will take your classes?"

"Dasa owes me a favor or three," Ahksell said immediately. "She can take over for me—and she just started gemstone resonance, so running back over base metals might conjure up a break through."

Lady Azadiya smiled, and readjusted her sleeves over her wrists. "Well enough."

"Can I take the carriage?" Ahksell asked.

"We can simply ride there! There's nothing wrong with my sister's horse," Ibram said. "Pick a nag from the sect's stable."

"A nag," Ahksell said. He had entirely too much fondness for animals, and it showed in the growing affront of his raised voice.

Ibram held up both his hands, and groaned. "Ahksell."

"Pick a *nag*," Ahksell said in an incredulous tone.

"Carriage it is," Lady Azadiya said.

I bram woke early, pulled on the clothes he'd left to air overnight, and then ran down the stairs, while trying to strap down his little wrist wallet one-handed. He had two such purses, of course, one hidden beneath his sleeve and the other larger one strapped to his belt before his sica. Both of them were sealed with alchemy, and needed the heat of his fingers to unlock. He had supplied himself with sufficient funds from his small pay to have enough for meat in his meals rather than only quash. If they were lucky, it wouldn't cost him more than a silver picaio or two before the whole affair was wrapped up.

Kholdo, their housekeeper, wasn't in the kitchen, but there was a tray of baked sweet buns steaming on the counter, brown-topped and fat with chopped dried cinnaks. Ibram tore free a particularly large roll on his way past, licking honey from his fingers as he ran through the house. He grabbed a cloak from the hook by the front door and slung it over his shoulders.

The year was still slogging its way through spring, and so the sky was as grey as a stone, and inclined to drip with rain. When he reached the front gates, Ahksell greeted him with a sleepy wave from the driving bench of one of the sect's smaller carriages. A bay horse, almost a pony, with a thick mane and a short muscular neck snuffled the air and shook its head in the harness. Ahksell hushed it. He was dressed in the quilted deep green wool gambeson and grey wrapped breeches the Sect of Seven Fires handed out to roaming alchemists, with all those diagonal buttons pulling double duty as fashionable protection. Ahksell's plain brown half-cloak was tossed off one shoulder and Ibram couldn't see the seven-foot pyrus wood gar that said he was out on official business. No doubt, it was strapped down within the carriage. He examined the overlapping scales draped along the carriage's low curved roof and the leather flap that covered the single window. Two men might sleep comfortably within it, if they didn't mind breaking their backs through a night on wooden benches.

"Take it that Ladyship doesn't want me accepting the Monbriths' hospitality again?" Ibram set the bun between his teeth, and then tucked his thumbs in his broad leather belt. His cloak flapped at his knees and slid off his shoulders.

"Good morning," Ahksell said. He picked up a glass apple from the driving bench and took an enormous bite from its remaining flesh. The sunlight dappled on its iridescent skin.

Ibram yawned, caught the falling bun, and shook his head. He bent down to pick up his cloak. "No hard feelings about yesterday?"

Ahksell shrugged, and another glass apple appeared, hovering about his other hand. "Figure it's the duty of the young to make up for the mistakes of their elders."

Against his will, Ibram laughed. He hauled his sleepy carcass up onto the driving bench, and sat down on his cloak next to Ahksell, making sure he didn't catch his belted sica under his own thigh. The short inwardly curved blade had been a present on his sixteenth birthday; it wouldn't do to break it now. He set the bun in his lap.

The hovering apple descended back to a sack on the floor. Ahksell's head was a good two or five inches above Ibram's own when they sat together, but he was willing to ignore the blunder in etiquette in favor of opening up the wrapped flask he found at Ahksell's feet. The shaggy horse chuffed the air. Ahksell tossed the apple core into the bushes by the house gates, and licked his fingers clean. He clicked his tongue and flicked the reins.

"Walk on, walk on, Antio," he said, and then glanced at Ibram as the carriage rolled down the road. "Did you get the chance to look over the notes from court?"

He had, but it was far too early in the morning for disasters of that sort. Ibram considered the horse's long back and coarse mane in front of him. "You named the horse 'Antio'?"

Ahksell shrugged. "It's pretty."

"It's old Vissilian for 'flower'."

"Don't you like flowers?"

That wasn't the point, and so Ibram ignored it. Horses should be named as their owners wished to go on, like...Strider, or Jumper, or Dash. He tore off a small chunk of the sweet bun, and stuffed the piece into Ahksell's mouth. Then, he took his own bite. "To the matter at hand," Ibram said. "I did read the court's papers. They were thorough, but I can't say I learned more than I knew before. At least, not about Master Tolk's demise."

Ahksell chewed and swallowed his bite of roll. "That's what Mentor said."

Ibram nodded and dug another chunk of bun free. He propped the flask between them on the bench, and unscrewed the top. Steam floated out and scented the air with smoke-laden shay.

"Didn't she let you read them?" he asked.

Ahksell shrugged. "Not more than the young mistress' letter," he said. "I'm not supposed to be here in an official way anyhow." Ibram nodded. Ahksell glanced at him. "Supposed to be keeping my eye on you."

So Lady Azadiya was worried about a default in Ibram's conduct. Ibram stuck his chin in the air. "Or perhaps you're to learn from my example?"

Ahksell laughed, and elbowed him in the side. Ibram rocked with the blow, and poured himself a cup of shay.

"Well, since I'm mentor here," he began, and Ahksell laughed loudly enough to startle a bird from a tree. Ibram spoke over him. "Since I'm mentor," he repeated. "Let me proffer a few facts that you might keep in mind for this debacle, as we go on."

"Oh please," Ahksell said, pulling the reins slightly left as they joined the main road. "Enlighten this poor Learner."

Ibram hiccupped into his shay. He coughed, turning his head away, and then took a long swallow before he put the cup between his knees. He took up another piece of bun, and sunk his teeth into the plump belly of a cinnak, dried to bring out its sweetness. Kholdo soaked them in cider and Ibram could feel the burn in the back of his throat. Ahksell let go of the reins for long enough to pick up another piece himself.

"Harken Tolk," Ibram began, and then cleared his throat. "Was one of those odd job folk you see traveling the province—"

"Where they don't have a smithy, nor the money to keep one just for pot repairs," Ahksell interrupted. "I have been around the world a time or two."

"I've been around the world. You've been around the province."

"You have been back for two years. You can no longer be vainglorious about your little jaunt. Besides, my travels are more to the point in this instance," Ahksell said. "I'd never heard of Master Tolk, though. Was he new?"

Ibram shrugged. "Not especially. Mistress Monbrith told me he started showing up after that trouble in Kandrilat three years ago. Suppose not everyone could afford to stay once they put the fires out."

"A disastrous fellow, I see," Ahksell said. "He must not have been well-liked."

"He wasn't popular," Ibram allowed, "but he hadn't been a nuisance, either. The Monbriths have an old smithy in the back of their land, hasn't been used regularly in years."

"So perhaps he was thinking of staying?" Ahksell asked.

"Mistress Denrind—that's the headwoman—said she'd spoken to him of the possibility, but it never came to anything. Fontis is on the trade route from Delbrite, and the reason why a village needs a blacksmith is the same—"

"Reason why anyone might buy a new tool in Delbrite or mend an old one when the traders come through," Ahksell interrupted. He considered the horse before them for a second, and then said: "Or go to Itol if the need is pressing."

Ibram nodded and ate more of his bun. "Nice trees, though."

Ahksell slid a glance his way before he refocused on the road.

"Why do you bring those up?" he asked. "Do you not see enough forests here in Lityen?"

He nodded at the leafy monstrosities around them, and Ibram shrugged. "Just something Ama and Father mentioned at dinner last night."

"Oh?"

"Well, it can't all just be shop talk about Katka's latest commission," Ibram said.

Ibram's younger sister was his father's heir, as Ibram was his Ama's. It had been written into their marriage contract and divided by age in the Western fashion rather than by sex as was the Vissilian way. He had a passing familiarity with Father's work as a maker of jewelry, but all the hammering gave him a headache.

"I rather like your father's workshop," Ahksell said. "It's wonderfully warm in the forge during the winter."

"And boiling in the summer," Ibram agreed. "It could just be a coincidence," he said after a moment's thought. "One of Father's customers is a minor Tyal—the family down the river—and she mentioned they'd purchased a stand of lillia trees in Fontis. It's probably nothing. I don't believe they would seek trouble so soon after signing a contract for that orchard."

Ahksell nodded. Ibram chewed a cinnak, sugar and warm spice on his tongue. The presence of minor nobility might possibly complicate matters, but only in part. So far, there was nothing to connect the events except for their being new in the area.

Besides, with a judge there, the Tyals would want to be on their best behavior. By ancient decree, nothing bigger than a village could exist in close proximity to an alchemist sect, ostensibly for their own protection. Major landmasses had in the past been rather accident-prone during the old days of unlicensed alchemy, after all. In practice, this meant no noble house could ever hope to build up the kind of large strongholds found in other parts of the province and around the empire, but younger children—some perhaps born of a different mother—might find enough space to become the scion of a cadet family. The Tyals certainly wouldn't profit from Fontis' shaming.

Ibram took a drink of shay. "I was told Master Tolk would come into the village as soon as the snows passed. Just as much a sign of spring as the male Attendants filtering back up the living mountain to replace the women."

Ahksell rolled his eyes, and then waved at a farmer in Vo Wolly colors guiding his flock of fluffy horned mouflon down the Imperial road. Commerce being what it was, no one with a working brain could pass up the opportunity that a traditionally isolated section of the empire with money to spend presented to the general populace. So the closer a body came to a sect, the more small communities bloomed all up and down the valleys, and then skittered off every which way into the wilderness. You could walk a mile and travel through four or five different villages without breaking a sweat. Fontis lay nearest the imperial boundary where it rather awkwardly tapered to deny the sect full river access, hence the sudden space between it and Delbrite that required a lonely draughtshop masquerading as an inn. The entire village still sat less than a day's ride from the base of the living mountain.

Ahksell slowed Antio to a stop to let all the mouflon safely past. Their other minder, bringing up the rear, shouted her thanks over her shoulder as she followed her flock. Ibram leaned back and put one foot up on the carriage.

"And he stayed through summer?" Ahksell asked. He flicked the reins and the carriage rolled onwards. "Walk on, walk on."

"Rustam Monbrith told me he'd been learning Master Tolk's business, so the old man stayed on longer," Ibram said.

"Then he would have to leave in the winter." Ahksell shook his head. "We have milder seasons in the valleys, but surely in the winter an old man might stay. Even if Fontis can't afford a live-in blacksmith, there's no need to freeze to death over it."

"And yet he refused," Ibram said. "Perhaps he had grown to love the road too well."

Antio moved along in her steady gait and Ibram glanced around them. It was a fine enough day for travel. Horrible reason, though.

"So on the first day after the Hunt of Embrin..." Ahksell prompted.

"The fifth day," Ibram said. "On the fifth day after the Hunt of

Embrin, Rustam Monbrith, second youngest twinkle in his parents' eyes, goes out to pick syah berries, and comes back with a corpse."

"Wait a moment, hold on," Ahksell said. He turned a bit on the driving bench. "The eldest is called Satya, and her brother is 'Rustam'?"

Ibram chuckled.

"There's another of them, is there not?" Ahksell's grin dawned across his dark face. "A brother, yes. Tell me—"

Ibram shoved his laugh down to his gullet, but smiled. "It's really not—"

"Tell me!" Ahksell barely managed to talk through his own laughter. He crowded closer. "Tell me the name!"

"It's not that interesting!"

Ahksell put the reins in one hand and slug his arm around Ibram's shoulders. "Rollim? Aihic? Tolgeram? Oh tell me it's Tolgeram, he's my favorite. All those oxen!"

Ibram wormed his way free and pushed Ahksell back. "You're the only ox around here, let me breath!"

"I'll find out when we get there!" Ahksell snapped on the reins, and the carriage rattled into speed.

Ibram groaned. "It's Diarmit!"

Ahksell threw back his head and howled, loud enough to startle the traders walking their pony train on the other side of the road. Ibram shook his head and felt his own amusement bubble free in answer.

"A triumvirate of royalty!" Ahksell giggled. "Do they pray to the Empress like those dualists in Bastilat?"

"*No*," Ibram insisted. "They can't help how they're named!"

"Ah well," Ahksell struggled, but contained himself, though the corners of his mouth stubbornly twitched. "No, I suppose not. We'll have to blame the parents."

Ibram snorted and took another drink. Antio in her harness had ignored them completely, and he contemplated the flick of her ears as the rig continued down the road. Slowly, he recovered his breath and Ahksell began to whistle.

He stopped after a few bars of "The Cook's Whistle Needs a Firm Blow". Ahksell frowned at him. "And that was it for Harken Tolk? That was all you found out?"

Ibram shifted in his seat. "He was a pristine corpse in his seventies! Mistress Denrind had no problem declaring the event an act of age, and neither did I. He had nothing on him worth stealing! Nor could anyone say they hated him enough to be happy at his death. Most of them were...irritated at the bother."

"Then there was no reason for this Monbrith to run off?"

"None that I can see," Ibram said. "The whole family were upset, of course, but not so badly you'd think they were covering anything up."

"Well," Ahksell said. He frowned down at the reins in his hands. "We've got a bit of traveling to while away yet. What's your best guess? I'm betting on Isconian spies from across the Thundering Ocean. We'll be imperial heroes!"

Ibram laughed and refilled his cup of shay.

╋

The sun had warmed the air by the time Ahksell turned the carriage past the meager freestanding gate that marked the entrance to Fontis. Usually, a pair of local militia members bracketed the gate as a simple show of force, but they were absent from their posts. Instead, a squad of warders dawdled near the timber logs sunk into the ground.

Coming up the slight hill, Ibram heard the market in full swing to either side of the road before he truly saw it. The rows of small densely packed buildings of Fontis' residents were obscured by stalls and bustling crowds. It almost felt like a feast day market. He counted at least six more stalls than usual, and all the shops behind them appeared to be up and running. It seemed as though all three hundred villagers in Fontis had turned out to shop at the same time. Still, there was a bite to the atmosphere that Ibram couldn't just put down to the wind. Ahksell slowed the carriage to avoid hitting anyone as they inched through the crowd. The warders were out in force amongst the populace. Ibram could hear sharp voices, a certain urgency in the tones, but not the words spoken. He tucked his chin into his chest and kept both eyes steady.

By the well, Ahksell managed to work the carriage past of most of the folk wandering about. Ibram nudged him with his elbow. The circuit judge's caravan was obviously still encamped in the village. As they turned right, he counted three expensive coursers tied to a post outside the headwoman's front gate with four extra servants surrounding them. How many warders had this judge brought with him from the Cohort of Peace anyway?

"What's the headwoman's name again?" Ahksell asked. "I'm assuming we're stopping there first before we go and see the Monbriths."

Ibram sat up and yawned ostentatiously. "Just get over there into the livery yard," he said.

Ahksell obligingly set them down in the arcaded yard outside the headwoman's manor, next to the Scribes' Bureau and near the shay shop. Even as small as their carriage was, they barely managed to fit. The yard and the bays beneath the two-story curved wood and clay building surrounding it was crammed full of rickety wagons and wheeled huts. The small rooms above must have been full to bursting. One mobile stall by the troughs looked like it had seen its day of joy during the reign of the Empress' father. Ibram hummed to himself. They stepped down from the carriage, and Ahksell handed Antio's reins to the stable girl who came running out. Ibram stretched out his back while they came to terms behind him.

"The man who invents a better mode of travel is going to be right up there in the heavens with the Founder," he muttered.

"Poor lordship," Ahksell said. He went to the back of the carriage, opened the low door, and pulled out a leather satchel which he slung over his shoulder. "Next time recline inside the carriage."

Ibram smacked him on the shoulder, and Ahksell hit back. Road dust bloomed from their rumpled clothes. They each sneezed.

"Quick brush down, and then off to the body?" Ibram suggested.

"Yeah, think so."

The stable had a bowl of communal water set out, and Ibram sacrificed his own handkerchief to it. They each wiped their faces, and brushed the worst of the dust from their clothes. Ibram paid careful attention to the leather belt that ran cross-ways over his chest and connected by hooks to the wide leather belt at his waist. The silver torch buckle on his chest carried no weight outside the province, but it was the Sect's mark and carried some measure of localized authority. He loosened his gambeson to wipe underneath the neck of his tunic, and then did up the buttons again. It was going to be too hot for this heavier gambeson soon, and he'd still have to wear it on official business. He wrung the rag out and then tossed it back on the carriage.

"The corpse should be in the manor," he said. "They usually bring them for viewing in the public courtyard for the trial."

A mule brayed. Ibram looked up, but couldn't see a beast about. It called again and was answered, and Ibram realized it was the pair from the mill behind the shay shop. Master Kolesar also ran the village's bread oven. They began walking.

"Surely they wouldn't leave it out for this long?" Ahksell asked.

Ibram shrugged. "There's a special cold room," he said.

"How many..." Ahksell swallowed audibly, and Ibram glanced over. "Have you seen many dead bodies?"

"Enough, on Ladyship's business," he said. "One of us usually has to be brought in when a stranger dies for formality's sake. You got your bag of ginger?"

"Oh—" Ahksell pushed him in the back with both hands, thrusting him forward just as they crossed through the wide main entrance gate into the receiving hall.

An official detached themselves from the huddle of people by the interior doors, and bowed with her hands on her stomach. Her light brown hair was braided around a length of ribbon, and knotted ribbon of the same greenish color hung at her throat. She wore a blue knee-length open-front surcoat with a red braid belted at her waist over her green tunic and wrapped breeches. He bowed shortly in return, and Ahksell set his arms at his waist and curled his hands closed. When he loosened them, she straightened.

"Good day," she said, and inclined her head towards Ahksell. Clearly, she recognized the uniform, but without his gar she could dispense with added formalities. He smiled in return, and Ibram saw her green eyes widen slightly.

"Good day, Mistress Islozia," Ibram said. "Did you drop enough rose cake to the Wheelmaker and make my return inevitable?"

She snorted before she could help herself, clearly, and Ibram grinned. The good official recovered too quickly, however, and soon he was faced with her severe eyes and skeptical eyebrows. Ibram kept his hands free and open at his sides.

"Have you come on business with our headwoman, Master Ucalegon?" she asked. "I'm afraid she's with a magistrate from the Court Civil at present, but if you'd like to wait, I can provide a cooling shay in our anteroom."

She gestured to a small room made of old wooden planks built into the side of the hall. Previously, Ibram had been advised that that space was where they kept prisoners or drunks to think over their bad decisions for a night. Through the hole where a door should have been, Ibram could see a small table with a glowbulb on it, surrounded by low seating.

"Alas, I cannot succumb to your hospitality. Actually, I was hoping for a glimpse into your cold room," he said and gestured with an open palm to Ahksell. "There's been an interest."

Mistress Islozia's eyes flickered between them and finally rested on the buckle on Ibram's chest. She glanced back at the small group of villagers behind her, and then turned to face them with straightened shoulders. Her hands folded right over left as she bowed again.

"Please follow me," she said, and twisted on her heels.

Ahksell raised his eyebrows at him, but Ibram shook his head quickly. He took the lead as they followed Mistress Islozia passed the main interior gate and into the public courtyard. He'd been there before, of course, but it was worth noting how small the little open-air space felt once it was crowded. Two squads of loitering warders in imperial purple and black uniforms beneath their chainmail watched as they passed by on the wooden terrace. By the raised dais at the far end where the headwoman usually dealt with business, an elaborate tent had been erected. It was surrounded by servants and more warders, and Ibram would bet his next pay-pouch that inside that swirl of lesser people sat Judge E'grard himself and Aynura Denrind, the poor woman usually in charge of day-to-day life in bureaucratic Fontis. He hoped E'grard was a conscientious man, and not made Mistress Denrind give up her office as well as most of her household. Mistress Islozia started to detour down the steps towards the swarm, but Ibram put up his hand.

"Best to just show us to the cold room first," he said. "We're all already acquainted."

She wobbled, but nodded, and led them into the cold room where the body lay. Ibram shivered as they crossed the threshold. Mistress Islozia took up a long stick which had leaned just inside the door, and touched its tip to the glowbulb attached to the ceiling. It was a cheap version, bright but harsh, and Ibram blinked rapidly to get his eyes to adjust. They stood in a moderately sized cold room that had clearly been hastily converted from storage. He could still see the dusty outlines where crates had been stacked for the household's access. The row of large marble tiles along the wall had symbols inset with a silvery metal. They looked like the ones the sect imported from the northern alchemists for kitchen preservation.

Ahksell stepped out further into the room like a toy chariot pulled by a string. The body lay before him, fully encased in a cold casket, on a trestle table. Ahksell bent at the waist to peer down at it. He probably wasn't getting a good view of the corpse. The casket's glass facets were lined in frost, and as Ibram came near, his skin prickled in the cold coming off it.

"It's an older construction," Ahksell said. He swallowed noticeably, and then wiped his left hand on his gambeson. He reached out; his fingers hovered over the framework.

"It's usually for the summer fruits," Mistress Islozia said. She walked up to stand next to them by the table. "I don't think we've ever had to use it for a body before, not in my own lifetime anyway."

Ahksell waved his hand over the casket. Steam wafted above the hoar frost covering the top. "It's not too cold for that?"

"Oh, a bit," she said. "But no one minds something chilly in summer, do they?"

Ahksell put his back to the casket, and nodded quickly. The conversation turned to fruit tarts, and Ibram left them to it. He moved to the head of the table, and looked through the flat square panel of glass over Harken Tolk's face. The cold casket had done its work from what he could tell; Tolk didn't look much different from the first time he'd seen the body.

Ibram squinted and leaned in for a closer perusal. The old man looked peaceful. Certainly not anything how a murdered man would look, he didn't think. His face was a little frosted now, but it retained its features well. He'd been a solid sort, with a roughened face and a receding hairline, and a weak but clean-shaven chin. His hair had been neatly clipped sometime in the past. Through the slack mouth, Ibram could see his teeth had been adequate. He moved around to the other side of the table. An official seal in wax covered the knot of rope that held the casket closed. He lifted it up in his right hand and twisted the wax circle back and forth. The seam was a little untidy, but it was solid enough; barely a shaving fell off when he scratched it with his thumbnail.

Ibram cleared his throat, and looked over. Ahksell ignored him; he and Mistress Islozia were deep into their discussion. Ibram unbent his spine, and cleared his throat again.

Ahksell began to mime some kind of squeezing action with both hands; he swirled his arms. "And there was this…I'm not actually certain what it was, but the cook said it had sugar and egg whites, so I'm fairly sure it was liquid once, and—"

"Ahksell," Ibram said loudly. "The corpse would like a word."

He let the wax seal fall from his hand. The pair of them startled visibly, and turned as one unit. Ahksell's face cut to Tolk's body, and then quickly away. Mistress Islozia smoothed both hands down her front. Surely Fontis' officials were used to handsome Attendants fluttering in and out of the village boundary by now? This was practically the main thoroughfare out of the province, after all.

Ibram held one hand out to ward off the glare of the light above them reflecting off the casket. "Well?" he asked. "Can you…" He waved his hand, squinted through the resultant shine, and went back to shading his eyes.

Ahksell breathed out sharply through his nose. He smiled tightly at Mistress Islozia, and approached the corpse. He narrowed his eyes at Ibram, but said in a perfectly even voice, "I'll need the casket taken off in order to examine the body."

"Oh," she said, startled. "I'm sorry, I was... Here, I'll just get that for you."

With a small smile in Ahksell's direction, Mistress Islozia came over to stand by Ibram. She lifted the ring attached by a chain to her belt, and sorted through the sealing rings and keys. Ibram glanced up at the open door across from him. He couldn't see anyone outside, but the warders had doubtless told their officer an official had let two strangers in to see the body.

He stepped back as she snapped a brass ring onto her first finger at the third knuckle. When the small beveled flint touched the strike plate she quickly ran the charged blunted needle at the hinge around the seam of the wax seal. Smoke drifted out between her cupped fingers. The melted resin and beeswax smell made Ibram huff air through his nose and step back. Horrible stench. He waited until Mistress Islozia had caught both wax halves in her hands before moving in to undo the knotted rope and slip it free of the casket.

Ibram tossed the rope to the table, and then put both hands on the casket's latch. Mistress Islozia stepped out of the way.

"Has anyone else seen the body?" he asked, as he flipped up the bar that usually held it closed, but not locked. "I was hoping when I'd left that you might find he had family somewhere."

Ahksell had his satchel open, still with the strap on his shoulder, and one leg raised up to act as stabilizer. He was digging through whatever he was carrying, and already had some kind of metal wire framework dangling from his fingers. Ibram felt the corners of his lips threaten to curl, though whether it was up or down he couldn't say himself. Ahksell had balance a Kilk traveling show would kill for, and he would act like it was nothing at all. Mistress Islozia made a stifled noise beside him, and Ibram looked over.

She met his gaze, a trifle flushed. "No," she said and coughed. "No, we found no one. The closest we could get were the Monbriths, and Zosi Kolesar, of course." She looked to Ahksell. "He runs the shay shop in town."

"Is that so?" Ahksell had his head in his satchel now.

"I remember Zosi," Ibram said. He grinned, and Mistress Islozia chuckled. Zosi Kolesar was a transplant from Delbrite, a widower of some years, and spent all the time he wasn't serving customers, regaling them with life on the river. "I didn't know they were close."

She shook her head. "Oh no, I wouldn't say close. When he had a mending job in town Harken used to set up shop in the yard out there, and then go for a bite to eat in the shay shop. You know how it is."

Ibram nodded. Most of the homes in Fontis didn't have room for an oven, so if they wanted their daily bread they visited the shay shop. Over time, Master Kolesar had inherited quite a little business from his parents-in-law.

"It's a pity no one knew Master Tolk," Ahksell said, quietly, and Ibram looked up at the change in tone. "Must have been hard all on his own."

Ahksell frowned at the contraption in his hands, concentrating on threading yellow and white yarn over and around the wire frame he held in his fingers. Ibram tilted his head, but let it pass. Ahksell was funny in his moods sometimes, and it was best to let him feel how he felt rather than try and shake him from it.

"What have you got there?" Ibram asked. "I'm sure Mistress Islozia needs to know for her records."

"It's Hessele's Cage," Ahksell said as he frowned in consideration of his contraption. They waited, but that was all he said on the subject. Ibram debated within himself whether to ask for more information than that, or simply let Ahksell get on with matters. Alchemists could be very open about some parts of their craft and then turn around and claim they couldn't reveal the mysteries of the real world in the next breath.

Ahksell looked to Mistress Islozia and smiled. "You might want to step back," he said. "I'm opening the casket now."

"By which you mean, I am," Ibram said.

Ahksell raised both hands, which were tangled in yarn and metal; his gaze turned rueful. Ibram sighed. Mistress Islozia went wide-eyed, and nodded. She quickly went to the foot of the table away from the casket. Ibram raised first the top half of the glass lid, and then the second, laying each carefully on the other side. His neck prickled with cold as he leaned over the body. He waved away the vapor that poured out as the freezing temperature inside the casket met the comparatively warmer air of the cold room. At least it smelled like nothing still.

"Bit much for plums, isn't it?" he asked.

"Mistress Denrind ordered the temperature lowered to make sure the body was presentable for his honor," a man said from the doorway.

Ibram looked up just as Ahksell whirled around; his satchel swung down to his hip. Commander Ahmose Osthanes stood in the doorway, armored in chain mail with his Imperial silver falcon hanging as a medallion around a thick chain. His dark hair was wrapped at the base of his neck in a leather tie.

To set the needle to it, his appearance meant Ibram should bow and explain himself, but since he was already standing over a dead body, he figured the position to be self-explanatory. Commander Osthanes stared at Ahksell's uniform, and then made a clear survey of the cold room as he walked in. He could see there was no gar taking up space in the room, and that meant no official meddling, or so Ibram hoped.

"One of my warders thought he saw an alchemist and his assistant come in for a visit. Back again, Ucalegon?" he asked. "I thought you'd done your duty here."

Ibram stretched his right hand out and then curled it into a fist where no one could see it on the other side of the table. He leaned back on his heels. "Oh, it's outside my duty to question where I'm sent, isn't it?" he asked. "Be known to Attendant Ahksell Solari of the Preceptory of Yseult."

The good commander bowed his head and upper body towards Ahksell, who returned the gesture. "Allow me to introduce myself, Ahmose Osthanes, watch commander in the 78th Cohort of Peace."

Ibram had run into the man a time or two, usually on business for Lady Azadiya, and rarely within the section of the province where Ibram had some small authority. Commander Osthanes was a staunch Imperialist, of the quiet opinion that alchemists and nobles had too much power within their territories when jurisdiction should be left to the imperial bureaucracy. As a result, he was still only a commander, and not a captain. He and his cohort of peace usually spent their time in Delbrite, protecting the populace from suspected water bugs and the occasional drunken trout. Ibram supposed the august wisdom of the Court Civil had demanded he come out on escort duty, though it was a surprise to see this particular commander again.

"Good day, commander," Ahksell said. "Thank you for looking after the body so well until I could get here to examine it."

Ibram swallowed his chuckle back down his throat before it escaped him, and instead took a deep breath. He relaxed his fist. Outside the door, he caught the shadow of another warder, probably newly stationed in front of the cold room. Osthanes looked Ahksell's way, and arranged his face into a pained grimace Ibram was almost certain the commander believed to be a polite smile.

"May I ask why you are examining the body, Attendant Solari?" he asked.

"Well." Ahksell bent down—he had to, after all—to get a closer view of the body, and only Ibram saw how hard he swallowed. Their eyes met, and Ibram nodded sharply. Ahksell's mouth twitched upward. "Fourth Mentor Hobon—"

"That's *Lady* Azadiya Hobon," Ibram noted with a smile. A double blow to Osthanes' sensibilities.

Ahksell unfolded the wireframe until it was long enough to cover Harken Tolk's body completely. "She thought there might be more to the situation here in Fontis then any of us knew previously, since Master Monbrith has run off. She asked me to come and visit, and see if there's anything the body wishes to concede."

Osthanes blinked slowly at that. "You heard about this mess, did you?"

"We're very grateful for the interest of the Sect of Seven Fires, Commander," Mistress Islozia said, sharply. "I'm sure no one in Fontis would say otherwise."

"And the Sect of Seven Fires is very grateful to everyone in Fontis," Ahksell said gently. "No one wants to see it sanctioned."

Mistress Islozia turned pale at the reminder, and fiddled with her ring of keys.

"I have no input into the judge's ruling, but we'll find him," Commander Osthanes declared. "A boy on foot, alone, can't get far.

Once he's back and explained himself, I'm certain things in Fontis will settle out."

Whatever 'settling out' meant to the commander, his pronouncement dropped into the conversation like a stone. Ibram nodded without committing himself to anything. It would, to be sure, only be a good thing if Rustam was found, but he didn't imagine Judge E'grard's displeasure would allow him to brush off the whole ordeal. Mistress Islozia turned her ring of keys over in both hands. Ahksell quickly looked down to his wire frame. He tested the tension on the length of twisted white and yellow yarn woven through it, and then opened his satchel again. He took out a loop of open-hinged rings and pendants, and began sorting through the mess.

"I need the amethyst and the snowy agate," he said with a bit of force in his voice. "I think it's...yes! Here it is. You see, a body loses its resonance as it ages, and when someone dies it becomes practically nil as the world begins to absorb the emanations, but if I can connect my own—ow! Oh, that's where the flint went— anyway, if I can use the amethyst to gather myself and then the snowy agate to concentrate Master Tolk's remaining life-force—"

"Master Tolk is dead," Osthanes pointed out.

"Nothing ever truly dies, Commander," Ibram said. He walked around the table to its head. "Don't you remember your lessons from the Preceptory of Bedris?"

"There were no alchemists in the Speaker's Temple," he replied.

"Well, here's your chance to build upon that education," Ibram said.

He gestured to the covered corpse. Ahksell shook loose an arrow-shaped pendant of black and white agate which hung from a short chain, and a ring dotted with four square cut amethysts. The commander did not appear to be impressed.

"Just as long as it doesn't harm the body before the trial," Osthanes said. "His honor still needs to set the soul to rest."

Ibram nodded. It was a little sad that Harken Tolk's effects hadn't yielded any idea of which deity to send his soul off to, though at least he was named. Vissilians believed the soul needed correct paperwork burnt for a dead body so their pantheon could decide whether they went into the realm of the divine or dissipated into oblivion. Ibram had often wondered if the Heavenly Crossroads would really accept a man just on his Vissilian writ of travel. Possibly that was a treasonous thought, but Osthanes couldn't read minds, so Ibram allowed himself the freedom.

"Funny that Rustam Monbrith could even think to run with the warders in place," Ibram said, as Ahksell tied the agate's chain to the ring. He stood back when the pendant began following the path of the twisted yarn. "How'd the boy slip through your fingers, there, Commander?"

"The caravan suffered an unfortunate delay near Sigisbrite," Osthanes said. He pulled a leather strap studded with silver and began rubbing the rivets with his fingers. It was new, by the looks of it; Osthanes' last Speaker's Patience Strip had been leather and bronze. "By the time we met up with Judge E'grard's party, and court had been assembled, he'd escaped."

Ibram tsked. "Of all the luck, huh? And think of it, you might have run into him on your way into Fontis."

"No, we didn't—" Osthanes reared back. "What do you mean by that?"

Ibram spread his hands. "Nothing," he protested. "I merely—"

"Oh no, Ucalegon." Osthanes clenched his jaw; a vein appeared in his temple. "I remember you and your "merely" from the Hergian debacle."

"I dispute 'debacle,'" Ibram said. "I recall Master Hergian very fondly."

"Out," Osthanes snapped. He jerked his head to the doorway. "Kamos!"

"Now, think on it, Commander," Ibram said, glancing towards the short, squat warder with a thin mustache who had appeared in the doorway. "I might be helpful yet! Have you searched the forest, you know how boys like to climb trees. Has your squad come across any recent campfires?"

Commander Osthanes rubbed the rivets of his patience strip fiercely. "You know very well we haven't, or we wouldn't be in the building!"

Ibram spread his hands palms up. "Now, then, shall we not have a chance to pool our resources?"

Osthanes' stubborn chin stuck out when he was angry, and it stuck out just then. "Master Ucalegon is leaving. Escort him outside to the street."

"Wait just a minute," Ibram protested. He stepped back towards the table. "Attendant Solari's not done with the body yet, and it's a public building. I can be in here if I want to."

"That's very true," Mistress Islozia said. "Our headwoman prides herself on our open relations with the village."

"That's as may be," Osthanes said, "but I—"

"It's all right," Ahksell interrupted, without looking up from his stacked hands. He waved the pendant over Tolk's feet. "You can go and say hello to your friend Zosi. I'm just getting to the reverberations here."

Ibram's eyebrows raised of their own volition. Commander Osthanes thrust his creaking, rusty chuckle into the short silence that followed Ahksell's assertion. He gestured to his warder.

"Go on, take him," he said. He had a long and unattractive face, especially when he smiled. "You heard the Attendant."

Warder Kamos' beady eyes opened almost to their extremity. He gave Ahksell a wide berth as he crossed the room with one hand out and the other on his sword. Ibram lifted his hands from his sides, clearly away from his sica, and put them on his stomach. He bowed shallowly in Commander Osthanes' direction.

"I'll give Master Kolesar your affection as well," Ibram said as he walked past Ahksell's back. If Ibram was collecting imaginary friends, then so could Ahksell.

Ahksell made a humming noise that usually meant he'd noticed a voice addressing him, though he hadn't marked what was being said, and then Ibram was out the door with Warder Kamos falling in behind. The buzzing swarm of locals and purple-coated court officials and their warders continued unabated in the middle of the public courtyard. None of them noticed Ibram as he passed, which pleased him greatly. Ladyship wouldn't want to draw Judge E'grard's notice until the last possible second, since that would quite quickly herald his interference in her ambitions as well. Behind him, Warder Kamos cleared his throat.

"This way," he said unnecessarily, and pointed back down the way Ibram had arrived.

Kamos didn't take him by the arm, a courtesy for which Ibram tried to feel grateful. They walked in close tandem instead. Ibram rubbed his eyebrow with his thumbnail. Ignoring a warder escort was a skill that took many years of practice, but Ibram had learned it at Ama's knee, following her around on errands. When he was little, he'd pretended they were Ama's honor guard, there to protect them both on the sect's business. Now, he adopted the attitude that they were mere acquaintances who happened to share proximity on a little stroll. He quickened his steps with a free and easy stride, his head held high with a pleasant expression, while behind him Warder Kamos' chain armor jingled and jangled like the bells on a traveling musician's hat all the way out the door.

His musical companion abandoned him at the gate of the head-woman's manor. Left to his own devices, Ibram decided to return to the carriage. Freedom sat well with him, he was usually on his lonesome when out on Lady Azadiya's business.

He checked in at the livery yard to find that the stable girl had unharnessed Antio, and left the carriage sandwiched between two large open wagons that reeked of preserved vegetables. His cloak remained crumpled on the driving seat. He shook it out and wrapped it around his shoulders.

He had to speak with someone about Rustam's last movements in the village. He glanced to his left at the mouth of the livery yard. The shay shop Zosi Kolesar owned was set back from the main thorough-fare of the village due to the ovens, but it was a close enough walk. The Monbriths' draughtshop stood in the opposite direction, well outside of town. Ibram reached into the front of the carriage and gathered together the sack containing the flask and assorted remnants of their breakfast. The walk would take long enough he might need a snack for the journey. He slung the sack over his shoulder, and started on the road that led outside the province. If he kept to a good pace, he'd reach the Monbriths in time for the midday meal.

$$\text{❧} \quad 3 \quad \text{❧}$$

Ibram let the burlap sack dangle from his left hand and knocked on the long bar with his right. The Monbriths' draughtshop wasn't much to look at, just a plain six-sided wooden building with the bonus of a second floor where they could store people instead of winter grain. When he'd last visited, the main floor had been packed with customers, each gossiping into their ale about the body found out back. Now, the draughtshop was empty, save for the trio of warders in the furthest corner near a banked fireplace. One of the men nodded at him politely as Ibram looked over, and Ibram raised his hand in return. Osthanes was taking no chances, then. If Rustam came home, he'd be rounded up quickly. Ibram knocked again.

"Yes! Yes, I'm coming!" Satya Monbrith's voice wafted down from above. Ibram ducked and angled his head towards the stairs behind the bar that led up to the second floor and down to the cellar. He leaned back as her footsteps pounded down the stairs.

"How can I help you?" she asked, patting at her brown hair without looking at him.

She seemed tired as she came up to the bar. Satya tightened the already cinched knot of her heavy leather apron, and looked up. Her eyes widened. She was more pale than usual, so much so that Ibram could barely see the splash of freckles across the bridge of her nose. Her big brown eyes had deep shining circles beneath them and the point of her nose was red.

"Oh, you came," she said, with a low sigh, and put both hands on the bar to lean closer. Her faded green surcoat gaped over her undyed woolen dress. "I sent the letter as quickly as possible, but I wasn't sure—I mean—" She shook her head. "—thank you for coming."

"Never fear, Mistress Monbrith, the postmaster keeps a strong hand on the reins of the Scribes' Bureau in Lityen," Ibram said. He leaned one elbow on the bar. "I read your letter. You asked for my help specifically?"

He made the statement a question, because the fact had taken him by surprise. He hadn't thought he'd made much of an impression on her before. She'd put his name in the letter—misspelled, but it still counted—and he could concede in his own mind that her remembrance was flattering. Always nice to see the general populace appreciated his efforts. He watched her touch her hand to the side of her head. Her hair was taped into a braided bun at her nape by a wide green ribbon that looked to be new. She took a rag out of the pocket of her apron and wiped her hands, and then twisted the fabric in her fingers.

"Did you read it?" she asked. "My letter?"

"As soon as possible," he said. An evasion, but a truthful one. After what had happened in Lillis last year, he had made it a policy to never say more than he had to with anyone. "I was hoping you could tell me more. When did you notice Rustam was missing?"

"Another ale, mistress!" one of the warders called out.

Her plump lips pressed together. She looked down at the bar, and then reached underneath it. Ibram took a seat on one of the five high stools, and let his bag rest at his feet. Satya pulled out a clay pitcher covered by a beaded square of fabric. She carried it across the room and sat it down on the warders' table, next to the plate of half-eaten baked fenek and a quarter loaf of bread. The warders seemed more than happy to pour their own, judging by how fast they grabbed the jug.

"How long have they been stationed here?" Ibram asked when Satya returned to the bar.

"They're more or less permanent guests," she said. "They sleep in the communal room."

The last time he'd been here, that area had been enough for sixteen paying guests. "Room and board. A veritable feast," Ibram observed.

"Might as well eat up before it goes stale," Satya said with a grimace.

She put up two tall wooden mugs and then filled them from another ale jug by the barrels behind her, which she then sat on the bar. She pushed one towards Ibram and picked up the other for herself. Ibram drank a measure to be polite and wiped foam from the corner of his mouth. He restrained a shudder, ale was not his swig of choice.

Ibram nodded. "So, to my question," he said. "When did you sound the alarm that your brother was missing?"

She drank deeply. "I didn't," she said and wiped her mouth. "I'd promised Rustam I'd go with him to court that morning, so I was getting cleaned up a bit in my bedroom. I could hear Mother's pacing upstairs, when Diarmit came running in, yelling that Rustam wasn't in bed."

So the mistress and her heir had been getting ready, the youngest still abed. He tilted his head, and took another sip of ale. "Diarmit and Rustam share a room, do they?"

Satya nodded. "At the back of the house," she said. "Mother has the great chamber, of course, and then I have the room below, where the housekeeper should be." She smiled very tightly, as if she had been going to make a sour face and then abruptly changed her mind. "If we had one."

"What about your servant? Emil?"

Satya shook her head. "He was in the kitchen we have in the house, preparing breakfast."

Ibram sat back on the stool, and crossed his arms. This all fit the testimony she had given the court, which had continued as far as was able without its main witness, and the report of which Lady Azadiya had passed on to him. "Were you all going to court that day?"

"No, some of us needed to stay back," she said. "We had two

hostlers staying overnight. Mother was going to stay and see to them, and Diarmit was going to take over the day chores while Rustam and I went into town. We all—I mean, we were sad about Master Tolk, he'd been a good regular all these years. But none of us thought anything of him dying at his age."

"No, neither did I," Ibram said.

She spread her hands in front of her and looked deeply into his eyes. She seemed about to cry, but held it back by blinking rapidly. Ibram was uncomfortably aware of the handkerchief in one of his wallets.

"That's why this is so strange, isn't it?" she asked. "Why would Rustam run away like this? I told—I ran over everything he might be asked—and I told him it would be all right. And now..."

She picked up her rag again and began worrying at it. "Mother had to go and plead before the judge! And as soon as it spread that he'd run, all our guests left like The Wanderer was on their heels, and none of—well, look at the place!" Satya threw the rag down and flung her arm out in an arc at the room. "Every merchant we had is camping up in the village itself while the warders decide if they're allowed to leave or not.

There's no one who dares sup here now, and not one of—of our friends have come by since the judge issued his ruling. We've been chased out of the shay shop and the headwoman herself told us not to come into the market! I can't..."

Satya covered her mouth and hid her face in her shoulder. Ibram looked away to give her a moment's privacy. One of the warders was watching them without much attempt at subtlety, she had her chair leaned against the wall and stared out at the room over the rim of her ale mug. There was no hope of privacy, but he couldn't exactly ask Satya to take a walk with him through the forest. Ibram cleared his throat.

"Well, we have time, don't we?" he asked, just to get her to turn her head. "The judge's sentencing is only provisional until we've found Rustam, and E'grard allowed us a twelve-day for the search."

"It's not enough," she said. She swiped her sleeve over her eyes, and took a shuddering breath. Satya nodded quietly and finished off her ale. She poured herself another, and topped off his glass. Ibram grimaced, but she wasn't paying attention to his face, so it was all right.

"We've checked all his hiding places," she said. "We've spoken to all his friends... He's still young, but he's a grown man all the same. If only he'd just kept his head!"

She glared into her cup, red-eyed and exasperated. Ibram rested both elbows on the bar and revolved his cup in his hands. He glanced at her from the corner of his eye.

"That's what you think? He just lost his head?" he prompted.

She breathed in and out wetly, still cross, but shook her head. "I don't know," she said. "That's the worst part of it. I thought we had it all settled, and now everyone thinks— I don't even know what they think. Poison? Alchemy? Rustam's like me, Master Ucalegon. We're practical folk."

"Oh now," Ibram said. "I told you to call me Ibram, if you'll recall."

She ducked her chin into her chest and a small grin graced her moon-shaped face. "I didn't like to assume."

"You assume just fine," he said, and leaned in a bit. "And we'll have to work together on this, won't we? In your letter, you said you thought perhaps he became overwhelmed?"

She nodded and lowered her voice. "He's no good at large groups of people, never was. That's why I was going with him. We used to practice it when the Attendants from Bedris came by. He'd speak his reports to me, when I was in the crowd. I told him it would be just the same."

"It sounds like you two are close."

She nodded and swallowed her ale. "We are," she said. "Ever since Father died we've been each other's confidants, and now I just don't know what is in his head."

Satya tilted her face so that it caught the light from the windows, and Ibram rested his weight on his bent elbow. He nodded slowly. She was more talkative than she had been the last time he had visited, but he supposed it was better than the polite demurring to her mother of before.

This change in fortune was bound to be helpful. If he uncovered the reason why Rustam Monbrith had run away, then he supposed events might only naturally unfold such that he found Master Monbrith at the same time. Lady Azadiya couldn't be unpleased by such doubled success, and Mistress Monbrith was no doubt going to be appreciative too. Perhaps he might even get a free cider or two when next he came into the village. As well, it might be a nice poke in the eye for the Cohort of Peace that an arm-for-hire from the sect had managed what all their forces could not. He nudged his mug of ale a little ways away from him with his fingertips.

He leaned in closer. "Can you think of anything else I might need to know?"

The door opened behind them, and they sprang apart. Ibram angled himself to face the newcomer, and Satya stood incredibly straight. Ahksell stood in the doorway, taking up most of the space, and walked briskly inside. His satchel of wonders swung by his thigh in the same way an arm-for-hire might wear their weapon. Satya's eyebrows flew upwards as her eyes widened. She bowed with her hands on her stomach. It was a high bar, Ibram doubted Ahksell could see the courtesy.

"Please rise, Mistress," Ahksell said. He set his bent elbows at his waist and curled his upturned palms into fists. "That looks uncomfortable."

He was perfectly polite and his voice was kind, as Ahksell's voice nearly always sounded, but there was a discerning glint in his eye that Ibram disliked. He took an ostentatious gulp of his ale, and tapped the cup on the bar. Satya glanced between them as she rose, no doubt noticing that Ibram hadn't moved to bow.

"Mistress Satya Monbrith," Ibram said. "Be known to Attendant Ahksell Solari of the Preceptory of Yseult."

Satya flushed and then paled. She hurriedly pulled out a clean wooden mug and made her own disappear behind the bar. She poured Ahksell a generous measure and stood back with both hands clasping the ale jug. Ahksell nodded his thanks.

"I—I hadn't thought my letter would merit a real alchemist," she said.

Ahksell looked politely inquiring. "But you sent your letter to a whole sect of us, Mistress."

"Well, of course, but I thought..."

"I assure you, Mistress Monbrith," Ahksell said. "Fourth Mentor Hobon cares greatly for everyone in Vanima province. She would never refuse a call for help, be it from a great house or low. She instructed me personally on the matter."

Satya set down her ale jug, and then picked it up again. Ibram coughed. Ahksell was laying it on a bit thick; he never seemed to understand how odd that made strangers feel.

"The Fourth Mentor..." Satya whispered. She rubbed her thumbnail into a divot on the jug handle.

Ibram tapped the soft edge of his fist on the bar between Satya and Ahksell. Ahksell smiled at him easily, but Satya startled. Ibram opened his hand and smoothed his palm along the wood.

"Ladyship likes a puzzle," he said. "And she doesn't like the idea of losing Fontis for the next fifty years. Now that introductions have been had, you were saying..."

Satya blinked slowly at him.

"About Rustam," he prompted.

"Oh! Yes. Well, Rustam's my younger brother, Attendant Solari," she said, and paused while Ahksell nodded. "He's always been shy, and Mother wouldn't stop talking about the warders from Delbrite coming in, and the Court Civil and how the Imperial Eye was upon us. She's been making us all pray every night to The Advisor and The Speaker since Mistress Denrind told us Rustam would have to speak up at the trial. It shook me to the fibers, let me tell you, and Rustam's been green at the mouth for a month."

"Did the goddesses accept the offerings?" Ahksell asked while Ibram took another drink.

Satya's head wobbled. "They did," she answered. "Until two days before. The candles were unburnt."

Ibram sat back on his stool, and glanced at Ahksell. Oh hang, that had to mean something important, didn't it. Ahksell frowned. He was a Vissilian and kept their pantheon, after all. If that had happened at Ibram's little altar, he would just have assumed he'd forgotten to light them, but Father and Ahksell's deities were different. Ahksell took a deep slow breath and then leaned both elbows on the bar. He should have looked foolish, a great big ox like that bending to a small bar for a smaller woman, but he made it appear elegant instead. Ibram licked his teeth behind his lips, and took another tiny sip. He much preferred cider, but free ale was free ale.

"I'm so sorry," Ibram said. "That must have been frightening."

"It was certainly disturbing," she allowed. "But I told him that just meant they wanted us to stop pestering them! After all, all he had to do was tell the judge how he found Harken! He'd done that enough times during the evening rush!"

Ahksell chuckled. "I can imagine."

"It's why I sent the letter, Attendant Solari," she said. "After Judge E'grard granted us time to find him, I knew just what to do."

He smiled at her and she smiled back. Ibram put his mug back on the bar, and stood up; the stool bumped off the backs of his legs with a clatter on the wooden planks. Satya looked his way; her chest moved with her breath.

"Do you have any food?" Ibram asked. "I know you're no doubt still preparing for dinner, but we've been on the road and I haven't had time to eat all day. I'm sure Attendant Solari could use a hot meal as well."

She nodded quickly. "We do! We have that fenek stew you liked so much, and the bread's fresh this morning."

"Fresh bread?" Ahksell repeated. "I confess, there's nothing I love more."

"Our bread comes from our own oven and onto your plate! Hot enough to burn yourself. It's what we're known for." She nodded her head again.

Ahksell laughed. "That must be wonderful in the winter."

"Oh, it is," she agreed. "I'll just get that for you. Two bowls? And some baked potatoes?"

"Delicious," Ibram said.

"Here," Ahksell said. "For your trouble. And could you have someone see to my horse? I've unhitched her from the carriage, but I couldn't find your feed. Antio's just outside in your livery yard."

He reached into the satchel at his side, retrieved a pouch, and from that pulled out a stack of three picaio and set them on the table. Ibram raised his eyebrows at the sight of those long silver ovals, glittering in the light. That would pay for the stew, the bread, their drinks, food for Antio, and a stay that would have long overshot the Judge's allowance and lasted well into his village-wide interdiction. It was too much, and Ahksell knew that very well. Ibram spared a look out of the corner of his eye to Satya, whose mouth had loosened, slightly.

"Oh!" she said and sucked in a breath, and then waved her hands. "Oh no, thank you Attendant, you don't have to. We're perfectly fine —" She paused and bit her lip. "We're fine for now," she amended.

"Oh no, Mistress," Ahksell said. "This isn't just for the meal. This is for room and board for the night and the morning. That should be enough, shouldn't it?"

She paused and then swallowed. "Yes, Attendant," she said. "It should."

"Wonderful," Ahksell said. "Ibram, why don't you go choose the rooms while I get my baggage from the carriage. Then you can show me where Master Tolk was found."

Ibram wanted to frown, but kept it off his face. Ahksell was making those eyebrow movements that made him look like a frog with a tick. That usually meant he had something to say. He smiled at Satya and nodded. She nodded back.

"I'll just go air out the rooms," she said, and disappeared with a whirl up the back stairs.

Ibram turned back to Ahksell in time to see him disappear out of the front door. Curse the man and his silent footsteps. Why couldn't alchemists wear bells?

He wavered on his feet. Should he go after Ahksell or Satya? Ahksell had the carriage and whatever it contained, but Ibram had a sack of food scraps and a pretty girl clearing out a possible murder victim's last resting place. Not that they hadn't the opportunity to clean the room ten or twenty times over since Ibram's last visit two months ago. Reaching down, he tossed the breakfast sack over his shoulder and quick-stepped it over to the stairs.

The Monbriths' land showed all the hallmarks of what remained after a wealthy family fell into hard times. Several smaller buildings had been—and probably were now—in the process of being torn down when Ibram had made his first investigations. Now, there were only two large-ish places which still saw any kind of use. The draughtshop had clearly served as a bigger stable in better times, and it was still connected to the livery yard out front. It was the most profitable building on the Monbrith's land, built in a honeycomb style with the faceted roof done in wooden planks and bark shingles. They had an underground cellar to keep the stores cool and an upstairs level for the overnight guests who could afford a bit of privacy away from the main room. At the top of the stairs, Ibram found himself facing the long, tight corridor that separated the dormitory on the left from the two private rooms on the right.

If he remembered correctly, Harken Tolk's room had been the one furthest from the stairs by the large screened window at the end of the hallway. The sun beamed through the thinly woven metal twine, probably bought years ago in happier times. The Preceptory of Afsoun made that and charged a fortune per measure. Both of the private rooms' doors were open, and Ibram could hear the sound of Satya hitting something large, like a pillow or a mattress.

He walked towards the noise, and found the first room empty. Just as he reached the final door, Satya bustled out, holding a messily folded woolen blanket in both of her arms. They each stumbled back. Ibram grinned and glanced out the window. He could see across the smaller courtyard to where the family lived. A pair of goats were tethered outside the front door.

"Apologies," Satya said with a laugh.

Ibram raised his hands. "No, it's my fault," he said. "I should have known you'd get right to work."

She shook her head. "Well, it's best to get everything done as quickly as you can, isn't it?"

He nodded and dropped his hands. He made sure to rest them at his sides, empty-palmed. Ibram leaned forward to take a look into the room and then brushed past her.

"This was Master Tolk's room, wasn't it? I remember I stayed in the one next to it."

He glanced back at Satya, and she nodded. Her hands gripped the blanket tightly. "He liked the light in here," she said.

Ibram took stock of the little room. It held nothing out of the ordinary, a low bed large enough for two or an overly familiar three, a nightstand with a clay bowl and pitcher, and a connecting door for the floor's single lavatory. He strode over and peeked inside. A glowbulb snapped to life from the ceiling, highlighting the toilet, cloth stand, and a small cabinet with a half-burnt candle on top. He frowned. It was communal; there was no reason to suppose any evidence of Tolk would still be there, but it was a door he might not have thought to lock once he'd finished his business.

"Is there something wrong?" Satya asked behind him.

He shook his head, turned around, and closed the door. "Not a problem. It's a lovely room. Tell me, how's Diarmit and your mother? Are they worried?"

"Mother doesn't get worried, she gets angry," Satya said. "Which I suppose is the same thing. And Diarmit...well, it's even harder to keep him at his lessons."

"His lessons?" Ibram repeated.

Satya nodded. "I teach him in the evenings," she said. "He's too bright a boy to fall behind his friends in the village."

She seemed genuine in that respect, and even a bit frustrated. Ibram had spent his days up to his sixteenth year in a Bedris school before Ama had removed him to begin learning his trade. When Katka's turn had come around, he hadn't put up much of a fuss, but she'd been eager. Diarmit wasn't the first child taken out of school in favor of his responsibilities at home.

"Your family stresses education, I remember," he said. "Rustam was working for Master Tolk, wasn't he?"

She licked her lips and considered for a moment. "Not really working for," she said. "But alongside, definitely, when his other chores allowed it."

Ibram clasped his hands behind his back. He walked into the center of the oddly-shaped room. When this had been a stables, they'd probably stored tack and saddles in it or something. He nodded at the small round window to his right. "It does have a very nice view."

She hugged the blanket more tightly. "I think so," she said. "That window gets all the light. I think Harken used it to wake himself up in the morning. He'd always be down in the common room with the stiffs when I came in to serve breakfast."

Ibram chuckled. He opened his mouth, but Ahksell's voice beat him to the question. "Do you get a lot of stiffs, normally?"

Ahksell appeared in the doorway. Satya began to bow; Ahksell waved her off. He smiled, and her thin shoulders relaxed.

"The common room was full of them until now," she said. "Servants, farmers coming back from market... You couldn't walk from one part of the room to the other at night."

Ahksell nodded. "I hope it may continue so," he said. "When we find your brother, I'm sure the judge will understand the circumstances...whatever they may be."

Her entire body stilled and then swayed, before she remembered herself and nodded firmly. "Thank you, lordship," she said.

"Attendant," Ahksell laughed. "I'm hardly so high as that!"

Satya giggled, a little too quickly to Ibram's mind, and nodded. She gestured with her bundle of wool. "I'll just take this out and beat the dust," she said. "And then I'll bring up your meals, Attendant Solari."

Ibram waited until she was out the door and her footsteps had faded.

"I thought Ladyship wanted us to sleep in the carriage," he said. "Not that I'm complaining at the improvement, of course."

Ahksell shrugged. "I know, but I thought it would be better to see where Master Tolk spent his final days up close. The Cohort of Peace might have missed something."

"Don't you mean I might have missed something?" Ibram crossed his arms. He didn't like to be wrong about anything, much less in public, but the thought had to be allowed.

Ahksell coughed. "Best to be cautious now, don't you agree?"

"Oh, is that why you passed the young mistress a small fortune in picaio?" he asked, grinning.

Ahksell ducked his head briefly and then raised his chin in the air, a sure sign of embarrassment Ibram remembered from their younger years. "I just thought it was a good idea to be generous," Ahksell said, lofting his voice as high as his nose.

"Generous? You can't tell me you have much more than that in your pouch. There is no possibility Ladyship granted you a small fortune before she let you out the gates."

"Look, that shay shop was full of traders taking advantage of the—of our time limit to sell off their stock to a load of desperate villagers who think these are the last caravans they'll ever see. The warders have already stopped anyone leaving who doesn't have legitimate placement outside Fontis, and you heard Mistress Satya saying how the village is treating her. If she has a little money, she might convince one of the traveling merchants to sell her a bag of seeds or such before they leave, to tide the family over."

Ahksell scrubbed his left hand across the back of his neck and shrugged again. Ibram raised his eyebrows, and thought for a moment. He considered his response carefully before he allowed himself a cheering whistle. Ahksell scrunched his face at him. He made a fist, brought the backs of his first two fingers to his mouth, and flicked them at Ibram.

"Attendant Solari!" Ibram gasped and put his hand to his chest. "What would Ladyship say? And after such an act of charity?"

Ahksell was unmoved. "She'll say 'Ahk-la, how could you let Ibram go picking self-heal blossoms with a client!' and what will I have to say to that, other than, 'he left me in a cold room with a warder and a dead body?'"

"Ooh, I like how high you can get your voice, it sounds just like her."

Ahksell shut the door behind him, and crossed both arms. "You were supposed to be in the shay shop."

Ibram shook his head. "I don't remember that being offered as a suggestion."

"You were flirting with that commander—"

Ibram's mouth dropped. "I dispute this!"

"You were flirting," Ahksell said firmly. "You always do this, and it's very embarrassing."

"Ahmose Osthanes is the last—the utterly final person in a long list of folk who I would ever, ever flirt with."

Ahksell pointed. "So you admit you would at some point."

"He ordered me removed from the building!"

Ahksell's eyes popped wide. "On his very suggestion, you abandoned me to a corpse! And once out, you immediately went here!"

"To the client," Ibram said. "To find out what went wrong."

"We know what went wrong," Ahksell said. "Her younger brother made for the cliffs."

"Yes."

"It was all in the letter."

"Yes, but that's never all there is to these things," Ibram said. He shook his head, and then rolled his shoulders. "Ahksell, you are younger than me."

"Five years is not—"

"It is enough!" Ibram interrupted him, which he adored taking advantage of when they were alone. "You have been on one of these trips for Lady Azadiya how many times since I've been back?"

"Three," Ahksell said.

"And none of them have been a sanctioning, much less with a corpse."

"Neither have you."

Ibram raised both hands palms-forward. "I am not saying anything about it."

Ahksell rubbed one hand fully down his face. "Aren't you?" he asked through his fingers.

"All I am saying, is that Master Kolesar and his shay shop will be there, but Satya Monbrith will only be surprised at our arrival the once."

Ahksell narrowed his eyes, and Ibram spread his arms. "I am known to her," he said. "I'm closer to her level in society than you will ever be. I wanted a chance to get her perspective on the event in question."

"And did you learn anything? After you were done flirting with her as well?"

Ibram waffled his head left and then right. "I might have," he said, and wriggled his eyebrows. "Now, what did you glean from the dead man himself?"

Ahksell groaned, and rolled his head on his shoulders. He shrugged twice and then moved to sit down on the bed; it creaked beneath him. Ibram leaned against the wall, near the window.

"Master Tolk died perfectly naturally," Ahksell said. "Hessele's cage collected the barest wisps of any kind of resonance within his body, and what there exists is simply the natural decay of any kind of corpse. No harm to the body, and certainly nothing done to the soul."

Ibram frowned. "How can you tell? It could have been a curse. And even Satya brought up the question of poison."

Ahksell took a deep breath and sighed. "The white yarn would burn away would in the presence of poison, and it didn't so that rules out the lesser evil. I twinned the cage to yellow yarn spun with alfrin powder. Since the soul is paired with gold and gold is the higher balance of alfrin, the alfrin powder will gleam in resonance with any damage done to its mate. It's a simple sliding transmutation."

Ibram crossed his arms. "Oh well, if it's simple..."

"You know what I mean!" Ahksell protested. He deflated after a moment, and scratched his neck. "It's a little disappointing, isn't it?"

Ibram nodded slowly. If Rustam had run because he'd killed Tolk somehow, or knew who had and was frightened, it was still foolish, but it made sense for him to disappear. Yet if the man had simply died as all folk did, then they had never even left the starting point in their investigation. Wood creaked somewhere in the building. He glanced at the closed door, and waited, but there were no footsteps.

"Do you still have that list of Tolk's effects?" he asked. Ahksell nodded. "All right, what if it was robbery?"

"That's what Commander Osthanes said, too," Ahksell said. "And you must admit, Rustam might have taken something that you didn't notice was missing."

Ibram came off the wall and paced in an arc across the room. He turned with his back to the bathroom door. "But, again, there's no need for the boy to risk ruining his entire village."

"Maybe he didn't know he was ruining it." Ahksell lifted one shoulder. "Are the Monbriths popular?"

"Prominent business," Ibram said, after a moment's thought. "Not an ugly bunch...sounds like Mistress Monbrith the elder is very devoted to the Sovereign Twins, which usually means faith in the empire, so I wouldn't call them rebels."

Ahksell cocked his head; he must have picked up something in Ibram's tone. Ibram raised his hands and moved his head left and then right. "That certainly wouldn't make them stand out," he said. "They're close to the border."

It was moderately true that provinces inhabited by an alchemist sect were often singled out as areas of concern when the question of faith in the empire was raised. Three hundred years past, his Gracious Majesty Emperor Erenol II had decreed that no noble house could hold sway within two days ride of any area within a province already inhabited by an alchemical sect. Supposedly this spared the Great Houses fear over their heirs becoming victim to alchemasters, unlicensed alchemists, or the sort of large-scale accidents that sometimes struck down ambitious sects. Officially, this placed the sect under direct Imperial control.

Practically speaking, however, the villages existed under the clientage of The Sect of Seven Fires. They depended on them for trade and appealed to them when their own local bureaucracy failed. No one had raised a rebel army in centuries, but imperial cults were rare.

"Tolk traveled," Ahksell said. "He could know any number of unsavory elements."

"All the way to Iscona?"

Ahksell bit the corner of his sudden grin. He cupped the air and flung it at Ibram. Ibram rocked backwards under the blow and rubbed his chest. "Murderer!"

Ahksell laughed. "I'm only saying he traveled!"

Footsteps sounded in the hallway. Ahksell stood up from the bed as someone knocked on the door. Ibram walked past him to open it, and stepped back. Jorie Monbrith, the children's mother, stood outside.

"Mistress Monbrith," he said. He inclined his upper body.

She returned the bow and stood in the hallway, watching him. Her long earthy orange-red dress was belted by a thin brown cord. On her neck swung a small falcon amulet in bronze with blue enamel. That was new. Her mouth worked silently, thin lips pressing into a tight line.

Her greying hair was frizzing out of its wooden hair sticks, and her eyes were lined with red as if she hadn't been sleeping well.

"Good day," she said, finally. She held out a handful of copper faunts and two silver picaio. "I believe you left the common room before my daughter could return to you what is owed."

Ibram drew breath in through his teeth. "Mistress, I apologize, my friend and I only thought to help you defray the cost of this awful business."

"You may do so by finding my son," she said, with her hand still outstretched. "That is all I want."

Ibram nodded. He could hear Ahksell shuffling about behind him. He looked down at the money again; her hand did not waver. Ibram took Ahksell's money and closed his fingers over the coins.

"Thank you," he said.

Mistress Monbrith nodded. Ibram took a step back, but she remained, so he kept the door open.

"I would have you eat with us," she said. She took a deep breath and raised her chin. "My daughter tells me you have brought an alchemist."

❧

They followed Mistress Monbrith out of the draughtshop and into the family home. It was a smaller building, with the inner courtyard exposed and given entirely to gardening. The terrace had been newly repaired; the wooden beams were pale and unpainted. The walls inside and out of the building, however, had been painted white, freshly enough that Ibram couldn't see any smoke damage around the chimneys. The pocket door that led into the dining room was red to mimic tulia wood.

Their dining room was obviously used for many purposes, but it had been cleaned and set by the time they sat down to the meal. Clearly, the mistress had ordered as much of a feast as could be had at short notice, or possibly she wanted to use up the overflow from her lack of patronage. There was no way the Monbriths could eat the cost or the amount of perishable food usually necessary to run a business between the three of them.

Emil, their servant-of-all-work, went to close the sliding inner door once everyone had been seated at the table. Ibram took stock of huge cauldron of quash bursting with leeks and swimming in butter, the round of soft white cheese with a border made of roasted treeka nuts, the pot of fenek stew and the loaf of brown bread. Two pitchers of small ale sat on the table, with a smaller one of goat's milk by the youngest boy, Diarmit.

Mistress Monbrith looked up from her bowl. "No, leave it, Emil," she said. "I'd like the extra breeze."

Emil appeared startled, but left the door open to the courtyard. He bowed and withdrew through a pocket door which Ibram could see leading back into the kitchen. That, he left open as well, and took a seat against the wall, staring out at nothing. Ibram leaned back in his chair to get a more clear view of the courtyard beyond; Ladyship was strict on situational awareness. Nothing stirred.

Ahksell, who was now sitting with his back to the open air, smiled politely. "It is a nice day, isn't it?"

It was getting a bit late to name it 'day' but Ahksell was soothing like that. Mistress Monbrith smiled with the barest edges of her mouth, and then peered down at her stew. Ibram looked across the table. Satya was seated at her mother's right hand, as appropriate, and Diarmit was slumped in the chair nearest Ahksell. The space between them was conspicuous.

"Are you going to find Rustam with alchemy?" Diarmit asked suddenly. "Imriska said that Attendant Serisan told *her* class that alchemists can find anything on earth as long as it's living, and even then you can still find them pretty good because of their strings."

Satya flushed. "Diarmit!"

"You can, can't you?" Diarmit ignored his sister with the ease of long practice. "What if we gave you his shirt he left behind?"

"Diarmit, that's not how it works," Satya said.

"It's a little how it works," Ahksell noted, and the entire family startled. Ibram noticed Mistress Monbrith's fingers tightening on her carved spoon. "But your brother's clothes wouldn't be enough to find him unless they were cut from the same bolt of fabric."

"They are..." Mistress Monbrith cleared her throat and continued. "They were woven on the same loom, all of my children's clothes are."

Ahksell shook his head. "I'm sorry, mistress, but it's not enough of a connection."

"Can you make something into gold then?" Diarmit asked. He was about ten years old or so, and clearly drunk on being allowed to the table with company present.

"Of course not," Ahksell said and laughed.

Mistress Monbrith rapped her knuckles on the table. "Turning anything into gold is an offense against the empire, which is an offense against the Sovereign Twins and not to be spoken at my table."

Ibram made a face into his fenek stew. It was fairer to say that any alchemastering—unlicensed alchemy—was illegal in Vissilia, though turning something into gold by alchemy was the most serious charge. Half of all the cases brought to Lady Azadiya's attention were allegations of Mistress Baker cooking up fake panaceas or some chalk and paste hawker trying to make money off desperate folk. The punishment for conducting experiments outside of a sect was harsh. Ibram had never some across a real alchemaster, though he knew his amitai had.

"Speaking of the Sovereign Twins," Ibram said. "Mistress Monbrith, your daughter tells me the candles didn't light the last time Rustam paid the altar a visit."

Mistress Monbrith's hand reached for her pendant, and then fell. "Not the last time," she said. "Just because a question isn't answered on one night, doesn't mean it won't get a response the next."

Ibram ate his bread and cheese. It was a little difficult balancing both on his spoon, but the Monbriths ate in the Vissilian manner and so he would, too. He set down his utensil.

He swallowed. "So what did he ask for?"

If it was a fast horse, that might be reasonable to request again. He wasn't as familiar with the Vissilian pantheon as he should have been. For his own goddess, Yilka the Green didn't like callers, and so Ibram had never developed the habit of ringing her bells every new moon, or what have you. He looked down at his cup. There was no cider to drink, only the same ale brewed for the draughtshop, but it wasn't so bad if he drank quickly enough. He glanced up at a glimmer of movement across from him; Emil was shifting on his wooden stool in the kitchen.

"Questions before the Speaker are addressed for her ears alone," Mistress Monbrith said.

Ibram coughed into his ale, and swallowed painfully. He set the cup down, and opened his mouth. Then, Diarmit's heavy sigh caught Ibram's attention. The boy's face brightened. "Can you make something blow up?"

"That will do, Diarmit," his mother said, and the child made a face down at his stew.

"It's all right," Ahksell said. "As the Speaker says, 'knowledge shared grows in the telling' after all."

Ibram noticed the ruler of the household distinctly shift in her chair. Her shoulders loosened about her neck. Ahksell inclined himself towards the boy.

"I'd need quite a lot of ingredients to make anything blow up," he said with a laugh. "And I haven't brought them with me. I'm only here to help, after all."

"But you could—"

"You are a follower of the Speaker, Attendant Solari?" Mistress Monbrith asked. She took a precise spoonful of stew, raised it to her lips, and swallowed without eating. She lay the spoon back into the bowl.

"The Runner, actually," Ahksell said. "Fellowship is important in the sect, and oratory is no mean skill to acquire."

"He is an easy talker," Ibram interjected. "Which is probably why his parents went for the one over the other. I always wondered why The Speaker wasn't in charge of rhetoric, myself."

Mistress Monbrith turned a severe eye upon him. "The Speaker learned oratory from the Runner after the demarcation of the empire, Master Ucalegon. So the pantheon works each together as an example to all Vissilia."

"Your pardon, Mistress," Ibram said and took up a spoonful of stew. He chewed a stringy bit of fenek meditatively. "I'm just a poor dedicant to Yilka the Green, and can't be expected to know these things."

The entire table shivered, but for Ahksell, who was used to it. The empire didn't name their deities, after all, and there was something of a superstition concerning the matter. Ibram swallowed his mouthful, and dug his spoon into the bread until a piece came off.

"Are all the children dedicated to the Speaker in your family?" Ahksell asked a bit too loudly.

Diarmit snorted into his stew, and then he flinched in a way Ibram recognized with long-suffering sympathy as a sister taking quick measures with her foot under the table. Satya otherwise was not to be bothered, her attention given fully to the fenek stew. Their mother took an actual morsel of food into her body before answering.

"My late husband was given to the Speaker and I sought the Advisor," she said. "We divided the children accordingly."

So she was outnumbered in adherents, but fair was fair. Ibram supposed it was good that she retained the same superior inflexibility that she'd had when he'd been in town two months previous. He could only imagine what sort of man Master Monbrith had been before the Wanderer had taken him to the Crossroads.

"Is Rustam very religious?" Ahksell asked. He gestured across the table. "I can't help but notice your fine amulet."

"We're faithful," Mistress Monbrith allowed. "But it's difficult out here without a temple."

"We have the altar, though," Satya said. She reached for the cheese with her dining knife and cut off a chunk. This she layered on a bite of bread. "And if we need to speak with our cleric, there's always the shrine in Thelis, or the temple in Delbrite."

"It is very lovely," Ahksell said. He glanced at Ibram. "Do you make the trip often?"

Mistress Monbrith shook her head. "When my husband was alive, I would take the children into town for the summer festivals," she said. "But it's been some time since we've been able to make such a trip."

"Travel costs money," Satya said without raising her face. "As anyone who runs a business based on trade can tell you."

"Not every aspect of life must depend solely on its cost," her mother reminded her. It sounded like an old argument.

"Duty does take its toll, does it not?" Ibram said. "Maybe once this is all over, you'll have the opportunity again."

"I pray so," Mistress Monbrith said. She set her spoon down on the table. "What do you need from us in order to find my son?"

Ibram glanced at every face at the table. Satya kept her eyes on her food, but Diarmit was squirming ever so slightly in his chair. In the short silence, he reached out for the pitcher of goat's milk, and Ahksell pushed it closer to him.

"Did you particularly like Master Tolk, Mistress Monbrith?" Ibram asked.

She seemed surprised. "Particularly? No," she said. "He wasn't the cleanliest of men, and that becomes tiresome."

"He tried to be, Mother," Satya said. "He was getting on in years, you know."

Mistress Monbrith shook her head. "He always kept trying to bargain with me over his room rate."

"Because he was taking Rustam on as an apprentice," Satya said in the tones of yet another old argument. There seemed to be a number of them coming to light all at once. She glanced at Ibram, and flushed.

"You cannot run a business on a pittance, Satya," Mistress Monbrith said.

"As I well know," she replied, and stabbed her spoon into her bowl.

Mistress Monbrith pursed her lips; her nostrils flared when she sniffed. She leaned over her food, and drew up a spoonful of cheese and treeka nuts. She spread the pairing on her bread, returned the serving spoon, and then proceeded to ignore the food completely.

"Rustam liked him," Diarmit said, looking up from his cup. "He used to show him how all the hammers and pincers and things worked."

"I remember," Ibram said. "That's why your brother went out there on the day in question, wasn't it? Master Tolk needed a hand with the bellows."

"Yes," Satya said.

The family attended to their food with their heads down over the stew. Satya and Diarmit were sharing a large chunk of bread between them. Satya cut pieces off for them both precisely from the opposite sides. The middle, Ibram assumed, was usually left for their brother. Ahksell cleared his throat; Ibram looked up, but all Ahksell did was widen his eyes at him. Ibram raised his shoulders up no more than an inch and then let them drop. Ahksell rested his wrists on the table and licked his lips.

"I think we need to know more about Master Rustam," Ahksell said. "Diarmit, did your brother seem scared when he went to bed the night before he disa—left?"

Diarmit nodded. "He was acting funny," he said around a mouthful of quash. "He didn't eat dinner, not even the pyrus pudding Satya had made! And he kept looking out the window all night. It was really cold, too."

Ibram nodded. "Does your window show anything interesting?"

Diarmit shrugged. "Just the courtyard, and it looks the same all the time."

"Mine does too at home," Ibram said. "So Rustam didn't meet with anyone in the two months leading up to the trial? No one else has gone missing, have they?"

"No, nothing like that. Rustam has a—a sweetling," Satya said, with a glance at her mother. "But she told the warder that she hasn't seen him, and they searched—"

"They have searched everywhere," her mother interrupted in a hard voice. "They have searched the larder and our cellar, and they ripped through our home as if we were not loyal tax-paying subjects of the empire. The village has let them, that Denrind woman has *supported* them as if Rustam was a common criminal."

Satya bit her lips together, and Diarmit dragged his spoon through his food. Ibram nodded slowly. To be fair, Rustam was, actually, now a common criminal but he supposed that wasn't the proper time to remind them of that fact.

"Did he say anything to you?" he asked Diarmit.

"The warder already asked me that," the boy said.

"Well, what did you tell the warder?"

"Nothing."

Satya made a face at Diarmit, who pushed a huge spoonful of quash in his mouth. He chewed slowly. Ahksell picked up his cup of ale and sipped it.

Maybe it was best to ask the table at large. "Did he say anything?" Ibram tried again. "Anything out of the ordinary? Asking about the weather for traveling, maybe? Do you think Rustam knows about the troubles now here in Fontis?"

"Never." Mistress Monbrith tucked wisps of hair back into her bun. "If he knew, he would return."

"He said he was going to make it up to us," Diarmit mumbled, and Ibram whipped his head around and down.

"What?" Ahksell asked as he leaned over the table.

Diarmit squirmed in his chair, but his head lifted up. "You're all talking about the night before he left, right? Not when he did?"

"Yes we are," Ibram said, since they most assuredly were now. "Do you know something about that, Master Monbrith?"

Diarmit picked at his fingernails, the picture of discomfort. Ibram angled himself a little lower in his seat. He kept his hands in his lap.

"You and Rustam talked to each other in your shared room, didn't you?" he asked.

Diarmit nodded.

"When did he tell you he was going to make up for something?"

"Sometimes he can't sleep," Diarmit said, "and he keeps the candles lit which means I can't sleep, and then the mornings are awful. And one night he blew out all the candles and just when I was going to sleep he lit one, and I woke up."

"And Rustam was upset?" Ibram asked.

"I guess. He just said he needed to make it all right," Diarmit said and shrugged. "I thought he meant the lights, but then later he ran off."

Well, those were two different statements completely. Ibram opened his mouth to ask for clarification, but Mistress Monbrith cleared her throat.

"My oldest son said nothing to us about his leaving," Mistress Monbrith said. "As Satya put it in her letter, we had no indication at all.

The day before he was supposed to appear before the judge, Rustam went about everything normally."

"How so?" Ibram asked. He'd observed the Monbriths working when he'd stayed at the draughtshop, but he hadn't given much thought to their routines.

"He did his chores, and then he cooked dinner for the nightly crowd. In the evening, he helped Satya and I unload the shipment of liquor we had arranged to be delivered, and then he set about his work behind the bar in the common room. We'd had a lot of business since Master Tolk's death."

Ibram slugged back his ale, and managed not to grimace. "I didn't know you sold liquor."

"Only some," Mistress Monbrith said. "And we'll be needing a new distributor when all this mess is resolved."

"Mother," Satya hissed.

"Rank sojin and a woman who consumes her own product?" Mistress Monbrith scoffed. "The only reason we bought from her was the bargain she struck with your father. It's finally over, and we're well rid of her and her sour face."

Satya ate her quash so forcefully Ibram was half-afraid she'd bite through the spoon. The Monbrith women's previous reserve was gone now; all that politeness lost to the doom hanging over their heads. Her mother nodded to herself.

Ibram cleared his throat. "Lot of people came around to hear Rustam's story, I'm sure."

"Yes," Mistress Monbrith said. "I think that Anlines woman made him go over it three times at least."

That was odd, but he supposed long nights made for strange bedfellows. Ibram tilted his head a little. "Did Rustam often help in the kitchen? I would have thought Emil would handle those duties."

"Emil cooks our meals," Mistress Monbrith said, "but we prefer his help in the washing up when it comes to the draughtshop."

Ibram nodded. He licked his lips and frowned down at his fenek stew. Something wriggled in the back of his mind, and he would have turned his thoughts to it, but a slippered foot suddenly rested on top of his boot underneath the table. He raised his eyes and met Satya's gaze. The wriggle subsided, and the rest of the dinner devolved into going over the Cohort of Peace's movements since their arrival in Fontis. No point in working along old hunting trails, after all.

It was growing dark quickly by the time they finished the meal. Satya and Diarmit escaped to the family sitting room with a copy of *Speechcraft and Civility* for Diarmit's lessons, and Mistress Monbrith went to the altar to pray, taking Ahksell with her. She insisted that Emil escort Ibram back to his room in the draughtshop, even though there was no way for him to get lost between the two buildings. It was a polite gesture of course, but Ibram couldn't help but notice it also eliminated the possibility of him wandering off and perhaps finding something he should not. Emil handed Ibram a small lit candle before he led the way back to the draughtshop.

"I don't suppose you have anything to add," Ibram said.

Emil's face was like a still pond. He was an old man with white flyaway hair and placid eyes, and he probably knew more about the Monbriths than they did about themselves. That was how a servant kept their job, after all.

"Any thoughts about where Master Rustam might have gone?" Ibram tried again.

Emil nodded slowly as he held open the back door for him. Ibram noticed there were two. They'd used the one on the left down the back stairway from the rooms above, and he saw that the other led into the kitchen. The Monbriths had been landowners for a good long while; they'd had time to refit everything to their liking.

He followed Emil through the kitchen door and into the common room. Ibram walked at the old man's right hand. It was a longer journey than simply returning up the way Mistress Monbrith had led them down to dinner. Perhaps Emil wished to have some time to speak freely?

A light gleamed outside the front window of the draughtshop. Emil pointed and then lay his finger diagonally across his mouth. Ibram nodded.

"The warders have posted a guard every night since their arrival, young master," Emil said very quietly. "I would expect the other two are upstairs abed."

Ibram nodded. "Did they truly search everywhere?" he asked.

"They tossed a few grain sacks around," Emil said, "but I don't think they knew what they were looking for."

Ibram raised his eyebrows. "Do you?"

Emil shook his head. "I've known Master Rustam since he was a babe, master," he said as they threaded their way through the empty tables. "I can't say I'm surprised he ran."

"Really?" Ibram eyed Emil's back as they climbed up the stairs. "That's not his family's view of it."

"Oh, I doubt it would be," Emil said with a dusty laugh. "But they're a very particular family, don't you know. The Mistress is very passionate. He's like his father, Wanderer guide him well, quite gentle. More likely to go with the current than fight its pull, if you understand me."

"I do, Emil. Thank you."

They reached the top of the stairs and Ibram moved a little ways in front down the hallway. He turned to face Emil and raised the candle between them. The flickering light tossed shadows across his wrinkled face.

"Do you think someone told him to run, then?" Ibram asked.

Emil breathed out through his nose. His mouth tensed as he frowned. Finally, he shook his head.

"I know he listened to people he shouldn't," Emil said. "I know that Master Tolk was no good for him."

"Really? That's the first time I've heard anyone say that."

Emil took a step back in the hallway and shook his head. "We had no need for a blacksmith," he said. "I don't trust peddlers any further than I could throw a carriage."

"What was so wrong with Master Tolk then?" Ibram asked. "And why not tell me this before?"

"There was no need," Emil protested. "The poor man died, that's what happens when you get old. I know that better than all the rest of this household." He sighed and rubbed his gnarled hand down his front. "All I know is that Master Rustam offered to help Master Tolk in his work one day, and from then on, it was like Tolk expected Rustam's aid whenever he called."

"It's not so bad to have a trade," Ibram said.

"I've known those children since they were babies in my arms, and I—" Emil cut himself off abruptly, and then shook his head. His mouth turned downwards. He stepped back again. "You'll not tell them I said anything out of my place, will you?" he asked.

Ibram shook his head. "No, not at all."

"I have to clean the dining room. My apologies, young master. Old men have fancies, you know."

Emil stepped back and bowed quickly. His hair bounced around his face as he walked quickly away. Ibram glanced down the empty staircase, and then back to him.

"One more question, though," Ibram called out, "if you have the time."

Emil rose. His face arranged its wrinkles into furrowed caution. "Yes, Master Ucalegon?"

"Do you think Rustam would have anywhere in mind when he ran? Do you think he ran alone?"

Emil sighed, long and slow. His hand patted down his tunic and returned to speak quietly. He glanced at the door to the communal area where the other two warders slept. "Master Rustam didn't tell me anything before he left." He waited until Ibram nodded, and then continued. "I don't think he cared for anyone in the village enough to run away with them, excepting the young mistress, nor any of the customers. Nor do I know of any place he might have gone."

Emil chewed his lower lip, and Ibram set aside the question of whether he believed the old man or not for a later time. If Emil had been in the Monbriths' employ since the oldest children were infants, then there was no telling how much he actually knew versus what he was willing to divulge. Ibram rested his weight on his heels and tried to make himself look trustworthy as well as discreet.

"The family doesn't move about much, as a rule," the old servant said. "Master Diarmit's the wildest of the bunch, and he never goes farther than the Suugan's house in the market square. Mistress Monbrith is very much interested in improving the family land, and Mistress Satya spends much of her time dealing with the business. But

I will say... I don't think he would have done something like this unless someone—some *wretch*—put the idea into his head first."

The question, though, was who would be so foolish, or malicious enough, to goad the boy into running. No one in Fontis certainly profited from Rustam's escape. Ibram bowed his head and smiled.

"Thank you, Emil," he said, and the old servant bowed. "I'll wish you a good night."

"Young master," Emil murmured.

Ibram waited until Emil had disappeared down the steps again, before turning and going into his own room. Like most places that merely sold space for a night or two, rather than a dedicated inn, the doors could only be locked from the inside. He pushed the door open with his left hand, and raised the candle in his right.

It all seemed in order. Ibram swung the small wooden sliding bolt above the door handle closed, and then took closer stock of the room. The burlap sack he'd brought with him was still lying on the floor by the pitcher stand. He set the candle next to the larger bowl and made a circuit around the room. There was light enough still from the window. He ran his fingers along the screen; it was well strung and not at all rusted. Even the nails in the window frame seemed newly placed.

Fontis was a prosperous village, but the Monbriths must have been seeing the greater share of the profits. He frowned. There had to have been something he had missed upon his first introduction to the events taking place in Fontis, but Ibram was a tup if he knew what it was. He looked across his view to the dense forest that encircled the Monbriths' property. He could smell smoke from their kitchen fire on the air, but the little house was dark and dim, no light in the windows facing him at all. He chewed his bottom lip.

Ahksell must have still been visiting the altar with Mistress Monbrith. Perhaps Ibram should have gone as well, but he always felt uncomfortable in other people's holy spaces. His family had no dedicated rooms in their house, just a tree in a rock for Ama and himself and a cupboard full of candles and icons for Father and Katka.

He didn't count himself a pious man by nature. Ama and Father paid their respects and had taught him and Katka the same, but no one made him pray all the hours of the day or promise this for that as if the gods owned a candy store and dispensed joys for faunts. Ask the gods for air, Ama always said, and you might not enjoy how hard the winds blow.

But all that talk of goddesses and what they might or might not have said to Rustam Monbrith had given Ibram pause. Yilka the Green had three faces: luck, prosperity, and work, and it seemed like she'd denied him the first two in favor of the third. Surely, a small hint wouldn't be too much? Ibram turned around and went to the lone table in the room. He pushed aside the pitcher and bowl to give him a little space. Then, he reached into his belt wallet, and pulled out the little pouch where he kept his bells and dice.

He poured them out into his palm. The tangled chain of bells he set on the table, and then returned the three four-sided dice to the pouch. Carefully, he unwound the clapper-less bells from their chain so that they would make no sound by knocking against each other. Then, Ibram dangled the charms from the fingers of his left hand. The bells were no bigger than the nail of his little finger, saucer-shaped and molded from bronze with wedge-shaped impressions of the words for luck, prosperity and work in the Western script.

He raised them up before him, and tapped the rim of each one with his first finger; they vibrated but made no sound. He closed his eyes and breathed in deeply. Let him see what he had missed before, or forgot, or failed to understand. He wasn't asking for the answers to be given! But let the three faces of Yilka the Green, who understood the value of time and the redress of injury, turn to him and smile. He would do the work himself; he would correct his mistake.

He quickly caught the vibrating bells in his left hand, and with his right emptied the dice pouch onto the table. All three four-sided dice tumbled onto the wood in a clatter. They were painted a deep green with a daub of paint to create a single white point on each, and sort of resembled the little dumplings Ama and Kholdo made on feast days. Two landed white points up for agreement and the third, green for disfavor. He sighed, and scooped them back into the pouch. Well, it wasn't an outright refusal.

Ibram put away the bells, closed the pouch, and returned it to his belt. He turned away from the table and stretched his left arm over his head, and then his right one. His spine was threatening mutiny after all that time spent sitting. He sat down on the bed—Satya had replaced the blanket—and pulled off his boots. Ibram wriggled his stocking toes and stretched out his feet. He stood to stretch his back, and knocked into his right boot. The leather shaft fell under the bed.

Ibram groaned and crouched down. Of course it fell where doubtless the dust balls were already invading inside and the creeping crawlers were skittering out of their hiding places. He reached his hand underneath the bedframe with a grimace.

"Hang it!"

A bite? A loose nail? Ibram whipped his hand out from under the bed. He braced himself on the frame, and stared down at his palm. A drop of blood welled up on the pad of his middle finger. He sucked it into his mouth, and fell to his knees. He looked under the bed, dragging his boot out of the way, but thankfully, no beady black eyes stared back at him. He put his non-bleeding hand out under the bed. He felt carefully, sweeping in slow descending arcs, and paused when something poked his littlest finger. It seemed caught between two floorboards.

Ibram drew out whatever it was, and frowned at it. He pinched it with two fingers and held it in front of him. It looked like a curl of metal, not very thick, but wide in the middle and pointed at the ends. It seemed to be a bit like a shaving—like he'd seen in Father's workshop—but it wasn't a curlicue, more like a half-moon. He turned it up to the light. It almost looked like it had been part of a design, one end was finished.

A knock came from the connecting bathroom door, and Ibram turned towards the noise. He tossed the little piece of bother out of harm's way, and stood. Ahksell knocked again, more loudly.

"A moment!" Ibram called out.

He brushed himself off, and then quickly unbolted the door from his side. Ahksell stepped into the room. He'd already dressed down for the night; his linen tunic with thick protective red embroidery at every hem hung loose over his breeches. Ahksell held out a small sailing light, only instead of a candle, it contained a tiny glowbulb. He pinched the glass casing and a warm ochre light filled the room.

Ahksell leaned over and blew out Ibram's candle, and then gently tossed the sailing light into the air.

"How does it rise without the heat from the candle?" Ibram asked. He tracked the little light with his eyes as it flew slowly over his head.

"Kalev wouldn't tell me," he said. "Afsoun has profitable secrets."

"And he outranks you."

"And he outranks me," Ahksell agreed. "Was your room searched, too?"

"Your room was searched?" Ibram stepped forward, and gripped the hilt of his sica. "How can you tell?"

"I left my satchel up here, and when I came back, the little lock had turned blue. They didn't break it, and no one could cut the bag open without some very specialized equipment, but they certainly tried to open it. And before you ask, no, they didn't leave anything behind to disturb my sleep. I checked. How about you?"

"Not as far as I can see, but I don't think I've got as complex security as you do." He gestured at the sad little bag of mostly eaten breakfast.

"You're right," Ahksell said. "Next time I'll put a better lock on my food parcels."

"A thought I've been trying to impress upon you for years." Ibram slackened his hold on his sica and flexed his now free hand. Perhaps he should have brought his sword. "Do you know what they were looking for?"

Ahksell shook his head. "Not a clue," he said. "There's no reason to go through my belongings."

If Ahksell could shine that much silver about, Ibram wasn't so certain of that, but he let it pass. "Can they get into the carriage?"

"Not without doing serious damage to themselves," Ahksell said. Ibram felt his eyebrows raise; Ahksell shrugged. "It's got a lightning lock upon it. Two of them, actually, one for the door and another for the window."

"All right, well then, if we're threatened in the night, we can always escape to the stables, I suppose."

"Oh stop," Ahksell said, and yawned. "Why do you think someone would search either of our belongings?"

Ibram unbuckled his belts, and tossed them on the bed behind him. He began unbuttoning the diagonal knotted buttons of his gambeson. "I have no idea," he said. He licked his lips and thought for a moment. "Nor who could have done it."

"Emil?"

He withdrew his left arm from his gambeson and then his right, and looked around for someplace to drape his clothes for an airing. "Was in my line of sight all through dinner."

Ahksell raised one eyebrow, which made Ibram want to stick his tongue out at him. "Where you were sat across from the young mistress?"

He rolled his eyes. "I will just remind you that, though compared to yourself I am the approximate length and width of a pebble, in the normal order of the universe, I am certainly able to look over the head of a woman as tiny as Satya."

He turned in a slow circle. There had been a little airing cupboard in the room next door, maybe he could borrow space in that from Ahksell. Ahksell chuckled, and he looked over

Ahksell pointed. "There's a little hook by the window that might do." He stared at the storm shutter for a moment. "When do you think it happened?"

Ibram squinted at the window until he found the small bent nail sticking out in the wall. It would have to do. He hung up his gambeson and shook his head. "Any time after we left the rooms," he said. He adjusted the first strap of his felt wrist wallet and ran his fingers under the second, his linen tunic always got caught up there. "We would have heard someone come up the stairs, or even just enter the room. These old buildings have ears built into the logs."

"So it could have been the family...or even someone we don't know!" Ahksell frowned in thought. "We left with Mistress Monbrith, and the young mistress came into the dining room later. Then Diarmit under Emil's guiding hand, and in the time it took us to make some small talk with Mistress Monbrith—"

Ibram cleared his throat to get Ahksell's attention, otherwise they would be talking in circles the rest of the night. "At this point it could be anyone. It could be a warder for all we know."

Ahksell breathed in sharply. "Surely not!"

Ibram spread his hands. "This is why Ladyship sends me alone, you realize."

Ahksell's frown could have powered the glowbulb in the sailing light for six thousand hours, and Ibram grinned in the face of it. Ahksell walked closer. He smoothed his hand down the embroidered edge of his tunic.

"It's not a bad room, though," Ahksell said. "On the whole, I mean."

Ibram raised his eyebrows. "Suppose not," he said. "I slept in yours last time I was here. The mattress was new tick, so that was nice."

Ahksell nodded. "They must run a very popular business. Did you know their altar is covered by white linen? A double layer in fact, one to the floor and another covering that."

Ibram felt the urge to whistle and, since they were alone, followed through on it. Ahksell closed one eye in a wince. He scratched his shoulder beneath his tunic.

"At home, Father and Katka just have the little table and icons in an alcove," Ibram said. "Is it real linen? Or that coarse weave they make in Istapool?"

Ahksell nodded. "It looked real enough," he said. "White as snow, too, which must have cost a fortune to import."

"Well, what did it feel like?"

Ahksell rolled his eyes. "Runner's bloody toes, I didn't touch the altar, Ibram," he exclaimed. "You know better than that!"

Ibram laughed and shrugged. "Well, you brought it up..."

"It takes two days to even get permission to clean it!"

"Who do you have to ask permission from?"

Ahksell waved his left hand. "The...well, in the temple you would ask a cleric to petition the goddess for permission to move the altar clothes, but here I suppose you would just go straight to Her."

"Sounds tiring."

"How are you like this?" Ahksell asked. "Your father's devout enough."

Ibram shrugged. "It's not my business, really," he said. "I have a working knowledge of all the pantheon I need, but Ama and Father like to keep us very separate in worship. Except for feast days, of course."

"Well the next time you stand in a corner and guess your future with dice, I'll be sure to remind you of this moment," Ahksell said. He raised and dropped his eyebrows. "Anyway, I suppose they must have more customers than I'd have thought."

Ibram laughed, and Ahksell grinned. He sobered quickly, though. "You should know, after you left the manor, *I* was invited to speak with the judge," Ahksell said.

Ibram sat down on his bed. The mattress sagged, the ropes hadn't been tightened in the frame. He pinched the bridge of his nose to try and squeeze out the pressure building in his head.

"What did his honor say?" he asked.

"That he allows it would be most helpful if the sect offered their aid, but because of the 'long tradition' of imperial precedence, it must remain mostly unofficial. I'm all right, though, because otherwise he would have to send for an alchemist from Hema—"

"Hema," Ibram muttered. "Throne lickers."

"—which would take an awfully long time and no small expense," Ahksell said a little loudly. He walked over and sat next to Ibram on the bed. "And so while we are not officially a member of his party, nor outside his authority as a representative of the empress, we are most welcome to come to the aid of our client within the established time frame."

"Can we leave?"

"And return, if need be."

"A twelve day to find the boy," Ibram said, and exhaled deeply. "And we've lost three already." He eyed the little sailing light on its meandering path. Ahksell leaned his great warm bulk against Ibram's side and Ibram braced himself lest he be thrown from the bed. He grinned despite himself. "All right," he said. "We shall just have to save the day."

❦

In the morning, they breakfasted with the family on the remains of the last night's quash and bread and cheese. The Monbriths clearly wanted to maintain a sheen of normalcy, but every gesture was strained and Ibram soon found his shoulders creeping up the length of his neck at each abrupt pause in conversation. Finally, the whole lot of them went to their chores, and Ahksell and he were freed to return to the village. The trio of warders from the night before were up and patrolling the area around the draughtshop as they walked out. Ibram could see one making his way in the direction of the syah berry patch.

They made sure Antio had been fed and brushed before abandoning her to the stables. It was no difficulty to walk when the weather was as fine as it was that morning, crisp air and bright sun. Ibram turned his face up to the sky as they walked. He took a deep breath and stretched his arms over his head.

"What's your worst thought?" he asked. It was a game Ladyship liked to play when faced with a problem. Ama had always thought it a bit too much like fearmongering. Ibram, on the other hand, rather liked getting the worrisome thoughts into the light.

Ahksell hummed to himself. "Terrible but true?"

"Absolutely. I'll start: Rustam Monbrith is dead."

Ahksell snorted. "His body would have been presented to the judge immediately as proof of good intent."

"Not if he was murdered," Ibram pointed out. "Then he must be said to run away out of guilt."

"Why murder him at all?"

"Why run at all?" Ibram asked. "You next."

Ahksell kicked a stick off the road into the underbrush. "Rustam Monbrith has no love for his family or village, and has run off for some selfish purpose of his own, possibly to become a river man. Yours?"

"The same." Ibram laughed and faced the paved stone road ahead. "But does the thought carry weight?"

They walked a few moments in silence. "No," Ahksell finally said. "I don't think it does."

Ibram nodded. "They're fearful, but not angry."

Ahksell scoffed. "Satya Monbrith's angry."

"Is she?" Ibram shook his head. "No, I didn't think so."

"At dinner with her mother? Those strange looks at breakfast?"

Ibram shrugged. "Tempers flare in uncertain times."

Ahksell sighed. "Well, what about Diarmit? Do you think he's hiding something?"

"If he is, he doesn't know it." Ibram beat his fingers against his sides. Emil had said Diarmit was the wildest of them, but he was also the youngest. Honestly, the conversation hadn't been much help. He sighed. "Rustam was..."

"Is, unless you think him dead."

"No, you're right, the warders would have found the body by now." Ibram shook his head; he glanced left and then right. "He's a sweet boy, but he doesn't say much, and he was very shaken by finding Tolk's body. He likes people, especially when they have a story. I remember I told him about that time I almost got caught trying to get inside Asfridlat, took his mind right off the corpse."

Ahksell shuddered. "I hate that one. Could he have gotten lost somehow?"

Ibram considered the forest they walked through. Like most of the province, they were in the bed of a valley, and surrounded by hardwood trees, dense and thick with foliage. In all his travels, he'd never seen its like: layers of greenery from the tiny, bright yellowish leaves on the budding lillia trees to the stiff needles so deeply green they might as well be blue or black depending on the light. The smell of resin and growing things was the perfume of home to him, and he'd missed it dearly. Far more, in fact, than he'd thought he would.

Ibram kicked a small stone out his path. "Anyone here would know their way around the village and its surrounds. Otherwise, they would have a guide from the headwoman's household, I would think. Can't have a Cohort of Peace stumbling about in some farmer's cabbages, can they?"

Ahksell nodded. "True enough, and let's be honest, there's no family in Fontis would dare hide him."

"Consider the length of time," Ibram said. "Two months ago a man dies of old age and a boy of eighteen years becomes the First Finder. It brings him a certain celebrity, but his overly religious mother—"

"We have no idea if Mistress Monbrith is overly religious," Ahksell said. "She could simply be returning to her religion in a time of trial."

"But the altar didn't work, did it?" Ibram asked. "What does it mean when candles are unburnt?"

Ahksell blinked and leaned a little away from him. "That the goddess is signaling displeasure," he said. "You bring the offering and leave when the candles light with the goddess' blessing."

"All the candles? Not one? Or two? Is there a kind of code to it?"

"Ibram," Ahksell said.

"I am merely suggesting that the only reasoning we have heard for Rustam to run away was that his goddess didn't light the candles for his family offering, even though Satya told us that they had been praying to the Sovereign Twins since this whole business began. The servant thinks someone put Rustam up to running...maybe it's his goddess?" Ibram rubbed his eyebrow. "So why did that frighten him so violently that he would sentence his mother, his sister and brother, and his entire village—including his sweetling—to a slow death by sanctioning?"

"We don't know he knows about that."

"A fine isn't much better."

Ahksell shook his head without speaking. Dogs barked excitedly on the road ahead of them, and Ibram looked up. He could see a four-some of warders herding a group of villagers from town marching towards them, dressed in mail over their purple and black-striped gambesons and with their pointed helmets on. Four brindled blood-hounds scampered around them all, short tails wagging. Ibram narrowed his eyes. He couldn't quite see, but most of the villagers' faces didn't look familiar. He cleared his throat, and spit to the side of the road, and then nudged Ahksell with his elbow. Ahksell nodded, peering ahead to their approaching company. It only took a few moments before they were met by the warders, and then Ibram recog-nized the man who had escorted him out of the headwoman's building.

"Good day, Warder Kamos," he called out before the other man could open his mouth. "Off to search the forests?"

"Much good it will do us," Kamos answered in a brusque voice. He gestured with his left hand at the trees. His tightly curled hair was wisping free of the comfort scarf knotted around the base of his helmet.

"Visibility should be good today at least," Ahksell said. "And every portion of the forest you do clear narrows the field."

Kamos paused, and then nodded. The group around him stirred. "Suppose that's true, lordship," he said.

"Attendant," corrected the woman behind him. Kamos twitched with annoyance, and she turned her face to stare directly at Ahksell. "Are you here to find the Monbrith boy?"

Ahksell nodded. "I am here to help, Mistress…"

"Terin," she said. She had a sharp, clean face, with hair that didn't know if it wanted to be yellow or brown tied up in a light blue woolen kerchief. Her breeches and heavy tunic were both brown and worn, but the leather belt and dagger at her waist was in good repair. "You'll not find him in the market, though, not if he knows what's good for him."

The group of villagers agreed in angry mutters behind her. Ibram studied their faces. None of them looked happy to be dragged from their duties, and neither did the warders. He cocked his head.

"Is Commander Osthanes still at Mistress Denrind's house?" he asked.

"He is," Kamos said. "Though I doubt he'll want to see you before his morning meal."

Ibram nodded. "Ours is a special relationship. Still, I'm sure he'd have no objection to my going into the shay shop. A man must eat after all."

"Aren't they feeding you in that burrow down the road?" Mistress Terin demanded.

"Family always tells," one of the villagers muttered. "One apple rots the barrel."

"No, no," Ahksell patted the air with his hands. "The Monbriths have been nothing but helpful."

"I'm just striking up an old acquaintance," Ibram said and raised his voice slightly. The villagers stirred amongst themselves, though the warders merely seemed bored. A hot, angry crowd forced to search for a fugitive all the hours of the day was nothing that should be pointed towards the draughtshop. He narrowed his eyes and cut a glance to Warder Kamos. He seemed to be in charge.

Kamos met his gaze and then looked away with a dour twist to his thin mouth. He gestured pointedly at his fellow warders. "And we've no time to spend asking a man for his dining preferences!" He began walking down the road. "Move out!"

The warders ushered the villagers down the road and off into the woods by the tiniest beaten footpath. Mistress Terin looked back sternly before she disappeared. Ibram frowned.

"Let's get moving," Ahksell said and pushed lightly on Ibram's shoulder.

He nodded and quickened his pace. They met no one else down the road, but occasionally he could hear the rustle of underbrush as they grew closer to Fontis. He glanced up at the treetops, but there was no wind. They must have deployed more warders than Ibram had first seen.

$$\text{❧} \quad 4 \quad \text{❧}$$

The main square of the village to either side of the road was bursting with the traders Ahksell had mentioned, yelling out prices for foodstuffs and wares that made Ibram's purse feel too light on principle. They had no want of custom, either; every merchant had no less than five good folk vying for their attention. Ibram dodged a woman carrying a coil of rope over her shoulder, and frowned at the crowd. Instead of free and easy laughter, he heard arguments and quick negotiations around them. It might be worth taking a stroll and seeing what disagreement came up most often.

Ibram saw a veritable caravan of yellow-clad Tyal servants running from group to group. He nudged Ahksell's elbow and cocked his head in their direction; Ahksell blinked at them and then made a face.

"If Ama's correct," Ibram began.

"She usually is," Ahksell interrupted.

"Well, if she *is*," Ibram continued, "then they've scrambling for workers to tend those lillia trees."

"Do you think one of them saw something?" Ahksell asked. "Where are they camped?"

"Outside of the village," Ibram said. "I don't remember where."

Ahksell reached out with his left arm and crooked two fingers. He frowned and tapped the air.

"What are you doing?" Ibram asked.

Across the road, one of the Tyal's servants startled and looked behind herself. She scratched the back of her head and frowned in confusion; Ahksell waved his entire arm at her. Her eyes widened, but she began making her way towards them.

Ibram sighed. Ahksell was easily the tallest man in the market square; it was like standing next to a water mill in full blast. "We could have just gone and spoken with her."

"Or spend our morning chasing after her in a crowd," Ahksell said.

"Show off."

"Ah, good morning, Mistress!" Ahksell declared as the woman reached them.

She bowed deeply. Her long red braid fell over her face. "Good morning, Attendant," she said. "Is there something the Tyal house can do for you?"

"Not at all," Ibram said, "but we hoped you might be able to answer a question or two."

She turned her head quickly in his direction, and frowned. She was probably more bothered at his speaking first rather than Ahksell, but it was better to nip any thought of future debts in the bud. Favors were for merchants, not alchemists. Ibram gestured to his left, and then at himself. "Be known to Attendant Solari. I'm Ibram."

"And I am Rozenn," she said. Ahksell set his arms at his sides, palms up, and she straightened. She cupped her shoulder with her hand. "Thank you, Attendant. Did you...I beg your pardon, I don't mean to be rude..."

"Yes, I was hoping to get your attention," Ahksell said. "I was wondering if you or any of your fellow servants were in Fontis when the boy Rustam ran away?"

Rozenn breathed in sharply. "We were within the border, yes," she said, and tucked her hands behind her back. "Our mistress sent an advance party to oversee the arrangement of her new grove."

"So you were in the village?" Ibram asked. "Or did Mistress Tyal have you camping in the trees?"

"We're camped at the grove," she said, with a quick glance between the two of them. "When the news came in the warders herded us into the village proper. We're staying in the stables now. They didn't even let us take our stores."

Ibram looked past Rozenn to where the other servants darted from group to group. If the judge's order went through, this mess represented a huge loss to whichever branch of the family purchased trees they would no longer be able to harvest. Rozenn coughed lightly.

"Are they—I mean, Attendant, is there something I can help you with?" she asked. "We're none of us from Fontis, and surely the warders will be letting us leave soon?"

She phrased it as a question, but Ibram could see her mind working behind her sharp green eyes. An Attendant would naturally have more knowledge than a mere servant, but a servant who knew something direct from an Attendant's mouth was a girl with picaio in her pouch. He smirked, but Ahksell seemed at a loss to answer.

"The Attendant can't divulge the warders' business," Ibram said, sternly. Rozenn's back stiffened. "Where are these lillia trees? And did you see anything the morning of the trial?"

"No!" she exclaimed and backed up a step. "No offense meant, of course, Attendant. I only thought you might know when I could go home to my family, you see. It's difficult being away."

Ahksell softened beneath the fluttering of her eyelashes. "Of course, Mistress," he said with a smile. "No offense was even registered. Ibram just didn't get enough sleep last night. It makes him testy."

She giggled. "Yes, Attendant. Thank you."

"But could you tell us?" Ahksell asked. "If you saw anything that day or the night before it could be helpful."

She shook her head and tossed her braid over her shoulder. "No," she said. "We're mostly here to put up fencing and mark out foundations for the processing huts to be—I mean, that we hope to be putting up near harvest time."

"So there's no way anyone might sneak past you in the grove?" Ibram asked.

She frowned at him and then snuck a glance at Ahksell and

attempted to look winsome. "I won't say no," she said, "but I can't think it likely either. There's a stream to one side of the trees and where we made our camp gives us a good view of the approach from the village."

"So you'd notice a man running," Ibram said. "But what about one who looks like he belongs on the road? Are you sure no peddlers walked by at all?"

"As to that, we could see a few foot travelers on the road far off," she allowed. "But he'd be going the wrong way, don't you think, Master? All the warders are saying so."

"The wrong way?" Ahksell asked.

Ibram sighed, and rubbed the back of his neck. He hadn't thought of that. Rozenn bobbed her head.

"Our mistress' grove is on the way to Hunter's Blind," Rozenn said and turned her pale cheek up to Ahksell. She had a gap in her teeth when she smiled.

"So if Rustam had planned his escape past your camp, he'd be going closer to the sect rather than away from it."

Ahksell nodded. "He'd be easier to catch inside the boundary than without it," he said.

"Which is why all the warders are searching east," Rozenn said, and cocked her head. "Did you not know that, Attendant?"

Ahksell opened his mouth and then cleared his throat. He tugged on his right earlobe in embarrassment. Ibram edged in front of him quickly. "The Attendant indulged me, Mistress," he said with a smile. "I was questioning the vast amount of trouble the warders were going to in order to find the fugitive and put forth a theory of my own that he might have taken shelter in your grove."

Rozenn flushed in alarm. "Certainly not!" she declared. "Attendant, I assure you my mistress' chamberlain would never harbor a criminal!"

"Oh I know!" Ahksell said and clasped his hand down on Ibram's shoulder. "But you know how it is. Sometimes you have to...simply let questions be asked. So they can be answered."

"They're like that up the living mountain. Thank you for your time, Mistress Rozenn," Ibram said. He backed up a step or two when Ahksell pulled on him. Rozenn frowned at them both, and Ibram shook himself free. He pointed. "Oh, look, is that your chamberlain now?"

Rozenn turned full around to peer into the crowd. Ibram bumped into Ahksell and then dragged him across the wide imperial road and ducked into the crowd. They paused at the edge of the cobblestones. Ibram groaned a laugh and rubbed the nape of his neck.

"Well, that's that for your mother's lillia tree connection," Ahksell said with a snicker.

"Oh?" Ibram asked and dropped his arm. "What happened to my mother always being right?"

Ahksell raised both hands. "Well, she never said the two were connected, did she?"

Ibram snorted and crossed his arms over his chest. Ahksell sighed in a great gust and looked about them. The crowd was thick here, but one of the stalls—something like a hut on wheels—was closed.

"Well, who should we speak to now?" Ibram asked.

Ahksell shook his head. "I have no idea," he admitted. "How do you usually start?"

Ibram looked up and down the road. He had no idea where to start, if he were truthful. Who was most likely to have the knowledge of what they needed to know that they hadn't not already spoken to? A small family jostled past them, tossing Ibram briefly off his balance. He jerked his head at Ahksell, and they began walking through the crowd again.

"Rope! Strong rope to last you years, good master! A flick for three feet!" a vendor shouted as they passed by. Ahksell whistled lowly and their eyes met. Five silver picaio was a hell of a price for three feet of rope unless it was strong enough to pull a longship inland, but the woman's stall was crowded with customers.

The trade stalls were set up to take advantage of the natural bisection of the square by the road that cut through the village. A flock of automated songbirds dipped and whirled above a stall dripping with other animated statues, trilling a lively melody. Another sold elixirs from the southern alchemical sects, properly sealed and examined. They looked to be cleaning supplies, mostly. As they passed, the merchant poured out a measure from his own wares onto a large rusty charger and purple smoke-filled bubbles congealed in the air as the charger polished itself. It was almost like a fair.

Ibram considered the gate wall, barely visible at the other end of the main road. It was illegal to block an Imperial road, so how were they going to enforce the sanctioning? Was the judge going to order the villagers to build walls on either side of the road, and doubly seal themselves away? How would the Monbriths or the other freeholders fit when their homes lay outside of the proper village? He saw Commander Osthanes at the main entrance to Mistress Denrind's home, and turned towards the man. It was never too late for a lesson on logistics, after all.

A whip cracked loudly by his ear; he jumped. Ahksell grabbed him by the arm, and pulled him to one side as a horse drawing an empty carriage trundled by. "Pay attention, Ibram!"

He shook himself free. They were under the overhanging eave of the stables before the shay shop now. "I am! I was only thinking."

"Of what?" Ahksell asked. He crossed his arms.

"Of speaking with the warders," Ibram said. If he'd been off by himself, he might have tried worming his way into the warders' commandeered offices for a chat with Commander Osthanes or a viewing of the report. Having Ahksell along muddled his usual method of begging forgiveness before asking permission. He was just a lowly arm-for-hire, not a true member of the sect, after all; Ahksell had a reputation to protect.

Ibram craned his neck back towards the headwoman's manor, but the commander had disappeared. "I suppose that might be more difficult to arrange than a servant girl, though." He frowned and rubbed the back of his head. "Now, I think we should split off and maximize our efforts."

"Really?"

Ibram nodded. "I'll go in to the shay shop and see what the village thinks of this whole mess. It might be that someone has an idea of why Master Rustam fled. You go call upon this sweetling they mentioned, and work your charms." He reached up and brushed down Ahksell's shoulders. "Make sure to stand in low light, but villagers love those courtesies of yours."

"The Speaker blesses your manifold compliments," Ahksell said.

"Well, you tell her I appreciate it," Ibram said. He shooed Ahksell off with both hands. "Off with you! Bring back knowledge!"

Ahksell snorted and stepped back into the throng of oldsters and children that made up most of the crowd. Probably the able-bodied folk had been rounded up to search the surroundings, though Ibram doubted it would help. Unless Rustam had gone to ground somewhere close by, even an untutored man could travel very far quite quickly if he was properly motivated. He could be anywhere by now. Ibram sighed and rubbed his eyebrow. He put his back to the trading stalls and walked down the wide alley that led around the side of the building towards the shop door. He kept to one side to avoid the steady stream of traffic.

"Wait, Ibram!" Ahksell called out behind him.

Ibram whirled on his heels and retraced his steps to the main street just as Ahksell came pounding back through the crowd. He bumped into a villager and caught them in both hands before they fell, lifting the man clear off his feet.

"Oh, my apologies, are you all right?" Ahksell set him down; the villager staggered backwards. Ahksell grabbed him and then began patting the other man free of dust.

"No, Attendant, please the fault was all mine!" The villager tried to bow in thanks and Ahksell drew him back up, still patting.

"No, no, not at all, I wasn't looking where I was going. I'm so tall, I always do this," Ahksell spoke over him. "Are you sure you aren't hurt? I really didn't see you there at all."

The villager—who was of a perfectly normal height, which meant he came to a little above Ahksell's elbow—turned a deep red. Ibram rolled his eyes and glanced around the growing throng of watchers in embarrassment.

"Truly, you look a little sunburnt," Ahksell said, and Ibram saw his hand stray to the pouch on his belt. "Here—"

A vision of explaining where Ahksell's money had gone to Lady Azadiya flashed flooded in Ibram's mind. The light of greed had no sooner lit in the villager's face, than Ibram had stepped forward and clamped his hand on Ahksell's arm.

"Attendant Solari!" Ibram called out brightly. "How good to find you again. Do you know, there's something very important I need to show you over this way?"

Ahksell looked down at Ibram's hand, and then up to his face; his eyes widened. He patted his new friend free of dust one last time and detached himself from the little spectacle. The villager's reddened cheeks deflated. Ibram smiled at him with all his teeth.

"So good of you to understand," he said, already dragging Ahksell away. "A pleasant day, master!"

They wove through the onlookers and back to the mouth of the alleyway leading to the shay shop. A drumbeat began to beat in the back of Ibram's head. Ibram let go of Ahksell's arm, and crossed both of his own over his chest.

"Do you want me to pass the hat around?" Ibram asked. "I think you and he have the bones of a good act there."

Ahksell raised his hand up by his right shoulder and touched his thumb to his middle finger. Ibram's eyes widened. He grabbed his hand and yanked it down before they truly caused a scene. Ahksell jerked free and glared at him.

"What's their name?" he asked.

"What? Whose name? That villager?"

"Rustam's sweetling," Ahksell said. "Who am I looking for?"

Ibram opened his mouth, and then paused. "Well, didn't you ask?"

"I'm asking you." Ahksell put his hands on his hips. "Didn't you ask?"

"Of course, I asked! It's..." He put his own hands on his hips. He cleared his throat. "So, neither of us asked?"

Ahksell spread his hands and raised his eyebrows. Ibram nodded. He glanced back out into the marketplace, but no one was carrying a sign indicating how intimately they knew Rustam Monbrith, and so he turned away.

"Well, maybe they'll know in the shay shop," Ibram said.

Ahksell groaned and turned him bodily around. He pushed on Ibram's back, and followed him down the alley. They reached the half-open door together, but Ibram went inside first. He blinked to adjust his eyes to the lower light. Zosi Kolesar, the owner, had a few glowbulbs hanging from the ceiling behind the bar, but most of the light during the day came in from the wide open windows. It was hot inside; the air smelled like bread.

The customers all seemed to have a lot to say to each other. He caught the edges of a dozen different conversations as they walked up to the bar. Ibram grimaced. All the talk was some variation on the same topic: what would happen to Fontis if Rustam was not found, and what would happen to the Monbriths even if they did. It made a man's stomach turn over.

Master Kolesar was handing his serving woman a pitcher and cups on a tray. Ibram leaned against the bar and tapped on the scruffy varnished wood to grab Zosi's attention. He was a swarthy man, thick around the middle, with a shock of white hair in a short braid over his left ear like a sailor. Ahksell settled at his back and Ibram shifted forward just a little.

"I remember you, young man," Master Kolesar said. He smiled and leaned both hands on the bar. "A bad time for a return visit, I should think."

"Oh, you never know," Ibram said. He made sure the light caught on his torch-shaped buckle. "Looks like you've got your hands full with all these customers, but since I'm visiting, I thought it best to see how you've been doing."

Zosi's eyes narrowed. "We've got the Cohort of Peace in town, you know," he said. "I figure their hard work will be enough."

You could take the man from Delbrite, but you couldn't remove Delbrite from the man's thinking. No matter how big and worldly the town was allowed to be, it had a lot to answer for, in Ibram's opinion. Every time he left the sect's corner of the province he was reminded of their bizarre insistence that the warders would take care of everything; it grew very tiresome. He resisted the urge to groan and nodded instead. Behind him, he heard Ahksell sigh and then felt him turn. He glanced back to see him resting both elbows on the bar.

"Two cups of cold shay, please," Ahksell said.

Zosi made a considering sort of face as he took in Ahksell's uniform, and then bowed shortly. "Of course," he said. "Gella! The midday special, frozen!"

So they weren't too proud to take advantage of those icing cantrips imported from the north. The serving girl turned around and went into the back. Zosi made to step away and Ibram cleared his throat; he took a rag out of the tie of his apron, and began wiping down the bar instead. Ibram ignored the dampening of his elbows.

"Surely it's the duty of any good Vissilian to aid in each other's time of misfortune," Ibram said.

"I suppose that's true," Zosi said. "Can't work the hauling rope by yourself."

"Exactly so," Ibram said, and nodded. "And that's why we're here. Besides, I enjoyed my time in Fontis last I visited."

"It's a good little village."

Ibram grinned. "And any travel is good travel, in my thoughts. What was it you said the morning I left? Something about the river?"

Zosi scrubbed a spot on the bar with a particularly hard swipe, but a smile began taking root on his face. "When the river calls, all good sailors answer."

"And I do miss answering the call." Ahksell poked him in the back, hard; Ibram ignored him. "Well, on the road anyway."

"Making the switch is a hard task," Zosi said.

"But you've made a success of it," Ibram said.

Zosi waved his hand. "My husband's family did the work, I just maintain it."

"Even a successful business can fail without a steady hand."

Zosi tossed his rag down to the bar. "All right, young master," he said. "What is it you want?"

Ahksell poked him in the back again, but Ibram shrugged him off. He smiled. "Master Rustam's movements the night he disappeared. Did he come into the shop?"

"I already spoke of this to one of the warders, you know."

"Ah, but they aren't from around here," Ibram said. "Might be we together can figure out something they cannot."

He kept up a pleasant face while Zosi studied him for a breath or two. Gella came by with Ahksell's order on a slim wooden tray. He thanked her, and then Ibram heard the clatter of coins on the counter. Zosi pursed his lips. "Those Monbriths don't come in for the ovens," he said. "They've got their own, so we don't see them as much as others in the village. Usually Mistress Monbrith will send one of the children when they're low on loose shay or a pound of caffa."

"They buy caffa?" Ibram asked.

Zosi nodded. "We get the occasional noble passing through, it's best to be prepared."

"So it wasn't anyone's particular job to come into town? I thought Rustam might be a bit eager to stretch his legs."

"Ach, well, Rustam." Zosi's face screwed up briefly in distaste. He sighed and looked about the shop. "These are almost all newcomers, you know? Bleeding us dry in case it's their last chance."

"Well, it seems like you're doing some bloodletting in return," Ahksell said. "I see those prices on your board here are newly marked."

Zosi looked up sharply, and then chuckled. "No point in keeping the sails tied up when the wind's blowing, is there, Attendant?"

Ahksell laughed. "No, I suppose not."

"Besides, I'm sure they'll find the Monbrith boy, he's not the sort of person to run around in the woods for any length of time."

"No," Ibram said and turned back. "He didn't strike me as the lonely hunter sort either."

Zosi leaned his hip on the bar and crossed his arms. His tattoo of a compass bulged. "Are you going to be joining one of the search parties, then?"

"I might," Ibram said. He had absolutely no intention of doing that, of course. What could he do in a forest that a pack of locals and a couple of squads of warders could not accomplish? He turned to his left and grabbed the cold shay Ahksell had ordered for him. "Do you honestly think they'll find him?"

"I can't think why he'd run," Zosi paused. His eyes flickered over Ibram's shoulder to where Ahksell stood. "Unless there was a question of violence and he'd lost his nerve, of course."

A tiny circle of quiet had grown about them as folk recognized the alchemist in their midst. Customers were beginning to lean as close as they dared. Ibram glanced about the common room to the rows of packed tables. He saw money changing hands.

"Oh no, no," Ahksell said. Ibram knew without looking he'd

adopted that unfairly earnest expression of his again; he drank his shay and sucked an ice cube into his mouth. "Master Tolk died quite naturally. I checked the body thoroughly and the pronouncement has been accepted by Judge E'grard."

A shiver ran through the crowd. Ibram watched a sour-faced old mistress scrape the money she'd collected in the center of her table back towards her companion. The crowd noise grew around their little corner of the bar, and Ibram put his back to it.

Zosi relaxed backwards from the bar, and tucked his rag back underneath the tie of his apron. "That's all right, then," he said.

"Was it a fear?" Ahksell asked. "I never heard Rustam described as the type to get into fights."

Discomfort drew lines down either side of Zosi's mouth. "Well, there was a bit of a scuffle the week before the judge showed up," he said. "Between Rustam and the Suugan boy."

Emil had mentioned the Suugan family, had he not? In connection with the youngest boy, Diarmit. The back of Ibram's head tingled, but he kept his face mild and pleasant. "Just a couple of children scuffling?" he asked.

Zosi shook his head. "Tieri Suugan bloodied his nose," he said. "Though Rustam's sister was quick to stop it. Still, the mess washed out clean once the Terin girl put their heads right," he said. "We all thought no more of it until he disappeared."

"Terin?" Ahksell asked. "Not Mistress Terin? We just met her on the road."

Zosi chuckled. "Aye, she's got a pot to heat with that whole family now. It's her daughter they were fighting over."

Ibram took another drink. "So which did she choose? Tieri or Rustam?"

Zosi began wiping out the empty wooden mugs behind the bar. "Oh, Rustam, of course. Tieri's nothing but a bruiser, and Hasi's bright as a new struck faunt." He sighed. "The three of them are practically the only ones their age in the village. Bound to happen, I suppose, but it's made life hard in the square since...what with all that happened later, I mean. Mistress Terin's taken the suspicion very badly, and Mistress Suugan's closed the family shop."

"Suspicion?" Ibram asked.

Zosi cleared his throat. "Well," he waved his hand in the air, "that Hasi knew Rustam was going to run, perhaps. They being so close and all."

"Young love," Ahksell said, very much as if he was a wise old man with a harem at his back.

"You'd know all about that, would you, Attendant?" Zosi asked him.

Ibram laughed before he could help himself, and ducked his head down. Ahksell kicked him in the ankle, and Ibram straightened up. "Well, Attendant Solari's a popular soul," he said. "But why has Mistress Suugan closed up shop?"

"Why, for the other rumor going about the village," Zosi said. "Seeing as it was her boy who fought Rustam, they thought...well, perhaps Rustam might have needed to get out of Fontis for a bit and misjudged his time." Zosi looked about the room and then leaned in to speak quietly. "Or perhaps he didn't leave at all, if you understand me."

Ibram nodded. He looked down into his cup, and then took another sip. Zosi kept his cold shay sweet. He didn't prefer it, but it was drinkable, and Ibram had a secret fondness for cold drinks.

"If you don't mind," Ahksell said suddenly, and Ibram looked up. "I see a little corner table opening up. If we clear the bar, Master Kolesar might finally be able to take a few orders."

Ibram stood back and bumped into someone behind him. He craned his neck and saw, indeed, that a line had developed that threatened to swamp poor Gella completely. He held his cup against his chest, and made himself bob his head politely.

"As you say," he said to Ahksell and then grinned at Zosi. "Always nice to talk with you."

"And you as well, youngster," Zosi said, and raised his arm towards the front of the building. "Keep that door closed!" He yelled.

Ahksell picked up his own shay, and Ibram followed in the wake of the trail he blazed. Folk squeezed against each other to give Ahksell a path to the last open table. The table was beneath an open window, with a fine breeze coming in that only smelled a little bit like the horses from the nearby stables. Ahksell took the chair that put his back to the door, and Ibram sat against the wall. He moved aside the small bowl of roasted treeka nuts left on the table. He popped one in his mouth and sucked off the salt. Not bad for something grown halfway across the empire.

"Worst thought," Ahksell said and leaned in. He drank his shay.

"We're going to run out of money if we keep eating everywhere we need to question people."

Ahksell pressed his boot down hard on Ibram's foot under the table. "If you don't want yours..."

He reached out for Ibram's cup; Ibram smacked the back of his hand with his fingers. "I didn't say that!"

"You want me to say it instead?" Ahksell asked.

Ibram scrunched his nose at him. He lifted his shay to his mouth and took a large slurp. Ahksell wrinkled his nose; Ibram smacked his lips.

"Come on," Ahksell said. "Worst thought."

"Rustam Monbrith ran because he might have won the affections of the Terin girl, but the bully was still after him." Ibram wrinkled his nose. "But one bully against the entire Cohort of Peace and the Court Civil?" he asked himself immediately. "Surely not."

Ahksell shrugged. "He's young."

"Eighteen is a ripe age for foolishness, but he's not stupid," Ibram said. "And if it were the—the Suugan boy then why did he wait to run?"

"He could be dead."

Ibram shook his head. "No, I still think he's alive for all the reasons we spoke of before."

"If the whole village thinks it likely, though, perhaps we should keep the thought in the back of our minds too." Ahksell shook his head. "Tieri Suugan...We could go and speak with him as well. Did you recognize the name? Where does he live?"

Ibram exhaled in thought. "I...vaguely, yes. They're friends, at least Diarmit is friends with whoever is his age in that family."

"So they all probably grew up together. Ahksell grunted and looked into his cup. "Not going to do too well if we can't find Rustam, are they."

Ibram glanced outside the window. The beaten path that led to the wide alley and the village square was mostly clear now, with only a few groups of stragglers headed in for a drink. One of the mules in back of the shay shop neighed; the sound of millstones grinding drifted out across the common room.

"We should retrace Rustam's footsteps," Ibram said. "Like when you're out hunting and you need to follow a trail."

"His mother said he hadn't done anything out of the ordinary," Ahksell pointed out.

"True," Ibram said, "but I can remember doing several things in the course of my day that I never felt the need to tell my mother about when I was eighteen."

Ahksell laughed. "Before or after you left Lityen?"

"Both," Ibram shrugged.

Ahksell shook his head and sighed. "What about the court records?"

"Satya gave testimony that Rustam had disappeared and what he'd taken with him," Ibram said. He thought back to the papers he'd read. "The mother...just a repeat of what she told us at dinner. And no one spoke to Diarmit or Emil."

"Maybe they have now," Ahksell said. "We could ask the warders."

"We aren't officially part of any investigation," Ibram pointed out. Ibram took a sip of his drink and rolled the liquid in his mouth before swallowing. "Do you think it's worth it to go and speak with the Suugans? It could be nothing, to be sure."

Ahksell revolved his shay cup in both hands. "I think we should," he said after a moment. "At the very least it's better to clear up a rumor from the source."

"Ah, but what if he lies?" Ibram crossed his arms. "I don't suppose you have an elixir for that?"

Ahksell chuckled, but shook his head. "If I could concoct something like a truth potion," he said. "I'd be living it up in a crystal and marble palace on the Summer Sea dressed in golden samite from head to foot."

"You've put a lot of thought into that fantasy, I see."

"What alchemist hasn't?" Ahksell asked. He shrugged. "Our Founder was gifted the right to establish our sect just for creating the imperial sewage system. The Sect of Purple Spires gained its license for conceiving luminescent sand. The closest anyone has ever come to formulating a truth serum just makes someone chatter until oblivion takes them, but if you could figure out how to control their speech? To make them only reveal the truth? The alchemist who accomplishes that can ask for anything."

Ibram dimly felt the need to shudder building at the base of his spine, and suppressed it. Ahksell blinked at him, and then smiled suddenly. The corners of his eyes crinkled.

"Not that you'll get many such things out of Yseult," he said. "The most concocting we ever do is for our own personal use."

Ahksell waggled his shay cup, and the ice sloshed inside of it. Ibram sniffed and finished his drink. He stood away from the table with a screech of chair legs. Ahksell leaned back.

"Well, you certainly don't need anything to make you talkative," Ibram said, and cleared his throat. "Let's go and see this bully of Rustam's now. We might be able to actually accomplish something today."

W hatever progress Ibram had hoped to make in the morning, it slowly melted as the sun rose higher in the sky. They walked the length of the market with nothing to show for it but sore legs. The Suugans had not been at home to visitors on account of being swept up by Commander Osthanes' warders in the dim hours of the morning, and that sat ill with Ibram. If Tieri knew anything about Rustam's disappearance—perchance he was the reason for it—he might be using the knowledge for his own gain in regards to the lovely and also elusive Hasi Terin. To be sure, if Osthanes caught up to Rustam before they did then half of Fontis' problems were solved, but the fact still remained that not one person could attach a motive to Rustam's flight. Fontis was high on emotion and low on information, for which he supposed they could not be blamed. Still, Ibram resented it.

They'd walked from one end of the village to the other, and no one seemed to know anything about the how or the why. Most of them wanted to cooperate, but couldn't say who they wanted to help more: the sect as exemplified by Ibram and Ahksell or the Empire as represented by the warders. The entire village was sitting in the doorway of a cell, and couldn't figure out which way the bars swung. Ahksell's presence seemed to reassure the villagers they talked to, but it also appeared to alarm them. At length, they returned to the shay shop to regroup.

It was no less packed than it had been in the morning—all the more so, because of the traffic in and out the door. The noise had everyone raising their voices to be heard, which made the bellowing even worse. Ibram had despaired in line, but the sight of Ahksell's uniform magically cleared a table once they'd acquired their food. Ahksell appeared uncomfortable at the courtesy, but Ibram was unrepentant; his feet hurt.

"I'm telling you, if they let him go, then the Suugan boy had little to do with it," Ibram said.

Ahksell pursed his lips and stirred his spoon in his bowl. "Or they simply can't prove he did."

"When has that stopped anyone from cooling their heels in a cell?"

"They don't have cells in Fontis," Ahksell pointed out.

Ibram shrugged and looked down at his plate. The midday meal was goat braised in its own broth with large chunks of onion and a strong whiff of garlic. Pepper oil congealed in slick pools on its surface, but he was damned if he could stomach that right now.

He poked a floating carrot piece with his spoon. "They could—"

"I'm telling the story!" an old woman yelled and Ibram turned his head at the interruption. She pounded her table with one bony fist. "Not a one of you deserves the warning but I'll not be swept up for oblivion on account of your ignorance!"

"Keep your breath to cool your quash, Madji Anlines," someone shouted from the crowd. "There's babes in here don't need to have your shrieks giving them nightmares."

Anlines? The family name sounded familiar. The crowded common room laughed. The old mistress set her hand to her right shoulder, her finger beneath her thumb, and flicked. A few customers rose from their chairs in a cacophony of wood scraping against the floor and were pulled back down by their tablemates. Some even gave her the filip right back; Ibram rolled his eyes and bent over his food. The only reason someone ever began speaking loudly in a common room was when they wanted to perform to a trapped audience; he absolutely refused to encourage her.

"Sour old goat," a man hissed.

"Do you know what they do?" the old mistress' reedy voice cut through the throng in the shay shop; the crowd quieted. "I do! I'm old enough that my father could remember Mandibrite. I remember his stories!"

"There's no such place," her tablemate argued. "All you remember is fire tales and fantasies, Madji."

"May oblivion disperse my soul if it's untrue!" Madji insisted loudly. She knew she had an audience. "Not true! Mandibrite was in Nivenia and they raised the University of Cornwarke on its bones! My grandfather used to trade there, good ranchers in the lowlands with a fair price for wool."

"It was the father but a moment ago," Ibram muttered at his food. He looked over to Ahksell and found him looking back. Ibram bent his head over his lunch; the sun through the window warmed the side of his face.

"Now then," Zosi called out. "Madji, we've spoken about you telling tales in here."

"And wasn't I shown to be right in the end? This whole village had done better to toss that family out past your so-called imperial boundary. And if you want my money to keep your shay shop running, you'll let me finish, Zosi Kolesar!" The old woman's voice grew even louder with conviction. "I know what happened to Mandibrite and I know what'll happen to you!"

The entire shop was silent now; he could hear the clack of the old woman's heavy wooden beads. Ibram refused to turn around. He shoved a spoonful of stew in his mouth and chewed. The almond milk in the broth was badly sieved; grains filled his teeth.

"Not that it will help you much," Madji said. "Too trusting that's why this village is doomed. It was the same in Mandibrite. My father told me they found a body up there, drowned in the pools around the Mand river, and none knew her name, nor where she'd come from."

"Drowned in the spring thaw, no doubt," her companion said, but her voice trembled.

"That's what they all thought," Madji said. "And no one said anything against it, nor the girl who found her. My father told me, they were always finding bodies in the pools, folk who missed a step in the ice and paid for it, but when the judge came up to give the trial and send the poor soul on with The Wanderer, the first finder was naught to be found."

A stone would have made more noise in the mud than was present in the crowd now. Ibram made a careful survey, looking from corner to corner as well he could without moving his head. Every man and woman was listening; even the babe in the sling seemed to hold its breath. He heard the scrape of a chair, and knew that decayed curse-bird had stood to address her audience.

"That judge," she said with relish, "wasn't as gentle as His Honor in this headwoman's house. She delivered her judgment and as soon as court was finished, wrote out the dead woman's writ of travel and burned the corpse to speed the process. Then she ordered out her alchemists and her warders."

She paused, swallowing her drink in wet gulps, and the tablemate cleared her throat. "Madji, that's enough."

"You don't need alchemists to raise a wall," the man with the baby sneered.

"They did something," Madji insisted.

Ibram met Ahksell's eyes. They sold table beer in the shop at lunch, more porridge than alcohol. Unless she'd been at the table a day and a night, this high talker wasn't drunk on anything but the sound of her own voice. Ahksell rubbed his hand down his face and leaned his chin in the cup of his palm.

"My father was there loading up the wool, and he said the warders went to each caravan and searched the carts. They pulled out those that tried to sneak away in empty barrels and killed them where they stood. They locked the traders who'd helped them in a storeroom and drove the rest out," Madji said with a smack of her lips.

Ibram leaned back in his chair for a better view. She had the look of a woman from deep within the interior of the empire, medium-height with a sharp pale face, puffed with ill-temper at the eyes, and a high peaked scalp. Her grey hair was cut short and flat to her skull. She wore a plain white kirtle and brown surcoat with a string of heavy multi-colored beads connecting her cloak about her shoulders. If

Ibram put some effort into it, he might be able to grab hold and pitch her out an open window before her companion could stop him.

"The whole town," she said, "with naught to trade and nowhere to go, and the judge drove off in her carriage with the howls of the headman ringing in her ears."

"There's been a university in Nivenia for longer than you've been alive," Zosi said. "You don't know what you're saying, old woman."

"I do!" Madji insisted.

Ibram flicked his eyes up and met Ahksell's troubled gaze. He frowned, and Ahksell looked down to his own meal. Ahksell made a fist and drew his arm back across the tabletop. He shook his head. Why wasn't Ahksell saying anything? This firetale sounded easy enough to refute. After all, what good was a wall when no one was watching it? Easy enough to make a battering ram and escape once this intemperate judge had moved on, and even then Ibram had never heard of Mandibrite before now.

"She acts like she believes it," Ibram said loudly enough to be heard while Madji drew breath. "But I don't."

Lies were only lies when they could be proven false, after all. No one in the shop could say what sanctioning actually was, not even him. Ibram took his eyes off his food to stare at the top of Ahksell's bent head. Ahksell glanced up but still refused to meet his eyes. Ibram squinted; that smacked of an Attendant who knew too much in his opinion.

"Is that so, young master?" Madji called out. Her voice sharpened. "You're going to sit there in your sect garb and call me a liar?"

Ibram swiveled in his seat and leaned back against the wall of the shop. He saw a few people eye the torch buckle on his chest and then look away. It was certainly a wondrous day for people refusing to meet his eye. He inclined his upper body and her wrinkled mouth stiffened into a thin line.

"I hope I call no one a liar without thought, old mistress," he said and heard someone stifle a laugh. "But I swear I never heard such nonsense as this. A judgment passed like that and no one but you and your grandfather left to spread the word? Or was it your father now?"

Her face grew taut with anger. "My father," she snapped.

"It's a fine true tale with no one to say it *didn't* happen." He waved her off and slumped in his chair. Better to try and calm folk while he still had a job to do. "But a whole village gone and naught but you to tell of it in living memory? I hate to ask anyone their age, Mistress..." Ibram spread his hands, and heard laughter from a few corners of the room. Madji flushed.

"If you want to practice your craft, Mistress Storyteller, I'd say try the patch of earth near the well," Ibram said. "It happens I saw a puppetry show there when last I visited. Won't you be able to pass the hat better out in the open air?"

Madji Anlines reared back as if struck. She turned white around the mouth and red everywhere else. "You'll shut your mouth when the time comes, *barbarian*," she hissed.

Ahksell's chair screeched as he pushed it back, and the room suddenly remembered it held an alchemist. Ibram's shoulders threatened to hunch, but he shoved them level before they met his neck. Madji's tablemate began gathering their things. Ibram grinned into her beady-eyes, and made certain to show all his teeth. His heartbeat louder in his chest.

"Out, Madji!" Zosi barked. He pointed to the door. "You go sleep this off in that distillery you call a wagon of yours!"

The baby began to wail. Their father took them outside, loudly shushing. Ibram leaned back slowly in his chair. He turned his head. The old mistress was standing by her chair and drinking deeply from her mug. She put it down on the table and wiped her mouth.

"No one better try to put a toe in my wagon," she said, and her tablemate got to her own feet. She looked about the room and raised her hand to Zosi in a conciliatory gesture. The woman put her hand on Madji's shoulder and began pulling her through the crowd, who let her through. "I'll not be shut up here with the likes of you!"

Ibram watched the pair of them leave and then followed their path through the window. He inhaled slowly and let the breath out again.

"That Madji's been after her own product again," Zosi said with a forced laugh. "It turns her nasty."

The angle of Ibram's eyesight was off, but he could just make out the folk lingering in front of the shay shop. The father swayed the babe in his arms, him staring at nothing as the baby snuffled in his shoulder. Ibram turned in his chair to check the common room. There were a few warders in the crowd, he realized. They looked uncomfortable. Across from him, Ahksell set his cup on the table and curled his left hand into a fist.

He stood abruptly, and Ibram sat back in his chair. The air felt close. His shoulder muscles tensed.

"Nothing has been sealed yet," Ahksell called out and Ibram felt the regard of the crowd sharpen as the patrons took in Ahksell's bearing, his deep green gambeson and clear eyes. If he'd held his gar instead of his satchel, it would have been a scene out of a traveling romance show. "Where a man has gone, he can be found, and every person who can help has reached out their hand. *We* are here to help."

He looked about the common room like he wanted to peer into everyone's eyes and reassure them personally. Ibram looked to the bar. Surely, Zosi didn't allow this much pontificating in the usual course of the day. But Zosi was silent, grey-faced, with his chin lifted. Gella the serving girl had her tray clasped to her chest, and her eyes were glistening. Ahksell peered out over the crowd and then down to Ibram, wide-eyed. Ibram gestured to Ahksell's audience. Ahksell's shoulders moved in a barely noticeable shrug. Ibram grinned and bobbed his head slightly. It wasn't a great ending, but he supposed it got the point across. Ibram tossed back the last of his shay, and bid farewell to his stew. He stood away from the table.

"Off we go, then," Ibram said. His voice seemed overloud, but he put as much jollity in it as he could force himself to pretend. "Our thanks for the meal."

Ahksell fell into step with him through the shop and outside. Ibram nodded politely to the father with the baby as they passed him, and they walked in silence until they reached the main square. The traders were still hard at work, and the lines seemed to have shifted. Even the street eatery, which Ibram had only seen at festivals before, was drawing a crowd. Ibram blinked. It was the same folk, just in different places.

"You're not a barbarian," Ahksell said. He grabbed him by the arm.

Ibram cleared his throat, and patted his hand where it held Ibram's sleeve. "I know that," he said. "It didn't bother me."

"She shouldn't have called you that."

Ibram shrugged and worked himself free of Ahksell's grip. "I favor my mother," he said. "Give it another six hundred years or so and I'm sure us Westerners will find someone to call barbarians, too."

Ahksell frowned; his forehead still creased with worry. Ibram waved him off and looked out over the market again. He shook his head at the crowd.

"So those buttons on your gambeson," Ibram said, for want of better ideas to change the subject. "How do they work anyway?"

"My what?" Ahksell asked.

"Your buttons," Ibram said. "The ones with all the enamel work that do things to people."

Ahksell barked a laugh. "That's not quite how I'd put it."

"How would you then?"

Ibram glanced over, and Ahksell shook his head. "I can't tell you."

"Of course," Ibram said. He cast around for something else to say. "Why can't I get my hands on them? Might come in handy, you know. I might need to blow something up or lock something away."

Ahksell shrugged. "Ask at Afsoun," he said. "I know they test them out with their agents."

And what was a little life-threatening danger to an arm-for-hire? Ibram nodded. He glanced down to the front of Ahksell's gambeson where he carried the little contraptions. Alchemical things always had grandiose sorts of titles: 'The Torch of Everlasting Illusion' or 'Thesengrim's Collapsible Filtering Cup' or something like that. "Do they have names?"

Ibram stepped out into the throng and Ahksell followed. He shrugged again. "They're just little shields that clip on," Ahksell said.

"So you could put it on anything? Is it the design?"

They passed a leatherworker putting out a tray of braided mouflon ties with glistening locator stones caught in the middle. Ibram tsked in jealousy. If Rustam had worn one of those things, they'd have been able to find him in two snaps of a lady's favor.

"Ibram, I can't tell you how to make Persep's Injunctions."

"Ah ha!" Ibram gave a little jump mid-step. "They do have a stupid name!"

Ahksell snorted and smoothed his hand down his front. His face relaxed into less anxious lines. Ibram took it as a small victory; there was no need for Ahksell to look upset...beyond the task at hand, of course.

"This one is for restraint," Ahksell said and tapped a silver button with interlocking circles of blackened iron and yellow enamel swirled within it. "You might practice some."

Ahksell still seemed fretful about something. His expression reminded Ibram of the time Katka had sworn Ahksell to secrecy over Ibram's birthday present; he'd lasted half the day before spilling his guts. Ibram led him past the candle-maker's stall. They looked to be down to selling bundles of rushes now.

"Do you know how a sanctioning works?" Ibram asked. Another change of subject seemed in order, it might as well be one which returned them to the matter at hand.

"I have a basic understanding of the mechanics," Ahksell said. The strain returned to his face. "Mentor requested a book of law from the library and we looked it up. I didn't like the implications."

Ibram nodded to himself; of course they had. "Well, how will they do it?" He lowered his voice. "With the road in between it won't be an easy task. Besides, there's not enough ready lumber to seal the whole place away, and I haven't heard any forest cutting."

Ahksell sighed. His cheeks flexed as he tensed his jaw. "They don't need to cut anything—well, they might if Fontis was more in the interior—but I overheard Judge E'grard with his retainers. They have an order in for wood from the lumber depot in Delbrite, and...well, since Fontis is where it is...we're to take care of the actual raising."

Ibram blinked. "We are?"

"No, I mean," Ahksell stopped talking. He looked around in the sort of furtive way that demanded instant attention from anyone looking, and stepped closer to Ibram. "That's why the Second Mentor of Salacia went to see Lady Sebbina, because Judge E'grard put in a preliminary order for the Sect to raise the borders in case Master Monbrith couldn't be found."

He jerked his head up at an eruption of cursing from the folk in the square. That Madji woman had lost her tablemate and was stumping through the crowd, not minding who she knocked into along the way. A man with a now-sore foot put his hand to his shoulder and flicked his middle finger at her back; a nearby young mother covered her infant's eyes, but the rest of the onlookers roared with laughter. Madji ignored them, and then a group of Tyal servers crossed her path and Ibram lost her.

"Don't tell me the old woman from the shop was telling the truth." Ibram frowned. She had had quite the story to tell. What kind of border needed an alchemist dedicated to the study of the abyssal plane to close it? Was it like a lightning lock? Ibram's chest felt a little hollow.

"How have we never heard of it before then?" Ibram asked. "Is that why you're here as well? To survey the land?"

"No!" Ahksell reared back and then returned to hunch over Ibram. "Don't be silly, I have no idea how they're going to do it. Mentor offered to explain it to me, but I didn't want to know."

"Then why lie to everyone back in the shay shop?"

Ibram frowned. He didn't like to think that Ahksell could tell a falsehood and Ibram wouldn't know it. He'd always been a poor liar when they were younger, or so he had thought.

"That's not it at all." Ahksell shook his head. "Mandibrite was hundreds of years ago, her father couldn't have been there."

"Then explain yourself," Ibram said and crossed both arms. "How far off the mark was she? And how would she know anything in the first place?"

"How do merchants know anything?" Ahksell asked. "They travel, they talk, it's nothing new! And I've no doubt she picked it up in some student bar near the university. Students love grisly tales like that, and so does she."

Ibram clicked his teeth together and frowned. "I suppose," he said slowly. "But why wait to tell me? Aren't we here for the same purpose?"

"I'm here because Mentor doesn't want Fontis shut away," Ahksell said. "You were in the meeting yourself!"

"Then how soon are we to expect your folk from Salacia?" he asked, but kept his voice low. "And why that preceptory in the first place?"

Ahksell sighed. "I don't know yet," he said. "Nothing was decided when we left."

They stood in a pocket of space, untouched, but if they stayed longer someone—even just a trader—would begin to wonder what two well-dressed strangers talked of so seriously. Ibram breathed in the afternoon air, and waved his hand in front of his nose. He could smell the horses in the stable.

"And if we hurry, we might never need to know," Ibram said.

Ahksell cleared his throat. "Let's go speak with Mistress Suugan," he said. "We have to begin somewhere."

Ibram nodded, but then paused with one foot above the ground. He set it down in place and tilted his head. "No," he said. "I think we should talk to that old mistress."

On the other side of the imperial road, Ibram eyed the line of trading stalls that had popped up in front of the actual houses in the village. Smoke from kitchen fires rose up in the bright air. A trio of children ran around the village well, and then raced each other to the leather goods stall, laughing.

Ahksell wrapped one hand on the strap of his satchel. "Why? She can't possibly know more than she boasted of back in the shop. Anyway, she was half-decanted."

"Now, we don't know Madji Anlines was drunk," Ibram said, even though he'd have laid out a flick on the strength of the odds. "Many people get a little dramatic before lunch."

"Zosi said she likes to sample her own wares," Ahksell reminded him. "He said she lives in a distillery."

"Which is just plain wrong, really. You'd die of the fumes."

Ahksell stretched his arms out, and skimmed the head of a passerby. The man startled; Ahksell took no notice. "What possible relevance does she have to finding out why Rustam ran?"

Ibram shrugged and then caught himself raising one hand to his eyebrow. "I don't know," he admitted. "But doesn't what she might have to say sound interesting?"

"This isn't a fact-finding mission," Ahksell said, and looked around them quickly. "I mean, strictly speaking it is, but not every fact! We should be concentrating on—on Rustam's character! And why wouldn't we need to talk to the very person who got in a fight with him before he ran?"

Ibram sighed, and rocked his head left and then right. "I know we need to speak to the Suugans," he said. "But I also think we need to speak to that strange woman. We spent all morning listening to gossip and that was the only piece that stuck out to me. If she collects stories, then maybe she collected Rustam's, and if she did…"

"She might also speak to his state of mind," Ahksell finished for him. He sighed.

Ibram dragged up the left corner of his mouth. "You just don't like her," he said.

"She's unpleasant," Ahksell said. "And she's got a sickly emanation about her."

"That would be the sojin, probably," Ibram said.

"Not that kind of emanation," Ahksell said and tapped his left temple.

Ibram grimaced. "Did you drink something funny when you got up this morning?"

"I drank it when I was fifteen," Ahksell said, "and now my eyes—"

Ibram raised his hands and interrupted him. "I don't want to know," he said. "You drink weird brews professionally and it makes you see colors that aren't there, and that's perfectly fine. But I want to know about Rustam, not you melting nails with your mind or what have you."

"Well, that's just silly," Ahksell said. "Why would anyone want to melt nails with their mind?"

Ibram groaned. Ahksell rested his hand on Ibram's shoulder. He leaned down. "Look, Mistress Ale-pot isn't going anywhere, is she?" he asked. "Yet if Master Kolesar told us about that fight between the two boys, then he no doubt told the warders—that is to say, if someone else hadn't spoken to them first! Mentor would tell us that every moment counts, would she not?"

Ibram sighed. Ahksell wasn't wrong, Lady Azadiya's dislike of mistakes was nothing to her disdain for paltry information. Yet something was poking at Ibram from the back of his mind, a magpie instinct to pick up every piece of information on the off chance it was shiny enough to have merit. He flexed his shoulder in Ahksell's grip, and Ahksell let him go.

"Let's go see the Suugans," Ibram said grudgingly. "Suppose it doesn't matter in what order we speak to our suspects."

"All right," Ahksell said. "But try not to order any shoes."

He grinned when Ibram pointedly ignored that unkind remark. Ahksell's footwear came from the preceptory's stores. He didn't need to take any interest in cobblers like the rest of them. They started off again. The Suugans lived just off the market square, nearest the well, he believed. He tried to remember the diagram he'd drawn up in his mind when he was last in the village. Ladyship liked to know everything about a village when one of her agents visited, and no detail was too slight.

Ibram pointed to his right, and then led the way forward to the opposite side of the square. He nodded to one of the warders passing on patrol. Osthanes must have brought quite a few with him—or perhaps called up reinforcements when Rustam disappeared. The situation became precarious.

"Ucalegon," Osthanes yelled behind them. "Halt where you stand!"

Think of a man, and Laumye the Blue would direct you to him. Ibram winced. Ahksell stopped when he did, and stood by Ibram's elbow. Ibram saw a break in the crowd near the wagons.

"He didn't mean you," he hissed, and tried to shoo Ahksell on his way, but Ahksell refused to be shooed. He stood by Ibram's side and turned to face the oncoming warder marching towards them.

"Good day to you, Commander Osthanes," Ahksell said.

The good commander wavered a step in his tracks, before visibly straightening himself. He walked the last few steps alone. The warders following him, a pair of darker-skinned southerners with extra scarves wrapped around their necks, halted when Osthanes did, and took up ready positions behind him. Ibram glanced around; a small area of space had opened about them.

"Good day, Attendant Solari," he answered, and bowed shortly. A watch commander in the Cohorts of Peace was of a slightly lower social standing than a sect Attendant, but not by much. He already had his patience strip in hand, and the brass rivets appeared quite shiny.

"How goes your search, Commander?" Ibram asked. "We ran into your man Kamos on the road into the village. Is Rustam hiding behind any trees?"

Was that a chuckle being strangled behind Osthanes' heavy grimace? Ibram thought it was. He chanced a grin, which was not returned.

"We've ruled out most of the trees in the immediate vicinity," Osthanes said. "But the judge wants to see you, so you'll have to come with me."

"The judge wants to see me?" Ibram asked. He cocked his head. "Why?"

"He missed the opportunity yesterday, and he simply can't go another day without your company," Osthanes said.

"Ah well," Ibram replied and looked about himself. "Are you certain the judge needs to see me now? I have a little business to attend to, and really, how could there be anything I can tell his honor that his last little conversation with Attendant Solari couldn't answer?"

"I don't know," Osthanes said. "But it's not my place to question, now is it?" Ibram opened his mouth and Osthanes beat him to it. "Nor is it yours."

He grabbed Ibram by the shoulder and yanked him in the direction of the headwoman's manor. Ibram raised his hands and allowed himself to be led.

"Here now!" Ahksell objected behind him.

"There is no point to ruining my clothes," Ibram said as he recovered from a completely unnecessary shove. "I'm coming along peaceably."

"You and crowds are an unlucky combination in my memory," Osthanes said as he marched them forward back across the road through the crowds.

Ahksell groaned. Ibram wriggled his body to look behind himself and raised his hands in a helpless gesture. "Now, that is nothing to do with today," he said. "Big cities always make me yearn for fresh air and exercise."

"Delbrite is not a big city, and no one goes to the docks to take the air." Osthanes held his patience strip between thumb and forefinger, the leather already looked ancient with wear.

Ibram smirked. "If you will keep rubbing like that, you're going to break your patience strip."

Commander Osthanes looked down at the trinket in his free hand; his grip on Ibram slackened for a moment. Ibram twisted to one side and freed himself. Osthanes sighed with his entire body. Ibram straightened his gambeson and brushed down the sleeves.

He glanced up at the front gate to Mistress Denrind's home. Fontis' size had one grand quality to it, no one had been witness to that little spectacle for long. He frowned and tucked his hair behind his ears.

"Commander, there is no need for this," Ahksell said. He drew himself up to his full height, forcing the commander to look up when speaking to him.

"Are you coming in as well, Attendant?" Osthanes asked sourly.

"It's a public building," Ahksell said.

"That's as may be," Osthanes said. "But it's not a public interview. I'm afraid you'll have to stay outside."

"I will."

Ibram allowed himself to be hustled past the entrance and through the reception hall into the public courtyard surrounded by warders and his own personal chaperon. The crowd of officials he vaguely recognized from previous visits were strung along the walkway surrounding the cleared dais and tent, which was itself standing empty. They walked straight beneath it, going up and down the little steps on either side.

"I know this is the quickest way to the other side of the courtyard, but isn't this a little disrespectful?" Ibram asked.

"You're a little—just keep moving," Commander Osthanes said and propelled Ibram up the next small flight of stairs, and down the right into the interior rooms.

"So his honor did take over Mistress Denrind's office," Ibram murmured.

Ahksell nodded. Commander Osthanes glowered at them. "His

honor felt that due to the extension of his visit, he needed the extra room," he said.

Ibram hummed to himself. They passed by several doors, some open and some closed. Clerks walked the halls and avoided their eyes as they passed by the halls. The public rooms in Mistress Denrind's manor had been partitioned into window-less work rooms and offices with large document-laden shelves. Clay basin lamps had been nailed to the walls for light.

Ibram skimmed his eyes along the metal clamps holding the lamps as they walked. Mistress Denrind—the headwoman—made do with candle lamps and braziers in her own home, while the Monbriths had glowbulbs in their bathrooms. Did all the money in Fontis stop at their draughtshop? He would have thought a competitor would have sprung up in the village, if a place like that could turn up such profits.

Ahksell detached himself from Ibram's side and took up a position next to one of the guards who bracketed Mistress Denrind's office. He had both hands clenched around his satchel and glared at the hapless doorman. The young man stared up at him and then sidled across the door to his partner on the other side of the entranceway.

It was just like Ahksell to worry, but Ibram didn't think anything too serious was about to happen. Ahksell had already had one conversation with Judge E'grard, and now it was simply Ibram's turn. Still, he probably should have asked for a little more information last night. E'grard was one of those middle of the empire names, perhaps? Places where all those tiny scrabbling kingdoms had been violently shown the delights of peace back when the empire was new. Very few alchemist sects and several large universities. A judgeship usually meant a noble house, but in the Court Civil a particularly genius commoner might advance a little higher than their company.

Osthanes knocked twice on the door, and then paused.

"Enter!" a crisply accented man's voice called out.

The commander opened the door and Ibram walked inside. Osthanes closed the door behind them both. Ibram had been inside Mistress Denrind's office before, of course, when he was first introducing himself on Ladyship's business. It was handsomely, if not expensively, decorated with painted murals of a garden on the walls. A tapestry of the founding of the empire hung behind the old wooden desk.

Judge E'grard sat there now, a slim man with greying hair, dressed in a black tunic and wearing an elaborate full-length purple and black robe held at his shoulders by a heavy gold chain of office. On the end of the desk, perched on an upholstered wooden chair, sat Mistress Denrind, the headwoman. Last time they had spoken, she wore a sturdy light orange tunic and grey leggings, with only her chain of office to differentiate her from her people. Now she had dressed that small silver chain in a mauve surcoat, embroidered at the hems with thick silver thread, and tightly laced over a fine linen tunic caught at the wrists with wide beaten metal cuffs and soft gray wrapped breeches. Ibram ran his hand down his cheek; perhaps he should have shaved.

The pair of officials looked up from the desk, as did the assistant standing in the corner. She looked to be a kind of secretary, perhaps, dressed in a simple wool kirtle with a silver falcon's badge on her shoulder, and a braided leather belt dyed purple. On the desk, he could see a map with pins stuck here and there in a kind of loose circular pattern. Possibly, this indicated where the search parties had already cleared an area. Ibram placed his hands on his stomach and bowed from the waist. He waited, and heard the sounds of paper rustling.

"The arm-for-hire Ibram Ucalegon, your honor," Commander Osthanes introduced him. "Attached to the Sect of Seven Fires."

"You may rise," Judge E'grard said. "Can't be speaking to a man when he's got his face set to the floor, now can we?"

That was a lofty middle of Empire accent if he'd ever heard it gallop. Trained in Cornwarke, perhaps? If he'd spent time down in the universities of law nearer the capital, then he'd have more of a purring curl to his voice. Ibram rose and dropped his hands to his sides. He rested his weight on his heels.

"Good day, your honor," he said. "Mistress Denrind."

"Welcome back, Master Ucalegon," she said. "I deplore the circumstances, but..."

"And I as well," Ibram said. "I'm sure Attendant Solari passed on Lady Azadiya's own sympathies."

Commander Osthanes made a stifled noise behind him. Mistress Denrind smiled thinly. "He did indeed," she said. "We are, as always, deeply grateful for the attention of the Sect of Seven Fires."

"Indeed so, Mistress," Ibram said.

The assistant moved in the corner of Ibram's eye; he turned his head. She touched the back of her hair bun with one hand. The judge cleared his throat.

"As a matter of protocol, Master Ucalegon," E'grard said. "Be aware that our words and actions are observed by my court recorder, Alia Otten."

The woman in the corner nodded her head and smiled briefly. Ibram smiled back. A court recorder could be an asset or a hindrance, depending on how this matter turned out. They took potions that expanded their capacity for memory, developed for and entirely controlled by the imperial family's own alchemists. The courts were often granted those sorts of indulgences by Her Gracious Majesty. Everything Ibram said now could be repeated by Alia Otten, and then be taken as his own sworn testimony in a court trial.

"Now these pleasantries are out of the way," Judge E'grard said, and Ibram refocused his attention. "To the matter at hand."

Ibram bowed shortly, but politely. "Of course, lordship," he said.

"Your honor is sufficient for me," E'grard said, which didn't tell Ibram anything either way.

"Forgive me, your honor," Ibram said. "I don't have much to do with the Court Civil in the normal order of my days."

The judge's broad pale face rippled for a second. He had sharp pale eyes, and Ibram kept his face pleasant in the face of their perusal. There was something cold about him, a calculation in his movements and expressions that made Ibram wary.

"Nor should you hope to, I'm sure," E'grard said. He leaned back in the large carved wooden chair, and rested both of his elbows on their arms. "Attendant Solari tells me you're here on the request of the Monbrith family."

Ibram nodded. "Just so, your honor."

"You are aware, I presume, of the facts of this crisis?"

"I believe so," Ibram said. "I wrote the first report of Master Tolk's passing for the sect, and spoke with Rustam Monbrith as part of my duties."

Judge E'grard nodded and tapped his fist on the desk. "An absconding First Finder is a serious matter," he said, "and one which I take most to heart. An offense against the empire is an offense against Her Gracious Majesty. In such cases, I have a great deal of latitude in my rulings."

"I understand, your honor," Ibram said, and tried to keep his face calm and his eyes from rolling directly from out of his head. He might not have been in a court often, but every schoolchild knew that much of Vissilian law. He had no idea why his honor wanted to remind him of that. E'grard's tone didn't speak of regret, and he didn't behave like a man justifying himself.

"I want you to send a message," Judge E'grard said, "to your mistress."

Ibram tilted his head. "Beg your pardon, your honor, but I serve no mistress."

Judge E'grard narrowed his eyes at him. "Do you not? But the Lady Azadiya Hobon is of quite noble birth."

He knew very well that was beside the point, and as tests went, this was a very low bar to cross. Ladyship might prefer her agents address her by her title, but she was forbidden her own household. Noble alchemists held titles only for the length of their own lives, and renounced any claim to inheritance. Tension grew like vines up the back of his neck, squeezing Ibram's head. What purpose did the judge have for bringing up the terms of Ibram's employment?

"I am employed by the Sect of Seven Fires," Ibram said. "I have no particular patron."

Judge E'grard made a low humming noise in the back of his throat. "And yet the Monbrith heir knew to which alchemist she should address her letter."

"With respect, your honor," he said. "The letter was addressed to me via the Imperial Scribes' Bureau stationed in the living mountain. Like many folk, I am seconded to a particular preceptory of the Sect, even assigned to a specific few members, but I am not bound to them."

"Indeed," Judge E'grard said. "Just as it should be...for a mere contractman."

"And by long tradition, anyone who lives within the imperial boundary may call upon the Sect of Seven Fires for aid, just as we might any major house of nobility," Mistress Denrind interjected.

The judge's mouth twitched, like it wanted to purse but only on one side of his mouth. "Indeed, Mistress Denrind, but tradition is not the law."

It sounded like an old argument, or at least one she'd already heard before. Mistress Denrind shook her head and sat back in her chair. "It is by tradition that we deal justly with our nearest neighbors," she said. "Or is following the law not traditional in your part of the empire?"

Ibram grinned down at the toes of his boots, but made sure to be solemn and respectful when he looked back up again. The flooring creaked from the corner, no doubt Alia also mourned not being allowed to sit down. Ibram took a moment to check the lighting in the office. Glowbulbs, but of the older sort that required touch to light and extinguish, dotted the walls. They were weak, however, and Ibram spotted a pair of fat-bellied oil lamps as well.

"We are well-supplied with trouble in the interior," E'grard said. "But I have often found the greatest laxity is to be located at the edges of our grand empire. You saw nothing out of the ordinary when Tolk was killed, did you?"

"I did not," Ibram replied.

"Attendant Solari has also relayed his findings in Alia's presence," Judge E'grard nodded. "A pity we have not the time to verify his conclusions independently."

The utter bald-faced gall of the man! Ibram's right hand twitched, but he stilled it before it became a fist. Still he couldn't help a certain amount of fancy from entering his mind. E'grard looked to be the weight of a cat, soaking wet, and his spread in that seat gave Ibram the clear thought that tossing him out a window and bundling him down the village well would take only a little maneuvering. It was a strange occurrence that being in Fontis should give him such aggressive thoughts, but he thought he could bear it.

"For the purposes of the trial, your honor, Solari's report is sufficient," Osthanes said, and the judge waved him off. He returned his pale gaze to Ibram, and considered him. Ibram waited the man out, with as attentive a face as he could manage. Rudeness was a tactic he'd employed himself, but couple rudeness with power and even Ibram knew to save his breath to cool his quash. His thoughts turned to E'grard's poking at Ibram's status as an agent. It seemed out of place. That a contract for a sect agent could be lengthy, and were at times drawn up to profit a particular person within the sect was no matter, legally-speaking.

"It's surely a point in the Monbriths' favor," Mistress Denrind said into the dense silence. "That they are also trying so hard to find their missing brother."

"They haven't joined in the search so far, Mistress," Commander Osthanes said.

"Nor are they allowed to," she replied with a flare of heat. "Someone has to stay at their draughtshop while the rest of us search."

"And the Monbriths have always struck me as folk who know their duty," Ibram said.

Mistress Denrind settled back into her chair with a severe angle to her mouth, and rubbed her hand over her chest. She nodded sharply. "That they do."

"Duty is, unfortunately, at the heart of this debacle," Judge E'grard said. "And I'll remind you, Commander, that looming obligation must never be outmatched by our recognition of Fontis' efforts to rectify their community's fault."

Yet recognition of work might not be enough to change the result. Ibram swallowed a little too heavily than he wanted, but his throat felt tight. The judge watched him over his woven fingers. "You know, young man, that I have given Mistress Denrind a twelve-day to recover the Monbrith boy in exchange for a reduced sentence?"

"I do, your honor."

The judge sighed deeply. "It's most regretful," he said. "I am often appalled at the feral nature of the cases I am called upon to judge, but when a man cannot even be called upon to see through the simplest of duties as a subject of the empire, I cannot in all good conscience ignore the event, despite the tragedy of it."

"Very true, your honor," Ibram said. "We are all subjects of the law just much as the empire."

The judge peered up at him, sharply. Ibram pressed his lips together and glanced at Mistress Denrind; she had turned very pale. He was conscious of Alia watching the entire room from her spot in the corner, unblinking. Beside him, Ibram heard the creak of the floorboards as Commander Osthanes shifted his weight. The judge snapped his fingers and gestured his assistant forward.

"Now, the message," he said. "It has been written and sealed. You will be pleased to tell Lady Hobon that I await her response."

Which meant Ibram would have to stay in Lityen until Ladyship replied to him. It would take the rest of the day to reach the preceptory. Time was slipping through his fingers already. Ibram smiled tightly; he nodded.

"Of course, your honor," he said.

Alia withdrew a long scroll sealed with wax from a pocket of her gown. She held it out over the table, and Ibram took it from her. He glanced at the wax seal: the Imperial Falcon. So it was an official message and not a personal one.

He tapped the scroll against his thigh. "May I help in any other way?" he asked.

Judge E'grard, already perusing the map marked with pins in front of him, glanced up. "No, no, not at all. Good day, Master Ucalegon. Commander Osthanes, I require an update on our latest search. Have you cleared the forest path to Thelis?"

"We have, your honor, and also finished dredging the pond in the field one mile over." Commander Osthanes stepped around Ibram, and then jerked his head towards the door. "You heard the judge," he growled.

Ibram bowed his way out with a quick eyebrow wriggle to Mistress Denrind, and was out the door. It shut behind him, and Ibram rubbed the back of his head. His neck felt compacted with tension. Ahksell detached himself from the wall.

"What was it?" he asked. "What did he want?"

Ibram waved him back and eyed the closed door. Some stray thought refused to walk itself out of the back of his mind, but he could feel it meandering. Ahksell ducked the swinging scroll, and grabbed him by the wrist to better squint at the sealed letter.

"A message?" he asked.

"To be read and responded to by your own esteemed Fourth Mentor Hobon," Ibram said. "Come on, we should talk."

Ahksell nodded. The two warders who had been guarding the door had disappeared. Ibram wriggled his trapped hand, but Ahksell ignored his bid for freedom. He frowned at the wax seal, and then charged down the little hallway and out to public courtyard, dragging Ibram behind him. Ibram ground his heels into the terrace floor a third of the way towards the front gate and jerked his wrist free. Ahksell stopped and twisted to face him.

"Now, there is no need to be hasty," Ibram said. He held the scroll loosely, so as not to crumple it. "We can walk."

"Back to the shay shop?" Ahksell asked as they started off on a less embarrassing pace.

Ibram considered the idea, as he stretched his neck on his shoulders. "No, no, I want to do one thing. Before I have to go back to Lityen, I mean."

"Go back to Lityen?" Ahksell's voice echoed as they breached the reception hall. "Go back to *Lityen?*"

Ibram raised the scroll; his thumb flicked against the wax seal. "That's what he wanted. I'm to stay there until ladyship sends her response."

"Runner's blisters," Ahksell groaned. "I thought he just wanted you to take it to the Scribes' Bureau for him."

Ibram shrugged. "He's a fool if he thinks replying to a message will slow Lady Azadiya down," he said. "And I think she will not be pleased to know Judge E'grard doesn't want us in this business after all."

"He seemed so pleasant," Ahksell said.

"He questioned your findings."

Ahksell gasped. "I gave testimony to those!"

"I'm thinking Judge E'grard might believe the sect is embarrassed by this farce. Or perhaps that they might simply challenge his ruling." Ibram rubbed his eyebrow. "If I have to go, then we're losing at least another day and a half to find Rustam."

"I can just about manage to search out clues without you," Ahksell said.

Ibram shook his head. "That's not the point," he said. "This is... well, it's my responsibility, isn't it?"

They'd reached the street. Ahksell sighed deeply. Around them, the village was shuffling past each trader's stall. Ibram smelled smoke on the air. Food cooking in the shay shop, no doubt.

"It's our responsibility," Ahksell said. "As part of the sect's duty to the dependent communities."

Ibram rubbed the back of his head, and shrugged. Ahksell sounded like a man repeating something he'd studied in school. He looked out over the market. It seemed like the crowd of folk had grown while they were inside, and not just traders. There were folk in Vo Wolly colors standing by the well, gawking. Ibram considered them.

"There's no reward for Rustam, is there?" he asked.

"Not that I'm aware of," Ahksell said.

Ibram nodded slowly. Folk from around the outskirts of Fontis, most probably, come to get as many supplies as they needed in case the village truly did disappear and took them with it. He supposed it was possible whatever wall was erected might cut right through the farm-lands surrounding them and seal them in their houses. Word must have spread everywhere the warders searched. He sighed. Uncomfortable and unprofitable thoughts were the enemy of truth. He hefted the paper scroll in his hand.

"Here," he said, and offered it to Ahksell. "Put this is in your satchel for a bit, yes? We should go and speak to that bully before I have to steal your carriage."

"It belongs to the sect," Ahksell said. "And give it here."

He lifted one leg for balance underneath his satchel and twisted his thumb over the latch. It opened, and Ahksell dropped his leg. He held the satchel out, and Ibram dropped the message inside. Ahksell then closed the flap, and they moved on through the crowd. They stepped into the long alley created by all the traders vehicles, which suddenly deprived the townsfolk of their view of the square.

"Do you think they're back from searching in the forest?" Ahksell asked.

"Someone is," Ibram said. "I can see a face in their front window."

He pointed as they ducked into the space between two stalls. The face—a young man with a blotchy complexion—noticed them. The long wooden shutter slammed closed at their approach.

"Unfriendly," Ahksell said.

Like the other houses near it, the Suugan's house was one level with a bare wooden wall and a small rain bucket by its entranceway. The window, now closed, had fading red paint on its frame; its daub was cracking. The door to the Suugan's small workshop and home was also very firmly shut. Ibram knocked twice, but no one answered. He leaned his head to the wood and knocked again. This time, he thought he heard a footstep.

He glanced behind him to Ahksell, who shook his head. He crossed his arms and looked up and down the little street created by the trading stalls and the actual buildings. A fourth knock would probably do nothing to open the door. A small crowd of whisperers had appeared behind them. Ibram stepped back to take in the shuttered window out front. The rain barrel stood outside with its lid firmly attached and a dipper resting on top.

Ibram stepped a little closer to the door. "Good morning to you, Mistress Suugan," he said loudly. If the mother was inside, better to be polite about introductions. If she wasn't, his being civil might make the young man from the window feel guilty and answer. Nothing like a hanging social convention to make a conversation awkward. "I wonder if you could take a moment to speak to us?"

Nothing, not even another footstep.

"I mean, I can tell someone's in there," Ibram said in a louder voice. "For all its charms, Fontis is not so large that the absence of a family from this ruckus outside won't be noted, and so if you wish, Mistress Suugan, I can stay out here and ask my questions. You don't have to answer, of course, but Attendant Solari and I have a duty."

He stole a quick peep behind himself. Ahksell stood a few steps back, looking skyward, and heaved a sigh. More to the point, several villagers were deliberately not paying attention, but remained careful to linger in the vicinity.

There was a small scuffle, and then something fell to the ground inside the house. Ibram wagged his eyebrows at Ahksell. Ahksell shook his head and sighed, deeply.

"Oh, light a candle about it," Ibram whispered.

"Nightly," Ahksell whispered back.

"Mistress Suugan," Ibram raised his voice again. "When you learned—"

"My mother is not at home," a young man shouted. "Go away!"

"Tieri was at the window," Ibram said to Ahksell in a low voice.

Ahksell nodded. "Must be Tieri."

"Tieri Suugan?" Ibram asked louder. "Is that you?"

"No!"

"If that is you, Master Suugan, then it's not too bad, because Attendant Solari and I would also like to ask you a few questions! Just a couple of small ones, you understand, nothing too taxing!"

There was silence, and then another scuffle. Ibram made his voice stern. "Now young master," he said. "You answer when you're spoken to. We've come all the way down the living mountain to speak to you. Don't keep the Attendant waiting."

The door opened a crack and revealed a teardrop-shaped eye. Ibram inclined his head and shoulders politely and waited until the door opened more widely and the young man behind it returned the courtesy. He moved aside for Master Suugan to put his hands on his stomach and bow more fully to Ahksell. The boy then stood and gestured them both into the house. Good manners appeared to have quite a hold on the Suugan family. Really, why had Ibram shied away from traveling with Ahksell here? He presented all sorts of opportunities lately.

The lower room of the Suugan's home was given to the workshop, clearly, with wooden forms and leather scattered around on a long table. It smelled of leather and dust, but the floor by the small unlit hearth was nicely swept and the rushes were clean. He nudged an awl that had fallen to the floor with his boot, and walked in the direction of the closed door that separated the area from what was surely the family's storeroom and kitchen. A small girl of perhaps ten sat down on low stool, tangling a string in her fingers. She stood to make her bow to Ahksell, very much on her small dignity, and he quite seriously curled his hands at his waist to raise her back up as well.

"Hello, mistress," he said.

"Be welcome to our house, Master Alchemist," she said, with nary a stumble on the words. "Would you like a drink?"

Her older brother crossed his arms and huffed. "There's no shay ready unless we make it, Imriska," he said. "And I doubt Attendant Solari will be here long enough."

Imriska? Ibram perked up his ears. He'd heard that name before... at dinner with the Monbriths. This was Diarmit's friend, then. A small village really did have its entanglements.

"But Father says we have to offer the customers a drink when they come in to the shop," she protested.

"They aren't here for shoes," Tieri snapped.

"Alas no," Ahksell said, with a sly look to Ibram. The siblings quieted, remembering their manners, no doubt.

Ibram stepped forward. "But I do see you and your parents have quite the successful business going on. If your mother is not in, Master Suugan, is your father at home to visitors?"

Tieri bobbed his head like a dipperbird. His eyes rested on Ahksell and then traveled to Ibram and back. "He's out looking for that idiot Rustam, just like the rest of them."

"Why haven't you joined the hunt?" Ibram asked. "You look sturdy enough."

Tieri flushed. He was a large boy, almost the bruiser Zosi Kolesar had described him as, but he put Ibram in mind more of a puppy. His mother clearly kept both children clean and well dressed. Tieri's shoulders were broad enough to do some damage in a fight, but his hands and feet were out-sized for his body, and he didn't hold himself like a fighter of any repute. A village scrapper, surely, but there was no real danger to him. Still, nerves or anger could drive anyone to vicious acts.

"Someone has to look after my sister," Tieri said. "And our mother wanted us to buy some necessities from the traders to tide us by. Are these the questions you wanted to ask me? Because I don't see what our shopping habits have to do with anything going on today."

Ibram nodded. "A fair point," he said. "Did you know Harken Tolk?"

Tieri shrugged. "Not really. I never had anything needing to be mended. I think my mother sent him a clasp with a broken pin, once. He fixed that all right."

"So you knew him enough to recognize him," Ahksell said. "But that was all."

"Yes, Attendant," Tieri said. "He came here for years. We were his only stop in the province, I think."

Ibram considered that fact, and then set it aside to remark upon later. "What we really wanted to ask you about was your friend Rustam Monbrith."

Where before Tieri had flushed, he then went pale. He jerked his head at his sister. "Imriska, go make shay," he said.

"But you just said—"

"Go make shay for the customers," Tieri ordered. "Mother will be furious if we leave a guest thirsty."

She puffed up like a croona bird. "If this is about you fighting, I already know everything about it!"

"This isn't about you," Tieri said. "And Mother put me in charge, so go!"

Imriska sighed very heavily. "Do you see what he's like?" she asked Ahksell. "Do you have brothers?"

"I do not," Ahksell said.

"You're very lucky."

"*Wanderer's claws,* you little brat!"

"Why don't I help you make the shay?" Ahksell said, and extended his hand to her.

Her eyes widened. "Can you make it out of the air?"

"Just hot water, unfortunately," Ahksell said. "But I can—" He raised his left hand, crooked his first finger and turned it palm up in a slow circle. "—help you reach the shelves."

Imriska rose up into the air as if pulled by a string. She squealed and clapped her hands as he lowered her safely down again, and turned in a gleeful circle. "Oh, oh! Attendant Serisan never does that!"

Ibram hid his smile by looking towards Tieri. He was fidgeting where he stood, playing with the hem of his sleeve. Ahksell laughed, and Ibram returned his attention to him.

"Come along," Ahksell said. "Show me to the kitchen."

Imriska straightened up to her full height, which was about Ahksell's waist, and grabbed hold of his sleeve. Tieri startled forward and Ibram waved him back. Alchemists from Yseult never stood on much dignity with children. She led Ahksell into the backroom, chattering about her lessons with Attendant Serisan, and closed the door behind them.

"I don't think our doors were meant for a man of that height," Tieri said in a wondering sort of voice.

"You'd be amazed at how little of a problem that usually is," Ibram said. "Now then, Master Suugan, about this fight you had with the Monbrith boy." He held up his hand. "And don't bother telling me you've already spoken of this with the warders. I don't care about that."

"Well, if they didn't see much in my fight with Rustam, I don't see what business it is of yours," Tieri said.

Ibram blinked. "Truly?"

Tieri shook his head and grimaced. "Why do you want to know anyway? Shouldn't you be out looking with the others?"

"I'm here on sect business," Ibram said. "I go where that business leads me."

"I don't see why I need to keep going over this," Tieri kicked the toe of his boot against the ground. "Father already punished me for fighting."

Ibram tsked. "Water torture?"

Tieri frowned at his strangely. "I'm stuck in the house," he said after a bewildered pause.

"Then you've had a lot of practice in telling me what happened," Ibram said. "Let's hear it."

"Surely someone's already told you," Tieri said. "We were out in the square, everyone saw us!"

"I've heard some things," Ibram said. "But I've been cautioned against hasty decision making before. I'd like to hear your side of the fight."

Tieri snorted. "It was a matter of honor."

"As bad as that?" Ibram said, and crossed his arms. He looked about him, and sat down on the low stool Imriska had vacated. He stretched his feet before him. "You must like the Terin girl very much."

"It's not like that!" Tieri scrubbed his shoulder-length hair and paced a few feet to a table covered in leather scraps. He picked up a large needle and drove it into the wood of the table.

"What is it like then?"

"I mean..." Tieri leaned against the table and sighed heavily. "Rustam's a fool. He's as big a fool as—as Hristo in the palace of Yngvarr!"

Ibram raised his eyebrows. Tieri wasn't so far out of his school days as Ibram'd thought if he could remember that old firetale. He shifted on the hard wooden stool. He watched the boy slump in place and kick at the rushes on the floor.

"That's a pretty foolish person, then," Ibram said. "If I recall correctly, Hristo the gardener stole flowers from his king to give to the queen. Had a terrible impact on the order of precedence at dinner, I'm told. Did Rustam steal the Terin girl from you?"

"No, you can't...I know you can't steal a person from anyone," Tieri said. "Mother made that very clear. But I thought...I only thought that Hasi and I were more friendly than we turned out to be, and there was Rustam, prancing about and buying her ribbons and telling everyone who breathed near him how he was going to describe the body at trial." He looked disgusted. "As if finding a body is so amazing! Have you ever seen a corpse?"

"Several," Ibram said.

"Well, they're boring," Tieri said. "And they smell."

"I must admit that is true," Ibram said. "So that's how the fight started? You'll forgive me, Master Tieri, but it doesn't sound much like an affair of honor."

Tieri gave an awkward wriggle of discomfort. He glanced towards the backdoor, where the sounds of Imriska's giggling could faintly be heard. "I tripped him during market day," he said.

"Rude, but not too horrible."

"And he got up and pushed me, of course. Mistress Wethe yelled at us to get away from her stall before we tossed all her stock into the dirt, but we had already started shouting, and—and it just all came out, you know? My bitterness about Hasi, and he got at me about my problem with numbers, because he knows it upsets me." Tieri took a deep breath. "So, I said the old body must have had a purse on him if he was spending that much money on frills for someone who spends her days trapping feneks in the forest and he…"

Ibram leaned forward. Tieri licked his lips and shook his head. He glanced at the backdoor again. Ibram narrowed his eyes.

"What did he say?" he asked.

"Didn't someone tell you?" Tieri began to play with his sleeve again. "Everyone saw."

"No, no one told me."

Tieri sighed. Ibram frowned. "Truly, what could he have said? It can't be as bad as all that, boy."

Tieri looked to the back door, and his whole body moved once with his breath. He nodded. "He gave me…"

"What, did he throw the ribbons in your face?"

"No, he… Oh just look."

Tieri raised his hand to his elbow, palm facing towards, and touched his thumb to his middle finger. He flicked his finger hard in Ibram's direction.

Ibram raised both eyebrows. "Hey now," he said mildly. "There are children and alchemists in the next room."

"That's what he did!" Tieri said. He dropped his hand as if burnt. "I'm very sorry, but that's what he did! In front of all those people!"

Ibram blew out a long breath, and sat back on the stool. "Well, I can see why you hit him, then," he said. "If he gave you the filip."

It was fairly rude for a village scuffle between boys. Ibram had seen grown men grow horns with spite over the insult in his travels, even in caravans where fighting was strictly forbidden. Boredom on the road led to short tempers, he thought, and it was true in villages as well.

Tieri's color was high. He tucked his hair behind his ears with both hands and then crossed his arms. He dropped them to his sides and then shrugged. Ibram leaned forward and rested his elbows on his knees. "Duels have been fought for less, haven't they?"

"I think so," Tieri said. "I know our parents haven't spoken since."

"Well, it's a damnable thing to do," Ibram said. "Quite the curse."

"I could have taken it if he'd just flicked at me," Tieri said. He put two curled fingers to his mouth and demonstrated as if Ibram didn't know what he was talking about. Maybe Tieri thought he was getting away with rude gestures while he could. "You see that all the time among the caravans—even though Mother hates it—but he made me so angry, and I felt stupid. I just couldn't let it pass, and then Hasi came to break it up."

"And you couldn't tell her why you were fighting," Ibram said.

Tieri nodded. "Wouldn't have been right."

"Did you speak to Satya at all?" Ibram asked. "She was there, wasn't she?"

Tieri huffed and then scrubbed his hand under his nose. "She doesn't want to talk to me. She just..." He shrugged again and shook his head. "I don't know. She dragged him off, and I thought they were going to start something almost."

Ibram blinked. "Really? They were that upset at each other?"

Tieri shook his head. "Those Monbriths all stick together," he said. "They think they're better than everyone else."

"And the warders accepted your story?"

Tieri flushed. "It's the truth!"

Ibram nodded. "To be sure," he agreed. "Listen, though, that was the end of it? What did the warders say to you?"

The back door opened, and they both looked towards it. Behind Imriska, Ahksell raised both of his eyebrows at once. Both of his hands were raised in front of him, palms up. Imriska came bouncing into the workshop with the shay pitcher and cups on a tray hovering above her head. She beamed at her brother and waved at the tray. Obligingly, Ahksell moved both hands forward, pushing with the heels of his palms, and the tray wafted into the center of the room with Imriska.

"Do you see, Tieri?" she asked. "Do you see? There's strings in the *air!*"

"I see it," he answered. His eyes widened. "Get out from under there before you burn yourself."

Imriska stuck out her tongue. Ahksell moved both hands to his left and the tray floated across the room to the table near where Tieri stood. He lowered his palms and the tray landed with barely a clatter of cups. Ahksell relaxed his shoulders and arms and shook his hands out; he sighed.

Ibram grinned. "Very smooth, Attendant," he said.

"Well, I was being tested," Ahksell said. "Imriska is very sharp."

The girl nodded firmly. "I saw Attendant Serisan move a desk once," she said. "But it was only a little bit."

"Well, I'll have to give her some advice," Ahksell said.

Which would no doubt go over well. Ibram shook his head. He pointed with his chin towards the shay pitcher. "I take mine plain," he said.

Tieri jumped a little, and then flushed. "I—ah—yes," he stammered. "I'll pour."

Ibram watched him begin to fiddle with the shay cups. "Who looked after you while your brother was with the warders, little mistress?" he asked.

Imriska had found her piece of string again, and was weaving it between her fingers. She seemed the type to always be in motion. Tieri paused in the middle of pouring and then went back to filling cups.

"Well—" she began.

"One of the warders," her brother interrupted her. "He kept an eye on her."

Imriska frowned, but he ignored her and began passing around cups. Ahksell smiled and bowed his head as he accepted one. He took a quick sip and sighed.

"That was nice of them," he said.

"Yes," Tieri said.

"They're boring, though," she said. "All he did was give me some bread and oil and leave me in the little room."

"Why'd he do that?" Ibram asked. He smiled at Tieri when handed his shay. Tieri frowned.

She leaned over and widened her eyes. "Because he's angry at the Tyals!"

"Imriska," Tieri warned.

"Well he was," she announced. "He said they were mean, only he used a very bad word, and that they made him work hard." She frowned. "I thought the warders worked for the empress."

Ibram glanced at Ahksell, who nodded. Out of the mouths of children and fools. Ibram crossed his ankles and drank his shay. Silence descended and Ibram let it linger. He watched Tieri Suugan stand by his work table and shift on his feet.

"Why do you think Rustam ran off, if it wasn't because of you, Tieri?"

"I don't see why you have to ask me," Tieri burst out.

"Warders are busy folk," Ibram said. "I just wanted to get a local's understanding of the situation. You know your neighbors best after all."

Tieri's hands clenched into fists. Ibram caught his eye and deliberately nodded in his sister's direction. Tieri wavered, face reddening. Ibram raised his eyebrows and waited while the boy composed himself. He poured himself a cup of shay and drank it in one gulp. Then, Tieri wiped his mouth with his sleeve.

"I think he ran because of something Satya said," he said at last. "She's the one in charge of him."

"He has a mother," Ibram said.

Tieri snorted. "She doesn't come into the markets like Satya," he said. "Satya's the one riding herd on Rustam and Diarmit."

"And you think she told him to run away?" Ibram asked.

Tieri nodded and then shook his head. "I think—no, it's just—Rustam's an oaf. He doesn't come up with ideas on his own."

"What about Hasi Terin?" Ibram asked.

"She'd never!" Tieri shook his head again, hard enough to move his hair about his face. "And even if she did, then why would she still be here?"

Ibram shrugged. "A fair point."

"Why are the warders angry at the Tyals?" Ahksell asked.

Tieri shrugged. "Ask them yourself, Attendant," he said. "It's not like they'd tell me."

Nor was it likely that the warders would respond well to their asking. Warders and minor nobility were rather notoriously closed-mouthed at the best of times. Ibram gulped down his shay and stood. Tieri turned nervous for a second and set down in cup in a flutter.

"I think we should get going," Ibram announced. "Have quite the journey to make, after all."

"You do?" Imriska asked.

"Oh yes," Ibram said and set his cup on the stool. "But thank you for the shay, little mistress, and for your time."

He and Ahksell left the Suugans' house quickly, and only Imriska appeared sorry to see the back of them. Above them the sky had given up its attempt at a clear day and grown drowsy with grey clouds as thick as a wool blanket. Ibram sighed. He didn't want to be a sooth-sayer, but something told him that of all the dice Yilka the Green had turned white point up for him, prosperity wasn't one of them.

$\maltese$ 6 $\maltese$

On their walk back to the Monbriths' draughtshop, Ibram kept his thoughts to himself and so did Ahksell. The sun was high in the sky, but the clouds were heavy and grey; wind bit through the wool of his gambeson. They met no more hunting parties on the road. The map on the judge's desk had seemed rough, but that many pins meant that his assumption about the number of warders in the area was most probably correct. They had more than enough to keep up the search, and then an equal amount to pen Fontis in like mouflon.

Ibram sighed as the Monbriths' home came into view, and Ahksell elbowed him gently. Ibram staggered to the side of the road, but corrected himself. He smacked the back of his hand against Ahksell's biceps. Ahksell turned to him in the road, and Ibram paused.

"What?" Ibram asked. "You have a pensive look to you, my friend, and it doesn't suit."

"I think I need to return to the preceptory with you," Ahksell said.

"What? Why? I thought you might talk to Hasi Terin while I'm gone," Ibram said. "Who knows, but she could know more than she'll tell a strange warder."

"Something she'd tell a strange alchemist?" Ahksell asked.

Ibram shrugged. "She might be scared. Frightened people keep silent in the face of amazing circumstances, you know."

Ahksell rolled his eyes. "I highly doubt that, and so do you. Now, what time are we leaving?"

"Why do you want to come anyway?"

Ahksell rubbed both hands over his close-shorn hair and hung them around his neck. He sighed. "I need to speak to one of the other attendants, and I think if I hurry we're still early enough in the season that I might catch her."

"A lady attendant?" Ibram considered the trees for a moment. "Are you allowed to court those?"

"I'm not courting her," Ahksell said. "I'm questioning her, it's different."

"What for?" Ibram said. "Is she from Salacia? Do you think they might head to Fontis before the judge's deadline has passed?"

"Well, I imagine they'll arrive a few days before anyway," he said.

"Oh," Ibram said.

Ahksell grunted.

"Is it that Serisan, then?" he asked.

Ahksell shrugged. They walked a few more feet in silence. Two of the warders were out front, loitering while armed. Fires had been lit; he could see the smoke coming out of the chimney towards the back of the draughtshop, and in the family's home. A third funnel of smoke curled up into the air, not attached to either place. Ibram grunted. The only burn site out this way was the old blacksmith's furnace Harken Tolk had used on his visits. Why was it afire now? A short gust of wind set Ibram to shivering; he rubbed his arms briskly.

"You keep forgetting your cloak," Ahksell said.

"I saw the sun this morning and became enthusiastic." Ibram stepped off the road into the soft ground by the livery yard. "I'm going to take a walk for a moment," he said.

"What for?" Ahksell asked. "In the hopes you'll get rained on?"

"No, I just feel like a walk. We've been in and out of doors so often. I want to clear my head for a moment."

"You want me to make our excuses to Mistress Monbrith, don't you."

Ibram raised his hands and walked backwards. "I'll be in soon!"

He dodged the stone Ahksell kicked at him, and then put his back to him. He walked around the side of the draughtshop in the space between the building and the fence around the livery yard. The sky was all one cloud, like a nubby grey blanket.

"I'm going to check on Antio," Ahksell called after him.

Ibram waved in acknowledgment. The track he was on had been pounded flat over the years, and so it was relatively easy to walk without getting too much mud on his boots. He heard a horse whinny and another answer, perhaps the warders' mounts. He turned the corner to walk in between the two buildings. Wind blew his hair into his eyes, and he tucked it behind his ears.

The goats he'd seen tied up the day before were not in appearance. Ibram tucked his hand around the hilt of his sica, and rubbed his fingers over the wrapped linen fabric. He felt... His stomach clenched. He didn't know what he felt. Perplexed? Upset? Frustrated? All those things and none of them. He didn't understand what could have made Rustam run. Ladyship would want a report when he returned, and Ibram didn't like the thought of having nothing to present to his employer, but more questions.

He wasn't the sort of man to leave a stone unturned or a line of thought undiscovered. At least, he didn't think of himself so. But there had to be something. He shook his head and continued walking. That third plume of smoke rose in front of him, and he quickened his pace.

Harken Tolk had been found dead, that was a fact. Ibram had been dispatched to view the corpse and record a preliminary report for Lady Azadiya, while Mistress Denrind the headwoman presented their joint findings to Judge E'grard when he arrived. Ibram cut a path around the outside of the family's home, glancing up at the darkened rooms and closed shutters.

There had to have been a detail he'd overlooked somewhere. He frowned. The dice had turned up two points, so either luck, prosperity, or work was compiling together on his side. He didn't mind work, but he couldn't stop himself hoping those points represented luck and opportunity. What pushed a man—well, a boy really—to run from a task he'd boasted about performing? Yilka's megrims, none of this made sense.

The wind blew and Ibram stopped a moment to orient himself. The syah berry patch was thirty feet away on his left, where they wouldn't invade the family's actual garden. The abandoned forge lay to his right, and between them both was a wide border of brown earth and soggy clumps of grass. Ibram walked into the syah berry bushes and stood in the middle of the double row. Apart from the one bush which was obviously crushed and then trimmed back in an attempt to heal it, all six plants were healthy and well-tended. They were old plants and grew up to the level of Ibram's chest. He toed gently at the ground. The sharp sweet berry scent wasn't as heady this close to the beginning of the season. He sneezed, regardless.

Ibram wiped his nose on his sleeve and looked around him. The road was visible, but not particularly close. The tree cover was dense. Master Tolk, according to Rustam, had been on his side with his arms flopped about as if he had fallen into the bushes and rolled to the ground. It had been a cold afternoon, but Tolk was in the habit of escaping the heat of the furnace and the cramping of his limbs with a quick walk in the middle of his working day. No one had minded.

Ibram dug his thumbs into the base of his skull and pressed firmly. He groaned, and dropped his arms. He turned around and faced the ancient shack. There was a door, hinged so that the top half could be opened for air while the bottom remained shut, but both were closed currently. The smoke was pouring up into the sky from the chimney in the roof. He turned back to face the bush.

To be sure, Harken Tolk had died of natural causes. When Ibram had first come to Fontis, the body had been dead no more than three days. Apart from what usually happened to the body in death, Tolk had been unharmed and unchanged. Indeed, Ahksell had found nothing. Ibram looked again at the plume of smoke.

"A thought, Ladyship," he said to himself and raised one finger. "Master Tolk has a heart attack while working." He waited for his imaginary employer to agree. "He staggers away from the nasty, dangerous fire because, well, anyone would if they could possibly manage it, and walks out through the backdoor.

Ibram faced the broken bush.

"Confused, he wanders into the berries and falls to the ground."

In his head, Ladyship began to tap her foot. He frowned. The stench of smoke tingled in the air, thin and sharp, not like a hardwood smoke at all. Strange to smell it now, the scent was so different from Father's workshop. Lady Azadiya the Imaginary raised her eyebrows.

"Yes, I know that doesn't matter," he said. He stared at the forge and then the short fat chimney. Harken Tolk spent most of his time in Fontis working. Working in the forge, or at the stables, and when he was at his work, Rustam had been with him.

Ibram breathed in suddenly and coughed. He bent forward, smoke caught in his throat, and pounded his chest. The syah berry bushes rustled about him.

"I never asked," he muttered. "I never asked exactly what they were doing."

And it wouldn't have mattered, except Rustam had vanished. Ibram had asked why Tolk was in Fontis, and the answer had been "making nails and what all" which was a very fair response, and all had seemed in order. But he hadn't looked for himself, had he? He thought back. He'd met Mistress Denrind in her office and she had told him what the Monbriths had told her. Then, he'd gone over the day with the Monbriths themselves in their home, seated around their dining table. They'd pointed out the forge, they'd shown him the bushes, and that had been sufficient for him.

Ibram groaned, and stood up. He pressed the heels of his palms into his eyes and then dragged his fingers up and out through his hair. He was an idiot, as dumb as a bloodhound in a puddle. Ama should have held out for a third child and hedged her wagers on the competency of her heir.

Either someone was able to kill Harken Tolk without attracting whatever emanation it was Ahksell said showed a man had been murdered, or something had happened which made Rustam disappear which was completely unrelated to anything they had learned, or would learn. Ibram frowned up at the smoke. Or there was something Rustam had found in the blacksmith's workshop which had made him skitter off like a cave sparrow in sunlight. The imaginary Lady Azadiya hummed to herself, and Ibram lifted his hands. All right, the fourth option: Rustam had known something all along—a crime or a dire secret—and he'd brazened his way through Ibram's interview, but quailed at the thought of an actual judge. Cangsa, maybe it was Isconian spies.

He clapped his hands together, and then let them drop. "Might as well ask," he said.

He walked back around the side of the shack. As he grew closer to the door, the smell of smoke grew stronger. Ibram inhaled and wrinkled his nose. If they were all lucky, the wind would blow most of the smoke across the forest behind it.

Ibram took a moment to survey the old place. It had lost a few shingles off the roof and the rest was covered in moss. The chimney was clearly all right, but the covered porch was a rickety shambles. Ibram stepped underneath it. The earth had been swept, which seemed a bit much.

"Hello?" he raised his voice.

Something dropped inside the smithy and rang out like a heavy ceramic. Ibram put his hand on the door and pushed it open. Inside, Satya Monbrith stood before the crackling fire, holding an overflowing bundle of orange vines in her hands. A sturdy wheelbarrow full of the same vegetation lay propped against the wall. A medium-sized crucible with a pouring mouth lay vibrating at her feet; she must have knocked it over.

"Oh no," she said. "Don't come in!"

Ibram stepped inside the smithy and let the door close behind him. Not behaving as he was told was a terrible habit with him. Ama despaired.

"Is something the matter?" he asked.

She gestured with her plants. "It's the strangleweed," she said with all evident disgust in the curl of her lip. "It's gotten into the potatoes again, and I don't want the wind to catch the seeds." She tossed her double-handful into the fire and shook her hands clean. "There!"

"But why couldn't I come in?" Ibram asked. It was a strange time to be planting potatoes. Strangleweed grew up most especially when the earth was first disturbed, bringing the dormant seeds more closely to the surface. "It's not poisonous."

"The draft," she explained. "This old place is a bit open-air, you see, even with the back closed up."

Ibram nodded. Indeed, light was coming through cracks in the daub. "And you decided to burn them out here?"

"I thought it would be better if I got them as far away from the garden as possible. The seeds are so tiny, and they get everywhere."

"They do indeed," Ibram said. He rubbed his eyebrow with his thumb. "I should warn Ama; she was just speaking of planting potatoes when I left."

"Do you farm at all?" Satya asked. She grabbed the crucible in both hands.

"Oh, let me," Ibram said quickly. He bent down and grabbed the crucible by its heavy lipped rim; their fingers overlapped as Satya pulled away. Ibram's fingertips tingled. Satya giggled above him.

"That's very kind, thank you," she said.

He braced his legs for balance as he rose up with the crucible. He cast an eye about the room. It wasn't properly maintained like Father's forge at all, but that made sense if it wasn't always in use. He turned to his right and walked a little closer to the roaring fire.

"I think it should fit here," Ibram said, and crouched down again to set it aside in the far corner at the bottom of the large clay and stone hearth. He rocked the crucible back along the dirty floor and something moved beneath a layer of foundry sand and debris. It looked like a circle, or perhaps a pendant, but Tolk hadn't been a jeweler. A discarded bit of work?

Ibram coughed and made a show of rubbing his hands clean, still crouched. "It's good to see tools well-used," he said. "Though I confess, I'm much more at home in a sitting room."

He reached down as if brushing his boots. His fingers flicked out to the floor, and picked the little disc up. It felt smooth, like it had been formed in a mold, and had a weight to it. He pushed it under his sleeve into his wallet. "That's what my father says anyway."

Satya grinned, a tiny bit nervously to Ibram's mind. "I always supposed Lityen was too much like a real town to have people who knew about work."

Ibram laughed. "Surely there's no such thing here, young mistress. A town in this province would be broken up as soon as it formed."

"Oh, you don't have to tell me," she said. She picked another clump of vines from the small wheelbarrow and threw them on the fire. "When Mother asked permission from Mistress Denrind to build another well, we had to swear in blooded contract that it was for our lodgers only—and that none of them intended to stay!"

Ibram nodded. "They get one of the Attendants from the Preceptory of Baran to oversee it?"

Satya shook her head. "Mother insisted on a lecturer from Delbrite. It took twice as long, of course."

"Did she?" he asked. "Is the study of the divine cosmology not enough for her?"

"Mother wanted someone with a more direct communication."

Not overly religious, Ibram's left toe. He made a polite noise and took a quick study of the room housing the furnace. He hadn't been to this place on his previous visit. It clearly hadn't been abandoned, though it could have used a lick of daub and a new roof. It was filthy, really, or...perhaps it had just been too quickly cleaned. There was a noticeable layer of foundry sand underneath his boots; Father was usually careful to put his in a barrel for reuse. He could see rusty tongs leaning on the wall and next to them, lay a set of empty rectangular metal frames. Ibram's eyebrows drew together. Father used those, he knew he'd seen something like them before. He packed them with foundry sand to use as molds. Ibram swallowed and licked his lips; his mouth felt dry all of a sudden.

"Did Master—"

"Who is Ama?" Satya asked. "Is that your wife?"

Ibram paused. "No, my apologies," he said finally. "I misspoke. Ama means 'mother,' actually. I am, um, partly Western."

"Oh," Satya said. She smiled in embarrassment and cast her eyes over the roaring furnace. "Well, obviously, I don't speak—"

"Oh no, no one is at fault," Ibram interrupted. "Please don't feel poorly about it."

"So, you are not married then?" she asked a bit too loudly.

Ibram stopped his jaw from dropping and took a quick breath. "I... no," he said. "I am not...married."

She swayed forward a step. "No...Western person on the horizon."

Ibram sidled to the right, a little more close to the furnace than was strictly comfortable. He glanced about him. The floor was scattered with broken twisting vines and tiny blossoms. Some of them looked quite dried out.

"No, no one on the horizon," he said, and reached out to brush some stray vines off the wide clay rim of the furnace. "Ow!"

Ibram yanked his hand away from the hearth and turned his back to Satya. He held his hand up to his mouth and sucked on the webbing between his first and second fingers. He stared at a line of increasingly wide-bowled ladles hung on the wall; they seemed cleaner. Well, they seemed more recently used.

"You've burned yourself!" Satya exclaimed. "Let me see, Ibram, here."

She cupped his elbow in her hand, but Ibram turned away again. He tasted blood and something thin but sharp poked his lower lip. He spit it back into his palm.

"No, no," he said. "It's fine." He grinned and wiped his mouth with the back of his knuckles. "I think Master Tolk was perhaps not as cleanly as he could have been?"

Satya dropped her hand and took a step back. Ibram's elbow tingled. He cleared his throat and smiled. "It's just a sliver," he said, though it felt larger in his grip.

He glanced down and opened his palm. A half-moon of copper metal lay there. He held it up to the fire, and the little filing gleamed.

"Are you sure you're all right?" Satya asked.

"Very much so," Ibram said. "I'm just a large baby, when it comes down to it. I was only startled."

He let the curl of metal fall to the floor. Satya smiled and nodded. "Well, if you're sure," she said. She cleared her throat and rubbed her hands together.

Ibram smiled. "I am."

Satya looked once around the small room. Ibram turned to face the fire. It burned too hotly for the time of year, but he supposed that was a lot of weeds she had yet to burn. In point of fact, the entire furnace looked like it was seeing heavy use. There were old coals on the floor.

"So Rustam and Master Tolk were out here quite a lot?" he asked. "Working hard?"

"Oh yes," Satya said. "Not that there were many big jobs to do."

"Lots of little ones can make a career as well."

She swallowed. "The extra money was a help," she said. "Rustam never told us exactly which job it came from. He just said he was helping Master Tolk with his repairs."

"All that hammering on your property?" Ibram asked. "No clue at all?"

She shrugged. "Hammering is just hammering. Why would we pay attention?"

"I confess, I know the feeling." Ibram nodded. He glanced at the furnace and then down to the crucible. It looked well used also. He wiggled his hand and felt the circle in his wrist wallet jump. A terrible thought built in the back of his mind, but this was twice now that he'd been pricked by scrap metal and there were very few reasons for a blacksmith to make flat circles. He stretched his hand out at his side. Yilka the Green had three faces, and all of them watched through sharp eyes. Maybe he could stand to be a bit more religious.

"Satya?" he asked.

She turned around quickly. "Yes?"

"I've been tasked to send a message back to the living mountain," he said.

Her face did a sort of flinch of startlement. Ibram looked down at the hard-packed floor. Now that he was looking, his attacker had a mate down on the floor amongst the weeds. It was strange. Father and Katka were cleanly when they worked in the smithy at home. Ore could be expensive this far away from the mines, and they tried to reuse as much scrap as possible. Though perhaps an old man, already feeling ill, wasn't as tidy. Especially if his heart had begun to pain him in here.

"You're leaving?" she asked, and he looked up. "What about Rustam?"

"No! Well, not permanently," he said. "But Judge E'grard wishes to converse with the Fourth Mentor, and I am dispatched. You know how it is."

She nodded slowly. "Yes, yes, of course...but you'll be back?"

"As soon as she responds," he said. "And Ladyship always has an answer for everyone."

She giggled rather like a hiccup, and Ibram pressed his lips together in a smile. Perhaps he had pitched it a bit to Satya Monbrith. She hadn't said much the last time she was here, but whatever Ibram had done his last visit must have made an impression.

He tucked his hands behind his back, and swiveled on his heels towards the door and back again. "Are you all finished here?" he asked.

"I—well, someone needs to watch the fire," she said. "And I have a few more handfuls to burn."

He nodded. "True, true."

"Is Attendant Solari staying?"

"No," Ibram said. He brushed off his hands and took another look at his palm. "He's coming with me. I've sure he'll be back as well, though. Possibly quicker than me, as his business is different and more mysterious."

"More mysterious?" Satya echoed. There was a brittle cast to her face and a trembling in her lip.

"When I am sent back up the living mountain, there is a reason," Ibram said. "But when he returns, it can be for any kind of whim."

"But he didn't tell you?"

Ibram shrugged. "He has not."

Satya nodded. She looked into the fire and then back to Ibram. "Rustam's a good person," she said. "I know what you must have been told in town, but it's not true."

"You mean the fight between him and Tieri Suugan?"

She bent and threw another pile of weeds on the fire. "You heard about that, then."

"You helped break it up, didn't you?"

She cleared her throat and swung back to pick up more plants. The flames licked higher. "Yes."

"Just a scuffle, wasn't it?" When her back was turned, he toed at some of the debris on the floor. Dust and those little seeds puffed up into the air, but a glimmer of metal lay on the ground, especially close to the furnace.

"Hasi Terin has a roving eye and a mouth only the Speaker could stopper," Satya said. "Tieri's just a fool, but she started that fight no matter what anyone tells you."

Ibram nodded. "There's always one, isn't there?"

"As I'm sure you'd know," she said and glanced at him out of the corner of her eye.

Ibram grinned. "Perhaps."

She hummed, and returned to her dead weeds. Ibram watched her for a moment. She had an easy form about her, compact and fluid. He breathed in deeply, coughed out the smoke, and waited for a moment.

"Did Master Tolk serve all the needs of the village?" he asked. "Since you're so close to the road here, I would have thought you would need the services of a blacksmith more often than, say, Itol or Lillis."

Strictly speaking, Fontis was a spoke on the hub that was Itol, which had its own village blacksmith who traveled between the smaller villages on demand. Though with the Tyal in the area, Fontis might gain one from proximity to a greater house. But the Monbriths would have profited from it more, and travelers' horses were always throwing a shoe or stuck in the stables when a wheel came off a carriage. They had farriers and a carpenter in Fontis, so why not a blacksmith?

"Well, I can only tell you what I told you before, Master Ucalegon," Satya said. "We asked Harken to stay many a time, and each time he refused."

"Because he liked the road so much," Ibram said.

"Indeed."

"What was he working on, before he died?" Ibram asked. He brushed his hand along the rim of the fireplace again, taking a little more care this time. Something glinted by his foot. "I hope whoever placed the order didn't have to go far to see it fixed."

Satya paused and then shook her head. "I don't remember, I'm sorry," she said. "It wasn't for us, I know that much... No, it was the

Alths. They're farmers, mostly. They live much further out of the village than we do to the north."

Ibram nodded. "It must have been difficult, cleaning up in here."

She laughed. "I don't know if I could call it clean, but I tried my best!"

"What happened to the piece he was working on when he died?"

Satya swallowed. She held her doubled handful of strangleweed before her and shook her head. "Rustam took care of it," she said. "He likes having a project."

Ibram nodded. "So it wasn't complicated?"

She shook her head again. "No, not at all. All we heard was a little bit of hammering and he took it out to them. Mother saw no harm in it. A deal is a deal after all."

She sounded a little bitter at that. Ibram tilted his head. "You would know, young mistress," he said. "I came away from my first visit firmly convinced in your business sense."

Satya chuckled anew. "Well, my thanks for that," she said.

"I'm sure your family is very proud."

Satya nodded back at him with a smile, but did not speak. She turned around for the last double handful of strangleweed, and Ibram bent down. He scraped his fingers around the bottom of the forge, where the stones dug into the ground, and three curling scraps of metal came up into his palm. He grabbed for the one with his blood on it and then the little one next to that as well. He smacked at the legs of his boots and his knees as he rose back up and found Satya watching him.

"You're right about that strangleweed," he said, and put his hands behind his back again. With his right hand, Ibram pushed the metal shavings under the woolen flap of his wrist wallet. "I have to get back to Attendant Solari, but I don't want to trail it behind me."

She nodded and laughed a little. "It wouldn't be good at all."

Ibram drew his hands through his hair. The back of his head throbbed. If he was correct, then he'd been very, very wrong before, and if he was wrong, they were still swimming upstream in a flood. He wasn't certain which outcome was worse. He beat at his sleeves and checked the soles of his boots.

"Would you like to walk with me?" he asked and made certain his smile curled a little too high for polite company. "I might get lost."

Satya chuckled and ducked her head. "Oh, I doubt that," she said, and gestured to the furnace which had several buckets beside it. "And as I said, I have to mind the fire. I want it a little lower before I add the sand."

Ibram nodded. "Well then, I shall say good bye for now," he said.

"Return soon," Satya said. She breathed in a trifle unsteadily, and had turned to watch the fire when Ibram left the smithy.

Ibram made his way swiftly back to the draughtshop, and entered through the back kitchen door. Emil looked up from a bubbling cooking pot near the fire, and watched Ibram as he marched through. He raised a hand as he passed.

In the common room, he found Ahksell standing before Mistress Monbrith and Diarmit, with one of the warders—whipcord thin and heavily mustachioed—sitting at their table in the corner. Diarmit was in a full bow with Mistress Monbrith's hand on his back.

"I'm really very sorry," Diarmit said in a wavering voice. "I just wanted to see if you had a flying potion to find Rustam and—"

"That's enough, Diarmit," Mistress Monbrith said. "An apology is nothing when it merely contains excuses."

The boy twisted to look at his mother. "But Imriska said they can fly!"

"Diarmit!"

Diarmit turned back around. "I am most sorry, Attendant," he grumbled. "I didn't mean to break anything and I hope you still want to stay and find my brother."

Ahksell caught Ibram's eyes, and Ibram could see the heavy sigh that wanted to break free in the set of Ahksell's mouth. He raised both hands as he came out from behind the bar. The thin warder watched him.

"I'm afraid that Imriska has some lively ideas about alchemy," Ahksell said gently.

"That girl hears only firetales and nothing decent," Mistress Monbrith said. Diarmit tried to rise; it seemed his mother had other ideas. "I told you not to listen."

"And alchemists cannot fly, Diarmit," Ahksell said with a certain amount of stressed finality in his voice. "If I could, I would spy out your brother in a second, but I cannot. That's why I'm going back to my sect for a little while. And please, Mistress, let him back up again. There was no harm done."

From Ibram's position, all the angles of Mistress Monbrith's face were tensed. Her mouth worked, but she dropped her hand and Diarmit stood up straight. Ahksell shook his head.

"Then what do you keep in it?" Diarmit asked.

Ahksell sighed. "It's where I keep ingredients that little boys should not be playing with, and neither should they be picking at locks."

The warder in the corner stirred; Ahksell raised his hand. Diarmit's pout was about to overtake his entire body. Mistress Monbrith took him by the shoulder.

"You could be hurt getting into locks," she said. "You remember the story of Ili and the Storm Cook?"

Diarmit's sigh was surely loud and heavy enough to rattle the windows. Ibram chuckled despite himself, and the little group all turned to him. The entire back of Ibram's head was prickling like someone had danced a pavane at his pyre. Regardless, he nodded to them all and tried to appear collected.

"I return refreshed and ready to break my back in that uncomfortable carriage of yours," Ibram said.

Ahksell smiled. "Well, how wonderful."

"I just need to grab my bag and cloak from my room," Ibram said, and then spoke quickly over whatever protest Ahksell was about to say. "I will not be more than a moment. Shall we meet in the livery yard?"

"Of course," Ahksell said, with a little wrinkle of his eyebrows.

"Mistress, fear not," Ibram said, already heading towards the stairs. "We shall return quickly!"

"I will see to the horse," Mistress Monbrith said behind him.

Ibram quickly walked down the hallway and into his room. He shut the door and threw the latch behind him. It was a foolish thought—no, it was barely a thought at all—it was simply a feeling that surged at the corner of his mind. An old man, not very sharp anymore, covered in little metal slivers and dust from minor repairs. He left messes instead of cleaning up his scraps. Yet didn't a blacksmith need every scrap of usable metal he could get? Father complained of that all the time, and so did Katka. Ibram looked around the room and then frowned. Where had he thrown it?

He got down on his knees a few steps by the far wall and leaned down on both hands. It might have been cleaned up already. Ahksell had paid enough that Mistress Monbrith could quite rightly assume he wanted his rooms swept every day. It was a miracle that piece of metal he'd stuck himself on before had been left at all. Ibram squinted and turned his head. There, once again in the crack between floorboards, curved a half-moon of metal. He picked it up, and looked at it. It was too big to be a sliver, really and he could feel a ridge right along the outermost curve.

He tucked it into his wrist wallet with the others, and stood. He picked up his mostly empty sack, and slung it over his shoulder. Then he strolled back down the hallway, and down into the common room. It was empty, save for the thin warder.

Ibram walked over to him. He bowed shortly, and the man bowed back. "Ibram Ucalegon," he introduced himself. "May I be known to you?"

"Warder Phiri," the man said. He sounded like a local.

"Warder Phiri, I am about to—Well, I'm on my way to Lityen on behalf of his honor Judge E'grard, but I forgot to inquire with my colleague Commander Osthanes before I went. Would it be possible for you to send him a message? Perhaps when you're relieved for patrol?"

Warder Phiri's mustache wavered. He crossed his arms, and leaned back in his chair. "Might be," he said.

Ibram refused to look around to see if he was being watched. That was ridiculous. Of course he was being watched. Emil was in the kitchen and Diarmit apparently had a career as a sneak to look forward to. He nodded.

"Please to let the Commander know that I wish him well on his search, even though it's not the season yet for potatoes, and also ask him if he knew where Harken Tolk traveled outside this end of the province."

Phiri raised his eyebrows. "Is that all?"

"It is," Ibram said and held the warder's gaze with his own. "Oh, and if you remember it, let him know that I've finally made a more complete search of the property and *Rustam* is not here."

Phiri's face grew scornful. "To be sure, I'll get right to that."

"Your service is a blessing. Good day!"

Ibram walked out with a raised hand to Emil, who was standing behind the bar now. He made his apologies to Mistress Monbrith and added his reassurances to Ahksell's that they would return soon. Diarmit was nowhere to be seen, and Ibram couldn't fault him for it.

The return trip back to Fontis went much more quickly now that Antio was doing all the work. The hardest part was weaving the carriage down the road with all the merchants beginning to close of shop. The foot traffic grew a little impenetrable at times. The warders at the front gate eyed them with great disdain, but let them past after searching the carriage thoroughly and in full view of the public. It wasn't long before Antio was trotting merrily back in the direction of Lityen. Once they were well away, Ibram turned to Ahksell.

"When you bought food at Master Kolesar's shay shop, did you get change or did you overpay again?"

Ahksell sighed heavily and rolled his neck on his shoulders. "I did not overpay."

"So Gella did give you coins?"

"She did."

"Show me."

Ahksell looked at him askance. "Show you?"

Ibram yanked on the strap of Ahksell's satchel, and Ahksell leaned the opposite direction. "Come on," Ibram said. "This could be important. And Mistress Monbrith's change as well."

Ahksell groaned and switched Antio's reins to his left hand. He laid his satchel in his lap and undid the latch, and then lifted open the flat. The satchel gaped open, a jumble of pouches and stoppered bottles. Judge E'grard's message scroll was looking a little dented.

"Go ahead," Ahksell said.

Ibram leaned over. He pushed aside Ahksell's folded traveling sailing light, and rifled through the little sloshing bottles. He pulled out a small pouch tied closed with soldered wire.

"That's not it," Ahksell said. "That's granite dust."

"Why would you need granite dust?" Ibram dropped the pouch back in and picked up another. He shook it and heard the clink of coins. He shook it again in Ahksell's face.

"Get off!" Ahksell said, and kicked at Ibram's ankle.

Ibram laughed and sat back on his side of the bench. Ahksell resettled his bag, and Ibram stretched his arms out over his head. He groaned and then collapsed back onto the bench.

"So we've solved the mystery of who got into your room," he said.

Ahksell nodded. "He's very eager to help, poor child," he said. "I imagine they're all feeling the frustration of being, well, locked away before they seal up the whole place."

Ibram hefted the coin purse, and opened the top wide. He peered inside. No gold, unsurprisingly, but he saw a good bit of older silver coins, and what looked to be a doubled handful of copper faunts. He frowned. An ugly thought was taking shape in the back of his head, and he wasn't certain he liked it. But it was only a thought, as of yet, and he wanted to speak to Father before he brought his suspicions to Lady Azadiya.

He pinched a faunt out of the bag, and ran his fingers around its edge. The coin was old, and it was no longer a perfect circle of copper. That wasn't strange at all, coins often grew out of their shape as they aged in circulation.

Ibram sighed. "It's just a thought," he said. He closed the coin purse and set it down on his thigh. He pulled up his sleeve, and double-checked the thick overhanging woolen flap the covered the top of his wrist wallet.

"Well, let me know when it becomes anything more," Ahksell said.

Ibram nodded. "When we get back to Lityen, can you drop me at my home?"

Ahksell glanced at him. "No, of course not," he said. "You need to deliver Mentor's message."

"It's just for a moment," he said. "I need to ask my father's advice about something."

"Something Mentor can't know about?"

"Something I want to ask Father about before I make my case to Ladyship," Ibram said. "It may come to nothing, but even if it does not, it won't take more than a moment."

"We need to get back to Fontis as soon as possible."

"Yes, which is why we're going to arrive in Lityen just in time for dinner," Ibram said. "And then we're all going straight up the living mountain like good little errand boys."

Ahksell sighed with far too much force to be taken seriously. Ibram rolled his eyes. He glanced around them on the road. Bandits were mostly unheard of in this end of the province but he could have used the distraction about now.

"What a shambles this all is," he muttered.

Ahksell shifted on the bench.

"Are you going to tell Mentor we didn't actually sleep in the carriage?" Ibram asked.

Ahksell snorted, or possibly that was Antio.

"Satya Monbrith asked me if I was married."

"I knew it!" Ahksell exclaimed, and then Antio was startled enough to attempt a rolling canter instead of a trot. It didn't last for long, but Ibram gave her credit for it. "I knew you pitched—"

"I barely said anything to her!" Ibram protested. "Or, to the point, I didn't say anything that prompted more than a polite response. I can't help what strange girls I meet in the course of my duties think of me, now can I?"

"You absolutely can."

"Well, forgive me, because I have no idea what I did in any case."

"What do you mean?"

Ibram sighed and put one foot up on the carriage. "The last time she and I were in the same room, she addressed me as "Master Ucalegon" and answered my every courteous question with three and four words. She was very polite but she didn't know anything. At the most, she was persuaded to tell me all she wanted was to focus on the future."

"And now?" Ahksell said as he directed the carriage around a curve.

"She called me Ibram and grabbed my elbow."

Ahksell nodded slowly. "Oh, well, you'll have to marry her now."

"That's not what I mean!" Ibram punched him in the arm; they both winced. He shook out his hand and crossed his arms over his chest. Ahksell sighed.

"What do you mean then?" he asked.

Ibram shook his head. "I think I'm being made fun of," he said. "Or Ladyship is, but I'm just not certain how."

"Well," Ahksell said. He pulled the carriage to a stop, and then handed over the reins. Ibram took them, startled. The little coin purse fell to the floor. "Have a think about it while you get us home." He jumped down from the carriage and brushed down the front of his gambeson. "I'm going to go take a nap in the carriage so I won't have to lie to Mentor when we get back."

☙❧

The drive didn't clear Ibram's head, but it did keep him preoccupied. He woke Ahksell up when they arrived at Ibram's family home, and they switched places. The sun still sailed, but its boat was sinking quickly in the sky, and the back of Ibram's neck felt damp with sweat. It hadn't even had the decency to rain.

"I'll meet you at the Preceptory," Ibram called out as Ahksell pulled away.

Ahksell waved as he ambled up the road, and Ibram turned to his front gate. The heavy iron gate was open and he walked up, feeling the tingle as he crossed the line of salt-soaked iron embedded in the ground. As he approached the door to the house, Kholdo was already there to draw it open. He bowed with his hands on his stomach, and Ibram slowed to a halt.

"Are there customers here?" he whispered. Kholdo had been

chasing Ibram around the courtyard, yelling Ibram's sins to the heavens since he was a child, but he tended towards formality at the front door or in front of strangers.

"Oh, it's you," Kholdo said as he rose. His hair stuck out at all angles in a perpetual wave. "Welcome back, Ib-la."

Ibram sighed. A knot was slowly tightening between his shoulder blades. He was so close to his own bed, and lunch had been less than thrilling from the front of the carriage. Kholdo stood aside and Ibram walked through into the hallway.

"Where is your cloak?" Kholdo asked.

"In the carriage," Ibram said.

"Whose carriage?" Kholdo frowned. "Are you courting?"

"I find the spring air bracing, thank you, Kholdo," he said. "Where's Father? Is he in the workshop?"

"Your mother and father have gone on a visit to the Banik's manor," Kholdo said.

He followed Ibram down the hallway and onto the wooden platform surrounding the inner courtyard. The ornamental garden still slumbered, and there was only one row of glowbulbs lit. Ibram glanced around.

"Katka!" he yelled. "Katka!"

Kholdo pushed him on the shoulder. "Your sister is in the family's courtyard," he said. "And cannot hear you."

Ibram groaned. "Fine, yes, thank you," he said. "Is there any chance of something to eat before I have to leave again?"

"When do you have to leave?" Kholdo asked.

Ibram blew his breath out between his lips. "Depends on how helpful Katka is," he said, and took himself down the lighted path around the courtyard.

"Supper is in the sitting room!" Kholdo called after him.

Ibram waved over his shoulder. He heard Kholdo's footsteps behind him, but with no one telling him not to run, he was through the entrance to the family courtyard in no time at all. He paused at the inner door and looked around. The shadows were lengthening, and the two apprentices were sharing a blanket and a bowl of something crispy looking while they read a scroll between them. They looked up when Ibram burst through.

"Where's my sister?" he asked, and the nearest red-cheeked little person took their arm out of the blanket to point towards the family bedrooms. "Thank you," he said as he passed them. "Katka! Katka! Get out of bed, lazybones!"

He turned in the covered corner, and heard the rumble of booted feet on wooden stairs. Ibram leaned against the wall nearest the open door, and crossed his arms and legs. Finally, Katka walked out onto the terrace.

"What's with all the shouting?" she asked.

Clearly, Katka had done with her work for the day. She wore a sleeveless blue linen tunic belted over loose green breeches with her scuffed leather boots. Her hair was still tied in a braid wrapped in a length of fabric around her head. She looked more like their father every day, to be sure. Katka had his muscles and his red hair, and the way she liked to be laughing and pleased with everyone she met. About the only aspect of their parents he and she shared was their equally stubborn chin. She turned around and crossed her muscled arms. Her face was still reddened from the heat of the furnace.

"How else am I going to pull you from your nap?" he asked.

Katka pursed her lips and Ibram sighed. "I need your help with something."

"You do?" she asked. "With what?"

Ibram came off the wall and looked about them. Katka snorted. "Are you worried Inzhu and Hedvi will tell?"

"Which... Never mind. And the answer is no," he said, but lowered his voice. "It's just a thought right now, but I was hoping to talk to Father."

Katka scoffed at him. "He's with Ama playing tica at the Baniks."

"Kholdo told me," Ibram said. "But you're just as good, right? You're a blacksmith."

She drew her head back. "We make jewelry, thank you!"

Ibram waved his hand. "Yes, but you make things with fire. We have furnaces."

"The Wheelmaker foresaw our souls and made sure I'd be born second, didn't he," she said.

"That's another question! Thank you. Now come on, Kholdo said there would be food in the sitting room."

Katka wrapped her arm around his shoulders, and kissed his forehead. Ibram allowed this, but sighed heavily. She let him go far enough that they could both walk comfortably. She waved at the apprentices, who bundled up their little station and trotted along behind them.

"They're eating with us?" he whispered, leaning up a bit to Katka's ear. He wasn't a short man, but must so many folk be taller? "Why aren't they in bed?"

"Hard work makes hungry bellies," she whispered back.

The sitting room was smaller than the dining room, of course, and used for times when the whole family ate together without guests. It was closer to the kitchen as well, and the warmer for it. They ate in the Western style here, with plates and bowls already on the table covered by a light cloth. Father had his little pile of cutlery near his chair at the end of the trestle table. Ibram took his seat with his back to the far wall and Katka took hers opposite him. The children arranged themselves on the bench to either side of her.

A stack of fluffy flat breads lay on a charger near a platter of hard cheese, apple vinegar preserved peppers and sticks of cooling green eorepple with smoked mouflon meat slices in the center of the table. Katka passed out the wooden plates and then the bowls. Ibram split Father's trident-shaped forks between the children, just in case.

"So...which of you is youngest?" Ibram asked.

Katka laughed. "Really, Ibram?"

"I'm hungry!" he protested. "Youngest eats first, and I want to begin."

"They've been here for a year."

"I'm youngest!" The littlest apprentice raised her hand, and Ibram studied her face. She had a pug nose beneath a thick swash of freckles, which had clearly been scrubbed clean. Truly, he had an equal chance at this.

"Hedvi?" he guessed.

"Yes!" they said.

"She's the youngest by a year," Katka said.

"So this is Inzhu," Ibram said, pointing at the other one, and the child nodded. She had pale skin and close braided pigtails over her ears like a Kilk girl now that Ibram saw her in the light.

Ibram passed Hedvi the bread. She grabbed the topmost round with her fork, and then he offered it to Inzhu, who took her own piece. Ibram laid the third round of flatbread on Katka's plate. His stomach growled. He put the platter down, and licked his fingers clean of salt and oil.

"Do they not feed sect agents in Fontis?" Katka reached over and gave him his own piece. Ibram passed around the triangles of hard cheese and sliced, smoked mouflon meat, and then the cups. The drink pitchers lay on their own platter, milky shay for the children and glass apple cider for him and Katka, heavily spiced to Ama's own recipe.

"It was a long trip back," Ibram said. He licked his lips and kept his eye on the pile of mouflon meat; it could go fast if Katka was hungry. "And in town we had our minds on other things."

Hedvi took up her fork. She speared the end of her cheese, and ate it, and Ibram clapped his hands together. He nodded at the table. Katka pinched a bite of bread and mouflon in her fingers and popped them in her mouth. He moved his own plate closer, and began pulling apart the mouflon meat into chunks. He loved the salt and the peppery glaze on Kholdo's smoked mouflon, but he hated trying to bite through it. He licked his fingers, and the children giggled.

Katka rolled her eyes. "So, what did you need Father's help for?" she asked.

"This. Well, these."

Ibram moved the platter with meat to the side by Inzhu, who was only eating the bread and cheese. She wrinkled her little nose. Ibram swiveled the platter so that the cheese and vegetables faced her instead. She helped herself to a handful of eorepple sticks and began crunching her way through them. He pulled up his sleeve, and dug into his wrist wallet for his evidence. He spread the little metal scraps and the blank disc on the table, and Katka leaned over them.

She frowned. "What about them?"

Ibram sighed. "I'm not certain, but I think they're important."

She picked one up. "Why?"

He glanced at the children, who were both frowning at the scraps. "Because the only difference I've found between my initial report to Ladyship—"

"Ladyship," Hedvi and Inzhu whispered at each other excitedly.

That was strange, but Katka rolled her eyes at him, so he continued, "And any kind of reasoning for the First Finder to run is the dead man's occupation." He gestured at the scraps. "He was a blacksmith. The boy was learning the trade, as far as I can tell."

"Oooh," Inzhu said. She stood up and reached over to pick up a copper scrap.

"Be careful with that," Ibram said around a mouthful of cheese.

"Is that all you've managed to figure out?" Katka asked. She offered him a pale red pepper, and he took it.

"It's complicated," he protested. "Anyway, this isn't a pendant, is it? I mean, those are thinner."

He nudged the blank disc closer to her with one finger. He bit through the red pepper and put the stem on his plate, swallowing quickly so the pickling liquid inside wouldn't choke him. He coughed and followed it up with bread. He turned his hand up and then shrugged.

"Found this on the floor, but the rest of those things are all over that place," he said. "I've been pricked twice by them. And these...little slivers here, that one has a finished edge, doesn't it?"

She hummed in consideration, and picked the biggest piece up. The silvery metal was a flat curl. She set it down and then raised the disc so that it caught the lantern light. She rubbed her thumb along its edge.

"There's a little bump here and also here," she said. "Probably hadn't been sanded down after it was cast."

She weighed the disc in her palm and then laid it back on the table. She dusted her fingers clean, and then began to eat again. Ibram waved his hand over the pieces. Katka caught his eyes and shrugged.

"I didn't pay attention before," he said. "I let other people draw my conclusions for me. The scraps alone I might ignore, but with the little disc as well? I have a horrible thought."

"So you were listening in on my lessons," she said, and smiled.

"I heard some things!" Ibram said. "How could I not? But these were in the dead man's bedroom and in his workplace, and... Cangsa, but I hope it's nothing. Honestly, to be sure, it could be nothing."

He rubbed his eyebrow with his thumb, and then covered his eyes with the flat of his palm. He laid his hand on the table, while Katka ate her food silently. The little apprentices each had their own scrap, and were frowning at them. Ibram poured himself a cup of cider and drank deeply.

"Mistress," Inzhu said. "Why would you cut something like this? It has a bird on it."

"What?" Katka asked. Her head turned around quickly, and Inzhu handed her the little copper scrap.

Hedvi held hers up to the single hanging glowbulb. "Do they all have birds on them?"

Ibram raised his head. Katka frowned down at the scrap she held. "Hedvi, leave that here, and go and get my lenses."

The child dropped her scrap back onto the table and scampered off. Ibram leaned closer. He poked through the metal with one finger.

"What are you thinking?" Katka asked quietly.

"The Monbriths have too much money," he replied. An image of all those recent signs of renovation at their home flashed into his mind. "And the village doesn't."

Katka breathed in through her teeth, and winced. Ibram nodded. He glanced to Inzhu and smiled.

"There's a bird?" he asked. "I just thought the finished edge was odd."

"Yes," Inzhu said. She leaned over a little too far and almost put her elbow in the flatbread. She pointed. "Here! It's silly. Why would you get rid of work you already done?"

"Did," Katka said absently.

She turned the copper to the light and Ibram squinted. Inzhu sighed incredibly heavily, and sat back down in her chair. Kholdo came in through the pocket door that separated the kitchen from the sitting room carrying a small cauldron in two rag covered hands.

"Potato and leek soup," he said. "It's just enough for you four."

"Hedvi's gone," Inzhu announced. "Me first!"

Ibram covered his mouth, and caught Katka's eye. She smirked at him. Across from them, Kholdo nodded in all due gravity.

"Yes indeed, Mistress Inzhu," he said. He walked behind Ibram, and then placed the cauldron nearest to Inzhu. The ladle he angled towards Ibram, who picked it up and carefully poured her a full bowl. She wriggled on the spot and reached out, but then pulled her hands back. Kholdo reached into the pocket of his apron and pulled out two spoons, which he laid on the table. She snatched one up while Ibram doled out soup for the rest of the table.

"Thank you, Master Kholdo," Inzhu said and carefully blew on her spoonful of soup.

"You're very welcome," he said. "Maybe you'll teach these two some manners."

Katka snorted. "She can try."

Kholdo shook his head. "You have grease on your mouth, Kat-la."

Katka scrubbed her lips with the back of her hand. Ibram laughed. The jolting thud of tiny boots pounding down the walkway grew louder, and Hedvi appeared in the doorway. The little thing caught her breath and thrust Katka's lenses in her vague direction.

"I couldn't find them," she said, while she got back into her seat. "But I did!"

"Straight to the point, thank you, Hedvi," Ibram said.

Kholdo moved over to his side of the table so that he could prod one unreasonably hard finger into the space between Ibram's shoulder blades. Ibram failed to hide his flinch to Katka's delight. He leaned forward and put his elbows on the table.

"What do you need your lenses for?" Ibram asked.

"Cool your soup for a moment and I'll tell you," she said to the apparent delight of the smaller folk. Katka held her bioptic lenses by the ear pieces. She set them on her face and picked up the copper scrap Inzhu claimed had a bird on it with her left hand, while she adjusted the little telescopes attached to the wooden-framed eyepieces. Ibram picked up his wooden soup bowl and carefully swirled the steaming liquid.

"Yes," she said slowly. "Inzhu's correct. There's a bird here, but it's only half of one." She breathed in sharply and held the scrap higher in front of her face. "It's been snipped, not very carefully, twice. The first to the right and then the second coming in from the left, I should think."

Ibram set his soup down. "Does that mean what I think it does?"

"It makes it like a triangle," Hedvi said, and modelled the shape with both hands.

"Which is why it's only half a bird," Ibram said.

A copper bird, cut in half. Ibram frowned and tore a strip off his flatbread. He chewed it. A horrible draining feeling was slipping down his chest to pool in his stomach. Kholdo took a seat at the bench and picked up one of the large silvery pieces.

"Where did you get these?" he asked. "This feels heavy."

Ibram reached into his belt and pulled out the money pouch. He cleared a little space on the table, opened the pouch, and poured out the coins. The girls gasped as he quickly sorted through the coins. He divided them, silver picaio from copper faunts and even a lone fat gold pick that he hadn't noticed before.

"Is that all yours?" Katka asked.

Ibram shook his head. "No, it's Ahksell's," he said.

Katka whistled. "And to think I lent him a faunt for the dunking contest last feastday," she said.

"What are you two doing betting on carnival tricksters?" Ibram asked, but then he shook his head. "No, a question for later, but look!"

He tapped his finger on the pile of faunts, a much bigger stack than any of the others. "Faunts are all stamped the same way, aren't they?" he asked. "Octagonal shape—or at least they begin so—with Her Imperial Majesty's face on one side and the flock on the other. Same as the picaio have the palace on the other side and picks have the tower."

He sat back and rubbed his eyebrow with his thumb. Katka raised her eyebrows at him, and he dropped his hand. He had to stop doing that, it was such an annoyingly obvious tell. He stared down at the scraps. These were coin clippings, snipped off from legitimate currency and hoarded until they could be melted into counterfeit coinage. Oh, he was in for it now. Not only had he overlooked a serious crime, but he'd allowed a criminal to escape unpunished. Lady Azadiya was not going to enjoy hearing about this.

"Bo Catha ocsin," Kholdo muttered. "Di calla hanar umera monoie."

Katka laughed. "Kholdo! It's not as bad as all that, surely."

"What did he say?" Hedvi asked, looking up from her soup.

"Is it rude?" Inzhu asked. She seemed a bit too delighted by the prospect.

"No," Ibram said. "Just dramatic."

"To be sure," Katka said. She took off her bioptic lenses and set them to one side. "Ibram already knows who did it, and he's dead. Still, I think you should leave these piles with me. If these coins have been clipped—"

Ibram leaned his elbows on the table. "This is so embarrassing."

"If these are clipped," Katka said. "Then I want to show them to Father when he gets back home. I think we should take a look at the other coins you've brought in."

She picked up one of the picaio and frowned at it, running her finger over the flat edge. Ibram nodded. It was a good plan. He could work out what he was going to say to Ladyship in the meanwhile.

"You're taking this to Lady Azadiya directly, aren't you?" Kholdo asked.

"Of course, I am," Ibram said. He lifted his soup bowl and blew over the top of it. Kholdo put his hand over the bowl. "Am I not allowed to finish my supper?"

"I'll make you a little meal for the road," Katka said, and began piling mouflon and cheese on the remains of his flatbread. "Take my horse."

"Oh, poor Gilma," Hedvi said. "She just got put in her stall!"

"Does no one know how to name an animal in this village?" Ibram sighed, and went to saddle his sister's horse.

❦

Gilma—named for the Western word for 'glittering'—was absolutely the opposite of her name, being a dull brown in color and monstrously stupid. She was spoiled and round and really a bit more of a pony now that he and Katka were grown, but she made her way to the base of the living mountain all right. Sadly, she was useless at providing any advice when Ibram began sorting through his options for how he should admit his faults in observation and deduction to Lady Azadiya. Thus, he left her in the stables at the base of the living mountain, and continued up to the Preceptory of Yseult in the usual way.

Lityen darkened at night, but the living mountain above shimmered like a jeweled mosaic. Hundreds of multi-colored torches directed traffic and blue glowbulbs lined the streets and pathways strung between the preceptories, while within the walls almost every building was alight. A bright orange flame ballooned into the air as Ibram's gondola rocked upwards and hung, shining, like a bubble. It slowly fizzled as he changed course at the clearing station and by the time he arrived at the preceptory, it had dissipated to a trailing ruddy afterglow.

Ibram walked quickly in the direction of Ladyship's tower. She had somewhat of a daily routine. If she wasn't in her office, than she was most likely on the training fields. He could smell charcoal and a sharp stinging smoke that told him someone had lit off an explosion or three during the day. He was lucky to have missed it. The sound of banging was interspersed with high-pitched whistles, which turned into small groups of learners practicing in the training fields with their gars. Yseult was responsible for making sure all the little alchemists in the sect had at least the basics of self-defense.

Wire-worked cages full of sailing lights glowed above the practice fields, nailed to the ground with long ropes tied to heavy iron stakes. He waved down an Attendant sitting with her legs crossed beneath her, balanced on furthest tip of a tree branch. She had a telescope in one hand, and a red handkerchief tied around her upper arm, which marked her as a referee. She dropped down into hearing range, and Ibram bowed shortly, but with his hands on his stomach.

"Do you know where the Fourth Mentor of Yseult might be?" he asked.

The Attendant pointed further down the field. "Mentor is providing an exhibition in the tower field."

He bowed again and she floated back up into position. She cupped her hands around her mouth. "Tenth position! Gars up and back to your marks!" she yelled with augmented force.

The group of learners she was overseeing stopped poking at each other with their sticks in a guilty wave, as Ibram walked off. The split rail fence that outlined each practice field in a long wavering quilt of staging areas was a mess of cloaks with satchels left on the ground. Yseult never seemed to sleep, there were always folks running around training or being trained. Ibram hadn't visited the other preceptories much outside of running errands or delivering messages, but there was an energy in Yseult that not a one of the other preceptories could touch.

Attendants had been paired off in a staggered melee in the fields approaching Ladyship's tower; the shouts and bangs of their sparring reverberated in the air as they fought. A few of the older alchemists and agents observing the athletics in the fields noticed him and raised a hand as he hot-stepped it down the road. Ibram kept an eye out for Ahksell, only pausing to bow in recognition if someone managed to catch his eye as he surveyed the crowd for Lady Azadiya.

The tower field held a rowdy crowd of Attendants and a higher number of Ibram's amitai than Ibram was comfortable with. Ivane and Yera were betting on the practice bout between two Attendants as he reached the gate that opened onto the field. Ibram saw Ahksell leaning against the fence, wearing his satchel and adjusting the shoulder strap. He was speaking with a plump woman who Ibram didn't recognize. Ibram opened the gate and walked onto the field. He ran forward, and raised one arm.

"Ahksell!" he yelled.

Ahksell turned around and waved. "Ibram! Over here!"

He lowered his arm and the other woman ducked out of the way of Ahksell's elbow. Ibram opened the gate and arrived to the pair just in time to hear Ahksell's apology. The woman appeared good-humored about it.

"Aren't you supposed to be the one with body awareness?" she asked. "Don't tell me I've been teaching the wrong lessons."

"Well, if you ask him to hold his breath underwater for the length of a short candle or slow his heartrate so your little sister thinks he's the ravening undead, then Ahksell's your man," Ibram said. "But elbows..."

Ahksell glared at him. "Be known to Ibram Ucalegon," he said. "Ibram, be known to Attendant Serisan."

They bowed to each other, with the Attendant rising first. Ibram smoothed down his gambeson. The name was familiar. He looked her over. She kept her hair close cropped to her head and wore gold hoops following the curve of her ears.

"Mentor's just finishing up," Ahksell said and gestured over to the center of the field.

Ibram's eyes widened as he stepped up to Ahksell's side for a look. They stood on a hill. Downward, in the center of a shifting crowd held back by his amitai, Lady Azadiya dueled two opponents at once, dressed in the green gambeson and dark grey breeches. Her reddish-brown gar whirled in her hands as she parried one opponent and slammed her boot into the second's knee. He stumbled back, stabbing his gar into the soft ground for balance and then jumped six feet in the air. Ladyship scuttled right, driving her opponent still afoot further down the hillslope in a flurry of overhand strikes that gave him no choice but to block as he lost ground. She jabbed him in the stomach, and then swiveled away from his attack.

Ibram gasped. The jumping Attendant flipped at the highest point of his arc, gar pointed like a spear towards Lady Azadiya's exposed flank. Her arm darted upwards, her hand like claw, and the jumper halted mid-air, flailing like a fish on a hook. He dropped his gar and flung his arms out; Lady Azadiya hurtled him to the ground as if she were bouncing a thrown ball. The ground rumbled beneath Ibram's feet. The crowd groaned and hooted.

Watching Ladyship fight made Ibram itch to join the circle and place a bet of his own—no doubt several had been laid—but if he did approach them now, one of his uncles or aunts would notice his nerves. Doubtless, they'd get the story from him first and he wanted to present himself to Lady Azadiya before he fell into their clutches; it was only proper. Amota Viran called out a new bet as Ladyship's remaining opponent began circling to her right, but only in Merrilian.

The Attendants were supposed to be learning their footwork, and had failed their last progress test it seemed. Thus, they would fight Ladyship until they learned, or realized how much they had yet to learn; Amota Viran held the odds poorly for either happy event. Lady Azadiya and the Attendant still standing began to circle each other while her downed opponent scrambled to his feet. Without looking, she jabbed her gar behind her and into his padded chest; the man fell back down. Ibram turned back to Ahksell and his new friend, who he'd remembered now.

"You teach in Fontis," he said. "I've heard good reports."

She smiled. "Yes, I do. I'm told you two have met Imriska Suugan?"

"And another of your pupils, Diarmit Monbrith," Ibram said.

Attendant Serisan paused. She and Ahksell glanced at each other. Ibram cocked his head.

"Did I stumble into something?" he asked.

"Diarmit doesn't go to the Bedris school anymore," Attendant Serisan said. "His mother decided to take him out to help around the draughtshop."

"Really?" Ibram asked. "When was that?"

"About three years ago," Ahksell said. "Once Harken Tolk started coming around."

When Ibram had been seven, he'd been plopped in the back of Attendant Olini's village school learning how to make cones and cylinders with bark and reciting the table of transmutation. He'd been in a class with the children of other agents, some even went on to become learners. It wasn't uncommon to be taken out of school to attend to your family's business, but the timing did seem too neat.

He nodded slowly. "Well, that begins to make a lot of sense," Ibram said. "Considering what I think was going in on that den of sin."

"Ibram!" Ahksell exclaimed.

"Well, all right, not sin as you might call it, but there's definitely illegal activity going on there—" The crowd behind Ahksell roared and the thud of bodies vibrated the ground unnaturally. The doubled effect shot right through Ibram's feet; his knees buckled, and Attendant Serisan caught him by the elbow. She helped him up with a rueful grin.

"How does she do that?" Ibram muttered. "Why does she do that?"

"When I know, I won't tell you," Ahksell said. He twisted to look behind them. "They're fine, see? They're getting back up."

Ibram shuddered, and Serisan let him go. Down the hill, the grass was torn in the center of the fighting ring, and Lady Azadiya was the only alchemist left standing. Amota Viran stood at her side, and several folk were already lined up before him, money in hand. Ibram swallowed at the flash of all those picaio and faunts. It wasn't right. How could he have missed it on his first investigation? Why had he been so complacent?

"In that case," Ibram said, "I need to go and greet Ladyship before I lose her to the celebratory feast."

"I'll go with you," Ahksell said after a moment's pause. "Sotiria, thank you. May we speak later?"

"I look forward to it," she said.

They bowed their goodbyes and then Ibram carefully made his way down the hill to the lower field. Ahksell caught up to him easily. Ibram waggled his eyebrows. Ahksell frowned at him. Ibram glanced back towards Serisan and then waggled them again. Ahksell laughed and pushed him a few stumbling feet.

"It's not like that," he protested. "I told you I was going back for a reason. She was the reason."

"How does that make it better?" Ibram dodged between two retreating groups of alchemists, and risked his footing in the grass to look back at Ahksell. "Did you merely want to ask what Attendant Serisan thought of Diarmit?"

"Well, in a way," Ahksell said. "I thought every bit might help in the search, but I also wanted to know what she knew about how many children in Fontis were of school age and..."

He trailed off, and Ibram stopped trying to walk through the thick of the remaining onlookers. Ahksell's eyebrows were drawn together in a clearly unpleasant thought. Ibram turned to look at him more fully.

"What?" he asked.

Ahksell shook his head. "I need to speak with Mentor before I say anymore," he said firmly.

Ibram raised his eyebrows. He glanced about, but none of the people walking towards the gate were paying much attention to them.

Amota Berac was standing a few feet from them, speaking to Amota Lakum. Both men were responsible for the younger agents attached to Ladyship's office. Berac noticed him, and tapped Lakum on the shoulder. The older man turned and frowned. Ibram avoided eye contact. Yilka's megrims, it was like Lakum knew he'd made a hash of things.

"To be sure," he said around the tightness in his throat. "As long as you let me say my piece first."

"What do you need to speak to Mentor about?" Ahksell asked. "Did you find what you were looking for at home?"

"Do not we all?" Ladyship asked.

Ibram whirled on his heels, slipped an inch in the grass and recovered himself. Lady Azadiya stood in front of them, leaning on her gar, with her long hair braided back and a soft cloth hanging over her neck. Her quilted green gambeson had a splash of mud across the belly, and her breeches and boots were filthy with grass and dirt. Ibram bowed low with his hands on his stomach and stayed there. He stared at the ground, and felt the back of his head throb unpleasantly; his neck crackled with strain as he stared at the torn earth.

❧   8   ❧

"Oh dear," Ladyship murmured. "Arise, Ib-la. Ahksell, what have you been doing to him?"

"Nothing, Mentor!" Ahksell protested as Ibram stayed put.

Ibram tucked his arms more firmly against his body. He clasped his left hand around his right wrist and squeezed. His chest felt heavy and his face bloomed with heat.

"Ibram, when I said 'arise' I meant you should stand and face me," Ladyship said. "I don't like to repeat myself."

Ibram swallowed and took a deep breath. He stood slowly, feeling the ache in his spine and the back of his head. He raised his face at the last, and she appraised him with the slightest tilt of her head.

"You two have returned earlier than expected," she said. "Have you found Master Monbrith so quickly?"

"We have not, Ladyship," Ibram said.

"Then you've discovered why he ran," she suggested.

Ibram eyed the small empty space that had grown around them, as it naturally did wherever Lady Azadiya stood. The tower field was still too open a spot for what he had to tell her. He swallowed and met her gaze. "I have...made a mistake."

She nodded. "Come, walk with me to the tower. Viran!" she called out behind her.

Her loud voice drew the attention of all of her agents, naturally, and several of them took note of Ibram standing with her. Ibram winced; it couldn't be too long before everyone knew of his error now. Amota Viran, the oldest ranking agent attached to Lady Azadiya, appeared out of the crowd like smoke. He was a tall man, but thin, and wore a Western coat with large bronze buttons over thick woolen trousers tucked into high boots. His burnished torch brooch was pinned to his cloak. Ibram smiled at him; he frowned back.

Viran began to bow, but Ladyship waved him up. "Come with me to the tower," she said. "Make my excuses at the evening meal, and choose a few of the agents to be at their ready. I have a feeling I will be needing a message or three sent."

"Raffasticates, damita," Viran said in his deep resonate voice. They all filed into place behind Lady Azadiya as she led the way across the field. Ahksell and Viran flanked her shoulders while Ibram fell to the back. The crowd parted around them, and they easily walked through the gate and then onto the pathway further into preceptory.

The tree canopy closed over them as they paraded down to Ladyship's tower, and the road was lined by strings of glowbulbs. Ibram rubbed his palms against each other. He hadn't come up with anything to say to Lady Azadiya while he was traveling up the living mountain beyond the bare facts of the matter, and it didn't feel like this walk would unearth within him any great explanatory powers either. The truth, he supposed, was the basic solution. He'd already admitted he'd made a mistake. Ibram grimaced. Now, he just had to explain the error in full. The thud of Ladyship's gar on the earth was beginning to over-take his own heartbeat.

Ahksell dropped back to walk next to him. The trees above wavered in a chill breeze. Ibram looked up at him, and Ahksell leaned over.

"What did he say?" he whispered. "Master Kalmar, I mean."

Ahead of them, Viran's head twitched, but did not turn; his hearing was unfortunately excellent. Ibram shrugged. Of all the languages Ahksell knew, he'd never had an ear for Merrilian. They walked down the turn that led to the tower and saw the lights in the top level aglow. Viran ran ahead to open the doors.

"It means 'of course' I suppose," Ibram said. "It's not exactly the same."

"How can it mean something, but only 'not exactly the same?'?" Ahksell asked.

"It means he was more polite than merely saying 'of course' usually signifies," Ibram said.

"Oh, it's the tense of the word," Ahksell said.

It was not, in fact, anything due to the tense of the word, but Ibram wasn't above a polite fiction to protect a friend's ability to claim ignorance. Amota Viran had said "by your command" or that was the meaning behind the phrase, and in Merrilian it held the ring of a vassal to his noble. He'd also addressed Lady Azadiya as his aunt, or more specifically, his father's sister.

Ibram shrugged and Ahksell accepted the explanation quietly, though he studied Amota Viran's back closely. Ibram made it a practice not to think overmuch about the collection of little quirks and odd behaviors Lady Azadiya's agents seemed to develop. In his mind, it was Amota Viran's own affair. He'd been an agent of the sect for longer than almost every other person attached to the Fourth Mentor and if he wished to claim a family kinship with Lady Azadiya, then Ibram wasn't going to touch on it. Merrilians substituted family titles for working relationships often, hence why Ibram was saddled with a host of uncles, aunts, and some few cousins who bore no blood relation to him whatsoever. He frowned. Judge E'grard's little dig at the way the sect structured its employment thrummed in the back of his mind.

The tower's common room was darkened to a warm orange glow with sailing lights orbiting the center fountain and above it almost to the ceiling. A large table had been placed near the couches, laden with stacks of flatbreads and a giant bowl of farmer's cheese jiggling next to platters of sliced meats and vegetables. Ibram smelled spiced wine and roasted chilies. Viran split away and walked down to the nearest couch, already crowded with those who worked in the tower.

Lady Azadiya sailed past the assembling horde of her ravening household, and led the way up to her office on the third floor. Ibram walked through with the usual shiver and moved to stand in the center of the room in front of Ladyship's desk. Ahksell stood next to him, but gave the strange hanging glop by the window a very hard glare. It coughed purple smoke, and he looked alarmed.

Ladyship waved her left hand sideways, and the alembic arrayed on her desk shuffled to the right in order to clear a space; clear liquid sloshed like oil in its belly. She leaned her gar against the wall and wiped mud off her hands on the sleeves of her gambeson. She unbuttoned the diagonal row of knots which held the quilted wool closed and then tossed it on her desk. Beneath, she wore a linen tunic crumpled with sweat, and embroidered with red and blue thread at the collar and cuffs.

She glanced at the small perpetual water clock sitting on her desk and then picked up a glass pipe. From a drawer, she removed a chunky stoppered bottle. Removing the plug, Lady Azadiya dipped the pipe into the bottle of pearlescent fluid and stoppered its open top with her index finger.

"Now, what's happened in Fontis?" she asked. "From these long faces, I think the news has gone from bad to worse."

Ibram bit his bottom lip. Ladyship removed a large rag from her desk, and carefully dripped the liquid in the pipe onto its folds. She set the now empty pipe back in the bottle, and then retrieved her gar.

He opened his mouth, but nothing in particular came out. Ibram sighed; the back of his neck throbbed. She waited him out, and began wiping the blunted top end of the wood clean of grass and muck. Ahksell nudged him, gently, with his elbow. Ladyship flipped her gar, and resumed cleaning. Ibram put his hands on his stomach. If someone needed to say they were sorry, then it was best to do it quickly and cleanly and lance the boil of shame.

"That's enough bowing, Ibram," she said without looking. "Should I wish for obsequiousness, I will visit the caffa."

Ibram dropped his hands. Ahksell squeezed his upper arm for comfort and then looked between them quickly.

"I don't think it's so bad, Mentor," he said. "We've been interviewing the villagers to get an impression of Rustam's last days in Fontis."

"And what did you learn?" Ladyship finished cleaning off her weapon, and leaned it once more against the wall. The rag was tossed atop the alembic, which rocked alarmingly but held. Then, she came around the side of her desk and stood before them with her arms crossed.

Ibram unstuck his tongue from the roof of his dry mouth. "Ladyship, I must apologize. I failed to notice a crime being committed while gathering information on the death of Harken Tolk, and my inattention has created the problem in Fontis."

"A crime?" Ladyship asked. She leaned forward. "Tolk was murdered, then?"

"No, Mentor," Ahksell said in an alarmed tone. "I ran Hessele's Cage with a snowy agate twice, and found nothing but a natural death. I think the man's heart gave out, that's all."

"Then what crime was committed? And to whom belongs the blame?" she asked. "The corpse or the first finder?"

"I don't know," Ibram said, and failed to hide his wince at Ladyship's frown. "It is my current thought that they were working together. But let me begin at my suspicion." He paused and Ladyship waved him on. "When I—no, Ladyship, I'm sorry. I had no luck getting my thoughts in order on the trip here."

Ibram took a very deep breath, held it, and then let it out slowly. Ladyship nodded. Ahksell shifted his weight next to him. Ibram held out his hand and turned it palm upward.

"When we arrived after Rustam went missing," he said, and watched himself making some kind of waving gesture. He dropped his hand to his side. "I found myself going over my previous interactions with the Monbrith family. Satya Monbrith, in particular, was more attentive—"

"She asked if he was married," Ahksell interrupted, and Ladyship's sharp chin rose alarmingly quickly.

"—and *her behavior*," Ibram continued, "as well as that of her mother's made me believe that either something had changed after I had left or that something had not changed, and I had missed it completely."

This was all moderately obvious, but Ibram felt the need to say it. He always tried to be complete in his reports of his successes, let him be equally as frank in his failures. Lady Azadiya watched him. Ibram's entire face flushed. He was sure she knew exactly how overheated he felt in the blaze of her silent evaluation.

"First, the Monbriths have more money than I believe they should, now that I am..."

"Paying attention?" Lady Azadiya supplied.

Ibram tugged at his collar. "Their windows are well-screened with metal cloth spun from Afsoun. The draughtshop shows new construction, and their own home has expensive linens on the altar. Ahksell saw them. Now, that they have glowbulbs is no great thing, but theirs light upon approach, while Mistress Denrind's own home has bulbs which light only upon touch in the rooms in which I have been allowed entry."

"How do you know this?" she asked.

"I...arranged for us to stay in the rooms above the draughtshop," Ahksell said.

"Instead of the traveling carriage?" she asked.

Ahksell nodded. "I thought it might endear us to the village if we spent a bit of money while we were there, and that it might also make up for their lack of business while the Cohort of Peace began warding everything off."

"It's Commander Osthanes again, Ladyship," Ibram said. "You might recall him from that time with the river barge and the mathematician?"

"Osthanes and Judge E'grard?" Ladyship tapped her fingers on her arm. "A most lawful combination. But you were speaking of the Monbriths having too much money at hand. Do you think they robbed the deceased?"

Ibram shook his head. "No, I read over the inventory created by Mistress Denrind, and observed the objects myself. Master Tolk had nothing out of the ordinary on his person when he died, nor with his effects."

She nodded. "I recall the inventory, but if they had already taken the money it wouldn't have been out of place for Tolk not to be seen to have any."

"Yes, Ladyship, but the renovations to the draughtshop I've seen couldn't have taken place all within the last two months. And there was no reason to suppose that an itinerant blacksmith would have the kind of ready coin that amount of construction would imply," Ibram said. "Which brings me to my next point—"

"And didn't the young Mistress Monbrith say she and her family were fine for coin, even though they had lost all their custom?" Ahksell interrupted.

Ibram swiveled to look in his direction, and crossed his arms. "Yes, but that was when you were trying to give her an entire handful of picaio."

Ladyship frowned at Ahksell. "An entire handful?" she repeated.

Ahksell shook his head. "I was only trying to help!"

She pointed at him. "Be lucky I do not explain your expenditures to the First Mentor," she said. "You know she's been going over the budget again. So, Mistress Monbrith refused money? Doesn't sound like any innkeeper I've ever known."

"No, she accepted," Ibram said, "but her initial protest was notable. It was her mother who returned the balance of Ahksell's money. Further, Ladyship, Rustam Monbrith was buying ribbons for his sweetling in the marketplace prior to his disappearance. Satya has one as well, and very nicely woven it is, too." He spread his hands. "That's why I went home before I came up the living mountain. If Rustam was working with Harken Tolk, and the Monbriths have too much money—more than a simply traveling pot-mender might earn, then it occurred to me that they might have that extra money for a reason."

She nodded. "Perhaps he was cutting into Tolk's profits and mending things for his neighbors."

Ibram cocked his head. He hadn't thought of that, to be sure, but it was of no matter. He took a breath and stood at attention. "Ladyship,"

Ibram said. "I believe, aided by Harken Tolk, the Monbriths' have been counterfeiting coins."

"A *counterfeiting* operation?" Ladyship asked. She stood away from her desk. "How do you know this?"

Ibram nodded. "That's what I went home about. I found silver and copper clippings, both in my bedroom in Harken Tolk's old room above the draughtshop and also at the site of the old smithy. I also found a copper disc."

Lady Azadiya groaned. "They were making blanks?" she asked.

"I wanted Father to confirm my suspicions, but he wasn't home. Katka did." Ibram turned briefly to Ahksell. "She has all your money, by the way. She said she wanted to look it over."

"What is she looking over it for?" Ahksell asked.

"Clipped coins, I should expect," Ladyship said. She put her hands to her hips; her linen tunic crumpled. "Are you certain, Ibram?"

"I know it's not evidence, Ladyship—at least not in an Imperial court—but I rang the bells and threw the dice to Yilka the Green for aid. I was pricked twice by these fragments."

"It's a serious offence if you're right," Ladyship said.

"Katka identified such markings on the pieces I brought back to say that they come from coins."

Her mouth pursed. "It would explain why the boy ran, if his nerve failed him at the end."

He nodded. Her face tightened; Ibram could see rapid thought firing behind her grey eyes. She clapped her hands together and Ibram jumped.

"We go to your mother's house," she announced.

"But they're at the Baniks," Ibram protested.

"I care not, I don't want them. I want to speak to Katka." She strode over to the doorway and out of the room. They followed her onto the balcony. She leaned over the carved lacquered wood and called out to the diners below, "Tana, send for a carriage! Viran! A messenger for Lady Sebbina and one for our First Mentor! Ruzena, gather my coat and cloak—and find me something to wear!" She whirled back to them. "Has Ahksell looked over the smithy? Is there any sign of alchemastery?"

Ibram's heartbeat wobbled in his chest. Alchemastering was what they called unlicensed alchemy, the sort that caused uncontrolled explosions and mass water poisonings, and there was a variety of painfully inventive punishments for it. He shook his head.

"Ladyship, there's no way Rustam Monbrith is an alchemaster," he protested. "He was barely a blacksmith!"

"So you have not," she said. "We'll have to see about that in Fontis."

Ibram looked to Ahksell. "I hadn't thought of asking," he admitted. "Where would Rustam learn alchemy, much less become an illegal one? Where would he get the tools?"

"Diarmit," Ahksell said, suddenly. "He asked if I was going to turn anything to gold."

Lady Azadiya sighed. "What will I do when the summer ends, and I must shackle Ibram to another of my Attendants?"

"Ladyship!" Ibram protested.

"You will speak of this to no one." She cut her hand lengthwise through the air, sharply. "You will go downstairs and greet your amitai, and make me something up to eat for the journey. When I am changed, both of you will accompany me for the rest of this night. If we are to suffer the embarrassment of counterfeiting under our very noses, then it will not be for long." She shooed them off with a sharp gesture and began walking away. "Go!"

🦋   *9*   🦋

Ladyship's carriage was drawn by two horses with an extra snap in their gait, and built for a much larger crowd than was sat inside it. Above her head, she had clamped her gar into the straps installed for the purpose. She had sent Ahksell out for his staff as well before they left.

Ibram glanced at it above his head. Across from him, Ladyship occupied the entire bench by herself, sat sideways so that she could see out the window while she ate her bread and meat. Ibram and Ahksell shared the opposite side of the carriage. Ibram leaned against the wall and peeked up at the tiny slats that created the long curved roof; it had been painted with a picture of a garden. Small glowbulbs were lit and attached to the interior corners, and the luminescent sand within them bounced with every jolt of the sprung wheels.

Ahksell poked him in the hip and made a bizarre yet demanding face. Ibram frowned at him; he shook his head. Ahksell jerked his head in Ladyship's direction and mouthed something at him. Ibram leaned back, and smacked his head into the side of the carriage.

"The judge's message!" Ahksell hissed.

"Runner's *corns*," Ibram swore. Ahksell poked him again. He glared at the man, and then sat up straight. He patted down his sides. Where had he put the message scroll? He felt at his belt pouch.

"What are you looking for?" Lady Azadiya asked, and licked her fingers clean. She set aside her empty plate. In the warm light, the golden pins keeping the top section of her dark hair off of her face gleamed in a corona around her head. She had let the rest of it out of its previous braid, and now the thick mess curled over her shoulders. Her blue coat was buttoned with large metal shields which did Kivan the Red knew what to the unwary, and her cloak was the same color with a pale gold lining that matched her turned cuffs.

Ibram cleared his throat. "I didn't merely return to Lityen to inform you about the counterfeiting, Ladyship," he said. "I was also instructed to deliver a message to you from Judge E'grard."

"You were?" She sat more forward on the bench. "Well, what is it?"

He paused. "He didn't tell me the contents. He wrote it out in a sealed scroll."

She held out her hand. Her long fingerless mitt was made of pale silk with embroidered trembleberries. "Then where is this scroll?"

Ah. Ibram swallowed. "Ladyship, I confess to being off my stride," he said.

"Ibram, you are not off your stride, you are in the next province," she said. "Did you lose Judge E'grard's scroll?"

"No! No, not at all, I never lose things like that." Ibram thought very hard and quite quickly. He had taken the scroll—

"He gave it to me! I have it, Mentor," Ahksell said. He opened his satchel, and began digging through the contents. Ladyship set her hands together in her lap and watched them.

"I am wondering who wrote me those detailed, observant letters on your travels if not you, Ib-la," she said.

"It was me," Ibram protested. "I am very detailed and observant. When I have time."

"Here!" Ahksell said, and held up a slightly bent message scroll. "I found it."

He handed Lady Azadiya the scroll and sat back. He turned to Ibram. "Also, I found your cloak in the carriage and took it back to my room. I can return it tomorrow if you like."

"Thank you," Ibram said, and rubbed his eyebrow with his thumb. He was going to scratch himself bald at this rate.

His recollection had been easier when he was traveling, to be sure. All he had to do was keep a list in his head of the kind of details Lady Azadiya required from wherever he had stopped for the seven-or-twelve-day. The terms of their agreement had been consistent, even if all he had accomplished was a short exploration of the land around the draughtshop before moving onward. Travel contained more empty moments walking down the imperial roads than a body might suppose. Ibram had filled that time with notes-taking, and letter composing in his head, and then merely had to write his draft at the end of the day.

"An agent who cannot adapt quickly to a changing situation is not desirable," she said.

"No, Ladyship," Ibram said quietly.

Lady Azadiya cracked the wax seal and unrolled the scroll. She held the paper up to the light and began to read. After a moment, she put the message in her lap, writing side down, and leaned back against the wall. Her eyes unfocused as she stared up at the painted ceiling of the carriage.

He and Ahksell glanced at each other. Ibram's fingers trembled and so he curled them into fists to hide it. His skin felt flushed and hot, a little damp at the base of his neck. If he'd been paying attention, or at least been less accepting, he might have caught the counterfeiting before Rustam had the chance to run. He had simply thought the whole incident a formality, and treated it accordingly. Ahksell knocked the toe of his boot against Ibram's, and held it there. The space between his eyebrows had grown an unsightly pair of furrows to either side.

"Mentor?" Ahksell ventured. "What does his honor say?"

She refocused on him. "I am invited to witness the sanctioning of Fontis as a representative of the sect," she said.

"But won't one of the mentors from Salacia already be there?" Ahksell asked.

Ibram frowned, and Ahksell must have caught his expression. He tilted his head. Ibram shrugged.

Lady Azadiya turned the message over and again in her hands.

"They will," she said. "Though, I expect it will be Perhara, rather than Ablemu, or Ritiescu."

Ibram leaned forward to put his elbows on his knees. "Perhara?"

"He's the Fourth Mentor of Salacia," Ahksell explained, as if Ibram didn't have the entire roster memorized. "Is he to be responsible for the actual enclosure of the village?"

"Seems a bit much, doesn't it?" Ibram asked. "I mean, why not just send attendants?"

Ladyship hummed to herself.

"Well, I mean," Ahksell continued, "not by himself, though I suppose if he got enough chalk together he might manage it. But if he's in Fontis that means we still might have time to find Rustam."

"Why?" Ibram asked.

"He doesn't like the Cohort of Peace very much," Ahksell said. "He won't like being summoned by them. Still, if the Judge requests his aid, I suppose he'll have to come."

Lady Azadiya frowned and began slowly winding a piece of her hair around her fingers. "Whereas I am asked on behalf of the work done by my agents."

Ahksell's forehead wrinkled. "But we haven't done anything yet," he said. "Not that he knows about, anyway."

"He's just being rude," Ibram said and slumped against the wall of the carriage. "He wants Ladyship to watch how we failed her."

Lady Azadiya scoffed. "I decide whether or not I have been failed," she said. She shook her hair off her fingers. "I tasked you with discovering why Rustam Monbrith ran. You have done so."

Ibram straightened a little out of his slump. "I did," he agreed.

"It remains to be seen whether your theory is correct, of course," Ladyship continued and Ibram slumped again. "But it suits the facts as we know them."

The carriage rocked as it traveled along the road. The night air was damp and still cold. Ibram rubbed both hands over his face and scalp and hung them off the back of his head. Ladyship watched the passing houses out of her window.

"We still must find Rustam," she said suddenly.

"We do?" Ahksell cleared his throat. "We do, of course."

Lady Azadiya smirked. "E'grard is a foolish man if he seeks to intimidate me with an offer of shay and conversation while Fontis is walled up. Though, to be sure, judging by his wording, he doesn't expect my acceptance of the invitation." She settled herself more comfortably on her bench. "Judges turn bitter with experience; I've never been able to stomach them."

❧

The carriage jolted down a turn, and Ibram saw a familiar copse of trees through the window over Ladyship's shoulder. He sighed and crossed his arms. Lady Azadiya rarely visited their home. Ama or Father either went up the living mountain to her on work business or she rambled across to their stall on market day as if she were a plain Attendant. He had no idea what to expect when they reached the house. He shifted again on his section of the padded bench. She made an inquiring noise and threw the judge's message in Ahksell's direction. It floated in an undulating wave and landed in his palm. Ahksell returned the scroll to his satchel and closed the flap.

"Tell me of Katka?" she asked.

"Katka?" Ibram repeated. "Why?"

"Of your mother, I am well aware, and of you I am learning," she said. "Your sister may be counted as more or less of a work in progress."

"More or less?" Ibram asked.

"Is that not the expression?" she asked. "Vissilian is so imprecise."

Ahksell's face began to lose its worried furrows, but he didn't interrupt.

"I suppose it works," Ibram said. "Katka is my father's first apprentice. She's been training to make the larger pieces, but Father says she'll be ready to try her hand at the finer designs soon."

"Her eyes are sharp?"

"She could count the facets on a crystal spider."

"Well," Ladyship said. "We shall hear her explanations when we get there."

Ibram shifted forward and braced his feet on the carriage floor. "I apologize again, Ladyship, if I had been more careful on my first assignment, Rustam would not have had the chance to run."

She tilted her head. "It would have been better to catch the counterfeiting before, but worse to never become aware of it at all. I will have to speak with Evren about you."

"Evren?" Ibram asked. "Amota Evren?"

"Doesn't he work in your archives, Mentor?" Ahksell asked.

Ibram's jaw loosened, and so he grit his teeth. "Why him in particular?"

Lady Azadiya quirked her lips. "I think perhaps we have gone too fast with you, Ibram," she said gently. "It might be better to spend time closer to the sect for a while."

"I've only been working by myself for a year," he said. "You had me with all the other agents before then, and there have been no problems, until..."

"Until now," she said. "This is really quite serious, Ibram. We must be cautious."

Ibram's blood stuttered in his veins; he flushed and dropped his gaze. He didn't want to be stuck in that airless room underground of Lady Azadiya's tower. He raised wide eyes towards Ahksell, who covered his mouth immediately and studied the ceiling.

"Here we are!" Ladyship stuck her head out of the window. "Hit the receiving bell, Lakum!" She sat back down. "For now, let me review the evidence for this counterfeiting. We can decide on other events later."

Ibram heard Amota Lakum drop down from the driving bench, and then hit the lodestone with the attached hammer. The gate opened a few moments later and Amota Lakum drove through. He pulled the horses to a halt as it closed behind them. Ladyship stuck out her left hand, crooked her first two fingers, and lifted hand and carriage door latch at the same time. The short steps attached to the door clattered out. She exited first and Ibram and Ahksell followed. By the time Ibram's feet hit the ground, Kholdo stood before them, locked into a full bow. Lady Azadiya extended her hands at her waist and curled her fingers into fists; Kholdo rose.

"Are Verena and her husband still with the Banik family?" she asked.

"No, Ladyship," Kholdo said. "They have just returned."

"Perfect, please run ahead and let Verena know I wish to speak with all the family, but unless necessary the two apprentices may go to bed."

Kholdo bowed again. "Raffasticates, Ladyship," he said, and hurried off.

If Ibram knew his own Ama, she had probably arranged the entire household in order of height by the time Amota Lakum had finished hitting the lodestone. They all walked up together, except for Lakum who stayed with the horses. The manor was entirely lit by torches, and the double doors were flung wide. Kholdo, still panting lightly, bowed to Ladyship at the inner door of the reception hall. Well, it was more like a short pause in a closet, but Ama called it their reception hall. Ladyship waved him up with a smile, and walked quickly out onto the terrace.

Ama had set up the table in the floating pavilion in the ornamental garden in the center of the public courtyard. She stood in front of it with Father and Katka next to her. Lady Azadiya walked down into the garden without pausing along the line of torches, and Ibram's family bowed at her approach. She caught Ama's face between her palms, an inch away from her skin, and raised her up. After a moment, Father and Katka straightened as well.

"Verena, good evening," Lady Azadiya said. "I apologize for the hour, but bad news obeys no one's clock."

"Not at all, Ladyship," Ama murmured. She was still dressed to go out in her best robe and breeches. Her polished leather boots and her hair bun glittered with cuffed clasps made of enamel and filigree flowers. She looked tired. "My husband and youngest child, if you remember."

"Master Cibulka, always a pleasure, and Katka! Why, you are grown a head and a half since last I saw you." Lady Azadiya beamed at her. "I am told you have sharp eyes."

"I... Actually, it wasn't me who first found the evidence," Katka stammered. "That was Inzhu, one of father's other apprentices."

Lady Azadiya hummed and smiled. "Truthful, as well," she said. "How is your memory? Perhaps I might have work for you."

Ibram sighed. Ama coughed. Katka's eyes, sharp or otherwise, were as wide as saucers. She held her hands clasped in front of her. She was still dressed in the clothes she'd worn at supper, but someone—probably Ama—had made her throw on a loose long-sleeved robe on top of the outfit. She looked behind herself and then at Ibram. From behind Ladyship, Ibram pointed at the pavilion and mouthed, 'ask her to sit down.' Ahksell smacked him.

"Lady Azadiya, please sit down," Father said, sounding quite grim. "I do believe Katka and I have something of great import to show you."

He stepped to one side and gestured at the pavilion with his right hand, and put his left around Katka's shoulders. Ladyship swept through and seated herself at the head of the table. Ama and Father followed and then Ibram jostled for a seat with Ahksell and Katka.

Ama had brought out the good table and chairs, the kind reserved for only the best customers. There was caffa and boiling water in small pots above a fire and next to that, a stack of the small cookies Ibram could never remember the names of with diamond-shaped dough folded at two points over dollops of timoleon jam. A large platter lay in the center of the table below a glowbulb clasped in a frame, which typically held jewelry pieces that Father showed to his clients. The metal scraps and the blank disc as well as the piles of Ahksell's coins lay on top of the platter, while two pairs of bioptic lenses lay next to it.

They all settled down, and Ladyship leaned forward. She rested her upper arms on the table. Father adjusted the glowbulb at little lower.

"This is what Ibram brought back from Fontis?" Ladyship asked. The rustle of her skirts seemed loud as she readjusted her seat for a better angle to view the coins.

"Yes, Ladyship," Katka said, and cleared her throat. "I took the disc Ibram brought back, and I weighed it alongside one of the faunts I have. They're about the same—near enough it could be excused on account of wear, even.

The first clipping is the copper piece that Inzhu noticed at supper. When I examined the others, they showed similar signs of being taken from properly minted coins. Here, you can see the birds on the obverse side of the faunts and the half of a bird on the clipping."

She handed Ladyship a pair of lenses and pushed one of Ahksell's coins next to the half-moon of copper for her to see the difference. Ladyship held the scrap steady with two fingers as she compared them. She nodded. Ahksell and he leaned forward and Ama quickly waved them away. Ibram sat back with a sigh.

"That was bad enough, I know," Katka said. Her voice grew stronger. Ladyship took off her lenses to watch her speak. "But Father has been telling me about the—the different ways a jeweler can do business, not merely in creating pieces, but in mending them sometimes, and also, uh, evaluating them. Which is why I had Ibram leave all his money here, before he went to tell you."

"It's my money, to be fair about it," Ahksell said. "And what does any of that have to do with this?"

Katka looked to Father, who nodded at her with a small smile on his face. He stroked his beard, and then folded his fingers together. Katka sat up a little in her chair.

"Ladyship, if I may ask, are you familiar with counterfeiting at all?" she asked.

"I am," Lady Azadiya said. "But Ahksell is not."

"Give us the summary, Kat-la," Ama said. "It's getting cold."

Katka deflated a breath, but steadied. "Oh. Well, obviously, there is clipping spare metal off of lawful coin as we see here. But Father always says that a blacksmith always has two or three tricks in their pouch, and I thought that, where there is clipping, there might also be some other kind of funny business taking place, too. So I went over the coins in Ahksell's pouch—you might wish to put the lenses back on for this—and most of them are fine, I think, but one or two of them looked like they had been manipulated."

"How?" Lady Azadiya asked. She picked up the lenses and put them back on again.

"I had to wait for Father to come home to be certain," Katka said. "I'm not so skilled yet."

"She's a good worker," Father said. He leaned forward and tapped a silver coin on the platter. "Smart and capable, just needs a little more finesse."

"To be sure, I'm thankful for her help," Ladyship said, and Ama beamed across the table at Katka, who blushed.

"Now," Father said. He picked up the picaio and Ibram heard a strange little clinking noise. Father separated the picaio into two rectangular pieces of silver directly under Lady Azadiya's gaze, and picked up one slice. "Do you see, Ladyship? Where they've tried to meld these two halves back together? It's melted too far here and deformed the edge."

"I do, yes." Ladyship sighed. Father flipped over the coin in his palm and then laid it on to the platter. In the center of the silver lay a dull grey ingot. Ladyship placed the other silver slice on top, and it looked like a normal coin again. Lady Azadiya sat back in her chair.

"Plugged," she said.

"The weight is the same here as well," Father said. He frowned down at the platter. "These are very precise fakes. Really, this counterfeiter had no business being an itinerant. Any city would be lucky to have him."

"But what greater opportunity for a criminal, than traveling from small town to village and passing on his false coin along the way?" Ama asked.

Katka reached out and separated two faunts. Each one had a smaller, but identical dull grey ingot. "These as well, and while I can't prove it, I would wager some of the older looking coins have been steamed in a bag to disguise the raw edges from clipping."

"Steamed?" Ibram asked.

Katka nodded. "You put coins into a bag and shake it. They rub up against each other and...sand each other, for want of a better term. Then you can beat the bag and collect the dust."

"You get the best of both worlds," Father said. "Newly minted coins which merely look damaged by time and enough dust to melt together a new coin."

"We must mourn the passing of a master crafter, then," Ladyship said. "Ahksell, which of these coins were given to you in Fontis, and which did you take with you?"

Ahksell leaned forward. "All the faunts are from the shay shop in the village or from the pile Mistress Monbrith returned to me," he said. "But every other coin I had with me when I arrived, except for these older picaio," he pointed at the halved silver ovals, "The pick and the two new picaio were given me by Attendant Yakino in the office of disbursement. I remember because they were from the stack of new minted coins the quartermaster received last twelve-day."

"If we open up all these coins and find them false, then what happens next?" Ama asked.

Ibram kept his hands in his lap and squeezed his left wrist. He cleared his throat and then shook his head. This was good; he'd been correct in his suspicions, but what did it mean for the larger investigation? Rustam Monbrith was still on the loose, and could possibly be trading in counterfeit money even now.

"Could we catch him like this?" he asked. "Rustam, I mean. Or is it the shirt problem all over again?"

"The shirt problem?" Ama echoed.

Ahksell shook his head. "I don't think so," he said. "It...Metal is far more durable than fabric, of course, and it retains its resonance longer, but I fear the likelihood of Rustam having a twin of one of these coins in his pocket on the run is too low. How do we know Master Tolk only minted false coin in the Monbrith's old furnace? Perhaps he was doing this throughout the region."

Ibram nodded slowly. "He does a little in every village he works in —by himself or with accomplices—and thus avoids what struck me wrong about the Monbriths. Small amounts, spread thinly in the course of his travels, and no one in authority is the wiser."

Father whistled lowly. "Or he could have been merely passing the coins onwards as part of a commission. Perhaps he was not skilled and someone in another town or village was."

"I do not envy you that thought," Ama said. "This could be—I mean, the entire province could be affected!"

Lady Azadiya breathed out, and her eyes unfocused. Katka leaned back in her chair and crossed her arms. She glanced about the table.

"So what does this mean?" she asked. "What happens now? Do we go to the warders?"

"We shall, we shall," Ama told her. "You've done very well, Kat-la. Your father and I are very proud."

Father patted her on the shoulder. Ibram cleared his throat. A little credit should have fallen his way, surely, for thinking up the possibility in the first place. He smiled when Ama glanced his way.

"There are twenty-five Imperial issuers of coin," Father said. "But the only mint in the province is in Chetilat; these all bear their mark. Ibram, did this dead man have any equipment on him? There would have to be molded blocks to pour out the blanks, and at least one set of coin dies, made out of iron, perhaps. They don't last long, so there should be at least one rolling about."

"I saw empty frames," Ibram said and set his hands apart. "About yea big."

Father nodded. "It would be enough for a brace of blanks," he said. "Foundry sand molds? You used to help me pack those when you were younger."

"I think so. What do the dies look like?" Ibram asked.

"Something like those carved jet earplugs they wear down in Swarilat, a bit like a mushroom head, especially if they were well-used."

Ibram shook his head. "No, Father," he said. He called to mind the paper Mistress Denrind had sent him off with. "He had the usual assortment that I can remember. Ladles, a crucible, a selection of hammers and tongs...he had one of those blocks in bronze like you have for making wire, but nothing so fine. Apart from that and his clothing and supplies for his horse and cart, there was nothing else."

"What about the smithy?" Ama asked. "Perhaps he hid the dies there."

"He'd need a lot of them," Katka said, "depending on how many he was making."

"Oh, a good coin maker can do a purse-full at least," Father said. "It only takes one blacksmith to hammer the design, but if you want to speed matters along, you need another to make enough blank discs. Keeps the production line going."

"Like when your father has Inzhu and Hedvi twisting wire for the pendants," Ama said.

"It's very messy in there," Ibram said, thinking back on the little smithy. "And mostly abandoned. I don't think anyone in the family was using it before Master Tolk started coming around. Besides, I doubt the Monbriths would have left such incriminating evidence lying about."

"They left these," Ama said and gestured towards the coin clippings.

"Do you really think the entire family is incriminated?" Ahksell asked.

"We shall have to see," Lady Azadiya said. "As long as nothing else happens and we find Rustam, we might all escape death by poisoning."

Katka gasped and turned pale. Ladyship waved her hand; her silver rings glittered on her fingers. "Oh don't worry," she said. "It hasn't happened to any of us yet."

She had obviously finished wrestling with her mind and had returned to the party. She pointed at the plugged picaio. "Master Kelemen, may I have you and your daughter write out your findings? We shall need three copies, one for the sect, one for me, and the other for the judge in Fontis. It shall have to be tonight, I apologize for the necessity."

Father bowed as much as he could in his chair. "Of course, Ladyship," he said. "We will begin now."

She smiled. "Thank you. As well, I need a description of the items Ibram and Ahksell will be looking for, and the dies you mentioned."

"They might have thrown them in a hole," Ibram interrupted suddenly. "I told Commander Osthanes there could be something buried in their vegetable patch."

Ladyship hummed to herself, and then nodded. "Verena, in the morning you must go to First Mentor Skorinin and give her our copy. She will take it to our Lord Preceptor and thus begin searching the sect's own funds. Then go to Fourth Mentor Tikari of Afsoun—ah." She turned her head, birdlike, to Father. "Was there any sign of alchemastering?"

Father swallowed and stroked his beard. The others about the table fell silent. Ibram's skin prickled with cold; he shivered.

"Not that I know all the signs," Father said slowly. "But I held them up to the forge beneath a tin and bezoar curtain and nothing turned green."

Lady Azadiya sighed very heavily. "It shall have to be Tikari, then," she said. "Damnable woman."

"She knows her transmutations, it must be admitted," Ama said.

Lady Azadiya rolled her eyes. "She couldn't float herself the height of a shay cup."

Ibram snorted, and Ahksell giggled nervously. With quick fingers, Ladyship separated the piles of coins, dividing the clipped and plugged items from the newer ones. One half of the sliced picaio and three faunts she returned to Ahksell's coin pouch as well as two of the clippings. She left the gold pick and the rest of the money on the table. She tossed the pouch to Ahksell.

"This," she waved at the platter, "you shall take up the living mountain with you, Verena. Tikari will need them to make an analysis."

Lady Azadiya sighed and tapped the heavy gold coin with one finger. Ibram pressed his lips between his teeth. Of all the coins, if that should turn out to be formed from dross, they were all in serious trouble. At best, Judge E'grard would accept Rustam as the alchemaster to be punished accordingly. If he wasn't found, not simply Fontis might be sanctioned. At worst, the Court of Chancery would become involved, and the entire area around the Sect of Seven Fires would be razed, as barren and forbidding as Asfridlat. No one in the empire wanted to return to the days of unlicensed, uncontrolled alchemy. Sure, wasn't that how the Bright Broken Peaks had received their name?

Ama, after a swift glance around the table, passed out the caffa cups and then poured for the group. She mixed caffa and boiling water in each small cup, and then handed them all out, beginning with Lady Azadiya. She held the plate of cookies out over the charger full of counterfeit goods.

"Katka, take a viveka," she said.

"Yes, Ama," Katka said automatically. She snatched the topmost cookie and bit right down the middle of the jam. Ibram snorted again; she wiped crumbs from her mouth. The cookie plate made the round, and he cupped his hand beneath the viveka to catch the crumbs. He licked his lips and chewed thoughtfully. Timoleon jam always made his lips pucker a little, but the sugar in the cookie balanced it out.

Ama placed the honey drop bowl in the center of the table alongside a carafe of milk and they all began doctoring their caffa. The atmosphere lightened as they busied themselves. Ibram dropped in two crystals of honey and a fat dollop of milk; he'd had a hard go of it lately. Father dunked his own cookie in his black caffa, which made Ama frown, but Ladyship didn't seem to mind. Ibram cocked his head and watched his father eat. He'd come home with two questions in mind, but the larger issue had, of course, taken precedence, and now he wasn't certain how to proceed. Ibram chewed the corner of his viveka.

Father looked up from his caffa and caught him staring. "Do I have crumbs?" he asked, and brushed at his beard. Even in his going out clothes, he looked rumpled and lived in, comfortable in every line of his thick shoulders. The only vanity he had was his beard, always carefully combed and even oiled on occasion.

Ibram shook his head. "No! I just had a question."

Father smiled at him and picked up another cookie. He was a very neat eater and polite, though most of the Western foods Ama and Kholdo made were spiced too heavily for him. The only food he insisted on was the roasted garlic and soured yogurt they had on the table for almost every meal. He ate it with almost everything.

"Well then, you must ask it," he said.

Ibram nodded. "I have been thinking about questions," he said, and ignored the ripple of amusement that resounded around the table. "And not asking them."

Father nodded, though Ibram could very well see the corner of his mouth threatening to perk upward. "It's always better to ask, I think."

"Then what kind of thing could you say to a goddess to make her blow out her own candles?"

Father dropped his cookie into his lap. Hastily, he picked it up again and began brushing crumbs from himself. He tossed the viveka onto the table with his other hand and stared at Ibram.

"Have you been lighting candles to a goddess?" he asked sharply.

"Ibram," Ama said, shocked.

"No!" Ibram protested. He leaned in. "Yilka the Green doesn't like that, but your god does, doesn't he Father? You and Katka light candles to the Wheelmaker, and the Monbriths have been lighting candles to the Sovereign Twins—oh, Ladyship, Mistress Monbrith is an incredibly pious woman. Tell her, Ahksell."

Ahksell blinked at him rapidly and then turned to Lady Azadiya. "Yes," he said. "I spoke to Sotiria Serisan, who's been teaching the children in Fontis. She said the youngest boy, Diarmit Monbrith, was taken out of school to work at home—"

"Not really a surprise, considering the amount of custom they must get," Ladyship interrupted. "Many folk are taken out of a Bedris school for that reason."

"Yes, but she did it three years ago." Ahksell leaned forward, hunching his shoulders as if to make himself smaller. All it accomplished was making him look like an earnest slab of muscle. "Seven isn't too young for a pot boy, of course, but that was when Master Tolk began coming around and Diarmit is curious and very talkative! As well, she told us—well, the younger Mistress Monbrith told us—that Mistress *Jorie* Monbrith had them praying ever since Tolk died, but that two days before the court trial was to begin, the candles didn't light."

"Damn me," Father said. "That is very bad."

Ama shook her head. Katka grabbed another viveka and dunked it in her caffa. Ahksell poured Lady Azadiya and himself another cup. "That's what I told him."

"But Satya," Ibram watched Ama's eyes narrow at him, "said she had the entire household praying the entire length of time between discovery of the body and the trial. So the candles were working perfectly well up until that time."

"What did they pray for?" Ladyship asked.

Ibram thought back. His eyes fell on Kholdo, where he stood by the open warming room door, outlined in the firelight. Now, Ahksell and he and Satya... They had been standing in the common room of the draughtshop, being watched over by the trio of warders. He chewed his lower lip.

"It was the Advisor and the Speaker," he began.

"They split the children as you did, Mistress Verena," Ahksell interrupted.

"No, it's different," Ibram said. "I'm nothing to Kivan the Red and less to, say, Catha the Grey."

"That is not quite true," Ama said and glanced at Lady Azadiya.

"Well," Ibram said, "if I went while I was still alive to Catha the Grey to work off the debt of my sins, a prayer from me would need more behind it than a prayer from a true dedicant." He shook his head. "No, the Monbrith boys were for the Speaker and Satya's for the Advisor, and she's the heir by right of birth order."

Lady Azadiya pursed her lips. "But you believe the Sovereign Twins both turned against Rustam?"

Around them, the wind picked up. The damp chill of the evening began to have a bite to the garden air. Ibram heard the bush roses rustle.

"Mistress Monbrith had all the children praying to both goddesses?" Father asked. "At the same time?"

Ibram opened his mouth and then closed. "I'm not certain," he said after a moment. "Satya didn't mention it."

"I am no expert in the Imperial pantheon," Ladyship said, "but I understood that was allowed, as long as there were dedicants of both sides in the party."

"Oh yes, Ladyship," Father said. "And the Speaker and the Advisor are often worshipped together seeing as they're so much closer than the rest of the pantheon, but all the candles going out—"

"No, they were unburnt," Ibram reminded him. He raised his finger in the air. "Two days before, they didn't go out, they never lit during... there's a litany isn't there? I remember you saying something about a standard prayer."

"I think something must have changed. The form of the prayer usually begins the same, but then you fill in your specific need, just like you and Ama," Katka said. "What was it?"

Ibram rubbed his eyebrow with his thumb. With a groan, Katka threw her cookie at him; Lady Azadiya caught it between her fingers and ate it. Flames began to lick up the sides of Ama's face and Katka and Ibram looked down at their caffa cups immediately.

"Your house has such delicious treats," Ladyship said mildly. "I should send my cook for Kholdo's recipes."

"Thank you, Ladyship," Ama said with a certain amount of strain in her voice. "Shall we begin writing those reports for you?"

Rain began to fall on the roof of the pavilion. The torches lining the path back to the terrace sputtered. Ibram breathed in deeply. He had always loved the smell of rain, especially in the garden. It calmed him. He pressed his fist underneath his chin and frowned out at the bush roses. How could he have forgotten to ask so many questions?

"Yes, I think so," Ladyship said. "If you have ink and paper, I will write my own letters to take with you back to the sect."

"Ibram, get your writing supplies," Ama said.

Lady Azadiya stood first, and they all followed. Father and Katka began gathering up the coins and clippings. Ama touched the clasp in her hair.

"Ladyship," she said. She waved at Kholdo. "Would you care to finish your caffa in the sitting room? Ibram won't be long."

"I would, thank you," Lady Azadiya said. "Ah, Kholdo. How much would it take for you to instruct my cook in the creation of this pastry?"

🥀   I O   🥀

They departed from Lityen in Ladyship's carriage with the rain pouring forth from the sky like a broken keg of ale. Lady Azadiya commanded that he and Ahksell report every step of their time in Fontis, who they'd spoken with and what they'd seen, but it didn't take up much of the trip. Ibram did most of the talking. Ahksell himself seemed bizarrely hesitant, as if he was puzzled by something, and Ladyship did not push him on it.

After that, there was nothing but light conversation and the noise of the road. Ibram had tried to stay awake, even if only to prove himself stronger than sleep, but it was boring inside the carriage. Lady Azadiya and Ahksell had both descended into some kind of contemplation with their eyes closed—which looked not unlike napping, but supposedly was not slumber—and there were only so many times Ibram could count the number of leaves painted in the vines of the ceiling. He awoke sometime later to find that he had been dislodged from his section of the bench by a bump in the road and wound up lengthwise with his head in Ahksell's lap.

Ibram sat up with a snort. He rubbed his face with his right hand and shook his head quickly to clear it. Sleep had over-warmed him, and he tugged at the collar of his gambeson. Across from him was the trunk shoved against the wall of the carriage; he frowned blearily at it. Ahksell continued to breathe deeply and rhythmically without noticing he'd been playing the part of Ibram's pillow. Ibram raked his hair back from his forehead with both hands and tucked it behind his ears. He glanced at the window, but with the waxed tarp in place, the most that he could tell of the outside was that the sun had made an appearance. From the pounding on the roof, it had not stopped raining.

Someone knocked politely on the door to the carriage. Ibram swung his right foot down to the floor to meet its match, and stretched his back out with his hands on his knees. Across from him, Lady Azadiya opened her eyes and then rolled her head on her shoulders.

"Lakum?" she called out.

"We're here, Ladyship," Lakum said from the other side of the door. "I've already let the clerks know of your arrival."

"Very good," she said, and then clapped her hands loudly. Ahksell's eyes popped open; he gasped in shock and then relaxed against the side of the carriage. She chuckled.

"Good morning, Mentor," Ahksell yawned. He interlaced his fingers, turned them out, and stretched his arms in front of himself.

"And to you," she said. She stood with a bent back and shook out her clothes, and then ran a hand through the loose length of her hair. "Now, to my reckoning, we have less than half the time of the judge's decree left to us. The more is lost, the further away Rustam might be and finding him is only the beginning of our concerns. I charge you to be circumspect today, the pair of you. I want to speak with the Monbriths after I'm done with the judge and the headwoman."

She unbelted her gar from its place on the wall, and held it lengthwise in her right hand. "Ibram, stay with your Amota Lakum."

Ibram mouth dropped open; he closed it before she noticed. Amota Lakum had been responsible for his official training as an agent. It didn't bode well for him that he was back under supervision.

"Ahksell," Ladyship said, "you shall remain with Ibram unless I say otherwise, but both of you are to do as Lakum says."

She nodded to Ahksell, who followed Ladyship's example and took down his own gar. Ibram moved to the front of the carriage to avoid getting buffeted by a length of hardwood taller than he was. Lady Azadiya's layers of clothing made a shushing noise across the floor as she went forward and pushed the door open. The stairs clattered outward, and she stepped out into the open air of the village. The rain had died down from a deluge to a strong shimmer, and he could see Amota Lakum stood by the door, carrying a large orange waxed paper umbrella.

"I knew you weren't contemplating the eternal," Ibram quietly, as he followed Ahksell out the door.

"I was," Ahksell insisted, just as quietly. "I just got tired."

Ibram jumped down, splashing mud on his boots, and Lady Azadiya's skirts moved themselves out of the way. He brushed the back and front of his gambeson. He looked about him, it was early enough in the morning that only a small stream of villagers were making their way down the alleyway in the direction of the shay shop. He could see across to the livery yard, which had lost half its previous occupants. He recognized Mistress Terin standing by the fence, with a pretty young girl who must have been her daughter; they were holding hands. He turned his head in time to see Lady Azadiya nod to Ahksell, who took his place at her left shoulder. Lady Azadiya walked forward with Amota Lakum pacing her with the open umbrella at her right.

The sound of Lady Azadiya's and Ahksell's gars pounded the earth in the same rhythm as they walked forward from the grounds outside Mistress Denrind's main gate and into the reception hall. It seemed like the noise grew louder until it reverberated against the walls. Ibram glanced down at the tiles, but there was no mud splatter and no cracked clay to match his hearing. He swallowed against the tightness in his throat, and walked at the back with one arm behind his back and the other on the hilt of his sica; he kept his head raised straight and high.

As they walked towards the inner gate that led into the public courtyard, Mistress Islozia stepped forward, put her shaking hands on her stomach, and bowed low. "Mentor Hobon," she said. "Be welcome to Mistress Denrind's house. I am to escort you to the headwoman's office."

Lady Azadiya stopped with a thud of her gar, echoed by Ahksell. Amota Lakum closed the umbrella, and rested its end tip against the floor. Ibram came to a stop.

"Thank you," Lady Azadiya said. She brought her left arm to her waist and curled her hand closed.

Mistress Islozia rose, but kept her hands pressed to her stomach. She visibly calmed herself before speaking, "His honor Judge E'grard and Mistress Denrind are in the larger office room," she said, rather repetitively. "If you will follow me?"

She backed up a few steps and turned right down the terrace. Lady Azadiya walked forward and the procession began again. Ibram glanced into the courtyard. The Cohort of Peace were still out there, mostly underneath the tent the judge had previously set up. He saw Warder Kamos and the trio who had been installed at the Monbriths' draughtshop, but not Commander Osthanes. He kept his eye on the warders as they in turn silently observed them walking past.

Mistress Islozia opened a thick wooden door and then stood outside of it. She bowed as Lady Azadiya passed through, and stayed that way for Ahksell. She only rose when Amota Lakum made to cross over the lintel. He tossed the umbrella to her, and she caught it with both hands. Ibram tried to smile at her, but she was still staring at her hands.

They had added a third chair since Ibram's last visit, hastily dusted, as if it had been taken out of an attic. The maps on the desk were in greater disarray, and the increased numbers made the room feel cramped. Judge E'grard and Mistress Denrind were stood in front of the desk this time instead of sitting, but his assistant in her plain woolen kirtle was still in the corner.

Ladyship came to a halt in front of them. Behind his back, Amota Lakum awkwardly twitched his hand to his right, and after a second, Ibram moved over to that side of the room which suddenly provided him with a wonderful view of the judge's assistant, standing with her tablet and paper and ink-filled pen at the ready. The door closed with a slight squeak of the hinges.

Mistress Denrind stepped forward and cleared her throat. She bowed and rose when Lady Azadiya curled her left hand. "Mistr—

Mentor Hobon," she said and coughed. "May I make you known to Judge E'grard?"

"Of course, Mistress Denrind," Lady Azadiya said. "How good of you to offer."

Mistress Denrind made the introductions, and Judge and Lady bowed in exacting politeness. The judge's pale eyes considered the whole group of them from Ladyship to Ahksell to Amota Lakum and then Ibram himself. Ibram tried not to stretch out his steadily cramping shoulders. He eyed the still and silent assistant. How did she do it?

"Thank you for your message, your honor," Lady Azadiya said as Amota Lakum pulled out the backless stool with raised armrests made of carved wood from underneath the desk. He took a moment to bend and firmly swipe at the upholstered seat; dust billowed in the air. Ibram saw Mistress Denrind wince.

Lady Azadiya swept her skirts to the side as she sat down. "I appreciated your invitation to see Fontis," she said. "It seems quite lively today."

She handed Amota Lakum her gar. He placed both hands on the staff and stood behind her. No one had offered to take her coat, nor send for a refreshment from her journey, but she made no mention of the impropriety. Still, Ibram felt it; he stiffened his spine.

Judge E'grard steepled his thin hands in front of him and nodded. "I understand the Preceptory of Yseult has some small influence in this section of the province," he said. "I thought it appropriate that its representatives viewed my ruling."

"Just as a noble house might, in their own lands," Mistress Denrind said, with a certain amount of trembling in her voice. She sounded worn and looked as tired as a frayed thread. There was a slight lull in conversation, almost a physical wince, though no one had moved. Ibram felt for the woman. The deadline was looming closer, and all they had to bring her was more disaster.

The judge looked at her sharply. "Except, of course, that a sect of alchemy by Imperial decree is not ranked amongst the Great Houses and requires no such traditional deference by law."

"Yet we serve the empire in our own way," Ladyship said mildly.

There was no hint of an accent to her voice now, only a pure and unvarnished stream of Vissilian such as would be at home in the court of the Empress herself. "And provide such aid to our neighbors as we should hope to receive in our own times of trouble."

"Yes, yes, of course," Mistress Denrind said. She flicked her hand nervously in Ahksell's direction and then back to her lap. "It has been very helpful to have your representatives here in the village."

"I shall pass your compliments to our First Mentor," Lady Azadiya replied. She smiled at Mistress Denrind, and the woman settled a little more comfortably in her chair. "You might not be aware, your honor, but my preceptory prides itself on our relationships with the local villages. Apart from Bedris, we work the most closely with them."

"So I am informed by Commander Osthanes, the leader of my Cohort of Peace," Judge E'grard said. He sighed and watched Ladyship, clearly evaluating something in the back of his mind. "I'm not certain how to address you, I fear. Should it be Lady Hobon or Mentor Hobon? I hope that isn't an impertinent question."

Ibram tightened his calves and squeezed his right hand into a fist behind his back. He shook it, quietly, and ordered himself to not tap his feet in impatience. Judge E'grard knew very well that they were running out of time, and these pleasantries were mere gilding. If only they could ignore the man.

All E'grard had to do was wait out the search for Rustam Monbrith, and then ride away, safely escorted by Osthanes' warders. And such posturing! Perhaps in the court system even Lady Azadiya had to bow to the judge's command of the law, but Lady or Mentor, she was already at least three orders of precedence higher than a mere judge from the Court Civil. He frowned; the assistant was writing something on her tablet.

"Not at all, your honor! When I am acting on the business of my sect, I use my title within the preceptory," Lady Azadiya said. "You may address me as Mentor Hobon, just as Mistress Denrind does. It saves confusion." She cleared her throat and looked to her left. "Attendant Solari, the reports."

Ahksell started. "Oh, yes, Mentor," he said. He opened his satchel and pulled out a small sheaf of loose paper and a familiar coin pouch.

"On to the point of my visit," she said.

"The point?" Judge E'grard said. His wrinkled eyebrows drew together, but his pale eyes remained sharp.

"Yes, as much as I appreciated your kind invitation to Fontis, I confess I arrived to confer with you about a different grave miscarriage of the law. One discovered by my own representatives no less," Ladyship said with some satisfaction. "I hastened to lay the facts before you as a loyal subject of the empire."

Ahksell set down the actual evidence in the exact middle of the table and then retreated quickly behind his mentor again. Ibram heard the clink of coins and recognized Katka's agitated approach to penmanship. Mistress Denrind appeared to be holding her breath.

"Mentor Hobon, you were invited to Fontis to witness the court's response to a violation of the law," Judge E'grard said. "What new offense are you bringing to my attention?"

"To be precise," Lady Azadiya said. She leaned on her left arm, which she had draped along the padded armrest. "I believe now we know why Rustam Monbrith's courage failed him before his appearance in your court."

Judge E'grard picked up the sheaf of papers and Mistress Denrind snatched up the coin pouch. She opened it with shaking fingers and upended the entire thing on the desk. The clippings and the copper blank disc fell together, but the slices of faunts and the picaio tumbled apart across the map.

"Oh no," she said, and held up one of the clippings.

"Ah, you recognize them!" Lady Azadiya clapped her hands. "Now, Ibram here," she gestured to her right, "found those clippings on the Monbrith property, and the plugged faunts arrived in my Attendant's possession from the village's shay shop."

"And the picaio?" Mistress Denrind asked.

"Was not in his possession before arriving in Fontis," Lady Azadiya said. "But I remind you, Harken Tolk arrived in Fontis three years ago. That is more than enough time for him to collect enough debris from around the province, and send his debased coin into the local economy."

"And this Master Kelemen Cibulka is to be trusted?" Judge E'grard asked. He peered up sharply from the report. "He's a jewelry maker, not a coiner."

"He knows how to evaluate goods," Ibram broke in.

Judge E'grard frowned at him. "Do you know this Master Cibulka and his apprentices?"

Ibram paused. Did Lady Azadiya want him to tell the judge he'd asked his own father for help collecting evidence?

"Of course he does," Lady Azadiya said. She had not turned her head. "How else would he know where to send these suspect items for evaluation? Now then, in my position as Fourth Mentor, I have sent the other half of that picaio and the rest of my Attendant's purse to Fourth Mentor Tikari of Afsoun. She will be able to confirm Master Cibulka's efforts and further provide an analysis of the remaining coin."

"Do you suspect alchemastery?" Judge E'grard asked.

Mistress Denrind turned incredibly pale, and held herself still in her chair. Lady Azadiya tilted her head so that the spread of her heavy dark hair could be seen over her shoulder. Ibram clenched his jaw. Father had said there wasn't, but what if Mentor Tikari said otherwise?

"I do not," Lady Azadiya said. "Nothing that has been uncovered by Mistress Denrind, my agents, or your own Commander Osthanes has suggested that the dead man was anything more than what he appeared to be: An itinerant craftsman of less than sterling morals. Now, should Mentor Tikari send word that this is untrue, I will with a heavy heart prostrate myself at the Court of Chancery and swear to root out these alchemasters with all the fervor of Stook at the Field of Daggers, but until that time, I humbly submit such evidence as I have ascertained to you, your honor." She smiled. "In due deference to your position."

Judge E'grard nodded slowly. He surveyed the papers in his hands and the clippings and plugged coins on the desk. His thin lips pressed into a white line of displeasure.

"Alia," he said sharply. "Get Osthanes in here."

His assistant started to life. She glided along the floor to the door and Ahksell stepped aside. She exited the office silently. Ahksell cleared his throat; his gar scraped against the polished wooden planks.

"Yes, I should like to know what progress has been made in the search for Master Monbrith," Lady Azadiya said. Her head shifted backwards. "Would it be possible for my agents and Attendant to leave? In our zeal to speak with you, I'm afraid we forwent breakfast. Young men, you know, are nothing more than empty bellies on legs."

Those pale eyes made a slow circuit of the back half of room. Ibram nodded at him, politely. Judge E'grard frowned.

"I suppose it's fine," he said. "They'll go no farther than the shay shop?"

"No, your honor," Amota Lakum said.

"Very well," Judge E'grard said and waved his hand in a dismissive gesture, already reading the report from Father and Katka over again.

Lady Azadiya smiled over her right shoulder. Amota Lakum released Ladyship's gar, took a step back, and bowed to her. The gar remained in place, and then Ladyship uncoiled her hand. The judge glanced up as the door opened, and blinked rapidly at Lady Azadiya's gar as the heavy staff drifted across the floor and settled against the wall.

"Now," Ibram heard her say as they exited the office. "Where do we stand on the possibility of a third accomplice?"

Ibram's eyes widened. Everyone had discarded the notion before, but now that an actual crime had been exposed the threat of an accomplice to Rustam's escape was greater. The entire family, again, under even higher suspicion.

Amota Lakum put his finger diagonally across his mouth for their silence, and led the way out and around the terrace. In the center of the courtyard, Ibram saw Alia speaking to Warder Kamos, who shook his head and pointed over her shoulder. Mistress Islozia stood by, listening to them; she seemed worried. He wanted to go over there and ask whether or not Warder Phiri had delivered Ibram's message about the potatoes and searching the Monbriths' property, but there was no time; Amota Lakum didn't look in the mood for quick stops. Ahksell knocked his gar into the floorboards as they walked past the crowd and out into the reception hall.

A tension had settled around the manor. The servants moved quickly, with their heads down, and more than one warder was grimly polishing their armaments. An open cart had been moved into the reception hall; he could see bundles of arrows half-covered by a felt blanket. In his mind's eye, he suddenly pictured Commander Osthanes ordering his troops to circle Fontis, with their arrows aiming inward.

Ibram tucked his right hand more tightly against his back and clenched his left hand on the hilt of his sica. Ahksell stumped next to him, and he glanced over. Ahksell canted his head towards him.

"Ibram," he said quietly, with an eye to Amota Lakum's back. "Is it polite that I call Lakum 'Amota'? Because I never have before, and he has not seemed to mind, but I don't want to be rude."

Ibram shook his head. "No, it's just a Merrilian thing, more of a Western formality. He's my uncle, my mother's brother, from a certain point of view."

Ahksell nodded, and then yawned suddenly and hugely. His jaw cracked. Ibram hooted with laughter, and even Amota Lakum turned at the noise. Ahksell ducked his head and covered his mouth with his fist.

"My apologies," he said, and then yawned again.

They followed Amota Lakum passed the crowd of whispering locals and out of the reception hall. The rain had lessened somewhat, and now seemed more of an omnipresent mist that instantly adhered to Ibram's face and hands as soon as it touched him. He shivered.

The stalls—less than half what had been there the day before— were open, but the crowd of people was the same size. A plump woman in a long brown cloak paused in the middle of crossing the square. Ibram saw the oval shape of her face and her dark eyes, but then she turned her head and walked away quickly. He knew that woman. What was Attendant Serisan doing in Fontis?

"To be sure, when I was twenty," Ibram said, without taking his eyes off the woman's form. She was trying to disappear into the crowd, but it wasn't big enough. "I could manage a late night."

"And yet, the tragedy of your twenty-fifth year is that now you drool when you sleep," Ahksell said loudly.

Ibram scrubbed his chin, and glared at him. "I do not!" he hissed. He whipped his head back to catch his quarry, but Attendant Serisan must have ducked behind a stall. She had disappeared. He returned his frown to Ahksell.

Ahksell pointed down to his knee, but Amota Lakum cleared his throat, and Ibram lost the opportunity to retaliate. He scowled out at the remaining trading stalls and the puddles in the road. Then, Ibram stepped up to his fellow agent's side.

"The owner?" Amota Lakum asked.

"Zosi Kolesar," Ibram answered promptly. "Widower, used to work a barge in Delbrite. Has one girl to serve, Gella. She's his daughter. Master Kolesar knows a lot of gossip, and doesn't mind spending a small portion of his day in conversation as long as you buy a little something on the menu."

"There's also a woman who likes mouthing off during the midday meal," Ahksell said. "He threw her out the last time, but she might be back."

Ibram blinked. "Madji...Madji Anlines. She's a drunk, Master Kolesar said, though I didn't think so at the time."

"Well, why not?" Amota Lakum asked as they walked down the alleyway to the shay shop.

Ibram shook his head, though Amota Lakum couldn't see it. "It just struck me she liked the sound of her own voice," he said. "She had a vicious tongue."

"He did say she lived in a distillery," Ahksell said.

"She must have something to do with trade," Ibram said. "I don't remember seeing her before, then, but..."

Amota Lakum turned his head towards him. "Yes?"

"I thought I remembered someone talking about spirits," Ibram said. He shrugged. "It'll come to me, I'm sure."

"Hounds may not catch their prey," Amota Lakum said, "but that doesn't mean they dislike to run."

"Well, he's got the running away part down," Ahksell said, and again his voice was much too loud. Ibram turned his head, and put the first two fingers of his left hand to his mouth, and then flicked them at Ahksell behind Amota Lakum's back. Ahksell flicked him in return, and Ibram turned around, unsettled.

He eyed Amota Lakum's long grey and black hair held in a single braid wound through with a leather strip; it bounced between his shoulder blades. Unlike most of the other amitai, Lakum was from the high mountains where the trembleberries grew, so his chest was like a barrel and his muscles heaped like boulders. He wore a quilted Western robe beneath his symbol of office, with heavy breeches and tall boots. He stood out more than Ibram did, and even Ahksell received fewer measuring looks from the villagers and remaining traders.

The shay shop ahead had all its shutters flung open to let the light in, the same as when they'd last visited, but there were more people stood outside, despite the weather. They all had their hoods up and spoke quietly in groups. Ibram felt unfriendly eyes upon his back as they walked inside the building.

Apart from a few occupied stools at the bar and some folk in the corners, the shop was empty enough that he could hear the sound of the mules in their harness at the mill out the back of the shop. Gella pulled back from her cleaning tables and bobbed a nervous bow. Ibram smiled at her as he headed directly for the bar where Zosi stood, wiping out bowls and cups soaking in a wide bucket of suds. He put his rag and cup aside, and cleaned his wet hands off on his apron.

"Good day," he said and leaned across the bar. "Good to see you again, Attendant Solari, Master Ucalegon. And a new customer is always welcome." He grinned, but lines of stress marked his face. "Here to break your fast?"

"We are," Amota Lakum said in his thick rolling accent. "What's in the cauldron?"

The entire shop smelled like bread so strongly Ibram couldn't imagine they'd had time to make anything else. Indeed, he saw tied sacks leaning against the wall that reminded him of bread bought for caravan stores. It seemed like Zosi was doing good, if temporary, business with those traders.

"Quash and bread in the main," Zosi said. "Bread's on special, but I've got some cheese and half a roasted fenek left if you're truly hungry."

"And shay?" Ahksell asked from over Amota Lakum's shoulder.

Zosi chuckled. "Yes, Attendant. A fresh pot, too."

"That will be enough then," Amota Lakum said. He leaned forward and rested both his arms on the bar near the pail. His head tilted so that his braid fell forward. "And a cup of small beer."

Zosi wiped his hands again on a corner of his apron. His eyes flickered up and then down. "Gella! Come and get these boys a good breakfast, the full spread."

"Even the fenek?" she asked.

Amota Lakum's broad shoulders shifted. Zosi nodded. "As I said."

Ahksell stepped on Ibram's foot lightly. Ibram freed himself, and stuck his chin in the air. He moved over to Amota Lakum's right side, and grinned.

"Good day, Zosi," he said.

Zosi smiled. "Good day, youngster. You back to help again?"

"We're going to try," Ibram said. "Would you be known to my Uncle Lakum?"

"This is your uncle?" Zosi asked.

"I have responsibility for him, to be sure," Amota Lakum said. "His mother worries."

Zosi laughed. "All parents do."

He moved the tub of dishware off the bar and set it down on the floor behind it. When he stood, he crossed his arms so that his tattoo bulged. Ahksell came to Ibram's side and rested himself against the bar.

"Ibram tells me you run a good shop," Amota Lakum said and ran his first finger down a little crack in the wood. "I wonder if I might ask you a few questions?"

Zosi cast his eyesight sideways and raised his eyebrows. "Your uncle, you say?" he asked.

Ibram nodded. "Oh yes."

"Suppose another sect agent's questions can't hurt," Zosi said.

Ibram noted he also hadn't said they helped, but he held his tongue. Amota Lakum hummed to himself and nodded. Zosi looked him in the face again and seemed to come to some kind of decision.

"Well, it will be thirty faunts for the meal, and another ten for the deposit on the plates and spoons," Zosi said.

"A goodly sum," Amota Lakum said as he opened up his coin

pouch. He started counting out coins. "You must make a fair cup of shay."

"And the bread and the small beer," Zosi said. The corner of his mouth lifted when Amota Lakum handed over his coins. He shook them in his hand, and then turned around to set them in the chest against the wall. "Those who have no room to make their own come to my shop, after all. Best to make it a happy trip."

Amota Lakum hummed and tapped his knuckles on the bar. "What's to do with those bags?" he asked.

Master Kolesar half-turned towards the stacks along the wall. "Just preparing," he said grimly.

Ibram watched Zosi put the coins in the separate open compartments that lined the hinged portion of the money chest. There was a stack of picaio amongst the faunts, but no glimmer of gold. Ibram swallowed and looked down at the bar before Zosi noticed him watching, no merchant liked that sort of scrutiny.

No gold had to be a good sign. Alchemastery with silver or even copper was bad enough, of course, when you could just get a permit for limited transmutation, but debased gold meant the death penalty. Yet no gold in the money chest in the busiest shop in Fontis suggested that the possibility of finding alchemastered picks had far lowered. He frowned. They would have to search the other shops in the village, wouldn't they? The stables and the weaver... Wheelmaker's Rut, every merchant still in town as well.

Tolk had been coming around for three years. He hadn't just spent money in Fontis, but all the little farmsteads and villages and most probably the towns outside the sect's boundary as well. Delbrite was seven days ride away and on the river, but it was still the main port in the province. There were days when that distance felt insurmountable, but knowing what could be happening even now made Delbrite seem incredibly close by.

Ibram wrapped out a quick rhythm on the bar, and Ahksell leaned on his shoulder; he stopped his fidgeting. The few people left around them were murmuring quietly, enough to make out the noise but not the words. That horrible Madji woman wasn't present, so at least they weren't to be granted another viewing of historical disasters through the lens of commerce. He'd never even heard of Mandibrite before, and the empire certainly didn't object to making sure all of its subjects understood the cruel necessities of lawful society.

Gella came around the bar with a tray of food and drink. The fenek, split down the middle so whoever got the either half received two legs and at least some of the breast, leaned on the round of brown bread next to the wedge of cheese. Three small steaming cups lay nestled to the bowls of nut brown quash. Ibram could smell the shay even from where he stood. He swallowed and licked his lips.

"Amota—uh, Uncle Lakum," he said. "Our food is ready."

"Riant, Ibram," Amota Lakum said, and Ibram winced. "Go and eat with Ahksell. I'll join you in a bit."

Ibram let Ahksell pull him away from the bar, and followed him and Gella to a table away from the window, but within its light. She laid down the tray, pulled out spoons from her apron's pocket, and then waited while they sat down. Ahksell leaned his gar on the wall behind him, while Ibram took the chair that put his back to the window.

"Are you here officially now, Attendant?" Gella asked.

Ahksell took a deep breath. "I suppose I am now, yes. My mentor is here to speak with the judge and Mistress Denrind."

Gella's blue eyes went wide. She clasped her hands and pressed them to her stomach. "A mentor alchemist in Fontis? Already?"

"Lady Azadiya was asked down to help," Ibram assured her. "She has nothing to do with...anything else."

Gella nodded, but her breath came a little too quickly. "Of course," she said. "I'll just leave you to your food, then."

She took a step back and Ibram put up his hand to stop her. "Wait, I have a question." He smiled. "You wouldn't mind, would you Gella? I know you're probably quite busy."

Gella smiled without showing her teeth. She glanced about the mostly empty room. "I'm sure I have moment. How can I help?"

Ibram looked at Ahksell out of the corner of his eye. He hadn't spoken to Gella when he'd been in the shop before, though she was much closer in age to him and Ahksell. She was quiet and sturdy, and Zosi was much more fun to speak to, but so far much of what he'd done in Fontis had only served to reveal the consequences of his omissions. He might as well start making amends now, before Ladyship devised a more fitting punishment.

A sudden vision of the arid, windowless room where Ladyship kept her records flashed into his face. He shuddered. That place locked from the outside, didn't it?

"Ibram?" Ahksell prompted, and Ibram came back to himself.

"Yes! My apologies, yes." He cleared his throat. "Gella, did you ever meet Master Tolk?"

She nodded. "Plenty of times," she said. "Master Harken would set up shop in the livery yard if there wasn't as much work to be found at the—the other place."

Ibram nodded. "I suppose they got most of the trade coming up the road."

"Not so much the town, but a fair bit of the trade," she said, and nodded. "It depended. The larger caravans might stay with them, but they wouldn't have stopped in Fontis properly anyway. We're more for the village and the small traders, truly."

Ahksell took a long sip of his shay. "So he'd come in and have his meals?"

"Oh yes," she said. "Same as all the rest of them, but he was a quiet man, really. Well, unless you asked him about his craft, and then he couldn't stop talking."

Ahksell smiled, and Gella's worried eyes relaxed a small bit. Ibram coughed to get her attention. "I can't say that I'd have the same enthusiasm for it," he said. "All that hammering and heat just gives me a headache. What could he have found so interesting?"

She laughed. "He said the heat was good for his old bones, mostly," she said. "And that he was sorry he'd ever come so far north."

Ibram thought back to his time up in Halfrilat, where the snow packed higher than even Ahksell and the natives locked up their visitors at the least inclination. "He thought *this* was the North?" he asked.

Gella shrugged. "North enough," she said. "Or possibly not Eastern enough. He said he missed the plains a time or two."

"Sounds as if he was far traveled," Ibram said. "I remember, when I spoke to Rustam, he mentioned he'd only ever been as far as Delbrite before."

Her mouth thinned. "Yes, Rustam was always underfoot before. Mistress Monbrith likes to keep them all out at the draughtshop, but you can't stop youngsters from finding trouble, as Father likes to say."

Ahksell cut half the bread loaf into thick slices and laid them near the cheese. He put the flat of his spoon on the breast of the fenek and began to cut through the meat with his belt knife. Ibram caught his eye; Ahksell's head twitched.

"So Rustam didn't know many folk outside Fontis?" Ibram asked. Villages and settlements in their corner of the province were more intertwined that most in other regions, and a trading waystation guested caravans full of strangers. If Rustam had known Harken Tolk well enough to commit a crime with him, he might have known another one willing to help him escape.

"Oh we all know lots of people from outside the village around here," Gella said. "But I don't know about Rustam. I guess now we know he's quick enough to bolt, but before I always thought him shy."

It narrowed down the possibilities if Rustam had no one to turn to for shelter outside of his family. So had his sister called him shy, when Ibram had asked her, but would a shy boy pick a fight in the market over a girl? Something had given Rustam the courage to take a risk. He frowned and chanced a quick look back to the bar. Amota Lakum was drinking from his mug, and Zosi had an eye on his throat. Yilka's megrims, this was embarrassing.

"Did Rustam ever come in with Master Tolk?" Ibram asked. He picked up one of the carved wooden spoons and poked it into the little pool of crumbled treeka nuts atop the nearest bowl of quash. He released the spoon; its handle stuck up in the air.

"Sometimes," she said with a nod. "Especially if he needed help with the bellows or pulling nails. They'd set up a little furnace and buckets from the back of Master Harken's wagon and just work all morning."

"So Rustam was his apprentice?"

She shook her head. "No one ever said anything about that, but I expect Mistress Monbrith worked something out in exchange for the labor. Master Harken never stayed anywhere else."

"She's a sharp negotiator then?" Ibram asked.

"I wouldn't say that, no. More like eager," Gella said. "But she's been turning more of the business over to Satya."

Ahksell glanced up from his breakfast. Ibram nodded. "I remember the young mistress saying something along those lines."

"It seems to be doing all right," Gella said. "I mean, that's what we all thought until all this ruckus began."

She made a helpless gesture with her hands and looked about the shop. Ibram sighed and put his elbow on the table. Ahksell nodded up at her.

"I'm sorry, Gella," Ahksell said. "I know this is difficult."

She swallowed hard, looked about herself again, and then leaned forward. Her voice was a harsh whisper. "I liked Rustam, Attendant. I thought he was sweet and a little too easily led, but now I..." She shook her head hard enough to dislodge a few springy strands of hair. "I'm so angry I don't know what to do with it all, and I know the Sailor says anger never guides us home, but I have four candles for the Wanderer to carve Rustam Monbrith for supper! I hope the warders catch him to save all our lives, but I—"

"Gella!" Zosi called and Gella's mouth closed. Her body snapped upright and the knuckles of her clenched hands turned white. She turned smartly on her heel. Zosi and Amota Lakum watched them from the bar. Zosi tugged on his grey braid; the worry lines across his forehead deepened. "You all right there, girlie?"

"Yes, Father!" she called out. "I'll just go check on the ovens now."

She hurried away without looking back, and Zosi watched her go. He turned back to Amota Lakum with pinched lips, and then Ibram stared down at his quash. He stabbed the mush with his spoon.

"Not an uncommon desire," Ahksell said. He tore off the fenek's plump leg rather than slicing through the tendon with his belt knife, and put it into Ibram's bowl with his own hand. Ibram breathed in and out through his nose.

"To check the ovens?" he tried to make his voice a bit livelier.

Ahksell tapped the side of Ibram's bowl with his spoon. "Your quash is getting cold."

Ibram stuck a spoonful in his mouth and chewed. They ate in silence. Zosi's hot shay was just as sweetened as the colder version, but Ibram drank it down anyway. He'd need a bit of fortitude to face the Monbriths when Lady Azadiya was finished speaking with Judge E'grard.

"Did you see Attendant Serisan in the crowd back there?" he asked.

Ahksell's chin dropped a bit in surprise. He picked up his fork and served himself a piece of meat. "No, I didn't," he said. He looked down to cut his fenek in half. "Why would she be here?"

He glanced up when Amota Lakum joined them at the table. He sat down in the seat facing the window, empty-handed. He must have finished his small beer at the bar. Ibram pushed the third shay cup his direction, and handed him a spoon. With a raised eyebrow, Amota Lakum took the spoon and looked at it and then the quash.

"Treeka nuts?" he asked, and set down the spoon. He took up the loaf of bread and tore the end off of it before setting the rest back down.

"This place is full of them," Ahksell said. He cut himself a piece of cheese and arranged it on his own slice of bread by knifepoint. "The Monbriths serve them as well."

Amota Lakum hummed to himself. He dipped the end of the bread in his quash and scooped up a mouthful. Ibram felt his face heat. He circled his own bowl with his spoon.

"It tastes mainly of salt," Amota Lakum said as he chewed. "Zosi has a way with him, but I can't speak for his food."

"He's probably too concerned to cook," Ibram said. He pulled at the fenek meat with the side of his spoon and a small chunk came away. It was cold and chewy; it had probably been roasted the night before and intended for the midday meal's stewpot.

"Did you learn anything from the young mistress?" Amota Lakum asked.

Ibram frowned. "Satya?"

Ahksell slurped his shay, and rolled his eyes. "Gella."

"Ah, well," Ibram said. He sat up in his chair. "Gella told us that

Rustam was a shy boy who she'd like to see quartered and flung to the four winds."

Amota Lakum chuckled. "Happily, she might get her chance."

"She lit four candles to the Wanderer over it," Ahksell said with a grim set to his mouth.

Amota Lakum turned that over in his mind and ate another scoop of quash. "Did they light?"

Ibram shook his head. "She said she had them, not that she lit them. She's angry, but I doubt she'll go through with it."

"Oh?" Amota Lakum asked.

"If she hasn't lit them by now, I don't think she will." Ibram shrugged. "It might be enough just to have the option. Four candles to a deity for a death, but not for a demon, who might actually go for the bargain? It proves she's not so angry as to be reckless."

"Or suicidal," Ahksell said.

"Might be better for everyone if she did," Amota Lakum said. "Rustam's had four days. A man can cover a lot of ground in that time."

Ahksell squirmed a bit on his chair. "She also didn't say if she knew of anyone who might take him out on their wagon."

"There was never a question of that though," Ibram said. "It's always been thought that Rustam ran away, not stowed himself like luggage."

"But we have to admit the idea of a third accomplice," Ahksell said. He picked up his piece of bread and cheese, and poked the air. "If Master Tolk worked with Rustam, then Rustam could very well have had help."

Amota Lakum ate his quash with the end piece of bread, and licked his fingers. He took up a piece of sliced fenek and bit it in half. He seemed content enough to listen to them, without letting slip what he and Zosi had spoken about. Ibram turned his spoon over in his fingers.

"But if it was a third accomplice, then that would mean Rustam always intended to run way," he pointed out. "In which case, why not flee sooner? Why wait until the night before?"

"Courage?" Ahksell offered. "Or maybe he had to wait until they arrived."

Ibram ate another bite of fenek. "A possibility."

"Did the court's papers mention anything about that?"

Ibram frowned. "I...Satya said—you'll remember this, Ahksell—she said they had two hostlers staying with them, and the court's report said they searched the entire grounds of the property." He began ticking places off on his right hand. "The draughtshop, the house, the small barn they have in the back for the goats... Cangsa, I think they even searched the wells. The two hostlers had a string of horses for the little—" He broke off, laughing. "That's who it was. They were transporting new coursers for Lord Halfrey. They didn't have a wagon between them, just a pack mule."

"So, the wrong direction and no place to hide," Ahksell said.

Something flickered in the corner of Ibram's sight, but when he turned his head, he only saw Amota Lakum wrapping a slice of bread around some cheese. He caught Amota Lakum's eye, and frowned when the man did nothing but blink back at him. Ibram looked away.

"Besides," Ibram said to Ahksell. "What about the candles to the Speaker going out?"

Ahksell shook his head. "What if they didn't?"

"Did not the Monbriths tell you about the candles going out?" Amota Lakum asked. "Much information seems to come only from them."

"That's what makes me think the others cannot be involved," Ibram said.

"What do you mean?" Amota Lakum asked. He was staring out the window.

Ibram drank down the last of his shay, and wiped his mouth. "Mistress Monbrith is religious. She's for the Advisor and she gave both boys for the Speaker, which is two steps away from joining one of those cults that think the empress is their triplet on earth, or some such nonsense. And at her very dining table, she wouldn't even let Diarmit ask you questions about alchemy."

Ahksell poked the air with his spoon. "Because he asked if I could turn something into gold."

Ibram opened his mouth to answer, and Amota Lakum raised his hand. The simple ring on his thumb glowed a brilliant silvery light.

"Save these thoughts for Lady Azadiya. Have you eaten your fill? Yes? Off we go."

He rose and began walking to the door. Ahksell and Ibram followed him, calling out their good byes as they walked out. The rain had finally tapered off, and the sky was a light grey, bubbly with clouds. Amota Lakum walked swiftly up the alley and onto the village square. Ibram could hear the sounds of men and horses ahead of them.

The entire area was full of saddled horses and buzzing warders in armor with their swords strapped to their waists. Commander Osthanes sat atop his grey courser amongst them, calling out orders. Amota Lakum barely slowed, just moved to the outskirts of the troop, and continued towards Mistress Denrind's entrance gate. Lady Azadiya's carriage remained outside. A villager stood by the horses who had been given nosebags of feed, while a bucket of water lay at their feet. As they approached the carriage, Lady Azadiya came out of the manor, holding her gar in one hand with the orange umbrella floating at her side.

"I do wish you'd remembered this damp thing," she said and gestured with her crooked left hand. The umbrella bobbled in the air.

They all bowed. Ibram popped up first. "Ladyship," he said. "I need to speak with Commander Osthanes before he leaves."

She glanced over to the milling throng. "You'll have to be quick —oh, no."

A hunting horn blasted the air twice, and they all winced. The warders rode as one body towards the other end of town; the commander had taken his place at their head. Ahksell put his hand over his left ear. Amota Lakum held out his hand and retrieved the floating umbrella. Lady Azadiya smiled.

"Thank you," she said, still in that high Vissilian accent. "I'm sorry about your conversation, Ibram."

"Where are they going?" he asked.

"To the Monbriths," she said. "To return shortly. Now, what knowledge have you brought back?"

"Mentor, may I speak with you?" Ahksell asked. "In private."

Lady Azadiya angled towards him. Ibram frowned and stared quickly between them. The back of his head tightened.

"Why can't we hear whatever you have to say?" he asked.

Ahksell tightened his grip on his gar. "Because what I have to say to my mentor doesn't concern you."

Ibram's shoulders stiffened. "What do you mean it—?"

"I have no objection to a private talk," Lady Azadiya said. "We'll go to the carriage."

"But—"

Ibram tried again, and Amota Lakum grabbed him around the back of the neck and squeezed. Ibram snapped his mouth shut. Lady Azadiya sighed. Ahksell's jaw flexed, but he turned to his mentor and bowed shortly.

"I just need a moment, Mentor," he said, "but the matter is pressing."

"Of course, Ahksell," she said. "We'll go to the carriage. Lakum, please take the horses to the livery yard, we shall not need them after all. The warders are tasked with making an effort at the Monbrith property."

Amota Lakum bowed without moving his hand from Ibram's neck. "Yes, Ladyship."

Ahksell unlocked the carriage, and Lady Azadiya climbed up inside; he followed her and swung the door shut. Ibram heard the lock sizzle as it engaged. Amota Lakum shook him a little and leaned in.

"Don't embarrass Ladyship like that again," he said quietly. "Come on, climb up on the driving bench with me."

Ibram twisted his neck but only managed to dislodge Amota

Lakum's hand from his neck to his shoulder. "Who's embarrassed?" he grumbled.

Amota Lakum pushed him to the front of the carriage. He tossed the orange umbrella up and beneath the driving bench, and then finally released his hold on Ibram. Ibram sidled over a few steps and pulled his gambeson straight; he resettled his belts. He crossed his arms and kicked mud off his boots while Amota Lakum paid the villager for the feed and water, and then climbed up onto the driving bench. He picked up the reins and raised his eyebrows in Ibram's direction.

Ibram felt his jaw work. He squeezed his elbows, and then put his foot on the metal footplate and hauled himself up into the driving bench. Amota Lakum flicked the reins and the carriage began to turn around.

"Good luck those warders cleared out," he said with his eyes on the horses. "This great pile of lumber takes an acre to turn."

Ibram ground his teeth. He put his hands on his knees and dug his fingers into his muscles. He couldn't hear anything behind them since the carriage was almost as well-warded as Ladyship's office, and the noise in the square still hadn't recovered from the loss of the warders. He could see villagers and traders peeping out at them. A few of the stalls looked to be closing down in a hurry.

"Do you know what they're talking about in there?" he asked.

Amota Lakum glowered at him. "That's not our concern," he said.

"What could Ahksell possibly have to say that I can't hear about?" he asked. "We've been working next to each other this entire time!"

Amota Lakum sighed as he angled the horses into the livery yard. "Could be anything," he said. "Doesn't matter."

Ibram scoffed. "This entire village is about be walled up and he suddenly wants to keep secrets?"

Amota Lakum's hands tightened on the reins. He glanced at him from the corner of his eye. "He outranks you now, Ibram," he said. "Best get used to it early."

Ibram stared at him, and then slumped against the backrest. He crossed his arms. Amota Lakum hummed to himself. He guided the carriage past the open gate and into an empty bay beneath the rooms above the stable. The horses whinnied to each other, clearly a bit uneasy at the new location. He lay the reins aside and jumped down.

"Lady Azadiya put you in charge of both of us," Ibram pointed out. He spread his hands.

Amota Lakum turned his face up to him and nodded. "I am very trustworthy."

Ibram sat forward and resisted urge to stamp his foot like a grown man. He rubbed his eyebrow, and then frowned at his thumb for the anxious betrayer it was. "Far be it from me to disregard the most trustworthy of all my amitai but—"

"It's because I never gamble." Amota Lakum interrupted. He began unhitching the horses from the carriage without waiting for the stable hand to come out. "I just hold all the money."

"But if you, oh blessed Amota Lakum, don't have all the information and I, your only wretched anefa—"

"I have six more, each less troublesome," he interrupted again. "And twice as many aneptai."

Ibram leaned his head back and groaned. "That is not the point! How is anything to be solved when I am not given the information I might need to solve it?"

Amota Lakum cocked his head and pet his horse on its neck. "And here I stand, fairly convinced that it is not information gladly given over which will solve the problem of Fontis."

Ibram glared at him, but Amota Lakum was unfazed. "To be sure," he continued, "it is agreeable when the culprit confesses before we have sat down to accuse them, but it doesn't happen often."

"I'm not stupid," Ibram said. "There's no truth telling augur in Ahksell's buttons."

"Nor in ladyships," Amota Lakum said.

Ibram wrapped his hand around the back of his head and rubbed the prickling tension out of it. He scooted across the driving bench, and then hopped down from the carriage. "I know I should have realized something was going on with the Monbriths far more quickly than I did. I am trying to make up for it!"

Amota Lakum swept his braid back over his shoulder. He turned and ran his hand over the horse's flank. "Do you know how to unhitch horses from a carriage? Without a place to tie, I mean," he said.

"Yes, I do," Ibram sighed. "Ama taught me."

"You have to be consistent," Amota Lakum kept talking as if Ibram hadn't spoken. "As well, you must take great care. The horses are vulnerable right now, because they're facing a place they don't want to go. It keeps them from moving at the wrong moment in the process, but you still have to keep an eye on them. If they startle, they could injure themselves, or you."

Ibram breathed out sharply through his nose. He braced his hands on his hips and glared behind him. The alchemists were still huddled inside the carriage and the stable girl had apparently abandoned her duties. He turned back around to see Amota Lakum lifting off the horse's neck yoke.

"Do you take care, Ib-la?" he asked in a soft and rhythmic voice. The horse chuffed the air and bent its neck; its partner shuffled a step in its harness. "Were you consistent?"

"The Monbriths are not horses and none of them looked likely to bolt!"

The carriage harness jingled. The horse closest to Amota Lakum shook its head in the air. He shushed it, put the neck yolk down, and began stroking its flank again.

"Take a step away and roll your dice, if you're going to get your blood up in here," Amota Lakum said. He kept petting the horse. "Shh, shh, he didn't mean it, girl."

Ibram turned on his heel and walked to the back of the carriage. He stood outside the bay and looked up at the grey sky. He took a long slow breath and looked out to what he could see of the market square. Behind him, the carriage door hinges squeaked. Ibram turned on his heels, and saw Lady Azadiya stood on the top step.

"That didn't take long," he said.

She looked about her and then down to him, and smiled. "Ah, there you are Ibram," she said. Her accent had returned to her, and she seemed much livelier. "Well now, I am invited in the strongest possible terms to attend dinner with his honor, Mistress Denrind, and

Commander Osthanes tonight. This will, of course, mean I am bored out of all patience but at least there might be wine."

Ibram began to scoff, and translated it into a cough when she raised her eyebrows at him. "Yes, Ladyship," he said. "Will we all be required for this event?"

"You shall," she said. "I hope you've practiced your table manners."

Ibram shrugged. "I've given them some thought in the past."

"Then this will be an adequate test," Lady Azadiya said. "I am given rooms Mistress Denrind's manor. Lakum will stay with me, while you and Ahksell remain at the Monbriths in flagrant disregard of my hint to sleep in the carriage rather than invite fleas home with you."

"If I hadn't slept in Harken Tolk's old room, I would never have discovered that clipping," Ibram pointed out.

"Instinct unmanaged is useless, Ibram, and luck only takes an agent so far."

Amota Lakum came out from behind the horses to stare meaningfully at him. Ibram averted his eyes. Ladyship still remained in the doorway of the carriage. She looked over Ibram's head to the world beyond.

"Now," she said, "before the jaws of polite behavior snap closed on me, to this little matter." She raised her right leg and pulled up her skirts to reveal her leather boot. "The buckle of my boot has broken."

"It was fine when you went in the carriage, wasn't it?" Ibram asked.

Lady Azadiya wiggled her foot; the leather strap flopped. "The Suugans have the repair shop in town, yes?"

Ibram swallowed and then quickly looked up to her face. "Yes, Ladyship," he said.

She let her dress drop and smoothed down the front of her coat and cloak. He waited for her to stump down the stairs with her gar and then cocked an eye back up to the open carriage door. Ahksell emerged with his head down. He leaned his gar directly against the carriage. Then, he walked down the stairs in a serious manner and closed and locked the carriage door without speaking. He picked up his staff and resettled his grip.

"We shall all go together," Lady Azadiya said. She leaned on her gar. "Lakum! How are the horses?"

Amota Lakum came out from the opposite side of the carriage. "Just unharnessing them now, Ladyship," he said.

She nodded. "Very good. Do you get them attended to, and then take up shop back with Ibram's older suitor. I want to know the second Commander Osthanes returns with the Monbriths. I am off to get my buckle reaffixed and the boys will do very well for that."

He bowed and she raised him up with her hand cupping the side of his face. He smiled at her and they stepped apart. "Come, come," Ladyship said. "To the boot folk."

She led the way across the square and Ibram followed behind her. He made sure to keep a step behind Ahksell, as protocol demanded since Attendant Solari was in Fontis on such important and secret business. This time the window shutter on the Suugans' home was shut tight. Ahksell looked back once as Lady Azadiya knocked on the Suugans' door, and Ibram bowed shortly. He turned back around.

The door remained shut. Lady Azadiya knocked again. Ibram stepped up to her shoulder.

"They did this trick on our first visit, Ladyship," he explained. "I think it might be quicker if you announced yourself."

She quickly looked over at him and then faced front again. "You do it for me."

"Oh." Ibram took a breath and then looked at the wooden door. He rolled his shoulders back and then cleared his throat. "Open the door!" he shouted. Lady Azadiya pressed her hand against her right ear and winced. "Open for Mentor Hobon of the Sect of Seven Fires!"

He heard a squeal that sounded a great deal like little Imriska, and then the definite sounds of footsteps behind the door. The door flung open and his theory was born out; there she stood, beaming upwards into Lady Azadiya's face. Imriska's plump cheeks turned pink; her mouth dropped open.

"Good day," she whispered.

"Good day, Imriska Suugan," Lady Azadiya said. She knelt down, heedless of the mud on her hems. "Is your mother at home? I have broken my boot buckle."

Imriska blinked at her, and then nodded her head as if it were on a string. She opened her mouth, but a woman joined her at the door. She wrapped her arm around Imriska's shoulders, and Lady Azadiya stood back up.

"Mistress Suugan?" she asked.

"Mentor Hobon," she said with a deep bow.

Lady Azadiya put her left arm at her waist and curled her fingers; Mistress Suugan rose. She and her son carried quite a resemblance with their fine brown hair and thin nose. They had the same teardrop-shaped eyes, but where he was broad, she was thin as a lillia tree. Mistress Suugan stepped away from the door, dragging Imriska with her, and Ladyship walked into the workshop. Ibram waited for Ahksell to cross over and then followed them inside before Mistress Suugan could close the door.

"Ah yes," Lady Azadiya said. "What an excellent workshop you keep, Mistress. I am sure you'll be able to help me."

"I—we will, of course, Mentor," Mistress Suugan replied.

Master Suugan rose from the bench next to his worktable where he and Tieri had been considering a flat piece of leather with a thin wooden cut out upon it. Side by side, it was clear from whom Tieri had inherited his heft. He was short, but broad and round. His face was set in dour lines, but Ibram thought that was only to be expected given the circumstances.

"Good day, Mentor," he said.

They made their politenesses and then Lady Azadiya stuck her foot forward. "My buckle broke," she said. "I was wondering if you might fix this?"

Master Suugan came forward and considered Ladyship's boot without touching her. Ibram took the opportunity of studying the injury himself. It looked very much like someone had taken a knife to the rivet connecting the buckle to the strap high up on Lady Azadiya's shin.

Master Suugan nodded slowly. "Aye, looks as if the rivet popped out on the loop ring. It should be quick," he said. "Would you like a cup of shay as you wait?"

"I would love some water, if you wouldn't mind," she said.

Master Suugan waved to his son. "Off with you, boy. A pitcher for the Mentor and her folk as well. I can handle the repair."

Tieri bowed hastily towards Ladyship, and left the room through the kitchen door. The Suugans stood in their places and stared. Ibram cleared his throat.

"It's good to finally meet you, Mistress Suugan," he said. "Your son says only good things."

"That's very nice to hear, thank you," she replied, and swallowed. She rubbed her knuckles up and down Imriska's arm.

Lady Azadiya gazed about the workshop. "May I sit?"

"Oh!" Mistress Suugan started forth from her corner. She dragged out the same seat Ibram had used on his previous visit and dusted it off with her sleeve. "Please, Mentor, here... May I take your coat?"

She stood back and clasped her hands in front of her. Imriska darted out of the corner and joined her mother, hiding behind her skirt. Lady Azadiya inclined her head and began unbuttoning her coat. She let her gar stand next to her. It never wavered, but Imriska stared as if it would burst into trumpet blossoms at any moment. She practically vibrated where she stood.

"Thank you," Ladyship said. She shrugged off both cloak and coat, and handed the bundle to Ibram. Beneath them, she wore a deep blue shift and an open-fronted silk gown so green it looked like it had been dyed yesterday, embroidered with floating leaves in gold and copper thread. Both gown and shift lay beneath by a leather belt held together by an intricately designed gold buckle from which hung a linen pocket, heavily embroidered in protective red designs. The gown was low cut for the season and she had covered the expanse of flesh with a chained necklace laden with gemstones that Ibram recognized from Father's shop.

She stood apart from every single person in the humble unadorned room. The older Suugans didn't seem to know where to put their eyes, but Imriska had taken to wriggling in glee. Ibram coughed instead of laughing, and found himself sharing an amused look with Ahksell.

Ibram firmed his jaw and focused on settling Ladyship's heavy coat and cloak in both of his arms. Ahksell shifted his weight on his feet to his left. She sat down without a pleased sigh. Lady Azadiya stuck out her foot. She lifted her skirt and shook the loose leather strap again. Imriska giggled and then clapped her hands over her mouth.

Lady Azadiya shook her head. "I am ever hard on my footwear, Master Suugan. It makes life difficult for the shoemakers of Lityen."

"I suppose they look on it as job security, Mentor," Master Suugan said.

Lady Azadiya laughed. "I should hope so! I am far too old to change."

She took off her boot and wiggled her toes. She wore grey stockings. Ibram swallowed and looked away. Mistress Suugan had put her hands on Imriska's shoulders; she appeared about ready to scream. Ibram might join her; they were wasting so much time.

"Do you still have what broke off, Mentor?" Mistress Suugan asked. "That might be easiest."

"Mistress Suugan, please sit," Ladyship said, looking upward. "You cannot share a drink with me in so uncomfortable a position."

Mistress Suugan's mouth parted a little. She looked around and then dragged a short bench from beside the wall over to where Lady Azadiya waited for her. She dusted off the seat, and delicately perched on the bench with her knees together. Imriska stood by her side.

"And, alas, no," Lady Azadiya answered her. "It popped off without my noticing, but I do have the buckle. Ahksell?" She turned her head, and Ahksell startled to life.

"Oh, uh, yes, Mentor," he said and held out his left fist. He opened it, crooked a finger then snapped it forward, and the buckle floated over to where Master Suugan was selecting a small hammer. After a moment, Master Suugan plucked the buckle from the air, and laid it on the table.

Imriska clapped. Her mother looked horrified, but Lady Azadiya smiled at the little girl and leaned over in her seat. "He is talented, isn't he?" she said in a mock-whisper.

Ahksell coughed and rubbed the side of his neck. Imriska glanced up to her mother, and took a deep breath. She turned to Lady Azadiya and screwed her courage up tightly. She nodded quickly. "He made all the shay things dance before! Why doesn't Attendant Serisan ever do that? All we do in class is sums."

Lady Azadiya tsked to herself. "Suppose sums are a kind of alchemy," she commented. "But I'm with you. Floating is much more interesting." She narrowed her eyes. "Do you like your Attendant Serisan's class, Imriska?"

The kitchen door opened, and Tieri entered the room carrying a pitcher and cups on a tray. He lay the tray on his father's worktable and poured out water in five cups. He left one cup by his father's elbow, and then passed around the rest. Ibram refused his, but Ahksell accepted.

Lady Azadiya took her water and then waited to drink until Mistress Suugan had received hers. Then, she drank immediately so that others could partake. Vissilians ate in order of rank, for some reason. Imriska stepped forward only to be drawn back by her mother to a polite distance.

"Yes," Imriska said. She nodded firmly. "I'm the best of my age, which is very important, even though it's too easy now."

Ladyship tilted her head. "It's too easy now? What changed?"

"Diarmit's gone," Imriska replied. "He was the only one who could keep up with me and now he has to wait around for me to teach him, and I don't always explain things as good as Attendant Serisan so when he comes—"

Mistress Suugan covered her daughter's mouth and Imriska cut off with an indignant squeak. "Not that he comes here anymore," she said hastily. "It's only that Diarmit's mother took him from the Bedris school."

Ladyship crossed her legs at the ankle so that her stocking foot didn't drag up dirt from the floor. She looked into her wooden cup. Across the way, Master Suugan began fixing her boot.

"I think you told me something like that, Ibram," Lady Azadiya said. "He was needed at home, yes?"

"Yes, Ladyship," Ibram said. "About three years ago."

Mistress Suugan scoffed into her water, and then cleared her throat. Lady Azadiya watched her hosts with mild eyes that Ibram was sure caught absolutely everything. Master Suugan looked up from his work.

"Now, beloved," he said.

"It isn't as if it's a secret, Hawyoth." Mistress Suugan shook her head. "I'm not saying Diarmit isn't old enough to work, Mentor, but he's been running loose in the village for three years now, just as his sister and brother used to do. After Imriska's schooling, he comes—" She broke off and looked down at her water, and then took a breath. "Diarmit would come to our door to hear Imriska talk about her lessons."

"He's a bright boy," Ahksell said. "Very curious."

Ibram restrained himself from yawning and then covered his mouth under pretext of shifting Ladyship's coat and cloak to his left arm. This was getting them no closer to finding Rustam, and in fact, rather further away. Lady Azadiya hadn't needed both he and Ahksell to accompany her to the shoe repair. She hadn't even needed help across the street. This was a waste of time. He took a half-turn about the room, and stopped against the wall. Now he could see everyone laid out before him without having to be too obvious about it.

Mistress Suugan nodded. "He and Imriska both are. Attendant Serisan wants to send her up the mountain when she's older."

"Up the mountain?" Lady Azadiya asked. "Imriska, you must be very smart, then."

Ibram bit the inside of his cheek. At the very least, they should be doing something besides sitting and talking about children. Ahksell was digging his thumbnail into the wood of his gar, no doubt in lieu of fidgeting his feet. Ibram sniffed and stood taller.

"I think so," Imriska said over her brother's sudden hoot of laughter. "I know all the base metals and their...their remembrances."

"Their refinements?" Ahksell asked.

Imriska nodded. "Those, too."

"Then I look forward to seeing you there," Lady Azadiya said.

Imriska beamed. Lady Azadiya took another sip of water and wiggled her toes. Mistress Suugan looked down into her own cup and pressed her lips together.

"It sounds like your families were close," Ibram said to break up the sudden silence.

Tieri shrugged. "There isn't so much space this close to the boundary line; we all run over each other in the course of the day."

"Like you and Rustam," Ibram said. "What about Satya, the heir?"

Tieri cast his gaze to the floor and shrugged his shoulders. "They're close in years, but Satya's nicer…smarter, too. She," he paused and then shook his head. "I remember, when Mistress Monbrith took her out of class, she put up an accursed fight."

"Why was Satya taken out?" Lady Azadiya asked.

Ahksell leaned on his gar and crossed his arms. Ibram pursed his mouth. Then Ahksell crossed his right foot over his left. Clearly, the only way to work through his behavior was to ignore him. He focused back to listen to Ladyship's conversation, since she was so determined to have it. Mistress Suugan sighed and took a sip of her water. Beside her, Imriska leaned against her mother, who put an arm around her.

"It's old news now, Mentor," she said. "I'm not certain how much use village gossip is to you."

"To be sure, I'm not one for gossip either," Lady Azadiya said. She looked at Mistress Suugan from the corner of her eye. "But perhaps the draughtshop was not doing so well? A family must pull together in times of trouble."

Mistress Suugan gazed across the room at her husband and son. Master Suugan was fitting a new piece to Ladyship's boot. She frowned.

"I suppose that could have been the case," she said, "but I've never heard of trouble down at the draughtshop. Not that Jorie Monbrith and I stop to chat in the marketplace, mind you, but I've known her since we were children. It's more that those folk don't like the land they've cut out for themselves."

"Ah, meant for greener hills," Ladyship said.

Mistress Suugan shook her head. "They won't sell up, and they won't go either."

"And now they've lost their chance," Ahksell said.

Mistress Suugan stared at him and then drank from her cup with a shaking hand. Tieri gazed down at his hands, and picked at his nails. The sound of light hammering grew.

"I admit that what Rustam Monbrith has done makes me shaking mad," Lady Azadiya said. "But he might yet be recovered."

"I don't think that will help much anymore, Mentor," Tieri said. "We'll still be shut away, won't we?"

Lady Azadiya frowned slightly, but it was no more than a small downturn of her mouth. "I think it likely that some penalty results from this mess," she said. "But I think we can deliver a much better ending than this Judge's first proposal, do you not, Master Tieri?"

Tieri blushed heavily and shrugged his shoulders.

"Does it hurt to be sanctioned?" Imriska burst out. "I don't want it to hurt."

The hammering stopped. Her mother half-rose to pull Imriska away, but Lady Azadiya raised her free hand. Mistress Suugan sat back down.

"No, it doesn't hurt," Lady Azadiya said, calm in the face of the Suugans' suddenly fervent attention. "It's not a painful process, but I think it might make you sad."

Imriska chewed her bottom lip and nodded. She really was too smart for her age, no wonder Serisan wanted her for a test up the living mountain. Not that she'd get the chance unless they all put a spark in their step. They couldn't escape some kind of punishment for Fontis with Judge E'grard in charge, but if they had Rustam in hand and willing to claim all responsibility that might mean the village would at least survive. Ibram breathed out heavily through his nose, and tucked his right arm under Ladyship's coat and cloak to join his left.

"Those *Monbriths*," Mistress Suugan muttered.

"Were they always trouble?" Lady Azadiya asked.

"She's just like her father. He was a common cleric around here, you know. The Lecturer in Thelis invited him to take orders, but he never did."

"He liked yelling at us all too much," Master Suugan said. He shook his head and laughed. Ibram noted it sounded a little too forced. "You children are lucky Mistress Monbrith didn't inherit his lungs. Her father could shout like the Speaker herself and he spent most of the time telling us all we lived on the edge of burning for sedition."

"I think they like to pretend they're some kind of example for the rest of us," Tieri said.

Ibram rocked back on his heels with a low whistle. He crossed his arms and looked about him. Ahksell caught his eye, but Ibram turned away. Lady Azadiya nodded slowly.

"Not that we ever thought of your folk up the living mountain in that way, Mentor," Master Suugan said as he looked up from her boot. "We know a clapper-less bell when we hear it."

It was a very Vissilian saying, and Ibram let it pass. Besides, Master Suugan might be wrongheaded in his meaning, but to Ibram it brought a fair point. Ibram licked his teeth behind his lips, and touched his belt purse where he kept his bells and dice. Maybe this wasn't such a waste of time. Hearing Mistress Suugan helped firm up Ibram's own opinions on the situation in Fonts, so possibly he'd tapped the bells and Yilka the Green's first face came up lucky. It would certainly help bring Ladyship to Ibram's way of thinking. If the Monbriths believed so deeply in the Sovereign Twins—whose worship was entirely wrapped up in the foundations of the empire—then they'd never touch alchemy. It could mean they just survived this whole debacle.

"Oh yes, no one ever believed him," Mistress Suugan said. "But he wouldn't have anything to do with the Sect if he didn't have to. He even sent her and her brother to the Speaker's shrine in Thelis when it was working."

"Is it not?" Ibram asked.

Mistress Suugan shook her head. "The lecturer died, but I expect, if she could have, Jorie would have sent her children there herself. As it was, she raised them all the same way, in the Bedris preceptory school until they were seven and no more. I don't think she ever saw it as more than a day free from looking after the children."

"Just as well he got his letters and sums," Lady Azadiya said. "But a child or two out of the way in a busy draughtshop is no mean gift either."

"That's...true, Mentor," Mistress Suugan said. "But I won't say she was ever grateful."

"Then it's just as well," Ladyship said and raised one shoulder. "Learning in an unfriendly atmosphere is almost as bad as planting seeds in sand, wouldn't you say?" She sighed, before Mistress Suugan could answer. "To be sure, it's all complicated now, isn't it."

"Yes, I suppose it is, Mentor," she said.

"And Imriska truly is a special one. Not every Learner in my preceptory would take the trouble to teach a rival lessons." Ladyship smiled at the girl and scrunched her nose. Imriska giggled.

"Begging your pardon, Mentor," Master Suugan said. "I've finished your boot repair."

"So fast?" Lady Azadiya asked. "You are a wonder of a man." She cast a roguish eye to the side. "Very well done, Mistress."

Mistress Suugan emitted a shocked giggle as Master Suugan walked over and handed Lady Azadiya her boot. Lady Azadiya took it, and examined her new boot strap, which looked exactly as any other piece of leather Ibram had ever seen. She seemed satisfied.

"Pay the man, Ibram," Ladyship said. "I believe three picaio should cover it?"

Ibram nodded. He moved her coat and cloak back to his left arm, and then undid the clasp on his belt wallet with his right hand. "Yes, Ladyship."

"Why doesn't he call you 'mentor,' Mentor?" Imriska asked.

"Ah well, it's not in his mind," Lady Azadiya said.

Ibram doled out the appropriate coin, and handed it over. Master Suugan thanked him with a nod, and then turned to the chest by the small fireplace. He knelt and opened its top with a key from around his neck. Ibram leaned on the wall and tried to subtly peer over his shoulder. He couldn't see much, but what coins there were seemed to be copper in color. He turned back to the room and Tieri was staring at him. Ibram frowned, and the boy turned away with a huff.

Lady Azadiya had leaned over to do up her boot; she stuck her leg out in front of her. "Do you know, I think Attendant Serisan was speaking truth when she offered to send your daughter up the living mountain, don't you?"

She pushed her hair out of her way so that she could look up at Mistress Suugan from the corner of her eye. Mistress Suugan's eyebrows drew together. She turned her cup around in her hand.

"Yes, Mentor, definitely," she said.

Lady Azadiya sighed and wrapped her laces around her calf. "But I suppose it is unlikely now, given the circumstances."

Mistress Suugan pressed her thin lips together into a white line. Her face said to Ibram she didn't know whether to feel sad or angry, and had resolved upon a version of both. Still, she had her dignity.

"Yes, Mentor, very unlikely," she said.

"But you and your husband would have no objection to us taking Imriska away, would you?" Lady Azadiya asked. She knotted her boot laces and sat up with a sigh. "We take very good care of those they send for testing. Food and shelter, and clothing if they fall in the lake and so forth. So if Imriska did go up the living mountain, she would have nothing to fear." She turned her face fully to view Mistress Suugan, and Ibram was only just placed to see her smile. She held Mistress Suugan's eyes. "Only at the right time, of course."

Slowly, Mistress Suugan's eyebrows drew even closer together and then relaxed. She took a deep, shaking, breath and then nodded. "Not at all, Mentor," she said clearly. "We'd do it gladly."

Ibram frowned, and glanced about the room. Ahksell stopped lounging against his gar. Master Suugan was standing quietly with one hand on Tieri's shoulder.

"Very good! I shall make sure Attendant Serisan keeps her name on the list."

Lady Azadiya stood and clapped her hands together, and Mistress Suugan clambered to her feet. She held Imriska in front of her, hands kneading her thin shoulders. Master Suugan bowed and Lady Azadiya curled up her hands.

"Thank you for the water and your time," she said, and revolved her ankle in the air. "Always better to take care of a problem before it grows worse. Ibram?"

Ibram stood away from the door. "Ladyship?"

"My things," she said. Ibram handed them over. She shook out the heavy mass of her coat and cloak and then slid her arms into the sleeves. "Where do the Terins live?"

Ibram paused. He put his money away, and rubbed his eyebrow. Ahksell sighed.

❧

Once out on the street, Lady Azadiya led them around the back of the remaining traders' stalls. She left her coat unbuttoned and walked with one hand grasping her gar as if she were nothing more than a wealthy lady carrying a walking stick. Ahksell followed in her wake, and Ibram a step behind while she admired what meager goods the traders had left. The little flock of wire and feather automated birds flew above her head to her apparent delight before returning to their seller's stall. She perused gloves and seeds and ribbons with every evidence of pleasure. The bubbleman called out for her approval on his soap sprays, and gained a mob when she readily gave it to him. Whispers and excitement trailed Lady Azadiya like ribbons, lightening the atmosphere in a way Ibram saw rippling out like a stone in a pond. The alchemists had arrived! All would be well now.

If only they knew how many alchemists were on the horizon, and what was their purpose. Ibram watched coins changing hands all around him. His headache stabbed up from the nape of his neck at every exchange.

Those men and women who sold staples and dried goods had been quickly sold out. Now, they were shopping, merely be biding their time until they were allowed to leave, but the frippery merchants remained in full array. Lady Azadiya drew a thin knitted scarf of dubious silk content through her hands while the merchant babbled about his connections in the west. She smiled and nodded, and completely ignored the squad of warders in sight down the way, standing guard at the entrance to the village. They walked on.

Ibram looked about him, but he couldn't see the village guards Mistress Denrind employed as a local constabulary. Most probably, they were still beating the forest to flush out Rustam. He kept one eye on Ladyship and the other on the remains of the crowd. A grim sort of a resolution seemed to hang about them as they went from cart to stall to wagon. Mostly, though, it seemed as if the rush of buyers had died away. He heard haggling, but not the clink of money being exchanged. The candle maker was down to selling short wick lengths and a pile of snuffers. The higgler had a rag bag at his feet and a selection of old clay pots.

"I wonder how they're turning people away on the road," Ahksell said with a cough. "It's still the empress's road, after all. Do you think they've set up a barricade? Or are they diverting travelers further up to Guill? What do you say, Ibram?"

"I don't know, Attendant Solari," Ibram said. "If you wish, I could run over to a warder and inquire?"

"Oh, Ibram, let up, would you?" Ahksell said. "It isn't as if I want to keep secrets from you. It's just they're necessary sometimes. You don't tell me everything that occurs in your head, do you?"

"My apologies, Attendant," Ibram said and barely restrained his eyes from rolling. That was just Ahksell blowing hot air up his chimney. "I would no more—"

Lady Azadiya tsked and they both shut their mouths. She walked down the side of the road opposite the shay shop and the carpenter, ignoring the hopeful calls of the traders left open. She paused at the far end and considered the warders ahead of her. One of them noticed her looking and sprang to attention.

She nodded politely to him, and then turned back around. "Ahksell, go and speak with Lakum about our project," she said. "Ibram will do well with me."

Ahksell opened his mouth and she raised her eyebrows. He subsided without speaking, though he didn't seem gracious about it. He glanced at Ibram, who turned his head to make a careful study of the closest selection of bruised fruit at the stall next to them. Ahksell huffed and Ibram whipped around to glare at him. He knew very well his place in the world, and what liberties he was and was not allowed. He didn't need it thrown back in his face by a man who used to thieve glass apples from his Ama's orchard. Ibram set his right arm behind his back and stood correctly, but the stretch of his shoulder blades throbbed with a hot ache. Ahksell bowed shortly, and then turned around to march over to the shay shop.

He watched him go. The nape of Ibram's neck tingled. "What project is that, Ladyship?" he asked. "Are they going to be questioning the Monbriths?"

Lady Azadiya surveyed the village as it could be seen before her. Most of the warders had not returned from the Monbriths, which was either a good sign, or a very bad one. Ibram stretched his neck to the left and right, trying to relieve the strain. Ladyship swept her hair over her shoulder and tugged on the buttons which affixed her cloak underneath the collar of her coat.

"No," she said.

"Then what other project can there be?" he asked.

"Do you ever place bets with your Amota Viran?" she asked.

Despite himself, Ibram chuckled. "Sometimes."

The amitai held a betting pool on almost everything that happened in the sect, and sometimes outside of it. It was an excellent way to see what local gossip was doing the rounds up the living mountain. He ducked his head and knocked mud off his boot. He grinned and looked over to see Lady Azadiya considering him.

"What odds do you think he would give on Fontis?" she asked.

He cleared his throat and sobered. They crossed to the other side of the road, and she began the same perusal she had rendered before. Ahead, he could see a hopeful junk seller hurriedly switching out boxes.

"I wouldn't take them," he said finally.

Lady Azadiya twitched her clothes out of the way of a passing villager. "Nor I," she said. "A judge whose mind turns directly to the old cruelties is one who must be managed carefully and from several directions at once."

"So this project of Ahksell's is in addition to our main reason for being here?" he asked.

"Leverage and connections may only take our cause so far," she said.

"A walled garden still lets in air," he repeated from memory.

Ladyship made a face. "That sounds so much better in Merrilian."

They walked past the junk seller who had an entire box of wriggling mulch beetles in cages next to chipped urns with identical 'wear and tear' on their painted curves. Lady Azadiya smiled at the merchant, but refused his offer of a necklace made from dangling wooden beads and yarn tassels.

"Has your Amota spoken to you?" she asked suddenly.

Ibram nodded cautiously. "Yes, Ladyship."

"But you don't think much of his conversation," she noted.

Ibram sighed. "He asked me if I knew how to hitch a horse to a carriage," he said.

"Ah, yes." She nodded and glanced at him. "Were you conscientious? Did you take care?"

Ibram looked quickly away and bit down the corner of his mouth to hide his smirk. She laughed, and Ibram grinned down at his shoes. He glanced up and Lady Azadiya was still chuckling. Slowly, he felt his shoulders come down. The prickling lessened at the back of his head.

"He loves that speech," she said. "I think he's given it to at least one person a twelve-day ever since he was your age."

They walked past a man selling bolts of fabric. Ibram was surprised, fabric seemed too expensive to be sold in the market like that. He paused. Amota Lakum was in the waning of his forties. No one had ever told him exactly how old Lady Azadiya was, and Ibram had asked often as a child. But if she had known Amota Lakum when he was in his twenties, that was another kettle of quash entirely.

Not that he had thought Ladyship was really in her thirties. After all, alchemists often didn't look their age after a certain secretive point. Ahksell hadn't reached it; he still looked twenty-three. Would there come a day when Ibram was old and grey and Ahksell was still young and spry? Lady Azadiya had sailed onwards while Ibram thought. He cleared his throat. If she wasn't going to make much of the announcement, then neither was he.

"He's been using that speech for that long?" he asked as he caught up. "You'd think it would need to be more effective."

She leaned her head left and then right. "It lands on fertile or fallow ground accordingly."

"And as I told him, I am not a horse, and neither are the Monbriths."

She snickered. "But all this thick air, you know, it makes people with something to hide as skittish as any rouncey. Get you up in the mountains and you either learn to bear it well, or you faint."

The back of Ibram's head began to pulse in time with his heartbeat. He swallowed and licked his lips. "I'm not saying I deserve to know everything all at once," he said quietly, with an eye to the traders. "But I can't do my job if I don't have all the information, can I?"

"And no more can anyone, Ibram," she said with a practiced

eyebrow raise. He felt his cheeks grow hot. "Which is perhaps not the larger point?"

"I can be trusted," he said. "I don't have to be kept in the dark."

"No one can know everything," she said. "Do you think Lakum knows?"

"I think you're going to tell him," he said. "Ladyship."

She nodded slowly. "You are correct, to be sure."

"Then by what right is whatever Ahksell had to say kept from me?"

"Are you entitled to Ahksell's every thought?" she asked. "Or mine?"

He twisted his neck to try and alleviate the ache. "No, Ladyship."

She lifted her hands and let them fall again. "Just so."

"But when not knowing stops me doing my duty?"

"I decide that, as your employer," she said.

"Am I not to be trusted then? You think I'd go around telling everyone something you wish me to keep secret?" He wrapped his hand around the back of his head. He dug his fingers into his twitching muscles; it helped only a little.

Lady Azadiya put her hand at her waist. "Trust does not always enter into my deliberations, Ibram," she said plainly. "I have a different job for Ahksell to do in Fontis, and it doesn't concern you."

"So we are in Fontis for some private concern and nothing to do with the—" She raised her finger and Ibram lowered his voice. "Nothing to do with the counterfeiting fugitive in our midst?"

"Rustam is not in our midst, that's the trouble," she pointed out.

Ibram took a very deep breath and then let it out, and dropped his hand to his side. "That isn't the point, Ladyship."

"I'm sure I have a letter to the contrary," she said.

Ibram stopped walked. *"Ladyship."*

Lady shifted her gar from her right to her left hand. "Ibram, a certain motivation is required from my agents. As of now, there is no need for you to have knowledge of every aspect of this tangle we find ourselves in," she said.

"Bah," he said.

She scoffed and pinched her fingers; he felt a distinct tug on his earlobe. "But," she said, "either way, this is not what I kept you out here to speak about."

He glanced around. The traders were clearly watching Ladyship's every move. "What then?" he asked.

"Tell me about Satya Monbrith," she said. "Leave nothing out this time."

"I never did so deliberately," he said.

"Your situational awareness is lacking," Lady Azadiya said. "It troubles me."

"I did well enough for you before," he grumbled.

"Yes, we'll have to sort through your previous reports," she said. "To see what you missed there as well."

He paused, and a rock took the opportunity to sink low in his belly. She nodded and turned back to view the remaining line of stalls. One of the merchants across the way was closing up her shutters and bolting up her service shelf.

Ibram rubbed a hand over his chest and his fingers bumped against the side of his sect buckle. He'd always been meant to take service there. If Lady Azadiya was truly upset at his behavior then the unthinkable suddenly became possible. He looked at her back, but the question "Where would I be reassigned?" would not come out of his mouth.

"But what if I want to know what Ahksell said to you?" he asked instead.

She snorted. "You are welcome to try and inveigle the truth from Ahksell whenever you wish, though I doubt either of you are in the mood for confidences."

"I am," Ibram pushed his shoulders back. "He might not be."

"Possibly," she allowed. "Now, Satya."

Ibram nodded though she could not see it, and focused his mind. This time he tried to call up everything he had previously thought concerning the young mistress, and not simply what he believed Lady Azadiya would find pertinent. She turned to face him while he thought.

"She's pretty. She's competent. She's...quiet," was all he could think of at first. "Or I thought so. When I took Rustam's statement, she insisted on being in the room, but never spoke a word. She only held his hand, which I was grateful for because it was clear he'd been knocked off his posts by finding the body."

"Still?"

He nodded. "Even days later, which is when I was ordered to Fontis. Her mother did most of the talking elsewise, and I...got the sense that she wasn't pleased with my visit, but that Satya didn't much care. When she did speak, it was all business. She wasn't interested in me at all."

Lady Azadiya's eyebrows twitched. "Which is why you thought her too smart for her surroundings?"

He huffed a chuckle and glanced about himself. It felt strangely exposing to be speaking so freely out in the open as they were. "No, it was because of how quick she was. If she was with her mother, business ruled most of the conversation—Master Tolk's routines and habits, you know the like. But I caught the children in the..." He blinked rapidly, and trailed off.

"Yes?" Lady Azadiya prompted.

"I forgot," he said. "I went to the stables to check on Gilma, and I could hear them in the hayloft above. She was running the boys through one of those lessons that Bedris puts out for a picaio. You know, for the noble house tutors."

Lady Azadiya nodded slowly. "A strange family," she murmured. "To hide they were learning when the Speaker and the Advisor stress education."

"Do they? I thought they just taught people how to read and then sent them back to their slot in the ordained...thing. Place on earth."

"Speech brought the Vissilians out of serfdom," Lady Azadiya said. "The Wheelmaker and The Warrior did the rest, as I recall."

"Just speech?" Ibram asked. "I thought the plague did most of the work for that."

"A plague, a famine..." She waved her hand. "The speeches came after, but these little things all pile up. But learning was what gained the Sovereign Twins' favor."

Ibram sighed. "Then she was hiding that they were learning from an alchemist preceptory? Doesn't make sense, does it?"

Lady Azadiya nodded. "Entirely possible given their mother's supposed feelings about the sect."

The vendor who Ibram had seen switching out their wares at Ladyship's approach leaned over his boxes of goods and waved at him. Ibram averted his eyes. The trader began yelling, "Silver! Gold and stones from the Summer Sea! Fit for nobility!"

"So a rebellion then," Ibram said and hunched his shoulders. "Satya gains a foothold against her mother's authority by learning from folk her mother hates and takes her brothers along with her."

"Does she seem the type?" Lady Azadiya leaned on her gar, and watched Ibram's face. Ibram shook his head and then nodded. He sighed.

"Rustam didn't appear the sort to run," he said. "One secret rebellion begets another. What if he was ordered to? What if Satya told him to flee?"

Lady Azadiya paused for a moment and considered the thought. "It remains outside of her best interests," she said finally. "If Rustam had not run, then we likely would never have known about the counterfeiting. At least, not until it was far too late."

Ibram flushed and swallowed heavily. "Master Tolk did die of natural causes," he said.

"And it seems clear that one or all of them cleaned up after him," she said. She gazed across the village square without truly seeing it. The wind picked up the open folds of her coat and cloak and sent them ruffling to either side. "No, whatever the motive, Rustam's courage failed him. When you visited with Yilka the Green what did she say?"

It was such a Western thing to say that Ibram almost laughed. Vissilians worshipped and Merrilians visited, which was really just worship under a different name. He touched his belt wallet where he kept his bells and dice.

"I heard no ringing," he said, "but two of the dice fell white points up."

She nodded. "Not horrible," she said and her eyes began to lose focus again.

"If I may, Ladyship," he asked before he lost her to her thoughts. It was getting chilly. "What does Kivan the Red say?"

She squinted at him in surprise. "I haven't asked him."

"Haven't you, Ladyship?" Surprised, he took a step behind him and cocked his head. "I thought you said he needed answers in this matter."

She waved her hand. "Oh he does, to be sure, but I'm not so far gone I need to stray out of the raven's nest. Catha the Gray has an egg—."

A commotion from the front gate and the shouts of warders covered the rest of Lady Azadiya's answer. They both turned to see the warders begin to scatter, and the remaining merchants hurriedly begin packing away their remaining stock. A caravan of three large carriages drawn by paired reddish-brown horses with perked ears close together on top of their heads ambled down the road into the center of the village. The noise of the carriage sprung wheels was loud against the cobblestones; villagers came out of their homes to watch the progression. As they drew closer, Ibram could see their drivers were agents of the sect like himself, but none were folk he knew. He frowned and looked to Lady Azadiya. She caught his eye and nodded. The Preceptory of Salacia, whose work was the demonic cosmology, had arrived early. Fontis' doom was that much closer to being realized.

The arrival of the Monbriths with their warder escort was almost an afterthought. Commander Osthanes came marching up to Mistress Denrind's front gate in the wake of Fourth Mentors Tikari of Afsoun and Perhara of Salacia along with forty-one of their Attendants, and simply could not compete. The Monbriths were consigned to the anteroom in Mistress Denrind's reception hall, and the commander himself was drawn into conference with Judge E'grard, the headwoman, and a triumvirate of alchemists. Ibram felt for him, truly.

It was some small consolation that Osthanes looked as comfortable as Ibram felt when they all adjourned for dinner. Ibram didn't have much experience in dining in High Vissilian style, but with Lady Azadiya, two other Mentors, a judge and a commander from Delbrite, Mistress Denrind clearly believed it fell to her to represent Fontis' honor and lay out as grand a feast as possible.

From his vantage point, Ibram could see them all without having to turn his head much at all. As Headwoman and hostess, Mistress Denrind occupied the top of the table, while Judge E'grard was placed at her left and Lady Azadiya to her right. Then followed Mentor Perhara, who up the living mountain would have occupied Ladyship's spot, and next to him sat Mentor Tikari, who within the sect would have taken Perhara's seat. Ladyship's title might not have been in use during this predicament, but her noble house made quite the difference outside the Sect of Seven Fires. Mistress Islozia picked at her place setting at the opposite end of the table next to Judge E'grard's assistant.

Ahksell sat next to Commander Osthanes and a few other Attendants were sprinkled about most probably to fill in seats. Ibram, Amota Lakum, and two of the agents who had driven the carriages had been ordered to stand at the walls and act as living statuary along with Warder Kamos and a few of his ilk. They had nothing to do with serving the food, of course, but ancient Vissilian custom required that every guest had someone dedicated to making sure they left the party alive if conversation turned nasty before dessert. No one had ever died in Ibram's memory, but he supposed nobles liked their traditions.

The food came in on wheeled platters, steamy and savory. Ibram could smell the roasted baron of mouflon the servants heaved it past them, glistening in an herbed oil and surrounded by whole baked carrots. His mouth watered, even though he knew there probably wasn't a pepper or spice to be found in that grand hunk of meat. They liked creamy dishes in the middle provinces, like that garlic and soured cream sauce Father favored, or tough meats stewed in wine. The bread was white and came in large rounds. He kept his sigh of hunger behind his teeth; he wasn't eating until his betters had, after all.

He cast a careful eye towards Amota Lakum to his left. They'd all had time for a quick wash, and so his long hair was neatly plaited again. His face was impassive, but his mouth had taken on a decidedly pinched frame. Ama said in the West it was considered rude to eat while others watched, and that everyone ate together to show their strength. The only way to tell who was higher in rank was what table they sat down to. Lady Azadiya didn't seem bothered, but Ibram could only see the side of her face. A servant standing by the cart of food prepared a dish and then wavered, clearly unsure who must be served first: Mistress Denrind, Lady Azadiya, or Judge E'grard.

The servant clutched the steaming plate, and looked beseechingly at her employer. Mistress Denrind coughed uncomfortably and sat up tall in her chair. Ibram's toes tapped in his boots. Would she go the safe route and pick nobility? Or would Mistress Denrind bow to the bureaucratic title and send the dish to the judge? He didn't envy her the choice, even though Ibram knew which decision he would make.

"I'll take that. Thank you, Adgna," Mistress Denrind said. "If you will make the second for Judge E'grard, please?"

She accepted the dish with both hands, and held it while the servant assembled a new plate of food. The servant moved quickly to Mistress Denrind's left side and, at the mistress' nod, they set both plates down at the same time. Ibram bit both his lips together to avoid an unprofessional expression. Not a shabby solution at all, both higher parties served at once, with deference paid to her ladyship in being served by the mistress of the house.

"You keep a good table, Mistress," Lady Azadiya said, and speared a small piece of boiled potato, sauced with something green, on her two-pronged fork. She ate it, and inclined her head again.

"Thank you, Mentor Hobon." Mistress Denrind waved the small group of servers hovering at the opposite end of the dining room forward, so other guests could eat. Some small movement caught Ibram's eye. He looked up, and saw Judge E'grard's face twitch again before it smoothed into politeness. Ibram's eyebrows drew together.

"Do you enjoy Vissilian food, Mentor Hobon?" Judge E'grard asked.

Mistress Denrind's eyes flicked between them nervously. Lady Azadiya picked up her glass of wine, and took a sip. Immediately, Commander Osthanes raised his up as well and tossed down a solid third. He must have been waiting for her permission like a courser at the post. A servant hurried over to refill his glass. On the other side of the table, Warder Kamos winced.

"I do, Judge," Lady Azadiya said. "I find good hearty middle kingdoms food to be quite distinctive, do not you?"

His mouth worked for a moment, and then the judge picked up his knife and two-pronged fork, and began to cut his mouflon into smaller pieces. "Yes, indeed," he said. "I must say, I am glad to see you don't find it difficult to deal with all our formality."

He raised his knife and fork a bit higher as if to show them to her, and then returned to his meal. The back of Ibram's head tensed. Westerners ate with their hands and the occasional spoon or knife as needed. It was considered a sign of trust in family and friends. Vissilians ate rarely with their fingers. Across from him, Ahksell shifted in his chair; his lip curled slightly.

"Ah— We are not called the garden provinces for nothing," Mistress Denrind declared with a slightly nervous laugh.

"And, of course, we who live in the Sect of Seven Fires are very fortunate that our surroundings provide us with such foods as these," Mentor Perhara said. He was dressed like a rich merchant in a green velvet tunic and green and gold breeches. His tightly curled puffball of hair barely wavered when he nodded.

"The soil is very good here," Mistress Denrind said, relaxing a little. "The rest of the province as well, but I do believe our valleys grow the best produce anywhere in Vissilia."

Mentor Perhara nodded, and Ibram despaired. He was trapped. Trapped in a room full of people making idle chatter about agricultural products.

"It's the volcanic soil," Mentor Tikari said. She had turned out to be a medium-sized woman, stocky in her plain green gambeson and grey wrapped trousers. Her fine brown hair was clipped to her shoulders and held back by wooden clasps. "You rain enough destruction down on a place, and after the plants and animals rot, you're bound to have something new pop up in its place."

Ibram almost snorted, but caught himself and slowly breathed out. Amota Lakum shifted his position on the wall. Ladyship sighed delicately.

"It's the way of things, is it not, Tikari?" she asked as she ate.

"It is," Mentor Tikari said, and sawed into her meat like it was a block of wood.

"And of course it brings up the problem of weeding," Lady Azadiya continued, "for where there is good soil there are always opportunists. I've seen so many upstart plants blown in on an ill wind to this valley only to be razed to the ground by our farmers." She shook her head and Ibram heard her laugh. "I'm quite inspired by their tenacity. You're from quite a ways away yourself, Judge, are you not? Aerdhalat, wasn't it?"

The judge took a sip of wine as if it was vinegar. "I am," he said. "I trained in the law at the university there, but my family is of Nivenian stock. We have no claim to a house, of course, but we might be said to be a very old family."

Ladyship's head bobbed. "Ah, but then are not we all? Tell me, Mistress Denrind, how long has your family lived in Fontis?"

"Oh," Mistress Denrind swallowed her food, and blinked rapidly. "Well, I would say forever, really, Mentor. We haven't always been in charge of the bureaucracy, of course, but we've been here since...well, at least six generations or so."

Mentor Perhara turned his head and angled it so that Ibram could see the side of his face. He had a short beard but his cheeks and jaw were smooth and brown. He wrapped his arm over the back of his chair, and drank his wine with the other. To anyone else at the table, it probably looked sloppy, but Ibram thought his posture seemed more studied than that.

"And Commander Osthanes," Perhara said. "Are you from Delbrite originally? Whenever I send an agent down to the city, they bring back such fascinating stories of you."

Commander Osthanes had been steadily eating his dinner like a man marching to his doom. He looked up at this remark, and his jaw briefly jutted out. He swallowed, and licked his teeth behind his lips. Next to him, Ahksell went briefly wide-eyed and then began studying the vegetables on his plate. He poked something green suspiciously.

"Warders are forbidden to serve in their home territories," Osthanes said in his parade ground bark. "To discourage corruption."

"A sound philosophy," Mentor Perhara said. He raised his glass in Osthanes' direction and then took a sip. "Do you find it works in the long term?"

"What about after you've served?" Ahksell asked when Osthanes tensed. "I mean, how long have you been stationed in Delbrite, Commander?"

The Commander's shoulders softened. "Fifteen years, Attendant."

Ahksell nodded. "Does that mean you could return to your family when you retire?"

Osthanes answered him, but Ibram stopped paying attention. There was always something about Ahksell that made whatever he said sound open and honest. Ibram strongly suspected it was because Ahksell never really said anything he didn't mean or asked a question he didn't want to know the answer to. It was ridiculously effective, though, it had to be admitted. Ama had despaired of Ibram himself ever learning how to do it. She'd taught him to sound encouraging and a bit sly instead. Well, to be sure, Katka said he sounded like a man desperate for a free drink, but what did she know?

He looked over the diners at the table. The other Attendants were quietly talking to themselves over their dinners. Mistress Islozia and the Judge's assistant ate silently next to each other. Mentor Tikari was signaling for another glass of wine, and Perhara also nodded at Osthanes. He held his wine glass out without looking and the servant refilled it.

"Is that where you devised the idea?" Mistress Denrind suddenly asked, and something brittle in her tone caught Ibram's attention.

"No, Mistress, I did not," Judge E'grard said. His pale face had turned a little red as dinner went on. "As a magistrate under Her Gracious Majesty, I pay no attention to firetales and nor should you. The basis for my sanctioning of Fontis was sound legal precedent. The traditional punishments are no less viable today simply because they have fallen into some disuse."

"Your provisional sanctioning," Lady Azadiya said lightly. She sipped her wine.

Judge E'grard's nostrils flared in annoyance. Mistress Denrind had sat back in her chair at his rebuke, but her spine grew strong soon enough.

"Then you will put your reasoning into your court summary?" she asked. She swallowed and looked down at her full plate as if nauseated for a moment. "I must confess, I found the judgement quite sudden."

"Oh, but Judge E'grard hasn't made a judgement yet," Lady Azadiya said brightly. She, of course, had no trouble with her appetite. "Forgive me if I am wrong, but the trial of Harken Tolk's discovery cannot be completed without the First Finder, is that not so?"

"It is, Mentor," the judge said. He stabbed his fork into his food.

Lady Azadiya nodded. "A man insensibly ill cannot be called to task for his inability to rise from his bed."

"Indeed," Judge E'grard said. "Though there is no such evidence in this matter."

"But you do agree there might be any number of reasons for someone to run away," Lady Azadiya said. "And those might sway your decision on his return."

"I find the law has no trouble ascertaining the honor of a criminal's choices when they are confronted by its inevitable outcome," Judge E'grard said. "The needs of the Empire often outweigh the cost of any single personal loss."

Lady Azadiya's head tilted. She took a small drink of her wine, and set the glass down next to her half-empty plate. Ibram couldn't see her face, but he dearly wished to. Across the way from him, Warder Kamos' mustache was twitching like he was biting his lips.

"And if Rustam is found?" Lady Azadiya asked. "What then?"

"Alia," Judge E'grard snapped. "The relevant section."

All eyes at the suddenly quiet table turned to the judge's assistant, who dropped her fork to the table with a clatter against the clay plate. She swallowed her food and dabbed the corners of her mouth with her fingers. Then, she sat up tall and stared in front of her.

"The Acts of Law, subsection seventy-nine, created in the year of His Gracious Majesty Diarmit the Just," she announced as they watched. "Whosoever finds said body must present themselves at the appointed time to the Courts Civil or Provincial and provide evidence as to the state of the deceased upon discovery. If the First Finder does not appear, all attempts will be made to recover them. A provisional punishment shall be laid at the door of their community which has so failed in its duty to instill proper values within its denizens that the guilt must therefore be shared by all. Said punishment shall be measured in accordance with the disputation of the body, the length of the disappearance, and the needs of the empire."

Mentor Perhara nodded and sipped his wine. "Very well remembered," he said. "I do so admire an adherence to the letter of a contract."

"It is not a contract," Judge E'grard snapped, while his assistant returned to her meal. "It is the law."

"So the law provides an example for us all," Lady Azadiya said.

"It provides direction, Mentor Hobon," Judge E'grard corrected her severely. His cheeks had turned ruddy. "Loyalty to the law is loyalty to the Empire."

"No one could doubt Fontis' loyalty to the Empire!" Mistress Denrind declared in alarm.

Judge E'grard ignored her. "And in the case of a missing First Finder," he continued, "we must find not merely the one who ran, but those around him who allowed him to run to be at fault. A community which sets a lax example to its members, and perhaps, even now encourages a looseness of behavior leads to social unrest within its province."

"But is not the law an imperial contract?" Mentor Perhara asked. "Our entire judicial code, for instance, was it not negotiated with the Divine by the royal family and then upheld by the Vissilian Empire in return for prosperity?"

Judge E'grard leaned forward over his plate, and began a lengthy argument that brought in several historical documents Ibram had seen moldering on a shelf in Amota Evren's underground lair. He settled himself back as Mentor Perhara and the Judge settled into a lively argument. The rest of them ate and spoke around the two combatants as the night continued, but Ibram noticed Lady Azadiya observing the discussion closely.

$\maltese$ 13 $\maltese$

Ibram kicked his heels against the wall and glanced to his left where Amota Lakum and Ahksell stood. More waiting. As if dinner hadn't provided them all with a surfeit of it, after Mistress Denrind had brought out caffa Ibram wasn't allowed to drink and small rounds of cakes iced to a smooth white finish and topped with berries that he could only smell, the entire dinner party had been dispersed to their rooms for the night. Lady Azadiya and her fellow Mentors had been given rooms near where Judge E'grard and Commander Osthanes slept in Mistress Denrind's family courtyard.

Ibram had been tasked with leading the agents and the attendants back to the Monbriths' property to sleep, as it was the only place left in the village large enough to accommodate them. He'd had to give up his room for senior attendants and bed down next to Amota Lakum with the juniors and the agents, packed like caskfish in the large common sleeping area. Ahksell had been allowed to keep his own room, of course, but he'd opened it up to someone he knew amongst the attendants.

In the morning, Ibram had hoped for new orders, or perhaps a suddenly discovered trail of clues to follow, but he had no such luck. Instead, he arrived back to Mistress Denrind's manor to find the pack of them all shut away in Mistress Denrind's office for a situation report. He sighed.

When he bent his head towards the door between him and Amota Lakum, he could hear the occasional raised voice, but not what was being said. Across from them in the small hallway stood two agents, four Attendants, and Warder Kamos, who looked like he'd rather be on pole duty in Delbrite, fishing drunks out of the river, than stuck outside Judge E'grard's office door.

Ahksell stood away from Amota Lakum and gestured with his left hand down the hallway. He inclined his head towards his fellow Attendants. The oldest stepped away from her colleagues and nodded.

"I'll be back in a second," Ahksell said, and then led the other alchemists away from the door. They grouped together with their backs to the rest of the party at the far end of the hallway, well out of earshot. It looked a bit like a group of lost travelers consulting a map.

Ibram crossed his arms over his chest and leaned the back of his head against the wall. "I don't suppose anyone brought a tica deck?"

One of the strange agents, a short woman in a red gown and brown leather bodice with her hair taped around her skull with a strip of white cloth, sniffed and turned her head away. Ibram shrugged. He'd discovered through a long and painful night that she snored and it went a long way in making him unconcerned for her opinion of him. He glanced around. Instead of torches, Mistress Denrind had installed dripless oil lanterns that cast a steadier yellow light down the entire corridor. Someone inside the office made an exclamation, but he still couldn't hear what was being said in the meeting.

"Kamos, you stand on watch often, you must have something to while away the time," he said.

"I often think of my responsibilities," Warder Kamos replied. "Silently."

"Oh, I as well," Ibram said. He nodded and let himself relax further against the wall. "Yes, many are the times I've been placed outside Ladyship's door and counted my manifold responsibilities within the sect." He began ticking them off on his fingers. "The escorting, the standing, how many loaves of bread I'm owed a year..."

That, at least, coaxed what might have appeared to be amusement in a lesser man from Warder Kamos' wide moon-shaped face. Ibram glanced down the hall, but the Attendants were ignoring them. He turned back and caught Amota Lakum's eye.

Amota Lakum pursed his lips and contemplated his boots. "Your boredom and your belly, Ibram? What heavy thoughts you bear."

Ibram shrugged as best he could given his position. "But I never complain, Uncle."

"Yet you deny your employer her proper title," the other strange agent said. "An agent needs to show more respect in front of outsiders."

This one was a man, old enough for salt to pepper his dark hair, with bowed legs like a plainsmen. He was lean and rangy, and dressed in leather from shoulders to toes. His clothes told Ibram either he came from money or saved a great deal more than Ibram.

Warder Kamos didn't appear to enjoy being spoken of in front of his face. Few people did, but the knowledge presented an opportunity. Ibram cocked his head and smiled. "Not all of us have the honor of working for the nobility," he said in his best impression of Ladyship's most polite voice. "It's no slight against you for forgetting what recognition is due to Lady Azadiya."

Bowed Legs came off his patch of wall with an ugly cast to his already plain face. He stabbed the air in front of Ibram's chest, and Warder Kamos cleared his throat. Bowed Legs ignored him, perhaps he hadn't spent much time listening to warders signal their displeasure.

"I serve the Fourth Mentor of Salacia," he said, and this time he poked Ibram directly over his sect brooch. "And he needs no border-land title to make himself feel better about his lack of skill."

From the corner of his eye, Ibram could see Amota Lakum frown and step forward. Before he could be taken hold of, Ibram grabbed Bowed Legs' fingers where they poked him, and bent them back. Ibram stood taller; the other man hissed and threw his weight against him, throwing them both into the wall.

"Stop this!" Warder Kamos exclaimed. "Right now, the pair of you."

He reached out and shoved between them with his back to Ibram. Bowed Legs raised his fist; his friend pulled him back with her hand on his chest. Warder Kamos pointed at him and swung wide so he could include Ibram as well.

"I'll have no raised voices or violence in here," he said sternly. Even his mustache bristled. "There's enough to do without finding cells to hold more folk, and I swear to the Wanderer I'll shackle the first one who so much as disturbs Commander Osthanes' state of mind."

"Uxio?" One of the other Attendants called out. "What's going on over there?"

The two agents wavered in their discontent silently. Then Agent Snoring, possibly Uxio or merely the spokeswoman of the pair, craned her neck to see her employer and gave a short bow. "Just a bit of restlessness," she said. "Nothing to worry about now, Attendant Sarausk."

Attendant Sarausk put his hand on his hip and leaned on his gar. "Come here, both of you."

The agents obeyed while Ibram leaned back against the wall and re-crossed his arms. Warder Kamos frowned at him, but Ibram made sure his own expression held nothing but innocent amiability. Wader Kamos snorted hard enough to disturb his mustache.

"What was that in aid of?" he asked.

Ibram shook his head. "Nothing but rudeness on his end," he said. "We work for different clients. You know how an arm-for-hire in good pocket can get."

"Suppose I do," Warder Kamos said and nodded slowly. The sounds of a quiet, but intense interrogation could be heard from the other end of the corridor. He shook his head and stepped away. "I would have thought you sect folk stuck together."

"Not necessarily," Ibram said quickly, before the opportunity died. "They're from Salacia, which gives me the shivers."

"Now, Ibram," Amota Lakum said. "They're as reputable as any other preceptory."

"Who would you rather have dinner with, Uncle?" Ibram asked with half an eye towards Kamos. He kept his voice low so the men would have to step closer. "Someone from Baran who'll talk your ear off about the correct amount of candles to light for a wedding contract, or one from Salacia, who knows which type of bezoar to rip out of an animal so a demon will sit down for a cup of shay with you?"

"Depends on what I've asked them to dinner for, I would expect," Amota Lakum said.

Warder Kamos didn't laugh, but Ibram could tell he wanted to. He turned his gaze sideways and then away. Ibram picked his thumbnail clean.

"Have you ever seen a sanctioning?" he asked, and moved on to his next fingernail.

He heard a hesitation, the little jingle of chain armor, but then, "I'm not as old as that, thank you Ibram," Amota Lakum said.

Kamos chuckled. "Don't expect that many people have, either."

Ibram looked up. "That's not what Madji Anlines says."

Kamos focused on him, in that hunting sort of attention a warder developed after a couple of years' service. "Who's that?" he asked.

Ibram sighed and hooked his thumbs around his belt. "I don't know, really," he said. "Some kind of trader. She was spreading a story about someplace called Mandibrite and how the warders locked people in their homes and then walled off the town, or something."

"Oh yes?" Amota Lakum asked. "When did that happen?"

Ibram shrugged. "Said her grandfather was there...or possibly her father, actually."

Warder Kamos glared in thought, and Ibram waited for the wheels to stop turning. He'd been wanting to speak to Mistress Anlines since her spectacle in the shay shop. There was something intense about her, like she had more invested in the story she had told than a typical boaster. Kolesar had said she took her own product. Something like a brewery? Most homes that could made their own beer, though.

"I'm told they're a horrible trial, though," Ibram started talking again. He'd let the thought temper in the back of his mind for a bit. "She made it sound horrible. She's probably moved on now, though. I know you've been letting traders out upon a search."

"Now there, you're wrong," Warder Kamos said. "We've had orders to stop everything coming out of Fontis, even traders."

So she was most likely still in the village. Ibram wondered which carriage was hers. Did old Madji have a stall, or merely a wagon to transport goods? If she smelled like a distillery... Ibram dug the toe of his boot into the floor while Amota Lakum made small talk with

Warder Kamos. There was always a market for spirits, usually for preserving and drinking. Mistress Madji Anlines might be a dramseller. Ibram blinked. Mistress Monbrith had said she and Rustam had picked up a shipment from their dramseller the night before he'd left.

"Really?" Amota Lakum asked a bit more loudly.

Ibram tilted his head towards him, but didn't look up. Could that have been her? Why would that have mattered, though? If it was, Rustam had probably told her—he'd told everyone—about the upcoming tribunal, but nothing had been decided then. A scary firetale about what happened if he didn't go to court wouldn't have made Rustam run, rather the reverse.

Warder Kamos resettled his sword in his belt. Ibram glanced up and caught Amota Lakum's evaluating face. He stood tall and shook off his thoughts for the moment.

"There'll be trouble," Kamos said. "But then there always is in such unsettled business as this. The Commander doesn't like it."

Amota Lakum chuckled. "Can't say I disagree with him."

"Well, he signed up for the trouble when he went into the cohort, didn't he?" Ibram asked.

"Did he, then?" Warder Kamos' voice grew the slightest hint of a bite to it. Ibram fought to hide his wince, and hoped instead he looked merely like an embarrassed young man. He had worked in Delbrite long enough to remember Ibram and Osthanes' earlier encounters, hadn't he? Amota Lakum tucked one hand beneath his chin; he looked smug.

Ibram spread his hands. "I can appreciate a man's abilities even when we act at cross-purposes," he said. "And now when we are all after the same prize, I find myself grateful for Commander Osthanes' doggedness even more."

"Surely so," Warder Kamos said and looked off down to where the Attendants were still speaking.

Amota Lakum took in a breath, and then shook his head. Ibram shrugged and raised his hands. "Actually, I was wondering... I don't suppose you've had to keep people out as much as you've had to make sure they've stayed in, have you?"

Warder Kamos' mouth thinned beneath his mustache. "We've managed, thank you."

"Of course, of course," Ibram said. "I was just thinking there are a lot of freeholders under Fonts' jurisdiction."

He nodded grudgingly. "True enough," he said, and then leaned in a bit. Ibram obliging leaned in a bit as well. "Commander's not a hard man, you know."

Ibram shook his head. "I've always thought so. A man of tempered justice, really."

"Well." Kamos nodded a little. He looked quite tired up close, and a bit less sour than he was resigned. "We've had to redraw the search line, you see. And marshal our forces."

"Not even a circuit judge can command the whole Cohort of Peace from Delbrite," Ibram said. "Nor should he."

Kamos grunted his approval. "The Advisor Herself would have to tell him that, and in writing. Commander's had to be very clear his remit is capturing the fugitive rather than chasing down every fool claiming their land's beholden to Itol, and he'll not change his goal until the judge's own time limit is past."

Ibram nodded, and then leaned away. His neck was killing him; it felt like puzzle pieces badly interlocked. "Good heart in that man," he said, keeping a careful watch on Kamos' face. "I don't suppose you're any closer to finding the Monbrith boy?"

Kamos' body sagged beneath his armor before he regained his posture. "Not to my mind," he said. "He's not in the forest around the village, and he hasn't circled back home."

"A pity," Ibram said. He jiggled his left heel. "I'd love nothing more."

"Don't think it would save them much, now," Kamos said and then paused. He eyed Ibram and Amota Lakum, and frowned heavily. He put a hand on his plain belt pouch and Ibram heard coins clink together. "You know about the new business?"

Amota Lakum nodded. "We do indeed," he said. "Ibram here uncovered it."

Kamos' face turned blank in surprise, and then he nodded in appreciation. "Good work," he said, and Ibram bowed shortly. "But it sealed their fate, didn't it?"

Ibram breathed in slowly and then out again. "Might get us closer to finding him," he said.

"Well, now we've got this problem I expect there won't be enough warders to keep up the search. Might have to turn the bloodhounds over to the villagers," Kamos said. He shrugged. "Depends on what the commander works out with his honor."

Ibram chewed on a corner of his mouth. "I guess so."

Footsteps fell out to his right. Ibram turned to find the Attendants had broken ranks and were now returning to their former positions. The two agents trailed behind them. Warder Kamos stepped back to allow Ahksell past him.

Ibram picked at a loose thread on his belt wallet. He hadn't figured on the judge would recall his cohort of peace to keep the traders and villagers in Fontis, or rather, to keep their money within the village. E'grard couldn't simply confiscate all that coinage, not without a riot on his hands. Ibram chuckled quietly. So he kept the warders close to keep order, and in doing so made certain that no one would be able to find Rustam and plead for leniency, or at the very least, a more direct punishment.

It almost felt as if Judge E'grard wanted to make an example of Fontis, no matter how he managed to do it. His comments about alchemists weren't directly confronting, but taken together with Fourth Mentor Perhara's early arrival, their impact grew larger in Ibram's thoughts. He knocked his head lightly against the wall. If Mentor Tikari said she'd found alchemastered coins that put the sword to any hope for Fontis, but if she did not, would E'grard accept the ruling, or demand another sect review her findings? Ibram's shoulders began inching up his neck; he stretched them back down again.

It had been two days before Satya's letter had reached Ibram through the sect. The third day, he had been given the letter and reassigned back to Fontis with Ahksell in tow. The fourth he'd spent in Fontis, and the fifth and six had been lost to delivering messages and finding out about the counterfeiting. Of all of that time, only speaking with Katka and Father could be described as progress, and they had a mere six days left to recover Rustam. The boy could already be in Delbrite by now, and then he'd be completely out of reach.

Across the doorway, Ahksell fidgeted with his gar, turning it around in his hands. Ibram watched his fingers move against the wood. There was another problem. An ache built up in the back of his throat, and Ibram swallowed it free.

He supposed he was being foolish. Amota Lakum was correct: Ahksell outranked him. Lady Azadiya was also right, he wasn't entitled to Ahksell's every thought. But even still, not knowing lay at the heart of every problem Ibram had encountered in Fontis up to this situation, where all the players stood in an office and Ibram lingered outside it. He narrowed his eyes. Ladyship had said he lacked motivation. Well, if he wasn't to be told, if he was not worth being *trusted*, then he would have to find out for himself. Knowledge was the best shield, as Ama always said.

He studied the tips of his leather boots. No one had mentioned Attendant Serisan—not that he could be certain he had seen her in the crowd—but a woman who looked very much like her was in Fontis, and most probably could not leave. Ahksell had gone back up the mountain especially to see her. He had then claimed he needed to speak with Lady Azadiya privately. About Serisan? She could have been teaching the Monbrith children under their mother's nose, or providing the lessons secretly. Ibram's eyebrows raised. She would also have some part of the skills necessary to teach a budding alchemaster as well, intentionally or not.

Bedris was a kind of catch-all preceptory, full of generalists and perfectly happy to admit the lack of distinction. Naturally, there was overlap in each one of the preceptories within the Sect of Seven Fires. All alchemists needed a solid grounding in the essentials before proving themselves equal to their specializations, but no one said so in polite company. He looked up and studied the two possible Uxios sulking in front of him. Maybe...no, starting one fight was enough for now.

Ibram bent his head again. From the corner of his eye, he saw Ahksell look at him, but he ignored it. Bedris created all the lessons, taught most subjects and managed the learners for the entire sect.

They... Ibram dredged up his hazy childhood schooling. They refined the mind so that it purified the soul to...do something.

He raised his chin and sighed. Perhaps Ladyship was right, and his memory was failing him. The underground archival room lurked in his future. He'd never had this trouble on the road before. At least, he didn't believe he had. Around him, the Attendants were starting to grow restless. He could see it in their shuffling feet and sidelong looks at each other, but if they'd wanted to continue their secret conversations, then they shouldn't have returned to Ibram's side of the corner in the first place.

He turned so that he leaned against the wall on his left shoulder, and crossed his arms. "Attendant Solari," he said. "Do you have a moment to answer a question?"

Ahksell blinked rapidly and then smiled. "Of course!"

"What is the Preceptory of Bedris' watchword?"

Ahksell's grin fell in one corner. "Their what?"

Ibram waved his hand. "Their, uh, motto, their rallying cry, the explanation of what they do."

"Why do you want to know?" Bowed Legged Uxio asked. Female Uxio shushed him, but he persisted. "Is this really the moment for trivia?"

Ibram rolled his eyes, but otherwise ignored him. "I thought I saw Attendant Serisan out in the market today," he said. "The question just came to my mind."

Ahksell's eyebrows drew tightly together. "I didn't see her."

"Is she the village's tutor?" A short Attendant with round green eyes asked. "Are they still holding classes in the middle of all this?"

Ahksell drew himself out of his semi-habitual slouch and gripped his gar tightly. His shoulders suddenly took up a great deal of space in the hallway. "Attendant Serisan was recalled as soon as the judge laid down his preliminary verdict," he said. "That's why I had to visit her up the living mountain."

"So she isn't in the market," Ibram said.

"No, she is not."

Ibram shrugged. "Just thought I saw her."

"You didn't," Ahksell said.

Ibram opened his mouth, but one of the other Attendants chose their moment to speak up. "You give your agents great freedom, Ahksell," she said. Her hair was a shoulder-length light brown held back by Northern-style bejeweled clasps, and her gar was of some type of dark wood that shown with a slick stickiness which did not appear natural.

Ibram swallowed his first retort, and then his second for good measure. Sadly, his third was no better, so he merely bowed and settled for rising without waiting for her to curl her hands. The skin around her eyes creased, but that was the limit of her expression.

"Agents contracted with Yseult are required to have the ability to think on their own," Ahksell said. "There's nothing wrong with a lively conversation."

Attendant Clasps drew breath to speak, but the office door opened, and she was forced to keep her breath to cool her quash. The whole pack of them moved back down the hallway to clear space for the Mentors exiting the office. Ibram shuffled to the right away from the threshold.

Fourth Mentor Perhara left first, walking lightly but with purpose. His gar was stained a rich brown. His puffball of tightly curled black hair waved as he walked briskly forward and snapped the fingers of his free hand. Both Uxios and three of the Attendants bustled after him.

He was either walking so quickly because Tikari had found alchemastering and now they were all to be put to the sword, or because she had not and now he had to find a spot in the stables to sleep for the night before anyone else did. It was impossible to tell from the brief bland glimpse he'd had of Mentor Perhara's composure. Ibram cleared back a step from the doorway as Fourth Mentor Tikari exited next. She was medium-sized and stocky, with short brown hair and sharp brown eyes set in a face made primarily of angles, as if Laumye the Blue had birthed her from a pile of pottery shards. The remaining attendant, a man with miniature braids caught at intervals by large carved beads, bowed his head. She waved at him irritably, and took a look about herself.

Ibram stood away from the wall as did Ahksell and Amota Lakum, and even Warder Kamos jingled in place. Mentor Tikari frowned at them all in equal measure and thrust her pale gar into the hands of her Attendant. She breathed out sharply through her thin nose.

"Which of you is Warder Kamos?" she asked.

For a moment, Ibram found himself glancing about the room as if perhaps Warder Kamos was not the man standing to his left, and he saw the others doing the same. Then, Warder Kamos gingerly raised his hand. Mentor Tikari huffed.

"Is something amiss?" her Attendant asked. He had a middle empire accent like the judge, full of unexpected dips.

She opened her mouth, and Lady Azadiya called strenuously from inside the office. "You three, in here!"

Mentor Tikari paused, still irritated, and jerked her head. "Warder Kamos comes with us," she said as Ibram slipped over the threshold. "I will explain on the way."

Ibram strode over to where Lady Azadiya stood next to Commander Osthanes, both of them pouring over a large map. Someone had done the polite thing and hung her coat and cloak on a small hook in the wall. Her gar lay beside them. The commander had his patience strip out and was rubbing his thumb over the largest rivet. Mistress Denrind and Judge E'grard were sat at the other side of the desk, sharing a stack of papers, and in between both parties, sat an open trunk full of blacksmithing equipment. Ladyship glanced up at his footsteps. He bowed to the room, and came to her side.

"Close the door behind you, Lakum," she said.

Ibram heard it close. "Ladyship," Amota Lakum said.

Ibram's head throbbed. He pressed his lips together, but he couldn't wait for Amota Lakum to ask. Besides, technically he'd already spoken first. "Ladyship, may we know the verdict?" Ibram burst out.

Lady Azadiya raised her head and nodded once. "Master Kelemen was absolutely correct," she said. "Mentor Tikari found no evidence of alchemastering."

Ibram's breath left his body in a rush of relief so strong he surprised himself. He grinned over his shoulder and Ahksell smiled back. Amota Lakum put both his hands on his hips and nodded to the floorboards.

"I should point out," Judge E'grard said as he looked up from the page he was reading, "that Mentor Tikari's report indicated no unlicensed alchemy present in the samples of debased coins which she was given for study from Master Ucalegon's *father*. We will not know her final judgement until Commander Osthanes' warders have confiscated all the suspect currency in Fontis."

Mistress Denrind squirmed in her chair next to him. "I think we should take it as a sign of progress," she said firmly enough, "and a confirmation of the vigilance of the Sect of Seven Fires in their own affairs."

"We shall see," Judge E'grard said and returned to his reading. Ibram turned his head and rolled his eyes. To be sure, E'grard was most likely a sweetie at home.

Lady Azadiya revolved her first three fingers in a circle and then tapped them back on the map. "Here is where you found the campfire, yes, Commander?"

Commander Osthanes nodded. "Yes, Mentor. A full hour away by foot; it was recent, but it was completely cold."

She tsked and he sighed. Ibram bent his neck to see where she was pointing. The map Lady Azadiya was studying so closely was of Fontis and the areas surrounding it. It was not very professionally made, smudges were indiscriminately scattered across the surface, and the village of Itol was obscured by an old shay stain. Small stones had been placed in a wave pattern flowing out from Fontis. Ibram followed the staggered red line marking out the Imperial Boundary and then eyed the rough sketch of the rest of the province to the east.

He nudged one of the little rocks with his fingertip. "Are these the areas cleared by the warders, Ladyship?"

"What sharp eyes you have, Ucalegon," Commander Osthanes said. He sighed sharply and shook his head. "It's those lillia trees."

Lady Azadiya hummed. "Yes, they are inconvenient."

"The new stand the Tyals purchased?" Ibram asked.

Lady Azadiya looked up. "Yes," she said. "How did you know that?"

Ibram shrugged. "Ama told me."

"Why would your mother know about minor nobility buying trees?" Commander Osthanes asked.

Ibram paused, a little taken aback. It wasn't common for Vissilians to speak anything other than their own language in his experience, but perhaps Osthanes had picked up a smattering of Merrilian on the docks. He shook his head.

"My mother takes shay with Mistress Kada Tyal," he said. "When she comes in to the shop, they often have a little chat."

Commander Osthanes grunted. He stabbed a wobbly mass of dots with his first finger. "We were only allowed access to the grove on the second day," he said. "Monbrith could have hidden in there untroubled and then made his escape as we were searching further."

Ibram nodded. "The servant we spoke with denied the charge," he said.

Osthanes grunted. "As far as that goes, they'd swear to anything if it seemed helpful."

Ibram shrugged. "That's as may be, but the trees will still be here if Fontis is sanctioned, won't they?"

"Mistress Tyal will get her harvest," Osthanes agreed grimly.

"So they've no real need to lie," Ibram said.

The lillia trees were on the outskirts of the village. It would have been easy for Rustam to hide there while Mistress Denrind arranged access from the Tyal's representative. Of course, that also meant Rustam would have had to evade the entire village and then slip past any workers already hired to work on the property.

"Did you post guards around the trees in case Rustam did hide in there?" Ahksell asked.

Commander Osthanes very clearly ground his teeth. "When we began our search, I didn't have enough warders to split my forces. We had to call up three detachments from the surrounding waystations."

"Locals would know the area better." Lady Azadiya said, and hummed again in thought. "Still, it's the wrong direction, is it not?"

Commander Osthanes pressed his thumb so hard over the rivet he was rubbing that Ibram could heard his knuckle bone click.

"Commander, did Warder, uh," Ibram paused to dredge the name up from his mind, "Phiri send you my message?"

Commander Osthanes huffed. "He did," he said. "It was just cryptic enough to be mostly useless."

Lady Azadiya leaned back a little in order to observe them both. "What did he ask you?"

Commander Osthanes looked up briefly to meet her eyes and then glanced away. "He asked us to check where else Harken Tolk might have stayed in the province," he allowed with a gruff fringe to his voice. "But then he reminded us that Rustam wasn't to be found on the Monbrith premises and decided to tell us his thoughts on gardening."

She nodded. "Well, if Rustam wasn't to be found, then what was?"

Commander Osthanes mouth dropped open a little. He fastened his lips together again, and rubbed his patience strip. Ibram wondered at it, really; it never seemed to help the man.

Lady Azadiya rolled her fingers. "Don't worry over it, truth is all in the delivery, to be sure" she said. "Ibram, what did you hope to learn?"

"I caught Satya Monbrith burning strangleweed in the old forge. She mentioned it had gotten into the potatoes."

"Your point?" Osthanes asked.

"It's the wrong season for planting, isn't it? And strangleweed only grows like that when you disturb the earth. I thought they might have buried something out in their garden." Ibram glanced over at the judge and Mistress Denrind in time to see them exchange papers and continue reading silently. "I had no chance to speak of my suspicions to anyone without being overheard by the household before I returned to Lityen." He inclined his head in Osthanes' direction. "I tried to be subtle, but wound up being too vague. My apologies, Commander."

"Speaker's sore throat," Osthanes swore and tossed his patience strip on the table. He strode to the office door, threw it open and leaned out.

"Grognor!" he bellowed and a slim warder appeared in the hallway with her pointed helmet under her arm.

"Grab your sergeant and tell him to get back out to the blasted draughtshop," Osthanes said. "We're digging up their rutting garden."

Osthanes walked out and slammed the door behind him without asking permission to withdraw. As one, they all turned to see Judge E'grard's reaction, but he merely ruffled his stack of papers loudly. He turned his pale sharp eyes towards Mistress Denrind, who smiled nervously.

Ibram coughed and gestured towards the map. "Don't suppose we happen to know where Harken Tolk went outside of Fontis?"

"To answer your question," Judge E'grard said, "since Commander Osthanes has decided his talents lie elsewhere, it's of note that Harken Tolk never deviated from his routine. He traveled in a circle beginning from the port at Delbrite. He went through Nyarribrite, Polia, Lecki, and then the empty band before reaching Fontis, and thence back through the boundary."

"He never went to Othy?" Ibram asked. "It's close enough."

"Not in two years according to the reports," Mistress Denrind said.

"How do we know that, your honor?" Ahksell asked as he walked closer. He settled a bit close to Ibram's back; Ibram moved aside to give him room.

"When I sent word that there would need to be a trial of evidence in Fontis concerning poor Master Tolk," Mistress Denrind explained, "I also sent along the same report I made to Mentor Hobon—the one I sent with you, Master Ucalegon. Unfortunately, the commander informed me upon his arrival that Rustam's failure to appear meant a more in depth investigation. Nothing seemed amiss, of course, until all this nonsense began."

"If it is such nonsense, Mistress Denrind," Judge E'grard said. "You should be far happier that my Cohort of Peace's search is now winding down."

Mistress Denrind's face went as blank as slate, and Lady Azadiya looked at her sharply. She raised her eyes in the judge's direction, and then casually returned to studying the map. She moved a few stones in what seemed an idle pattern from Ibram's viewpoint.

"You're halting the search?" Ahksell asked. "But it hasn't been the full twelve day yet."

Ibram watched Judge E'grard from the corner of his eye. The judge rustled the papers in his hands. All the wrinkles in his forehead furrowed together as his eyes narrowed.

"Attendant Solari, as helpful as your rituals have been," Judge E'grard said. "They have not produced any definitive results—or at least none that have discovered the fugitive."

"Yes, but we had to know why he left first," Ahksell protested.

"Isn't that how it's done? You can't mean to say you're finished ahead of your own schedule."

"I'll thank you, Attendant," the judge snapped his papers again, "not to seek to influence my decisions. I am a representative of Her Gracious Majesty and beholden to the laws of Vissilia. Commander Osthanes has done his job ably and his forces have acquitted themselves well, but it is time now to focus on what must happen."

Ibram looked up. Judge E'grard sat back in his chair, as thin and sharp as a pulled nail. He steepled his hands in front of his chest, while next to him Mistress Denrind read papers as if her life depended upon it. The judge squinted at the room.

"Every moment we have not found the fugitive is a moment where he has traveled further away from us," E'grard continued. "Now, with this new information Master Ucalegon has uncovered, the need for an increased militia in Fontis as a show of stability is even more important. I cannot confiscate these merchants' coinage by myself, relying on their magnanimity."

Ahksell dragged in a breath, but it went nowhere. He merely exhaled and looked away. Judge E'grard pursed his lips, and then sat back up with every appearance of satisfaction. He picked up his papers again, and returned to reading. Ibram let his attention fall to the map in the short heated silence that fell. He tried to think up something to say, since he had the opportunity of asking Osthanes questions while he had to be polite.

"How many campsites have you found?" Ibram asked. "I know the area's quite popular with travelers, and since they can't go through Fontis now they must be going around it."

Judge E'grard sighed loudly. "Too many," he said. "Of the brace of abandoned sites, only four were recent enough to merit attention. The rest were occupied, and they easily submitted to a search when commanded."

Ibram bit his lips together to keep from commenting on the probability of lightly armed travelers refusing a heavily armed band of warders herding a mob of angry villagers. He nodded most properly instead. The bounds of propriety held, but only just.

"And the surrouding villages have been warned of a fugitive,"

Mistress Denrind said. "I sent the letters to my counterparts immediately."

"So far," Lady Azadiya frowned at the map, "I am told you have had no reports but a great many reassurances from the local constabularies. What about the shrine at Thelis?"

"At Thelis?" Ahksell asked. "Why go that far away?"

"I was told by Master Kolesar that outriders had been sent to the interior and beyond the imperial boundary line," Amota Lakum said. "It seemed a curious decision."

"An early attempt by the commander to intercept the fugitive." Judge E'grard shook his head. "It's abandoned, but for the groundskeeper," he said with some aspersion. "Some old man who keeps it up from the village. He comes in a few times every seven-day, makes sure the rooms are swept and candle box is full, that sort of thing. He invited my warders in to check, but there was nothing in any of the three rooms."

Ibram wondered if Commander Osthanes enjoyed how the cohort was spoken of with such possessiveness by Judge E'grard. He considered the map before him. The imperial border had been marked off in ink, separating the sect and its environs from the rest of Vanima province in a rather skinny arc that stopped in the exact center of the Emerald Mountains range. The natural barrier marked the end of the province as well, and beyond it the hills and mountains of the West. He moved the heavy parchment to the side for a clearer view of the detail map Ladyship was studying.

"It's very methodical work," Lady Azadiya said. She drew her finger in an arc along the stones laid out on the smaller square of parchment; they scooted away at her approach and formed a scallop pattern.

"Mentor Hobon, the markers are there for a reason," Judge E'grard said sharply.

"Fear not, I'll put them back," she said. She tapped the map. "Now, before Tikari passed about her report, Commander Osthanes said that he had found fresh tracks near this pond."

"Yes," the judge said. "It leads to a farm out in the wilds."

"The Alths live there," Mistress Denrind said. "They've a boy about Rustam's age. He says the tracks are from when he was fishing."

"Alths?" Ibram asked and Lady Azadiya looked up at him.

"Do you know of them, Ibram?" Amota Lakum asked.

Ibram turned to his left. Amota Lakum had wandered over to the judge's side of the desk, a little behind his right shoulder. Ibram looked back to face Lady Azadiya.

"Satya mentioned them to me," he said. "She said Master Tolk was working on a commission for the Alths when he passed away."

"What sort of folk are they?" Lady Azadiya asked.

Ibram shook his head. "That's all I know of them, to be sure. They're farmers, they broke something a blacksmith had to fix, and they live out of the way."

"They're freeholders," Mistress Denrind supplied. "It's a large family of about...twenty, I'd say, in total. They are rather spread out, actually. The main farm is close enough for them to set up a stall during market days, but the rest of the family are scattered about in the hinterlands."

"Are they all within the imperial boundary?" Amota Lakum asked.

Mistress Denrind thought for a moment, but then shook her head. "I really could not say. I know they're mostly towards the Bloody Rocks. My counterpart in Othy administers to them when there's a need."

"The 'Bloody Rocks'?" Judge E'grard asked.

"The mushrooms that grow there bleed poison, your honor," Amota Lakum said. "It's a reddish kind of ooze."

Lady Azadiya frowned at the map. "So the main farm falls under Fontis' jurisdiction, but the rest of them do not."

Ibram pointed. "The Bloody Rocks are too far away for Rustam to reach on foot."

"Do we know he's on foot?" Amota Lakum asked.

"Yes," Ibram said. "They don't own a horse."

"The stables by the draughtshop are only for travelers," Mistress Denrind confirmed. "The Monbriths have nothing but pushcarts and no one in the village is missing so much as a donkey."

"What about the Tyals?" Ahksell asked.

"There's no incentive for them to help," Lady Azadiya said. "I would not have thought he could have gone to ground so easily, though, even if the boy knew the terrain."

"No, Mentor," Judge E'grard agreed in a heavy tone. "It's why I think someone must be hiding him. These Alths, maybe."

"And as I have put it to you before, who would do it?" Mistress Denrind asked. "There's no one in Fontis who profits from this."

"I have learned in my career, Mistress Denrind," E'grard said as he tossed his papers to the desk, "that criminals often do not think past their next opportunity, and never for anyone but themselves. No, Master Monbrith cares little for his family and less for his village. It seems clear to me that he has gone to ground with his accomplices in this scheme."

He hated to say it, but Ibram was beginning to share that same feeling. From the way Mistress Denrind bit her lip, and looked to the side, it looked as though she did as well.

$$\maltese \quad 14 \quad \maltese$$

By the time Commander Osthanes returned to the manor, smelling strongly of dirt and with a certain grim satisfaction lurking about his rough-hewn face, Judge E'grard and Lady Azadiya had exhausted their store of polite conversation. Mistress Denrind, in an attempt to cover for their silent animosity, had ordered a tray of shay and snacks. Ibram appreciated the food, if not the outcome. Listening to Judge E'grard chew was an unenviable position. His assistant, Alia, was called in as a recorder and they spent their time ignoring the room while E'grard spoke in long paragraphs about other matters which Alia duly inscribed.

Lady Azadiya had taken a seat on the remaining chair, and spent the rest of the time in silence. Occasionally, she moved her head or narrowed her eyes at nothing at all, but for the most part she gave no orders and generally behaved as if she wished to be left alone. Ibram stayed by the map, idly letting his eyes follow the small trail markers drawn about Fontis.

Commander Osthanes entered the room as abruptly as he had left it, and bowed perfunctorily to those assembled. "The ground's been disturbed," he said. "Whatever was there, isn't any longer."

He snatched his patience strip from the table and began counting off the bronze buttons. Ibram glanced quickly about the room. The judge seemed grim. Mistress Denrind was stoic, but pale, while Amota Lakum—if Ibram was not mistaken—was still attempting to read over Judge E'grard's shoulder. Ahksell shook his head.

"Was there nothing left?" he asked.

Commander Osthanes pursed his mouth. "Not unless you count the vegetables," he said. "It looked like whatever it was, was buried deep. Strangleweed all over the place."

"How much?" Ibram asked. "If we believed it to be a cache of some sort?"

"At least two medium-sized bags," Osthanes said, chewing each word as if it were gristle.

"I hope you've set to searching for them in the village," Judge E'grard snapped. "Given this counterfeiting scheme, there's no telling what damage a cache of that size could do."

"We don't know the bags contained false coin, your honor," Ibram pointed out. "It could have been—well, it could have been anything. Clothes or a murder weapon, even."

"No one has been murdered, Master Ucalegon." E'grard pounded his fist on the table. "The fugitive is alive and running, or else his corpse would have been recovered."

"We'll find out just what it was, never fear," Commander Osthanes growled. "I've put two squads to searching the village."

"As easy as it will be to find something covered in mud in Fontis," Ibram said. "How do we even know what we're looking for?"

"Perhaps you should have done your digging yourself, rather than pass on cryptic messages!" Commander Osthanes smacked his patience strip on the table.

"Here now," Ahksell flared up, "Ibram was only doing what the judge ordered him to do!"

"Mistress Denrind," Lady Azadiya interrupted just as Osthanes' mouth opened to respond. She stood and adjusted her tight sleeves where the cuff ended on her forearms. "May I have the use of one of your sitting rooms? I would like to speak to the Terins."

Commander Osthanes twisted sharply towards Ladyship, but shut his mouth. Mistress Denrind sat up more straight in her chair. The papers she was reading crinkled in her hands.

"Of course, Mentor," she said. She began to rise. "The south facing room off the courtyard is very fine. If you wish, I can—"

"Mistress Denrind, I fear I do require your attention to the matter at hand," Judge E'grard said. "We must discuss further terms in light of these new offenses. Alia, you will stay as well."

Mistress Denrind fell back into her chair with a scrupulously blank face. "Of course, your honor," she said.

"And I am perfectly capable of finding an empty room and lighting a few lamps," Lady Azadiya said. "Ibram, my things."

She stood away from the map and brushed off her hands. Ibram picked up her coat and cloak from the corner. She called her gar to her side with one outstretched crooked hand. Commander Osthanes wrapped and unwrapped his patience strip around his wrist.

"We've already determined they didn't know anything about Monbrith's escape, Mentor Hobon," Osthanes said.

"Oh, I am well aware," Lady Azadiya answered. "I simply wish to ask a few questions. Shouldn't be too long."

She swept out of the room, leaving Ahksell barely enough time to get the door open. Ibram fell out after her, and then it was a race to see who would get to her side first: Ahksell or Amota Lakum. Amota Lakum won, but only because he swerved to her right. Ibram simply followed the pack of them down the hallway.

"I don't like not having something to do," Lady Azadiya said. "Lakum, did you see?"

"I did, Ladyship," Amota Lakum said. "They're abandoning the road to Delbrite and they've stopped moving up towards Lityen. I think the dogs caught a scent in the trees, but lost it in a stream. Osthanes is growing desperate."

"They didn't say anything like that," Ahksell said.

"No, but when I looked at the map Commander Osthanes had moved his markers in a very distinct pattern," Ladyship said.

"Then why don't they want us to know?"

"They want to catch him first," Ibram said. "Warders are territorial like that."

"Well, you would know," Ahksell said.

Ibram shrugged. "I also know if not for the Judge's order, the majority of them would still be out there looking. They have a good quadrant covered."

Lady Azadiya hummed. "They've enough folk for it, but I've never liked running about the countryside until the karsac pops its head out of the den."

The dripless oil lamps clamped to the beams supporting the walls flickered as they passed them. In a noble's manor, this section of the public courtyard would have been given to a garden, but Mistress Denrind—or her predecessors—had enclosed it. Now, it was a warren of tight hallways and workrooms. They walked down the last small stretch of interior corridor. Loud banging sounds were trickling their way to Ibram's ears; it sounded like hammering.

They all came out onto the terrace, and stopped when Lady Azadiya halted. Ten or so villagers were in the middle of unloading a cart full of lumber before them in the public courtyard. Two stood on the wagon and then the wood was passed down the line to be stacked in the middle of the courtyard. The tent that previously been erected in the center of the packed earth had been taken down. Two or three folk were already nailing planks together.

Ibram's throat squeezed in on itself. He swallowed heavily and gripped Ladyship's coat and cloak more tightly. "That's a bit quick of the judge," he said.

The manor's servants were clustered underneath the little corner pavilions, whispering to each other or simply staring at the workers. Ibram saw Mistress Islozia leaning against the railing on the opposite side. It was quiet enough to hear the workers grunting as they lifted the planks from the wagon bed and laid them out.

"I told you he'd sent to Delbrite for the wood," Ahksell said.

Lady Azadiya tapped her gar lightly on the wooden walkway. She pointed to her right, and they all walked onward. She walked briskly, with her head up.

"Ah, I should mention, Ladyship," Amota Lakum interrupted the silence that pressed down around them all. "Ibram's been starting fights again."

Lady Azadiya looked over her shoulder.

Ibram grinned. "I did."

"Is anyone injured?"

"You would have heard the wailing, if there had been," Ibram said. "Just a bit of affronted vanity."

"There was no point to it," Ahksell said. "All you did was make Uxio mad at you."

"Which one is Uxio anyway?" Ibram asked.

Ahksell frowned. "That's not the point."

"See, I knew you didn't know either."

Lady Azadiya chuckled. "Did Perhara bring Uxio with him?"

"He did, Ladyship," Amota Lakum said.

She shook her head; her hair swayed down her back all the way to her knees. "He's such a romantic. All to the best, though. Why did you start a fight, Ibram?"

"So Warder Kamos would like me."

She laughed, and several people in the public courtyard looked up. Ibram tucked his hand behind his back and then grasped Ladyship's coat and cloak against his chest with his other arm, taking care they didn't drag on the floor, all proper posture. Ahksell turned to look at him, and he grinned back. Ahksell huffed and faced front again.

"Does he like you now?" she asked.

"He told me Commander Osthanes isn't exactly carving a trench around Fontis and keeping the freeholders inside it."

"Really," she said.

They turned at the nearest pavilion and walked further on past a thin, open slatted door that looked to be hiding a storage room. Then, she paused outside a closed pocket door. She knocked, and then waited, but no one called out. Lady Azadiya grabbed the flat bronze door-pull and tugged. She walked inside the darkened sitting room, and then turned around on the threshold.

"He said," Ibram paused and leaned his upper body forward. He lowered his voice. "That some of them are claiming to be within Itol's boundary, and Osthanes isn't challenging it. Says his job's to find a fugitive until such time as, well, time runs out."

Ladyship's eyes narrowed in thought. "A fine piece of knowledge to bring back to me," she said. "Well done."

Beside him, Ahksell snorted. She took stock of him, amused. Ibram looked over her shoulder into the darkened room. He thought perhaps it was a sitting room, rather than for eating. He could make out the outline of furniture.

"Ibram," Lady Azadiya drew back his attention. "Fetch Hasi Terin and bring her to the courtyard here."

"What if her mother objects?" he asked.

She shrugged her shoulders; her dress rustled. "You'll have to bring her along, then."

Ibram bowed. "Ladyship."

He passed her coat and cloak to Amota Lakum and then turned on his heel and retraced his steps along the terrace. He could hear Ladyship issuing orders as he left, but since they weren't directed towards himself, Ibram paid them little mind. He twisted his lips into a frown. If the Terin girl was anywhere near Fontis she was most likely in the market square or her home. Otherwise, she was part of a hunting group, and this was about to become a very long errand. He touched the hilt of his sica lightly, running his fingers down the knot that tied it to his belt.

Possibly Lady Azadiya had just handed him a very good chance to see if he could spy Attendant Serisan again. She'd been furtive when there were only two alchemists in Fontis, now with this many, she was probably frantic to hide. She must have cooked up something with Ahksell, but Ibram could only smell the food, when he'd much rather partake of the dish. He tilted his head as he turned a corner. The carpenters were still working in the rain.

He caught himself a hair's breadth from rubbing his eyebrow, and tucked his thumb around his hilt instead. Worst thought: Rustam Monbrith was a genius tracker, capable of evading both locals and professional search parties, and they would never ever catch him. He was...dead. He was so upset at his own cowardice he'd gone to the Bloody Rocks and eaten the mushrooms. He had turned from his goddess and sacrificed Fontis in a pact with a wind demon, who had flung him as far away as—as the Grasslands to live the life of a bandit king.

Ibram frowned. Perhaps that was enough worst thoughts, if they were not to be helpful. Besides, several persons were clearly lying, and the Monbriths were only the most obvious culprits. He still couldn't wrap his head around the idea they had been party to Rustam's flight, though admittedly he could see at least Satya helping her brother conceal his part in the counterfeiting.

Someone cursed the wood to oblivion. Ibram turned his head just as a laborer staggered back from his workgroup, sucking the edge of his hand. He regained his feet and spat to the side, glaring at the timber. He threw his hammer to the ground, and then crouched on the packed earth and put his hands over his head. One of his fellows went over and began whispering to him.

Ibram cleared his throat, and stuck a finger in the neck of his gambeson to resettle the fabric. He'd be easily frustrated if this was his task as well. But fellow feeling didn't matter right now, to be sure. He had been sent out on Ladyship's business, which would halt all this work immediately, and Judge E'grard would have to swallow the cost. Ibram walked quickly down the terrace and out of the manor.

A few feet away, a large crowd of villagers, warders, and traders milled about, shouting at each other. A few were so moved as to shake their fists in the air and yell, but the warders themselves seemed mostly in control. The mood was restive, but not violent. Warder Phiri, previously of the Monbrith's draughtshop, pushed a raving trader waggling a pouch in his face backwards; the man fell to the mud and sat there, stunned.

Ibram sighed. Speak a wish and watch it burn. It appeared the confiscation of the entire village's coinage was going well. He patted Mistress Denrind's front gate as he went by, and walked quickly over to the edge of the throng. He reached down to pull the man to his feet. The stunned trader, who was wearing a full robe and loose trousers in the Southern style, glared at him and shook himself free.

Ibram raised his arms as the man disappeared into the crowd without a thank you passing his lips. He rolled his eyes and then brushed off his hands which were admittedly a little splattered with mud. He turned to his left.

"Good day, Warder Phiri," he said.

"And to you, Master," Warder Phiri said. "Back from the living mountain, then?"

The urge to say 'no' was almost overwhelming, but Ibram fought it back. He nodded. "I wanted to thank you for passing my message on to the commander."

Warder Phiri's mustache puffed with air. "Not a problem." He gestured at the throng. "Though if this is your doing, I don't know as I should have agreed."

"Not mine, Warder, I assure you," Ibram said. "What's going on?"

"Commander's ordered us to form them all into a line once the searching was completed," Phiri said. "We've got the traders going through Mentor Tikari's apparatus first so we can lock them back up in their conveyances once they're done."

Unfriendly, but effective, Ibram supposed. He nodded. "And they're protesting."

"They're an unfriendly lot," Phiri said.

Ibram snorted. "Suppose they are."

"Why are you out here?" Warder Phiri asked. "Need to have your purse checked?"

He shook his head. "I've been ordered to find Hasi Terin of romantic fame. Have you seen her about today?"

"The furrier's pretty daughter?" Warder Phiri grinned. "The mother's still out looking, but the young mistress is kicking her heels by the dramseller's cart with one of the local boys."

A lightning bolt flashed up Ibram's spine. He reached out and grabbed Phiri's shoulder; the man leaned back with a frown.

"There is a dramseller?" Ibram asked. Thus far, he'd had only his thoughts and no opportunity. He looked about himself. "Which one? Who runs it?"

"Don't know about that," Phiri said. "Just going off the smell."

He pointed over Ibram's head to the right of the scrum. Ibram turned in a slow half-circle and gestured in the same direction. "Which one?" Ibram asked again.

"The one with the tarp or the one with the chimney?"

"Neither," Phiri said and shook Ibram off. "The jumped up herder's hut."

Ibram nodded. "Ah yes, with the shingle. My thanks, Warder Phiri!"

He waved over his shoulder as he began to maneuver his away around the outskirts of the angry traders. As he approached the side of the market, he saw Mentor Tikari and her Attendant standing behind a table someone had procured, flanked by Warder Kamos and three of his brethren. Anxious villagers stood interspersed around the empty stalls and carts, watching as the warders slowly bunched the traders into what resembled an orderly, if fractious, line.

The dramseller's stall truly was a renovated herder's hut, with a large cut out that included where the door would normally be and a shelf for service. The sign nailed above it had been painted competently, but age had withered its stain. By the looks of the place, the proprietor couldn't do much good business. Anything bought from its depths was even odds to blind or refresh you. Currently, it was shuttered completely, but Tieri Suugan and that young girl Ibram had seen with Mistress Terin that morning still hovered outside it as if expecting to be served.

Ibram swallowed. He walked as closely as he dared without drawing attention to himself and squinted as if in thought. According to the sign above the children, the dramseller's hut was owned by Madji, who had been so insistent on telling firetales in the Kolesar's shay shop. A small thrill of victory made his blood warm within him. He looked around into the crowd. It was a wonder the old mistress had stuck around. Liquor was an expense few could afford in villages, though perhaps Fontis was a special case for who it served. Maybe she had been caught when the warders had closed the village. Perhaps she'd chanced on the fact that with the draughtshop closed, the market might be ripe for her sort of wares despite her fears. Or maybe Madji knew more than she ought to about Rustam Monbrith and all his mischief.

Quickly, Ibram began to move through the crowd. He could go back for the Terin girl; right then he had to freedom to find Madji Anlines and ask her a few pertinent questions. The bigger groups of merchants, those who had already closed up shop didn't yield her grey head and heavily beaded form. He stood up on the end of a wagon and tried to peer further over the mass of folks lining up to drop their money in Fourth Mentor Tikari's chests.

He licked his lips and took a calming breath. To his left were most of the warders, directly in front of him lay Tikari and her Attendant. To his right, the large carriages of the other newly arrived Alchemists created huge barriers and tiny alleys between stalls and wagons that someone might easily slip through. He sighed through his teeth, and jumped down to the cobblestones.

Madji might be in the shay shop—Cangsa, she might have locked herself in her wheeled herder's hut until she was allowed to leave. But she couldn't evade a search. Ibram clicked his teeth together as he walked through the crowd. He kept his eyes open and alert, conscious of the fact that he made a ridiculous sight to the folk about him, who began to draw away at his approach. He craned his neck right and then left, but she was nowhere. He considered the low-hanging sun in the sky and turned left to cross the road in the direction of the shay shop.

As he moved, slipping between a large man making his way towards the well with a bucket and a small group of folk muttering to themselves, a flash of grey hair caught his eye. Ibram stopped and angled his body to that small group. Standing a little to the right of them was the old woman herself, grey-haired, and wearing a large triple strand of wooden beads. She was clearly saying something to them, but didn't appear to be part of their group.

Ibram grinned. "Mistress!" he called out. "How lovely to see you again!"

Madji startled noticeably, and took a step behind her as Ibram made his way quickly towards her. He gave her no time to do so, merely bowed and then rose with a smile. He'd seen mud crusted on her boots.

"And what do you want, youngster?" she asked with narrowed eyes.

"Ibram Ucalegon," Ibram introduced himself. "I have the honor of serving the Sect of Seven Fires in a small capacity."

"And what does that lot want with me?" she demanded. "I'm decent folk, I don't truck with unnatural equations."

Ibram ignored the inference, because it suited him, but remembered it to tell Ladyship. "I'm told you sell spirits," he said. "The best that could be had. You are Madji Anlines, aren't you? The dramseller with all the stories?"

The old woman sniffed. "I am," she admitted. "A good story sends the spirit down, I always say."

"Oh indeed," Ibram agreed with a nod. "So does my lady, Fourth Mentor Hobon."

Madji's wrinkled throat bobbed when she swallowed. "What does a mentor want with me?"

"She's a Westerner, don't you know," he said, stalling while he thought. "And fond of her homeland. She wanted to know if you featured Drethylmane amongst your stock?"

"Drethylmane?" Madji repeated. Her face slackened for a moment and then she glared at him. "You think I'd lack something like that? I'm a seller of distinction, you know, I deal directly with the houses of nobility."

"And so you would still, if you stock Drethylmane for Fourth Mentor Hobon," Ibram said and shrugged dramatically. "But why do any of us like what we like?"

Madji nodded slowly, but Ibram could see her counting up the picaio and picks already in her mind. Drethylmane tasted like summer berries that had been living in a bog for a few centuries and clung to its glass like oil in a filter. It also cost more than an artisan could make in two years of work; Ladyship doled it out only on very special occasions.

"I do have a flagon or so," she said. "Back at my wagon. Why don't we go there? We can speak on price."

"A wonderful idea," Ibram said.

He gestured Madji on ahead of him, and then followed her. She abandoned her group without looking back. Ibram breathed in and cleared his throat.

"You've already done your bit here?" he asked, and pointed to Mentor Tikari in the crowd.

Madji sniffed. "I have not," she said. "I'm too old to be standing around waiting on an alchemist's rulings. I've got my poor tired feet to look after, you know. Can't be standing around all day."

Ibram nodded, and did not say anything about how he had found her or how long she'd been out on her poor tired feet, watching the crowd. He tucked his hands behind his back and kept pace with her. The folk about them were growing a bit restive.

"I think we've met before, mistress," he said. "In the shay shop?"

She grunted. "Did we?"

"You told a story about Mandibrite and what happened to it."

She glared at him and then nodded. "So I did, and so I will again, youngster!" she declared. "Bad deeds must be talked about, or folks will think they got away with ought they shouldn't."

"I very much agree," Ibram said and smiled. "Still, I was surprised anyone knew about it. I mean to say, I'd never heard of sanctioning before."

They skirted the edge of the crowd, but were forced to stop as four or five traders were let away from the group around Mentor Tikari. Ibram wrapped his left hand around his right wrist. Madji scowled.

"No doubt the alchemists don't like to think on it," she said. "They like to pretend the whole of the garden provinces weren't under their fists before the empire liberated them."

Ibram blinked at that, momentarily at a loss. Vanima, Appenwai, and Ercule had all been kingdoms before they'd been provinces, but that had been over a thousand years ago. No alchemist had held so much as a minor clerkship in government office since. He unstuck his tongue from the roof of his mouth, and shrugged.

"You certainly seem to know about it," he said. "Can't have been too hushed up."

Madji grunted, but shook her head. She walked through a break in the passersby and Ibram had to follow. He eyed the quickly approaching roof of her hut. What to ask before they reached it.

"Do you spend much time in Fontis, then?" he asked. "It seemed like Master Kolesar knew you well."

"That old gossip." She spit to the side. "We've had our dealings."

"I wondered because I also have been here—off and on in my work, you understand—but I was at the Monbriths' draughtshop, rather than staying in town, like you."

It was a gamble, but Ibram thought it had good odds. Madji snorted, but turned one eye towards him in an evaluating sort of way. "You stayed out there as well?" she asked.

Ibram nodded. "I did indeed. Met the Mistress and all the children."

Madji snorted again and crossed her arms as she walked. "Fools," she muttered.

"Oh, you've spent time with them?" he asked.

She laughed unwillingly, more a bark of ill-humor than anything else. "I did business with them," she said. "Same as any of these others you can see." She waved a dismissive hand towards her fellow traders. "Always buying, you know, and never selling. But I had a standing contract; they're in my book. They did good business with the travelers, and the mother likes to have something special on hand for the better class of person, if you take my meaning."

"Oh yes," Ibram said. "I do. Ladyship often does the same for her guests."

He didn't imagine Lady Azadiya would be too upset at the ideas he came up with, as long as they were for a good cause. He stepped to one side to evade a young mother coming up from the well with a bucket in one hand and her baby in the other. His elbow knocked into Madji; she pushed him off.

"But they're a mean bunch," she said and fixed her clothing in two hard jerks with both hands. Her necklace clacked together. "Always moaning about the price when it's already agreed upon and trying to say I shirk on my orders."

"Dreadful," Ibram murmured.

Madji sniffed loftily. "I told that brat Satya. I told her if I am contracted for a case of ryer, than I bring up a case of ryer! Not my fault if the taxes get raised during my journey."

"Yes, of course," Ibram agreed. "Did you speak with the Monbriths often? I barely got two words, myself."

"Been their supplier since their father was alive," Madji declared. "And aren't I helpful? I put it in the contract itself, 'subject to change,' and it's nothing to them if my safety is on the line, is it? A lone woman traveling with nothing but her wits and good humor."

They'd arrived at her herder's hut—still with the Suugan boy and Hasi Terin adjoining—and Ibram honestly felt himself at a loss.

"Like as not they drove that boy away, you mark me, youngster," she grumbled. "I told him to be wary."

Ibram looked at her sharply. Her head bobbed next to him, short grey hair waving about her ears. Her expression was turned inward, like as not she was playing out an old scene in her head.

"I warned him what those alchemists do to a body in court," She said. "They're allowed all sorts of indulgences, get away with everything. One sip and you're babbling like a five year old with their hands in the honey jar."

Ibram frowned. "Babbling?" he repeated.

"That truth serum of theirs," she waved her hand at him and then jerked her chin up to stare at him fiercely. She poked a bony finger into his chest. "I don't say he listened to me, though. I never told him to run! It's that family. A vinegared mother births pickled children."

He breathed in and out, and felt the air in his lungs as if it was frost. That was why Rustam had run; because he thought the Judge would make him drink a—a potion of truth and he'd spill the shay about their counterfeiting scheme. But had she done it deliberately?

"Oh, that old potion," he said weakly. "I hadn't thought of that."

She nodded decidedly and stumped onward. Ibram followed. If she really believed it, then it might be that Madji had no more to do with Rustam's flight than unhappy chance. Yet she had links to every personage so far involved. Merchants did have to pay travel taxes when they moved goods across the provinces. Spreading a few counterfeit coins would ease the burden of a tax rise, and also made for a good excuse to carry away more money than previously agreed upon. He frowned while Madji unlocked her hut, and then hauled open the door. Ibram stood up on his tiptoes to peek inside over her head.

It was too dark, he could not see much but a few netted sacks of cheese and vegetables hung on the wall above a small stack of crates. He fell back on his heels. He squinted at what almost looked like a sack in the corner. Madji stood up on the small set of stairs which had fallen out, and looked down at him with her hand on her hip.

"How much do you want?" she asked.

"Want?" Ibram jerked back and stuck his hands behind his back.

"The Drethylmane," she said impatiently. "How much of it?"

Ibram rubbed his head, and dug his thumb hard into his scalp. "How much do you have?" he asked.

He didn't want to say her eyes lit up, but Madji's face softened like a grandmother faced with a newborn. It made Ibram want to back away slowly with his hands out, but he steeled himself. She practically cooed down at him.

"I'd say Old Madji's got a fair jug," she said. "Perfect for your Fourth Mentor. Is that her?"

Ibram turned around to follow the length of her arm as she pointed to Mentor Tikari. "No," he said. "As I said—"

The door slammed shut behind her. Ibram whirled around, reached up and pounded on the door. He glared up at the warped wood.

"Madji!" he shouted. "What about that order?"

"I've got you in my book, youngster!" Madji called out from within her cabin. "Never fear, I'll remember you when it's time to leave but I'll not touch coin until we see each other in Lityen!"

Ibram ground his teeth and glared at the door. He stepped back and then took a deep, calming breath. It was no use to try and force the issue just then. She'd already answered him about the Monbriths. Mud on the boots in a village was no kind of clue. Besides, why only take some of the bags and not others if she had removed any from the Monbriths' draughtshop? Still, he might ask Warder Phiri if he'd seen Madji around the place while on patrol.

"I thank you for your time," he called out. "I'm sure we'll have business soon."

No answer came from within, and it was difficult not to imagine the old mistress cackling at him. Ibram put his back to the door and smoothed both hands down his green and brown gambeson. He stepped out and faced the crowd once more. No one seemed to have paid him much mind.

Tieri Suugan and Hasi Terin had moved further on nearer to a simple pull wagon. The back held a small load of hay and not much else. A large dun horse was hitched to its front. Ibram crossed his arms. He took a moment to consider the girl he'd actually been sent out to fetch.

Hasi Terin from the side was pretty enough for a girl of seventeen years. She had a smooth cheek with a heart-shaped face, a loose mass of auburn curls beneath a linen kerchief, and her mother was clearly an accomplished furrier if the quality of her clothing was to be trusted. The young mistress wore a grey wool gown pinned up neatly in front to reveal a dull yellow lining and the red skirt of her kirtle. She looked like a girl at a harvest feast, not whatever a body might call the ruckus occurring currently.

"Mistress Hasi Terin?" he called out.

The girl turned in a swirl of hair and smiled automatically. She had eyes big as a fenek's and twice as limpid, and very red cheeks. "Yes, Master Alchemist?"

Ibram shook his head as he approached and she began to bow. He waved her up quickly, conscious of a few too many sect-related eyes on them. "I'm no alchemist," he said. "I merely work for the sect."

Tieri's face had taken a sullen turn at the sight of Ibram, which Ibram did not take personally. Life had tripped Tieri Suugan up early, but he seemed the only one amongst his peers who was suiting up to face it. By contrast, his prospective sweetling watched everything with eager eyes, while he looked at the same things warily. Ibram approved.

Tieri shrugged his wide shoulders and stuck his hands underneath his crossed arms. Ibram raised his eyebrows at him. "Good day, Master Suugan," he said.

"Good day, Master Ucalegon," Tieri said. He kicked his toe in the dirt.

Ibram clasped his hands behind his back and looked about them. He completed his little look-around. From this angle, he could see quite a bit of Mentor Tikari and her set up. She did, indeed, have some kind of apparatus on the table in front of her. Twin metal frames held a full distillation set with fires under both bowls. The right still pot was boiling with a purple liquid and the left one was half-full of a white steaming powder, and both were connected by a spiraling glass tube.

Two drips from either of the still pots stood above a doubled basin bubbling with gauzy white smoke and itself held above the tabletop by a cage. A warder pushed the candle seller forward by the haft end of her axe, and he produced a large leather sack.

"You have a good view of the action here," Ibram said. "How did you stake out such a good spot?"

"Oh, Mother told me the warders were withdrawing from the searching before she left," Hasi said. "I wanted to see what was going on."

"A curious mind is a beautiful asset," Ibram said.

Hasi giggled and tucked her hair behind her ear. She had rough hands with red knuckles, possibly the Terins did a bit of business in tanning on the side. She blinked up at him. Ibram wondered if she practiced that little innocent look in the nearest stream or if she had a piece of silvered glass at home. If anyone would, it would be a furrier.

"How did you get permission to leave the search parties?" he asked.

"Warder Tessai said I could have the time off," she said and pointed into the crowd. "She said it was a better use of her time if I took Mother's chest to the Mentor and let Mother get on with her searching."

Ibram looked obligingly in the crowd. She seemed to be pointing at the tall Vissilian woman holding the line in the middle. He nodded.

"Have you already done that?" he asked.

"Oh yes," Hasi said. "Mentor Tikari said everything was in order."

Ibram didn't turn his head at the news, but it was a close thing. It sounded to him like Rustam had made sure that his sweetling hadn't been supplied with the coins he minted, either he hadn't wanted them involved or he hadn't worked up the nerve. The only question was whether or not she and her mother were aware of it.

He drew his eyes over the crowd and then focused on the opposite side of the village square. Several villagers had availed themselves of the livery yard fence and were standing on its lowest rail to watch. A couple of young mothers with babes in slings were talking to someone in a hood. Ibram let his gaze pass over them, but took note.

Something belched loudly and there was a roiling groan of dismay from the assembled traders. Ibram followed his nose to the stench before him. At the alchemist's array, Mentor Tikari's Attendant trimmed the wick of the oil lamp below the purple still pot. The candle seller's coins were in the process of being carefully poured into the bowl. Mentor Tikari extended her gloved hand over it and waved the yellow smoke away in a half-circle. Ibram couldn't see hear what she said, but the candle seller staggered back as if Mentor Tikari had hit him. The warder made a careful note in his scroll.

Ibram squeezed his hand around his wrist, and then turned back to his companions. "Have you sent your parents' chest over to Mentor Tikari, as well, Tieri?"

Tieri shrugged his shoulders and kept them tight to his neck. "No," he said.

Hasi Terin swiveled her entire body to look between them with her hands clasped low in front of her. "I've been telling him it's no trouble at all, and Mentor Tikari is so kind. He doesn't believe me, though. I think he's scared."

"I just don't like it," Tieri protested. "I don't like what it might mean."

Smarter than Master Kolesar had given him credit for. Ibram nodded seriously. "Well, I'm sure there's nothing to worry about," he said. "As long as everything still goes to plan."

Tieri's head whipped up; he frowned at Ibram. "Were you looking for me?"

Ibram tilted his head down. "Alas, I am not, Master Suugan," he said. "I've been sent to find your friend here."

Hasi's smile, which hadn't yet fallen, beamed brighter. "And here I am! How can I help?"

Ibram took a step back. "If you'll come with me, young mistress," he said. "Mentor Hobon of Yseult wishes to speak with you."

~ 15 ~

I t wasn't a large surprise that the well of Hasi Terin's kindness dried
up as soon as she realized she'd been summoned to a meeting with
an alchemist, much less a mentor. She had to know what such an interview was in aid of, and that giving answers an alchemist did not like
might not go well for her. Ibram wasn't sure she knew the difference
between Tikari and Lady Azadiya, but he was equally uncertain she
cared. She pled her warder escort, and then her mother's absence, and
finally turned a pleading eye in Tieri's direction.

Surprisingly, the boy refused immediately and even claimed he had
errands to run for his own mother with a strangely intense look in
Ibram's direction. Ibram didn't know quite what to make of it yet, but
he turned his thoughts over in his mind as he escorted young mistress
Terin to Mistress Denrind's manor. Hasi Terin spent the walk coming
up with increasingly small talk which Ibram periodically acknowledged
with a noncommittal noise.

Ahksell met them in the public courtyard where the lumber was
still being unloaded. He didn't bow in Hasi's direction, merely frowned
in Ibram's. The sound of hammering had grown louder.

"Mentor has been given a room towards the back," he said. "Let me
show you through."

He flanked Hasi without being told to, which Ibram appreciated, and led them through to a different section of the public courtyard that shared a wall with the family's section of the manor. Ahksell gestured at the wide pocket door to Ibram's right, and Ibram knocked on it.

He stood back. "Ladyship?" he called. "It's Ibram. I've brought Mistress Hasi Terin with me."

"Come in," Lady Azadiya said, and so Ibram slid the door open.

He gestured to Hasi that she should enter first and then followed her inside the Ladyship's latest place of business with Ahksell close behind him. It was clear that Mistress Denrind had given Lady Azadiya her best sitting room, where she met with her own counterparts in other villages or special guests. There were old fashioned glowbulbs on the walls next to faded paintings. A small table had been moved beside the small couch Lady Azadiya sat upon, and a low bulbous drinks cask placed against the far wall. Her gar stood in the corner. Several carved and padded wooden chairs were arranged around the couch in a semi-circle.

Lady Azadiya watched them all file into the room. She'd put her hair up in the time since he'd gone. As part of her meditations Lady Azadiya often reset her hairstyle, when she needed to think or when she needed to calm herself. She would sit down and without aid of mirror or hands, weave her hair into braids or buns solely through her command of the physical world. It was like watching a musician play an invisible harp, those 'strings in the air' as Imriska Suugan had put it.

Ibram walked to her side and stood behind the couch. Without her usual hair prongs, her hair was caught up in a complex weaving around seven large-ish gemstones in a silver framework, like stones in a river. Ibram had no idea where she'd gotten it, but he wouldn't put it past her to have something set aside in her carriage. Ama said Ladyship was always storing little caches in the strangest places.

Ahksell closed the door behind him, holding his gar to the side. Hasi stood in the center of the room, and bowed with her hands on her stomach. Lady Azadiya angled her head to look up at Ibram. She raised her eyebrows. He nodded.

"Mentor Azadiya Hobon, would you be known to Hasi Terin?" he asked. "She's just been to see Mentor Tikari."

"I think I must," she said. She rolled her head on her neck to take stock of the girl. "You may stand, young mistress."

Hasi rose, but held her hands together in front of her. She was a little pale. Lady Azadiya smiled at her, and Hasi made a very good return attempt.

"Your mother, I believe, is out searching for Rustam Monbrith," Lady Azadiya said, and Hasi was nodded before she'd finished speaking.

"Oh yes, Mentor." She tucked her hair over her shoulder. "We all want to find Rustam as soon as possible."

Lady Azadiya hummed. "As soon as possible would be the best outcome," she said. "And Mistress Terin would know the terrain better than most. I'm told your mother is a very driven tracker."

Again, Hasi nodded like her chin was on a string. "She knows the second name of every tree, I think, or that's what she says."

"Your mother sounds quite smart," Lady Azadiya said. "What sort of furs do you sell?"

"Fenek, mostly," Hasi replied, with a gleam in her eye as she took in Ladyship's clothes and jewelry. "We have some lovely spindle wolf, from when the snows bring them down from the hills. One of the free-holders tends mouflon for the Vo Wollys, so we're always laying down traps along the family farm. Good couple of karsacs, too. Perfect for gloves."

"Variety is an excellent quality in a trapper. And I suppose she's taught you her business as well?"

Hasi relaxed her shoulders, but began picking at her thumbnail. She seemed to be growing comfortable answering questions as long as they were family-related.

"She is, Mentor. First it was learning how to prepare traps and then it was setting them."

"And tracking?"

"Of course!"

"So if you were tracking Rustam Monbrith where would you begin?"

Hasi Terin grew a wrinkle in between her eyebrows. "I'd just ask Mother."

"Really?"

"Well, Mother knows all the little trails, Mentor. She'd be able to find his footprints. I'm no good with people."

"Ah," Lady Azadiya raised a finger. "Now, that's not what I'm told."

Hasi's red cheeks wobbled. "Oh no, my apologies, Mentor. I just meant that I'm not good at tracking people. I just know animals. Not that there's been many, besides all these bloodhounds they've been using. Wonderful dogs, but they're scaring all the game away. You can hear them from a mile off."

Lady Azadiya's head inclined slightly. "But you know Rustam," she reminded the girl. "Can't you guess how he might think?"

Hasi rubbed her right hand over her left. "I don't really know much, Mentor," she said. "I told the warders everything I could. Couldn't you ask them?"

Lady Azadiya picked up one of her hair prongs with the doubled bronze points from the couch, and began twirling it in her fingers. "I don't advise refusing me, Hasi Terin."

"I'm not saying no, Mentor!" Hasi took a step forward and then rocked back. "I just don't know anything. I told the warders that."

"So I should ask them to tell me you know nothing?" Lady Azadiya asked.

"It does seem a bit too complicated, Mentor," Ahksell said.

"That isn't what I meant," Hasi insisted, whirling towards Ahksell and then back to Ladyship. "Really, I told them all I could."

"To be sure, maybe she and Rustam just weren't that close," Ibram offered.

Hasi's eyes fastened on him; she nodded quickly. "That's true, though. I mean, we knew each other. You can't help but know everyone in Fontis if you live here, whether you like them or not."

"And there's plenty of young men in the village," Ibram said.

"Well no," Hasi answered. "There's only twenty or so folk of my age, but it's mostly girls, and I'm not inclined."

"I'm sure Rustam bought them all ribbons as well," Lady Azadiya said.

"No, he didn't!" Hasi snapped and then shut her mouth quickly. She blushed.

"So he would only buy ribbons for you?" Lady Azadiya said. "I think that shows a marked partiality."

"He got one for Satya and his mother, too," Hasi mumbled.

Lady Azadiya hummed and twirled her hair prong. She leaned back on the couch, and then turned up her right palm, still holding the prong, to show off her forearm where her pale silk mitt ended at the elbow below her sleeve. She turned it over to expose both sides.

"What other kinds of gifts did he bring you? I once got a lovely pair of mitts from an admirer, you know."

"Oh, how pretty." Hasi leaned forward to admire the embroidery. "No, I never got anything like that. He'd take Mother and me to the shop for a cup of shay, sometimes. And he got me some nice yellow cloth for my gown, and some—some sweets once from the dramseller."

"The dram seller keeps sweets?" Ladyship asked.

"Old Madji says ryer comes from honey and whatever the brewers can't use, they make into little candies."

"Did he always pay?"

She blushed and nodded. "Mother asked him where he got his pocket money, and he said he saved it because the only thing he wanted to spend it on was me."

"It's a lovely thing," Lady Azadiya said. "To be ranked so high in a boy's thoughts."

Hasi swallowed and looked down at her well-scrubbed hands.

"And I'm sure it's exciting to be in the center of two boy's disagreements," Ladyship continued. "But now Rustam has disappeared and our time grows entirely too short. We must all put away such youthful pleasures."

Hasi raised her chin. "I'm not a child."

"Your behavior says otherwise. Do you know what a sanctioning entails?" Lady Azadiya asked.

Hasi seemed a little lost. She turned her head to the door and then her eyes to Ahksell, before her gaze fluttered to Ibram. He raised his hands, palms up, and then let them drop.

"I...saw the planks in the courtyard," Hasi said. "I thought...maybe walls?"

"Walls a strong girl could climb over or dig under, or even smash through," Lady Azadiya said.

A little smile began to creep up Hasi's mouth. Lady Azadiya sighed. "I am sure many of your folk share the same thought," she said. "After all, a warder cannot always stand at the ready, can they? And we could leave all the alarms we wanted, could we not Ahksell?"

"Yes, Mentor," Ahksell said quietly. Ibram frowned at him. Ahksell glanced up; Ibram didn't like the crook in his mouth. "It would not matter if no one from the sect was close by."

Ibram's neck vibrated with the strain of keeping his head high. Lady Azadiya's voice was mild, as if she were merely lecturing. Ibram didn't like the path he could see her leading them all on. The Preceptory of Salacia did not produce carpenters.

Lady Azadiya tapped her hair prong in the air, weaving some symbol by the sharp ends. "Yet we are loyal subjects of Vissilia, are we not?"

"Yes, of course!" Hasi exclaimed.

"So we would accept our punishment, and never try to run."

Hasi's breath shuddered in her chest, very obviously. "Yes, Mentor," she whispered.

"Do you remember your lessons, young mistress?" Lady Azadiya asked. "What is required for a precise transmutation of reality?"

Hasi shook her head. She scrubbed her hands. Ibram tried to remember his tables of transmutation, but couldn't, a sinking feeling dragged down his stomach.

Ahksell responded for her. "An honest exchange, Mentor."

Lady Azadiya nodded and smiled indulgently. "So why would the Preceptory of Salacia require stacks of wooden walls?"

Hasi stared at her blankly, but with wide eyes. "I'm sorry, Mentor," she said. "I don't know."

Lady Azadiya looked back at her, unflinching. "Because in six days' time, they will bargain those walls to contract with our local Abyss and the demons therein will remove Fontis from the face of the earth."

Hasi's hands clapped over her mouth just as a small shriek escaped it. Ibram rocked back on his heels; the back of his head prickled with a sudden burst of heat and pressure. He saw Ahksell look down at his boots and shift his grip on his gar. Only Amota Lakum and Lady Azadiya were unmoved.

"They'll send us into the Gorge?" Hasi screeched between her fingers.

Ibram swallowed heavily. He almost felt like howling a bit himself. He'd pictured a wall as well, perhaps transmuted to a gigantic size in some alchemical ceremony, and a few extra warder patrols. He should have considered the preceptory chosen for the task. He shook his head, and Amota Lakum frowned at him. Ibram chose to stare down at the jewels flickering within Lady Azadiya's hair.

"Oh no," Lady Azadiya said. She spun her hair prong over and under in her fingers. "That would be impossible. Just like the Heavens, the Gorge isn't a physical place, and neither are the Abysses within it."

Hasi shook her head; her hair trembled. "Then how?"

"You'll still be here." Ladyship bent her neck to the side. "You'll be able to cross the road to get to the shay shop, though I recommend extreme caution, and run to the well whenever you need water. You could speak to Tieri or Satya or your mother as much as you liked."

"I don't understand."

He could still hear the hammering in the courtyard, Ibram realized suddenly, even through the door. The smell of hewn wooden planks and sawdust seized the back of his throat. He rubbed his fingers together; his hands felt cold.

"Fontis will stay just where it is and so will you," Lady Azadiya said. "The village will be set aside in reality, and it will...vanish, for want of a better word. No one will stop, unless it's to make camp in what to them will seem an empty clearing.

Travelers will not see you nor hear you, no matter how hard you shout. You won't be able to touch them, or leave the grounds of the village. Food cannot be brought to you, nor aid if there is sickness or fire. It's as if..." she paused in her explanation and considered for a moment. "It's as if you are standing just to the left of all of the rest of us. You surely exist, you breathe the same air, certainly, but no one who was not also walled away can perceive you at all. As if your body were shrouded by a heavy oiled cloak and all around you is a heavy rain."

Hasi Terin swayed on her feet and gulped. Ahksell hurried over and helped her into a chair. He stayed by her as Hasi gripped the armrests tightly. Ibram gripped the hilt of his sica and took a carefully slow breath.

"That's why I recommend caution," Lady Azadiya continued in that horribly even voice. "We have learned that though you cannot touch us, we will be able to touch you. If you're run over in the road by a carriage that doesn't see a reason to stop then it will go very badly for you, and they'll not notice a thing. I think it has something to do with the contractual details, to be honest."

"Is that..." Ibram's voice croaked and he cleared his throat. "What about Mandibrite? Where they built the University of Cornwarke in its place?"

Ahksell looked up sharply. Ibram pressed his lips together. A town of, what, five hundred? A thousand folk? Pushed out as new buildings were erected inside their homes. Losing ground as new roads crossed through their shops or into their ovens. Running out of food while watching the university kitchens churn out cauldrons of stew and quash. Ibram shook his head.

Lady Azadiya looked up at him briefly. "I highly doubt anyone is still alive in Mandibrite. The judge there wished to make a severe impression upon a fractious province, and succeeded according to all accounts. And if they ever did lift its punishment, it would not go well for either Cornwarke or the original town."

That was Judge E'grard's aim, Ibram realized. All his snide comments about Ibram's work and the Sect of Seven Fire's influence, legal or physical. His honor believed the alchemists were becoming too high-handed, and so he made them prove their fealty to the empire in the most humiliating way he could. If he had to kill Fontis to do it, so be it. Harken Tolk's counterfeit ring was probably the gift Judge E'grard had never known he'd wanted. Ibram watched Hasi's face turn white and then green and back again.

"I don't," Hasi swallowed. "I don't like that."

Lady Azadiya nodded slowly. "Nor I, to be sure."

"I don't want that!"

She very nearly stamped her foot, and Ibram shook his head at her. She looked down at her hands. It was a child's response, and—

He lifted his head and gazed off while Ladyship allowed Hasi a moment to compose herself. She asked Amota Lakum something, but Ibram wasn't paying attention. Their voices turned fuzzy.

The children. His eyes flicked over to Ahksell and then away. He was conscious of his breath coming a little faster. Was that why Attendant Serisan was in the marketplace? And why Ahksell insisted she was not there at all? Serisan would know every child in the village—at least the ones of teachable age, and probably a good amount of the parents with infants as well. Ahksell had said he only wanted to speak with her about Diarmit, but if that were all, then he would not be lying to Ibram and she would not be hiding herself in the market. Ibram frowned and bit his lower lip. What were they doing?

"You can stop it, Mentor!" Hasi proclaimed loudly, and Ibram startled back to attention. "You will, won't you?"

"I would like to." Lady Azadiya revolved her hair prong between her fingers, and then set it down. The light glowed on its golden diamond-shaped head. "But I cannot do anything for Fontis without also finding Rustam, and as of now he has disappeared quite completely. You see why we need to find him now, don't you?"

Hasi rubbed her hands together, thumbs over her knuckles as if she was washing them in a basin. "I truly did tell the warders all I know, Mentor," she said. "And mother didn't let me keep the ribbon."

"But you and Rustam are still great friends," Lady Azadiya said, now more briskly. "Tell me all, young mistress. Even the silliest concern of yours may be the key to finding him."

Hasi sniffled a little, but she nodded and sat forward in her chair. They waited. She remained silent.

"Why did Mistress Terin make you send back Rustam's gift?" Ibram asked, with a glance down to Lady Azadiya.

"Oh." Hasi shook back her hair. "Not send back. Mother made me go to the draughtshop with her and return it."

"She doesn't like the Monbriths?" Ibram asked.

"She thinks I'm too young to court by myself," Hasi said, and even giggled a little.

"So she wanted to make sure you and Rustam did things properly," Ibram said.

Hasi kept on scrubbing her hands, one after the other. "I suppose so, but that doesn't mean I was improper before."

"Of course not, I wouldn't even think it," Ibram said, though he definitely had been. "So what did you do then? Even with a minder, a young couple needs privacy."

She raised her shoulders a tiny bit. "We would go on walks, mostly," she said. "When I was checking the traps with Mother, or when Satya had a free moment."

"Anywhere in particular?"

She shook her head. "Only in the forest, really. I told them warders, I don't go—I mean, if you don't respect the forest, you'll come to harm in it, that's what Mother says. I don't go far off."

Lady Azadiya hummed softly. "It's certainly safer not to go far off, I agree."

A small smile grew on the girl's face. "Especially when you've got two raw walkers with you."

"Oh?" Ladyship smoothed her hand over her skirt. "Rustam and Satya don't know the forests well?"

Hasi's curls got back a small portion of their bounce when she shook her head. "No, Mentor, not really. I suppose they'd be okay for foraging, but not for my kind of work. They weren't quiet and you have to be calm, or you'll get bitten if the animal is still alive. I..." she stopped and swallowed. "Mentor, I liked Rustam. He was funny."

"Lots of people have told us the same, young mistress," Ahksell said, and put his hand on the back of her chair. Hasi gazed up at him and sniffled, but seemed pleased. Ibram did not roll his eyes, but only because she might see.

"But did Rustam ever speak of traveling?" Ladyship spoke and regained Hasi's attention. "Maybe there was some place in the province he wanted to see?"

Hasi looked down at her restless hands; Ibram had the impression she was used to having some kind of tool or piecework to fidget with.

"Not really," she said, and Ibram repressed his frustration. "He and I have mostly been to the same places. We all go to Itol for the Hunt of Embrin, and we all stay in for the Feast of the Sundered Legion. We talked about Delbrite for a little while. He used to go there when he was younger, and sometimes Mother takes me along with her when she has to go further for a sale. He's more pious than I am—not through lack of respect, mind you! I'm just often busy, but it was nice to hear Rustam talk about his Speaker."

"His Speaker?" Ibram asked.

Hasi shrugged uncomfortably. "I just meant—well, the whole family likes to think themselves a bit grander than the rest of us, just because their uncle's a lecturer at a shrine or something."

Ibram nodded, and saw Amota Lakum across from him take notice. Ibram shrugged. That matched up with the information he'd had from Satya.

"They go nowhere else?" Lady Azadiya sounded as if she were becoming cross. "Time is catching up to us, you understand."

Hasi gulped and nodded. "Not really," she said. "Satya used to chime in and say…it was something like "Why would you need to travel when the Speaker brings all the stories to you?" and then they'd both laugh. Not like it was blasphemy, you know, just like it was something they heard too much. They weren't really mean about it, or anything."

"To be sure," Ibram said, when Ladyship didn't respond. The ache in the back of his head grew hot tendrils across his scalp; they pulled his skin too tightly.

"Did you speak with Rustam any time before he left?" Ahksell asked, after a quick look towards Ladyship.

Hasi turned in her chair to speak to him, but still kept an eye on Lady Azadiya. "Not the day of the trial, but we went for a walk around midday the day before it. He was all nerves over it. Said Mistress Monbrith wanted him to keep vigil before he had to speak to the judge and he couldn't meet with me until after."

"Keep vigil?" Ibram asked. "What's that?"

Hasi's mouth opened and closed; her eyebrows furrowed prettily. "Don't you know?"

Ibram spread his hands. "I'm terribly sorry, young mistress. Perhaps you could explain to me?"

Mistress Hasi had apparently never spoken to anyone who worshipped outside the Vissilian pantheon before Ibram. His answer didn't appear to help her confusion, but she scooted a little more forward in her chair. "It's when, um, it's when you have something important to do, so you sacrifice your time before whoever in the pantheon you follow. You bring candles and only drink water and you stay in there for, oh, a good long while. At least a full part of the day."

Ibram nodded and dropped his hands down to his sides. "Could you stay as long as all night?"

"It's supposed to be as long as it takes for the candles to light." Hasi giggled suddenly. "Rustam said his uncle waited four days once."

Mistress Suugan had mentioned Mistress Monbrith had had a brother, too. The Monbriths themselves had not, though, had they? He let the thought bubble in the back of his mind for a moment.

"Four entire days?" Ibram asked instead. He opened his eyes widely. "That sounds like it was important."

Hasi's head bobbed once. "Oh yes," she said. "It was about being a Lecturer."

Ibram attempted to arrange his face into sympathy; it seemed to work all right on her. "Well, thank you for telling me."

She smiled, pleased. Then, she looked about her and twisted her fingers together. She stood. "Is that everything?" she asked.

"Yes," Lady Azadiya said, as if she had suddenly returned to herself. "Yes, that will be everything. You've done very well, Hasi, thank you."

Hasi bowed very prettily, and Lady Azadiya waved her up. "Now, go and when your mother returns from searching, tell her to come to Mistress Denrind's manor. I wish to see those karsac furs you mentioned. I might be in the market. And the spindle wolf, too."

She'd gone through a full set of emotions in a short span of time, but Lady Azadiya's pronouncement made Hasi's eyes go wide so quickly Ibram feared she'd damage them. Her face flushed. She bowed again before anyone could stop her, and then flew out the door calling her thanks. Ahksell slid the door closed behind her and then returned to the center of the room.

"Furs, Mentor?" he asked. "Why should Mistress Terin care?"

She sighed. "Why is the shay shop still open for business? Because it's normal, Ahksell, and Fontis requires a great deal of normal right now."

"Yes, Mentor, I see."

"That's the first mention I've heard about Rustam Monbrith performing a vigil," Ibram said. "Satya said the candles went out two days before the trial."

"You hold a vigil, you don't perform it," Amota Lakum said.

"What's the difference?"

"Ib-la, did you study in the preceptory school or were you merely learning how to nap with your eyes open?"

Ibram gave in and rubbed the back of his head, digging his fingers into his scalp. The muscles in his shoulders began to relax. "To be sure, that remains a type of study."

"The Monbrith family has a history of divine requests, doesn't it?" Lady Azadiya said, and whatever Amota Lakum was about to say, he was forced to swallow. Lady Azadiya gathered her hair prongs, and stuffed them in her pocket as she stood up. She readjusted her mitts, the left and then the right. "What do we know of the uncle?"

Ibram frowned at his boots, and then looked up. He released the back of his head. "Not much more than what Mistress Suugan told you, Ladyship. I can't remember any mention of him to me or Ahksell."

Ahksell tossed his gar from one hand to the other. "Nor can I, if I'm honest."

Ibram nodded. "My apologies for changing the subject, Ladyship," he said. "But I think I've discovered why Rustam ran off."

"Besides the fact that he's a maker of false coin?" Amota Lakum asked. "Isn't that enough?"

"Yes, but nobody knew that," Ahksell pointed out.

"I think Madji Anlines did," Ibram said.

Lady Azadiya regarded him. "Who is that?" she asked.

"A dramseller," Ibram answered. "And a spreader of misery, to be sure. She's the reason Ahksell and I heard about Mandibrite in the first place. She doesn't think much of alchemists—or perhaps, it's more fair to say she thinks too much of you?"

"How so?" Lady Azadiya folded her hands in her lap.

"She thinks the Court Civil makes witnesses drink truth serum," Ibram said. "And told Rustam the same."

"Why would she think that?" Ahksell asked.

"Court recorders dose themselves with that potion at the start of a trial, don't they?" Ibram asked. "And judges toast whoever's on the throne as part of their covenant with the imperial house."

"But how did she come to tell you anything?" Amota Lakum asked. He crossed his arms over his chest.

"I saw her in the square when I was looking for Mistress Terin," Ibram said. He squared his shoulders. "I seized the opportunity of asking her."

"That wasn't the errand Lady Azadiya sent you out on," Amota Lakum said.

"And yet I profit from it, regardless," Ladyship interrupted. "So this dramseller is close enough to the family to offer advice?"

Ahksell snorted. "From my memory, you wouldn't be able to stop her, regardless."

Lady Azadiya picked at a thread on her mitt. "A dramseller generally maintains a set route," she said.

"She had a contract with the Monbriths, but now complains that they've let her go," Ibram said, and then frowned. "In point of fact, I seem to recall the Mistresses Monbrith falling out about that at dinner. I didn't connect the two until now."

"The dramseller, the blacksmith, and the draughtshop," Ladyship muttered. She considered the backs of her hands for a moment. "The one able to make the coin, the other two capable of moving a large amount of money without drawing overmuch suspicion."

"How though?" Ahksell asked.

"Madji complained about travel taxes," Ibram offered.

"All merchants do that," Amota Lakum said.

"Yes, but what if that wasn't true?" Ibram said. "She keeps on grumbling, because, as you say, 'all merchants do that,' but it doesn't truly bother her because she has a stash of false coin to throw about? She hasn't been through Mentor Tikari's process yet."

Ladyship breathed in sharply. "Well," she said. "A search of her wagon will answer that. Were you able to gain entrance?"

"I tried," Ibram said. "I claimed you needed a bottle of Drethylmane, but she slammed the door in my face."

"An entire bottle?" Amota Lakum exclaimed.

"Did she have one?" Lady Azadiya asked.

Ibram nodded. "She claimed she did, and I don't know why she'd lie in the face of money. She could have just refused to talk to me."

"The import tax on that bottle means you charge twice its worth, or go hungry," Ladyship said. "Consider it a point in the favor of her criminal involvement. Do the Monbriths stock Drethylmane as well?"

"I do not know," Ibram said.

Lady Azadiya stood and called her gar to her hand; it somersaulted over the couch and Ibram felt his hair ruffle in its wake. "Where do we stand on Rustam's lack of favor with his deity?" she asked.

Ibram shrugged. "We can go and ask right now if they know what it was he said in their prayer to change the Speaker's mind. I place the bet on Madji, now, though."

"They might lie," Amota Lakum pointed out.

"What do they have to lose now?" Ibram asked.

"Enough," Lady Azadiya said. "Boys, go out into the hall, I need to speak with Lakum in private."

"Ladyship," Amota Lakum said and bowed.

Ibram turned around and safely rolled his eyes. Ahksell reached the pocket door first and slid it open. The sound of hammering grew louder. "Mentor, what should we do next?" he asked.

"I'll have your instructions soon," she said. "Now out."

Ahksell stepped onto the terrace. Ibram followed him and closed the door shut. He touched his knuckle to the flat hinged door pull and then glanced to his right. Ahksell crossed his arms, hugging his gar to his side, and shrugged. His mouth sagged downward.

"You still mad at me?" he asked finally.

Ibram turned and leaned against the door. He tucked his thumbs into his belt. They stood almost at the corner of the courtyard, next to a pavilion. A light rain began to fall, not unusual for the season. It sounded like pellets on the roof.

"Do you think demons care about sodden wood?" Ibram asked instead of answering. "When Mentor Perhara calls to them, I mean. Does it have to be treated with something to make it acceptable?"

"Ibram."

Ibram chewed the inside of his cheek and breathed in through his nose. Those folk in the courtyard were building their own doom, maybe demons fed upon that. His eyelids felt heavy, as if he'd had too little sleep. He blinked and then pressed the heel of his right hand against his closed eye.

"It's strange to think you hide things from me," he said.

"As if I never did?" Ahksell said.

"Yes, but you hiding a bag of candies with Katka is a bit different, isn't it?" Ibram said, and then cleared his throat. "And don't say you aren't a child anymore, I know you aren't. No more than I am."

Ahksell shrugged. "Well, I'm not. I'm twenty-three."

Ibram wiggled the back of his head against the wood of the door. He'd known coming back home after all his travels would be different. But for the past two years, it had been more exciting than unsettling. He had explored the changes in Lityen more like how he'd felt his way into a new part of world, only this one had familiar faces and better beds. It had even been like keeping notes for Ladyship, really. Seeing what there was to be seen and reporting back. Now he had to reevaluate all the bits and people he'd thought he could rely on not to change; he confessed to himself the urge to stamp his foot was growing very strong. Well, maybe not in actual fact.

"I'm not owed secrets," he said finally. He was older; he could afford the concession. "I work for the sect, I'm not a part of it."

"I know that," Ahksell said. "I just..."

Ibram looked at him out of the corner of his eyes. "Just don't think I need to know?"

"I just don't think you should—" Ahksell broke off with a very heavy sigh. He turned to lean on his gar and hunched his shoulders. He was so bad with his height. Ibram didn't even want to know what anyone watching them from the opposite side of the courtyard might be thinking. Ibram snorted, and then poked Ahksell's back straighter with two fingers.

Ahksell swayed back on his heels, but otherwise refused to be moved. "I don't want you getting into trouble!" he whispered furiously.

"I'm already in trouble!" Ibram protested.

"Yes, but more trouble," Ahksell jerked his thumb over his shoulder. "Official trouble."

"Like I wouldn't be in official trouble right along with you? What's bad for the serf's bad for the free man, you know."

Ahksell glared at him. "You are not a serf! This is Vissilia, not Orilind."

"Thank you, Attendant, for your grip of geography."

"Ibram!"

Ibram poked him again. "Why is Attendant Serisan skulking around?"

"Why did you bring her up in front of your friend Warder Kamos?"

Ibram spread his hands. "Ah, but if she isn't here then it doesn't matter, does it?"

"It isn't what you think!"

Clearly, Ahksell believed Ibram suspected an assignation. Which Ibram was definitely going to consider at a later time, because it was hilarious. But he could pretend to think along Ahksell's line, if it got him actual answers. "Do the other Attendants know? What does Ladyship say?"

Ahksell was too old to pout, but pout he did, and Ibram felt a thrill of fire lick up his back. He grinned. "See now, if you just tell me—ock!"

The door slid open behind him; Ibram's hands flew out to his sides as he tilted backwards. Ahksell grabbed him by the front of his gambeson and pulled him back on his feet. Ibram shook him off and walked towards the railing, and then turned around.

Amota Lakum stood in the doorway. He narrowed his eyes and puffed air through his mouth. Ibram pulled down his gambeson and cleared his throat. Over his shoulder, Lady Azadiya was unfolding up her coat and cloak; she shook it.

"Don't lean on doors, Ibram," Amota Lakum said. "What if Ahksell hadn't caught you?"

"You would have?"

In the room, Lady Azadiya laughed. "Tell him to put his wit to better use," she called out. "I want Satya Monbrith brought to me."

"That will be difficult, Ladyship," Ibram called back. "Since she's in the custody of the warders, and they don't like to remove folk from it."

She waved her hand, light flashed on her rings. "Then take Ahksell and your amota and go and speak with her. I want an actual questioning this time, Ibram."

"And what will Ladyship be accomplishing?" Ibram asked, while keeping his eyes averted from Amota Lakum's frown.

"Ladyship," Lady Azadiya said, as she put on her coat and cloak, "will be shopping in the village square. If I am to have furs, I shall need boxes. I expect I have quite a long list."

16

Satya Monbrith and the remaining half of her family were confined in the anteroom in the reception hall of the manor, which had been reconverted back into its original profession as a jail. The door had even been replaced and now featured a series of incredibly sturdy locks, non-alchemical in nature, but still enough to do their duty. Their jailor turned out to be Mistress Islozia, who handed over the keys too quickly to be called graceful, and then struck up a loud conversation with the two warders hovering to either side of the purpose-built hovel.

Ibram set the key into the first lock. The sunlight flickered. A shrieking bang reverberated through the reception hall, and a seismic thundering wind blew open the metal gate. Ibram threw himself to the ground and covered the back of his head. His breath smashed out of his lungs as he pressed up against the vibrating cell wall. He heard shouts behind him and the sound of collapsing wood. Amota Lakum yelled, and a large body fell into Ibram from his right; they slid to the floor and rolled as the wind shrieked above them. Ibram's ears popped; all the hairs on his head stood up.

The wind died as suddenly as it came. Ibram raised his head. Next to him, Ahksell groaned. Amota Lakum was on the other side of the reception hall, leaning one-handed against the wall. Ibram pushed off the ground and ran for the door, bouncing off a warder or two on his way. Ahead of them, he could hear yelling and another bang, smaller but no less frightening. Smoke billowed into Ibram's eyes and nose before he crossed the main gate, putrid and metallic. He gagged, wavering to a stop. He put his hands on his knees and retched.

A large hand covered in a handkerchief cupped his mouth and pulled him upright. He breathed in, the cotton was slightly sweaty but not so immediately disgusting. Ibram grabbed Ahksell's wrist and nodded for him to let go, but kept the handkerchief for himself. Ahksell had his own already tied across his face.

Before them the crowd of traders had turned into a mob, startled by the smoke and no doubt sickened by the stench. The warders darted amongst them pulling folk apart and dragging them off to the side. Some of them walked, but some were dragged, kicking at the cobblestones. Horses neighed loudly in the livery yard; Ibram heard wood cracking. He tied the handkerchief over his mouth, and then tucked Mistress Islozia's keys up his sleeve into his wallet.

Thundering footsteps pounded behind them. Ibram pointed to the right and they ran to the side just as Commander Osthanes and his leftover squad burst out into the square, shouting orders and laying into the crowd. Amota Lakum was not far behind. He kicked the knees out of a man who'd crawled out of the melee with a bloody face, and seemed about to rejoin the fray. Ibram pointed at Ahksell and then the caravans; he waited to see Ahksell nod and then led the way to the side of the fight. He hunched his shoulders, and pressed the cloth more firmly against his mouth.

The stink stung his nose; his eyes watered. Ahksell pulled him to a stop by one of the larger wagons, where Ibram could see hands wrapped around the spokes of the wheels. He coughed. Smart folk to hide out of the way.

"What happened?" Ibram yelled over the noise.

"Someone must have tipped Mentor Tikari's table!" Ahksell bellowed. He pointed and then bent his first and fourth fingers of his right hand. He waved his hand strongly to the right, and the swirling smoke parted as if it had been sliced by a knife. It curled back, but not before Ibram saw Mentor Tikari and her Attendant standing in front of a ruined table, tossing woven mats over spots on the ground that seemed to be on fire. Some old mistress took a run at them, and Mentor Tikari pushed out with her hand, sending the woman tumbling back into the fray.

Ibram looked about them. Twenty alchemists poured out of their carriages, gars in hand. A squad of them jumped high and landed on covered traders' wagons, but stopped there. Ibram frowned. Where they trying to intimidate the crowd with their presence?

Ibram dragged Ahksell down to his level. "Can you take them down?" he yelled above the noise.

Ahksell shook his head. "Not all at once!" he shouted back.

"Well," Ibram threw his arm out. "Couldn't hurt!"

Ahksell nodded. "Can you circle to Mentor Tikari?" he asked. "I'll form a barrier."

Ibram patted him on the arm and let go. He stepped left. Ahksell walked forward and held his gar out sideways in both hands. He breathed in, leaning backwards, and then pushed forward. Ibram squinted through the smoke. He saw the crowd stagger away from the fires and the upturned table; someone yelled and then a man on the ground scrambled up. He stepped on a mat, and fell; the green fire crackled.

Ibram darted forward; he snatched up the misplaced mat and threw it on the flames. He scrambled backwards out of the smoke. On the opposite side of the square, he saw Mentor Perhara and his agents hurrying over just as a rushing wind began to pick up.

Warder Phiri passed him with a struggling man under one arm. Ibram looked behind him for Ahksell, and saw him holding position with his gar. The crowd rocked together in a knotted mass of bodies, not even appearing to notice the barrier keeping them away from the fires Mentor Tikari was methodically putting out. They shouted and lurched as one while the warders dragged off folk and tossed them into a kind of human-formed corral.

As Ibram peered through the chaos, the wind strengthened. His ruffled hair whipped back into knots as the smoke began to swirl in on itself. The rotten, musty stench became overpowering; he gagged and ran back to the caravans. Men and women stumbled away, and fell to their knees to avoid the miasma. An unearthly howl wavered up from Mistress Denrind's front gate. Ibram raised himself up on his tiptoes—he wasn't ashamed of it—and glimpsed Lady Azadiya. She slammed her gar against the ground, and cobblestones rocked forward as if caught be a wave.

The crowd lurched and fell. Ibram fell back against a wagon, and pushed himself to his feet. Ahksell relaxed from his position and leaned against his gar with a dropped head; his back heaved. The keening wail was deafening; Ibram covered his ears.

Lady Azadiya walked forward into the loosening throng, poking folk out of her path with her gar in one hand and whirling a paper cone on a string with the other; the sound seemed like it came from that. She frowned as she stalked into the middle of the fight, the cone blurring with speed over her head. Her gar battered the stones of the square, and the noise wavered in the air like the clap of gigantic hands.

In its wake, even the shouting stopped. The horses' panicked neighs seemed to quiet. The rain lightened. The smoke tightened into a funnel, and then into a snake and then into something like a string that curled about itself the closer she came near to Mentor Tikari and her fires until finally Lady Azadiya opened her hand, and the paper cone dropped into her palm. The string dangled from between her fingers to the ground. Ladyship slammed her gar into the ground to hold it upright. Then, she crushed the top of the cone in her fist, twisted the paper closed, and then held it out to Mentor Tikari. Cautiously, Ibram lowered his hands from his ears.

"Yours, I believe?" she asked, her voice rang out in the sudden lull of noise. She glared up at the Attendants who'd climbed a few of the covered wagons. "And what are you wastrels doing up there? Did you get a nice view?"

A few Attendants dived over the side of the carriages they'd been standing on, immediately, but most of them stayed where they were. Ibram detected a high incidence of squirming. Lady Azadiya snatched her gar up and then down on the cobblestones again, a dull thud that nevertheless sent shivers through the assembled crowd.

"Off!" she commanded. "Or I'll give you to the warders as far-seeing dogs!"

They weren't even from her preceptory, but no one stayed to argue. Ibram's ears popped as the remaining Attendants quit the field as fast as they'd arrived. He winced and rubbed the little divot behind his left earlobe. The rain returned, but Ibram shoved his hair back over his head and resigned himself to the growing damp. He gulped down a clean breath of air, let it out, and then did it again.

He'd wondered what she was doing to let Osthanes and his crew beat her to a riot. Surely it must have taken her a moment to make the cone or find the string. That little contraption of hers had done its business well. Ibram breathed in deeply and felt a weight he hadn't noticed before fall from his chest.

"Give me that before you burn yourself," Mentor Tikari said. She thrust her hand between them, and frowned. Ladyship dropped the cone; Tikari caught it. She shook her head and glared about her. Her Attendant continued to stamp out the matted fires.

"One of these...*dolts* refused to believe my results and upset the table," Mentor Tikari said. "The essential concentrates mixed too quickly in the resultant smash and what am I to do when fools present themselves?"

"We do, in general, try not to sicken the local populace, Tikari," Lady Azadiya said.

"Am I to be blamed for a garden variety explosion brought about by mundane ignorance?" Tikari sniffed. "Besides, they're not local."

"Only some of them," Lady Azadiya said. She looked around at the defeated mob at her feet. "Now, which dolt was it?"

Mentor Tikari made a face. "It isn't my job to keep track of fools."

Even from some distance, Ibram could see the way Lady Azadiya's face twitched. "Attendant Zorion?" she called, and the fire-stamper came to attention.

"Yes, Mentor?" he responded.

"Who knocked over this table?" Lady Azadiya asked, and several folk on the ground cringed.

"Mentor Hobon! Sonic devices are illegal!" Commander Osthanes stalked directly towards her, trailing a pair of bedraggled warders.

Amota Lakum was not far behind, and Ibram could see Mentor Perhara strolling fast towards the center of the now contained action. Ibram glanced at Ahksell. Lady Azadiya waved her hand dismissively, but by that point Osthanes had reached her. Ibram tried, but he couldn't hear her response.

"Should we get over there?" he muttered.

Someone tugged on Ibram's pants-leg. He turned around and looked down; one of the young mothers peered up at him from beneath the wagon. Ibram crouched down and interlaced his fingers. The person next to her—hooded, plump, clearly a woman—inched away on her knees. Ibram grinned, and Attendant Serisan tugged her hood further down her face.

"Is it safe to come out now?" the other young lady asked him.

Ibram transferred his attention to her. He backed up a step and held out his hand. "Perfectly so," he said. "Ladyship's out of her sitting room and all's right with reality."

She clearly didn't know what to make of that, but struggled out from underneath the wagon, regardless. Ibram helped her stand and then put his hands behind his back as she straightened her clothes and hair.

"Didn't you have a baby before?" he asked.

The young woman glanced up, still with her hands in her hair. "Oh! Yes, I mean. He's down for a nap."

Ibram nodded.

"He's with his father," she continued. "I...best get back home. Thank you!"

She bobbed a short bow and hot-footed it down the length of the square. Ibram watched her go, and then bent back down to look under the wagon. The space was empty. He frowned, and placed a hand on the ground to keep his balance while he had a closer look.

"Where did she go?" he muttered.

"Where did who go?" Ahksell asked.

Ibram twisted around and looked up. Ahksell's face was a study in innocence. Ibram squinted as he rose up and dusted himself off.

"I don't need more distractions," he said. "You," he poked Ahksell in his belly, "are distracting me from my duties."

Ahksell sucked in his gut and leaned on his gar, unrepentant. "In that case," he said. "We should go and see what's going to happen next."

Ibram looked towards where Lady Azadiya was now obscured by a loudly debating group of alchemists and warders. Amota Lakum and both Uxios watched on the sidelines. Attendant Zorion had strayed back to the remains of the table. He picked up a broken glass pipe and sighed very heavily. The Sect had an entire department dedicated solely to glass-blowing; Ibram had always privately thought the artisans there earned every faunt.

"Might as well," Ibram said.

They picked their way through the fallen crowd of traders, who were only now making small attempts at standing up and making an account of themselves. Several warders, including Warder Phiri, moved amongst them. No one seemed gravely injured beyond a little nausea and a few strained muscles, the usual cuts and bruises gained in brawling. A stout man sitting on the ground had taken a clip over the eye and was staunching the blood with his sleeve.

Ibram came up to where Attendant Zorion was carefully picking through the glass. He watched him for a moment, but he was only lifting shards and then setting them down again. The smell lingered; Ibram wrinkled his nose. He pressed the handkerchief tied over his nose more tightly to his face and gave a testing sniff; the handkerchief's fibers also reeked. Ahksell pointed his first and second fingers to the sky and swirled them to the right. The wind picked up around them, a fluttering breeze that angled the smoke in the opposite direction. Ibram sighed and untied his handkerchief, and then stuffed the fabric under his belt.

Ibram checked once over his shoulder that Ahksell hadn't been diverted by the argument to their left, and then refocused his attention on Tikari's helper. "Attendant Zorion?"

The man dropped his splintered table leg and unbent, tossing his hair back over his shoulder. "Yes? Can I help you, Master...ah?"

Ibram bowed shortly. "Ucalegon, Attendant. I work for Lady Azadiya."

"Ah," Attendant Zorion turned to his right and then back to Ibram. "Yes. She's in there."

He pointed, helpfully, and Ibram nodded. "Thank you, Attendant. I was actually wondering if you could tell me what happened here."

Ahksell walked out from behind his back and came up to the other side of the ruined table. He crouched down and picked up the overturned basin. He looked into its bowl and frowned, and then set it back down. One of the little mats Zorion and Tikari had been throwing over the fires twisted beneath his foot, and he tugged it free. Then, he smelled it and turned it back and forth in his hand. The mat crackled audibly.

"Is that one of my mats?" Attendant Zorion said; he blinked at the air, slightly to Ibram's left, but above Ahksell's head. "It'll have to be resoaked," Zorion sighed.

The mat sizzled in Ahksell's hand; he tossed it in Zorion's direction. The little metal square hit Zorion in the chest, but he caught it on the rebound, and wrinkled his nose. "It's bone dry," Zorion observed. "I've never understood that saying, you know. Bones aren't dry, are they?"

Ibram sucked his teeth, and rolled his eyes in Ahksell's direction. Ahksell raised his hands in a helpless gesture. Attendants, honestly; they could be so strange.

"I think they might be if they're old, Attendant Zorion," Ibram said.

Zorion shook his head and prodded a large broken plank with his foot. "Well," he said. "The problem really was that we had run out of the Grum's Unguent fairly quickly, so in order to transverse the precipitate from the resultant silt and filter the unguent from the slag, Mentor Tikari had me take out the bronze mesh filters rather than the silver. They can take more weight, you see."

Ibram nodded. "Sounds about right. Is that what upset all these folk?"

"No, I think it was the money."

Ahksell stood with a sigh. "He means 'how did the fight start,' Hilbert," Ahksell said.

Attendant Hilbert Zorion blinked into the space next to Ibram's shoulder. "Oh, thank you, Ahksell," he said. "I didn't see you there."

"I know you didn't," Ahksell replied. "Put your glasses on, please."

Zorion squinted. "Is there going to be shoving again?" he asked. "I haven't ground my new lenses yet; I only have my old pair."

"Shoving's over for now," Ibram said.

"Then, that's all right." Attendant Zorion reached into a rectangular leather case strapped length-wise on his belt, and took out a pair of wooden-framed spectacles. He set them on the bridge of his nose and squinted through them; he chuckled in surprise. Ibram's hope of interviewing a close witness shriveled like a cinnak in the sun.

"Did you have those on when the fight started?" Ibram asked, regardless.

"Of course I did," Attendant Zorion said. "I can't see three feet without them."

"Well, small gods for small favors," Ibram muttered, and Ahksell poked him. He cleared his throat and raised his voice. "So what broke first, the table or the alembics here?"

"Oh, it was probably Mentor Tikari, really," came the reply. "That motley seller was being incredibly rude, but she definitely smacked him first."

Ibram tasted cold air on his tongue, and shut his mouth as soon as he became conscious it had dropped open. His teeth clicked. Behind him, Ahksell groaned quietly.

"She hit one of them?" Ibram asked.

Attendant Zorion nodded. "He disputed her declaration. He said if there was bad money in his pouch, then it was no fault of his and then he knocked the testing basin and splashed the leaded chalk onto the torch, which is what made this horrendous stench."

"And she got angry," Ahksell said.

"He really was very rude!" Attendant Zorion gestured in agitation at the ruins of their array. "Look at this mess."

Ibram followed the arc of his arm with his eyes, and saw the glint of coins amidst the wreckage. Two warders with a large basket were wandering around picking them up. No one in the crowd was moving to touch them, otherwise.

"Surely you brought spares," Ibram said.

"That isn't the point," Attendant Zorion said. "We'll have to start all over again, and these—these—"

"Traders," Ibram supplied.

"These traders!" Attendant Zorion opened and closed both hands before himself. "He said we were making it up in order to keep the money!"

Ibram raised his eyebrows. "Where would he get an idea like that?"

Attendant Zorion shook his head. "I don't know."

"Was the motley seller the only person who made that claim?" Ibram twisted left and then right to look over the field of battle. The warders had gotten most of the crowd to their feet by then, but a few were being bandaged where they sat. He put his hand above his eyes to get the rain off them.

"I think so," Attendant Zorion said. Ibram looked back to him. "They were all getting restive, of course, but the first ten or so seemed to understand the seriousness of our task. And Warder Pendem gave them all a slip to send into the Bureau of Currency for a claim later so they certainly weren't happy, but no one did anything foolish about it."

Ibram sucked in a breath; he'd forgotten about that. Captured counterfeiters were liable to claims of remuneration from their victims, if it could be proven that the coins came from their forges. Hard labor to pay off the debt usually took precedence over the death penalty. With Harken Tolk dead, Rustam was the only one left unless they could find another co-conspirator to defray the cost.

"What about after the first ten traders?" Ibram asked. "Did they become, uh, rude as well?"

Attendant Zorion nodded and rubbed his earlobe. "I think they were bored," he said, watching Ahksell poking through the wreckage. "You know how waiting in a line just seems to go on forever, no matter how fast you work? They got to talking amongst each other." He frowned and his hand drifted to a large pouch on his belt. "Maybe we shouldn't have allowed that."

"You know that's not legal," Ahksell said as he stood up and handed Zorion a small stack of mats. "You can't just make people drink your strange infusions simply because you need silence to think."

"Mentor said my infusions are why she picked me."

Ibram reminded himself to never partake of a meal up the living mountain ever again. He let the two of them bicker for a moment, and stepped back for a wider view of the area. Now that the fuss had passed, villagers were out of their hiding spots to watch the show.

"Is there a motley seller available?" Ibram yelled. "I'm running out of pillows for my very large manor!"

Commander Osthanes' head leaned out of the gang of alchemists. He glared and pushed Warder Kamos in Ibram's direction, and then went straight back to arguing. Ibram heard the words 'assault' and 'custody' being growled. Warder Kamos frowned while sighing—quite the feat—as he stumped towards Ibram.

Ibram looked about himself hopefully. An older man dressed in a short red loose blouse tucked into his tan trousers like they wore in the southern plains caught Ibram's eye from where he was sat near the common well. He had a very swollen eye and a handkerchief pressed to his lip. To be sure, he looked like a man who'd taken a direct hit to the face.

Ibram ambled over to him, neatly sidestepping Warder Kamos, who swiveled to follow. He tucked his hands behind his back and nodded politely. The motley seller took off his handkerchief, stared at it, and then put it back on his mouth.

"You sell feathers?" Ibram asked. "Maybe a sack to put them in?"

"I do," the man said, grudgingly.

"You have any idea who angered Mentor Tikari so badly?"

The man grunted. "Not my fault," he said. "I'm locked up here for days, and now she tells me my coins's no good?"

"Ah," Ibram said. "So you tried attacking an alchemist. Perfectly understandable, it'll get you quickly moved out of the province. Don't suppose there's a smarter man we could be talking to?"

"She hit me first!"

"I should remind you, Master Ferglan," Warder Kamos spoke up with no intent to be helpful. "That you are not beholden to answer this man in any way."

"Oh come now, Warder Kamos!" Ibram pressed his hand to his torch brooch; Master Ferglan's one good eye took note. "A man gets into a violent argument with someone down the living mountain on Her Gracious Majesty's business and I don't get to find out why? That's the kind of tale I'll be able to dine out on at home."

Master Ferglan grunted and then winced. "What's to tell? I've been waiting in that line with my entire pot for the season, and she tells me a good quarter of it's not fit for trade?"

Ibram whistled. "That would make me furious. Did it make you that way? Did it make you furious?"

Master Ferglan removed his handkerchief and spit to one side. "Think I don't know how to weigh a picaio to tell if it's been plugged? I told her I wasn't a fool, and I wasn't going to be fooled by her."

Ibram nodded slowly, and cast an eye towards Warder Kamos. Kamos took off his helmet, rubbed his hair back, and smacked it back on his head. He shook his head.

"Well about that," Ibram said. "I'm not certain it was wise, you know. Fourth Mentor Tikari prides herself on her work."

He supposed that was a fair assumption to make, after all. In his admittedly small experience, alchemists did not start brawls with non-alchemists for small slights. Although, to be sure, the Preceptory of Afsoun was its own little world.

Master Ferglan's injured mouth moved silently for a second, the corner began to bleed a little. "Well—well so do I pride myself on my work!"

"Your work in assessing coins?"

"It's part of any reasonable merchant's duty," Ferglan snapped. He rolled himself to his feet, and Ibram and Kamos stepped clear to allow it. "Just because they need gold and silver in their—their experiments, doesn't mean they can have mine!"

"Wait just a minute," Ibram said. He cast an alarmed glance at Kamos, whose entire body had suddenly tensed like a hunting dog in Ferglan's direction. "Who said anything about that?"

Ferglan concerned himself mostly with brushing himself off and only briefly glared at Ibram. "It was all through the crowd," he said. "Everybody was talking of it."

"That the largest supplier of trade in this corner of the province," Ibram said, and crossed his arms, "which provides the only reliably safe public passage into the West, is somehow so deeply in need of silver and gold that they've corralled a small village in order to steal the coins of a single traveling motley seller like yourself."

Red blotches bloomed on Ferglan's cheeks. "I'll say no more to you," he snapped. "I see that torch on your chest."

"No, but you'll say it to my commander," Kamos said. He grabbed Ferglan by the shoulder and towed him away. Ibram turned on his heels in their direction.

"Who'd you hear it from anyway?" he asked loudly.

Ferglan twisted in Kamos' grasp. He raised his hand to his shoulder, and flicked his middle finger at him. Hasi Terin, her mother in tow, gasped as Kamos dragged him away. The rest of the folk in the square who weren't under the tender care of warders or mothers were growing restive. Ibram saw several pinched glares aimed in his general direction.

Ibram shook his head. "Malingerers," he muttered.

Around him, the rest of the mob lingered but was silent. He frowned as he considered the ones talking amongst themselves. Whoever had begun that rumor had a vicious tongue when idle, and he'd only met one who was that loose-jawed and recklessly malicious. He looked back to where Ahksell and Attendant Zorion were turning over broken equipment. The warders had kept records of who was in line, maybe he could get a look at that list to see if Madji had left her herder's hut.

"Ibram!"

He turned his head at his name. Amota Lakum raised a hand in his direction and waved him over. Ibram obeyed.

"How did you get that man angry at you so quickly?" Amota Lakum asked.

"It's not my fault," Ibram said. "He was already angry. That's the man Mentor Tikari slapped."

"She slapped someone?"

"Oh, it's all gotten very energetic around here," Ibram said. "Have you been talking to the Uxios?"

Amota Lakum frowned. "Ibram, there's only one Uxio."

"Yes, but which one?"

Amota Lakum's face settled into disappointment.

Ibram shrugged. "Are you all right? You didn't get hurt wading into the fray?"

"Not at all," Amota Lakum said. He did look a little wind-blown, but Ibram supposed they all did.

Ibram swiped a hand down his arms to shear off the water dewing up on the treated wool. He wiped them off on his breeches. He should promptly inform Amota Lakum of what Master Ferglan had said to him, but he'd only have to tell Ladyship as well. It made no sense to repeat himself. He shivered a bit in the cold and damp, and watched the back of Commander Osthanes' head bob like a water bird. The addition of Master Ferglan to the conversation did not seem to have helped matters. Mentor Tikari's voice raised sharply in counterpoint.

"Have you been able to make out what they're saying?" Ibram asked.

"Mentor Tikari says she was provoked," Amota Lakum said.

Ibram hummed in agreement. Amota Lakum smacked him in the upper arm. He winced and rubbed the spot.

"What?"

"Bad habits," Amota Lakum said.

"Enough!" Commander Osthanes finally yelled, and the group fell silent. "We're taking Master Ferglan back to the manor for further questioning. Kamos, with me. Pendem! Ingo! Round them all up!" He stared hard in front of him, where Ibram imagined Mentor Tikari stood. "We still have a lot of coins to get through here."

Ibram stood to one side while Commander Osthanes made his grand retreat to Mistress Denrind's manor with Kamos, Ferglan, and a second grim-faced warder in tow. Then, he observed the alchemists in their natural setting, talking amongst each other. Mentor Tikari was already stamping back towards Attendant Zorion and Ahksell, but Mentor Perhara and Lady Azadiya remained.

"I might have something for Ladyship," Ibram said, and then made a direct line to Lady Azadiya's side. Amota Lakum came with him. Ibram sighed up at the sky.

"Honestly, where were you?" she was saying. "It's not like you to miss a fight."

"Hardly a fight," Mentor Perhara said. He was smiling, but the expression appeared habitual. It never wavered. He nodded to Ibram at his approach. "I would say it was barely worth muddling in."

"Not every brawl involves a border dispute," Ladyship said.

"From your lips to the Speaker's Tongue," Mentor Perhara said. "Besides you know perfectly well I was attending to your favor."

He put such a stress on the word 'favor' that Ibram's ears perked up. He tilted his head and tried to assume the position of a polite yet inattentive servant. Across the way, he saw Ahksell bow to Mentor Tikari and then walk in their direction.

"My favor," Ladyship muttered. "Is it really such a hardship, Ziv? A few boxes moved and some supplies reassigned?"

"You know it isn't," Perhara laughed. "Even if I didn't share your enthusiasm for shopping, I enjoy the challenge."

She grinned with a few too many teeth and Perhara laughed harder. He glanced at Ibram and then stroked a hand down his short beard. Perhara inclined his upper body at Lady Azadiya.

"Am I to understand you still have some shopping to do?" he asked.

At some point, Ibram was going to have to let Ladyship know her subterfuge had lost its stealth, but it would have to wait until he could actually lay out what act 'shopping' was standing in for. Lady Azadiya raised her shoulder. She touched one of the buttons of her coat. "My list is still being prepared."

"Well, I'd light a fire under its compiler," Perhara said. "They'll start to notice that not all my Attendants are staying within Fontis. I'll have to recall them to their court-ordered tasks soon. The walls are going up fast as they're finished."

Lady Azadiya nodded. Ibram coughed discreetly. Lady Azadiya frowned at him. "Are you getting a cold, Ibram?" she demanded. "Stand over there."

She pointed a good foot away from her. Ibram shook his head and bowed to the air between her and Mentor Perhara. Mentor Perhara waved him up again.

"I'm fine, thank you, Ladyship," Ibram said. "But I do have something to report."

She turned to face him more fully. "Oh? What is it?"

"Someone's started a rumor that Mentor Tikari's here to steal everyone's coins, rather than assess them for Judge E'grard."

Lady Azadiya frowned heavily and Mentor Perhara sighed. He shook his head, and tucked his gar in the crook of his elbow. Lady Azadiya gazed to her right, where another group of merchants had formed. Ahksell came up and stood at Mentor Perhara's back.

"And it isn't known who began the rumor?" Ladyship asked.

Ibram shook his head. "I spoke to the merchant Mentor Tikari punched and he was just the first to express it to her. He said 'everyone' knew about it. But Attendant Zorion said they had gone through about ten caches before the crowd started to turn on them."

"Lakum," she said. "Find that book they were writing the names of merchants in. I want to know who has and has not heard this rumor of Ibram's and if they believed it. See if you can't find the one who did this."

"Of course, Ladyship," Amota Lakum said as he detached himself from the group.

Ibram turned back to the alchemists. "I think someone in this village likes stirring up trouble," he said. "And the only one I know of with a tongue sharp enough is Madji Anlines."

Lady Azadiya hummed to herself. "The dramseller again?"

Ibram paused, and then rubbed the back of his head. He'd not paid attention before and it had cost the entire village, but just saying things for the sake of having made the suggestion could be equally as bad. Lady Azadiya noticed and raised her eyebrows in inquiry.

"You think this dramseller is a likely suspect?" Mentor Perhara asked.

Ibram paused. He nodded, but then shook his head. "I think it's a few too many coincidences," he said.

Lady Azadiya nodded. "I will let Osthanes know then," she said. "Thank you, Ibram."

She frowned and then her face smoothed over. She looked to Perhara.

"How long will it take you to treat the wood?" she asked.

"The workers are unhappy making them, and no one in the village is feeling anything like joy," Perhara said. "They're already halfway imbued."

Ibram had only the slightest idea of what that meant, but shuddered from forming an opinion. His skin prickled all over. Perhara noticed and transferred his polite smile to him.

"It's like that, you understand," Perhara said. He waved his hand at Ibram's chest. "The more ill feeling in the well of emotion there, the more our realm of existence grows fertile for demonic resonance. Contact will be much easier."

"But it might not be needed," Ahksell said.

Mentor Perhara's smile was quite gentle, but he didn't turn to face Ahksell and merely slightly changed the angle of his head. Ibram felt chills up his spine. "I hope not," Perhara said. "It's much more pleasant to disperse such things, rather than make use of them. I look forward to your success."

Lady Azadiya tapped her gar very lightly on the toe of Ibram's boot. "Have you spoken with any of the Monbriths?" she asked.

Ibram tore his attention from Mentor Perhara to stare at Lady Azadiya. "No, Ladyship," he said. "We heard the blast from the fight and then I forgot." He raised his hand and felt something shift along his wrist. "I still have the keys to their cell, though."

He looked back to the manor. Hopefully, the explosion had merely alarmed them, and not damaged anything. He breathed out and considered the front gate. He might be the one of the last folk to ever walk beneath it, if he wasn't clever enough to figure out what was happening.

Lady Azadiya sighed. "Worst thought?" she asked when Ibram turned back to her.

Mentor Perhara immediately let his attention drift to something dreadfully important in the sky. He even touched Ahksell's shoulder and pointed to it as he dragged him back a few steps. Ibram cleared his throat and focused on the bridge of her nose, rather than Ladyship's eyes.

"I've forgotten something, and it will cost Fontis dearly," he said.

She nodded. "Then get yourself and Ahksell back to the Monbriths, and see what they have to say."

Ibram bowed as Ladyship walked off, calling Mentor Perhara to her side as she passed. Ahksell walked back to him, and sighed. "What a difference a fight makes," he said and huffed part of a laugh.

Ibram shook his head. He scrutinized the village square, slowly and obviously. Mentor Tikari had contrived to gain another table and she and Attendant Zorion were in the process of setting up their new array. The traders were milling about, more or less peaceably. The space before the table had been cleared of debris, and now sported four warders positively bristling with weaponry and zeal.

To his left, Mistress Islozia and Warder Kamos came charging up the field out of Mistress Denrind's house. Ibram pressed his hands to his face and groaned. Ahksell patted him on the back. He dropped his hands just in time to see Kamos detach himself from Islozia's side, and wade into the pack of merchants. Ibram hurried forward, Ahksell in tow, and ran past Mistress Islozia as she came within shouting distance.

"Anlines!" Kamos shouted. "Where is Madji Anlines?"

She'd been in her hut, the last time Ibram had seen her, and indeed, two warders had detached themselves to bang on the dramseller's door. No one answered. The merchants looked between themselves and shuffled in place, but no one spoke. Zosi Kolesar had come out of his shay shop and was looking about himself. Ibram pushed Ahksell forward.

"Finally, a moment for your height to have purpose," he muttered and then, louder, "Warder Kamos! Attendant Solari knows what she looks like!"

Ahksell shrugged Ibram off, and then glared around. "I cannot believe you," he said from the side of his mouth. He stood up on his tiptoes as the very definition of excessive effort. A stir developed in the middle of the traders towards the back, like a stone had been cast in a pond.

"Master Ucalegon," Mistress Islozia said as she reached him. "You were not given those keys in perpetuity."

Ibram turned his head, and there she stood, with her hand out flat. Ibram groaned. "Not now, Mistress," he said.

He gestured at the milling crowd, which had begun to startle under the approach of the warders, like a flock of mouflon seeing an encroaching dog. He heard her sigh. Ahksell suddenly pointed.

"There!" he called out. "In the back, going to the right!"

The warders began pushing against the crowd and the ripple of movement became a flood as merchants ran to the sides and the warders dashed into the current. Ibram darted forward into the throng and took an elbow to the chest for his trouble. He coughed and twisted to the side. Beside him, Ahksell waded into the merchants, who didn't so much make way as were forcibly diverted. Together, they worked their way inwards. They made it almost to the center, before drawing up short against the wall of warders blocking off the area.

Ibram frowned and looked left and then right. He leaned against a warder's arm caught tightly against his stomach. A flash of grey hair or the sound of a clacking bead flared up, but none belonged to Madji Anlines. The traders had calmed, as the warders grew increasingly frustrated.

"Looking for your sweetling?" a cackling voice called out behind Ibram. "Try the forest, eh?"

Ibram hunched his shoulders. The warder holding him back croaked "hup, hup!" and the rest of his fellows pushed the crowd back further still, stretching their arms in place. He craned his neck left and then right. They were in an area where the wagons and carts made all sorts of crevices and alleys to slip through. Was Anlines simply not answering her door? He grabbed Ahksell's upper arm and jumped to see better.

"I see her!" Ahksell yelled. He pointed. "Back by the yellow wagons!"

From afar, Warder Kamos' head turned fast as a bloodhound. Ibram jumped up off of Ahksell's shoulder and saw Madji Anlines duck between two sellers' mobile stalls. She couldn't be trying to make her way to her own hut; the warders were at the doors. He shook Ahksell's arm. The crowd rocked them both from side to side, pressing in at

Ibram's back. He looked up; Ahksell was the only one who still had his arms free at the barrier.

"Come on," he said and yanked on Ahksell's sleeve. "Grab her! Like you used to do with the apples!"

"What? Oh!" Ahksell raised his left hand into the air, made a kind of snatching gesture, and then heaved his arm upwards. The yellow wagon tipped forward with a thunderous crash against the cobblestones. Folk screamed; the crowd surged around them and Ibram fell into Ahksell. Suddenly, as if they were a school of fish, the merchants and villagers darted away and he and Ahksell now stood alone. Ibram straightened and glanced about himself, one hand on the hilt of his sica. The warders in front of Ahksell had turned very pale. He saw Madji Anlines thrown back against the other wagon, covering her head from flying debris.

The warders kept their restraining arms up, even though few folk had stayed after the wagon collapsed. Ahksell huffed; he'd kept his feet without a problem. He freed both arms, and reached out. His hands tightened like claws as he whipped his arms up. A thin high wail erupted; Madji Anlines rose into the air, twisting against an invisible vise. Her feet kicked out spasmodically.

"Catha's corpse," Ibram swore. "Don't kill her!"

"Down is easier than up!" Ahksell said. His eyes opened wide as he drew back his arm, and Mistress Anlines floated out into the larger square. The crowd—warders included—scuttled back as if she were on fire. Ahksell swallowed; his hands shook.

Warder Kamos approached her with both his hands raised as if she were a startled animal. "All's well, mistress," he said up to her. "Just keep on breathing."

She hung in the air, immobile, and Ahksell began to sweat. Warder Kamos tugged on her heavy tunic. Madji shrieked. Ahksell took a deep breath and then held it. Ibram rubbed the back of his head.

"Get her down! Deal with this!" The warder in front of him grabbed Ibram's gambeson and dragged him forward. Ibram stumbled and yanked himself free. He glanced up and then to the side as Ahksell joined him. The merchants swelled into the space they'd left behind, just barely caught by the warders closing ranks once more.

"He's going to let her go now," Ibram called out. "On your mark, Warder Kamos."

Ahksell drew his right arm back again, but kept his hand steady. He was panting a little, sipping the air between his barely parted lips. He lowered his arm while breathing out. Madji's body tilted feet-first, and when her shoes touched the earth, Ahksell bent over and braced both hands on his knees. Another shriek rippled out as the old dramseller was caught up by the Warders. Ibram grinned; he slapped Ahksell on the shoulder.

"Well done!"

Ahksell leaned down with both hands on his knees and took a deep breath. He shook his head and then nodded, breathing heavily. "Think I," he gasped. "Think maybe I need that class on stamina after all."

"Ah well—"

"I cannot—yes, yes, let me through!" Mistress Islozia's voice snapped irritably from Ibram's right. He turned in her direction, and saw a pair of warders escorting her past the cordon. She marched up to Ibram.

"Master Ucalegon, the keys," Mistress Islozia demanded.

The keys? Was that really so important right now? Ibram kept on eye on Ahksell as he continued to breathe deeply.

"A moment," he said, but dug the cell keys out of his wallet. He dropped them without looking, and heard her catch them.

"I do not know what is going on around here," Mistress Islozia snapped. "Dead men cause more trouble than they're worth!"

"Oh, I am in complete agreement with you there," Ibram said, keeping an eye on the festivities in the center of the square. "But, seeing as how this latest incident has rather derailed us all, do you think you might see clear to letting us speak with the Mistresses Monbrith now? As opposed to later?"

He glanced over in time to observe how she glared at him. He pointed to Madji, who was surrounded by warders. The villagers and merchants had been removed further from the area and now huddled into two groups, both equally unnerved.

"Please, Mistress Islozia? Ahksell's been very good," Ibram said.

Ahksell sighed, but Ibram thought he spied an unwillingly amused dimple in Mistress Islozia's cheek. He spread his hands and it disappeared. Ahksell rose up with an enormous groan and placed both hands on his back.

"You know, I feel I should receive a little credit for not losing the keys entirely," Ibram said. "There was a riot at the time."

She scoffed, but beckoned them to accompany her. Ibram clapped his hand on Ahksell's back; he grinned unsteadily. They followed her back across the square and into the reception hall. Mistress Islozia unlocked the door herself this time, and opened it as well. She leaned in.

"Mistress Monbrith?" she called. "I'm having your dinner brought in, now that the mess is over with for the most part, and there's visitors to see you."

She stepped away from the doorway and frowned impressively. "When you're done," she said, "knock on the door or call out; I'll hear you."

Ibram bowed. "I thank you, Mistress, and apologize for the inconvenience."

She sighed and made a gesture towards the pair of warders who Ibram assumed were assigned to guard the Monbriths. They acknowledged her and stepped closer. Both of them wore swords, which Ibram thought a little excessive.

"Hold there, Ibram!" Amota Lakum called out from behind him.

Ibram turned and leaned around Ahksell. Amota Lakum loped closer from the other end of the reception hall. He came to a stop and caught his breath.

"I'd like a chance to go in with you," he said, and smoothed back his hair. "See these famous folk for myself."

"Of course." Ibram swallowed, but nodded. He could not shake the feeling that Amota Lakum was more interested in reporting on him, than on the matter at hand.

Ibram went in first, and bowed politely to the Mistresses Monbrith. The low chairs had been removed but not the small glow-bulb. Satya and her mother sat on straw pallets around the low table. Diarmit sat tucked under his mother's arm. He'd been reading a scroll, and now was crumpling the paper in both hands.

"Good day, Master Ucalegon," Mistress Monbrith said. Her hair was coming out of its low bun in little wisps. She tightened her grip on her son when Ibram moved inside to allow for Amota Lakum's entrance. "I'm afraid you find us at a disadvantage."

Ama always said that was the best place to find a suspect, but Ibram was polite and made no mention of it. Instead, he nodded in sympathy, and then gestured towards the door. He sat down at the table, at the furthest corner on her end. Diarmit, now between them, stared at his scroll of paper.

"May I make you known to my uncle, Mistress Monbrith?" Ibram asked. "He also works for the sect."

Her sharp chin wobbled, but firmed quickly. She nodded once, and then looked towards Satya. Satya turned her face away.

"Mistress Monbrith, my uncle Lakum Abban."

"Good day to you, Mistress Monbrith," Amota Lakum said and bowed. He sat down near the far corner of the table so that he faced Ibram.

"Master Abban, my daughter Satya, who sits next to you, and my son, Diarmit," Mistress Monbrith said. "I apologize for the state you find us in."

Amota Lakum said something charming back, and Ibram kept quiet while his elders made polite talk between them. It wasn't so good that the whole family was penned in together, but he didn't want to push his luck and insist on speaking separately. They'd have to make the best of it.

"I hope you weren't unduly alarmed by the foolishness outside, Mistress Monbrith," Amota Lakum said. "I assure you, it has been dealt with."

She swallowed tightly. "We were concerned."

"A dispute between merchants," Amota Lakum said and waved his hand as if to clear the air. "They can be rowdy."

A bitter amusement filtered through the hardened planes of Mistress Monbrith's face. She nodded, and then looked down and pet Diarmit's hair. The boy studied his paper.

"Is there room for one more?" Ahksell called out as he began to twist himself down across the threshold. The small anteroom had very clearly not been built with folks of his stature in mind. Ibram glanced from him to Diarmit.

"Think he'll make it?" Ibram whispered from the side of his mouth.

Beside him, Diarmit twitched. His eyes peered up, and then back down again. He shrugged. Ibram mimicked him. He sighed, and interlaced his fingers in his lap. Ahksell didn't have his gar, no doubt he'd realized the little room wouldn't fit himself and it.

"I think he'll make it," Ibram whispered, just as Ahksell shuffled through and shut the door behind him. He stood, head hunched between his shoulders, and then made a face.

"See?" Ibram said.

A tiny giggle; Ibram took it as a sign of progress. Ahksell came further into the room, and plunked down between Ibram and Amota Lakum. Satya took a deep breath and then looked at her knees. Mistress Monbrith frowned deeply.

Ibram took a deep breath and let it out. Lady Azadiya would probably have started with something polite and leading, and then closed a trap over the Monbrith's heads. But Ladyship wasn't there, and quite frankly Amota Lakum's polite nothings hadn't made much of a dent in anyone's misery, and so perhaps what was best was a friendly sharp shock.

"So how long have you known Rustam was breaking the law and the Speaker's heart in one fell swoop?" Ibram asked.

"Ibram!"

"Master Ucalegon!"

Amota Lakum and Mistress Monbrith spoke at once, took stock of each other, and then looked away. Ibram caught Satya's eye and wiggled his eyebrows. She didn't seem too impressed. A pity, but he couldn't win every heart.

He sighed and plopped his hands in his lap. "Are you saying he didn't? Because Fourth Mentor Hobon of Yseult is very likely to disagree." He leaned in Mistress Monbrith's direction, but kept a weather eye on Satya. "She feels a little put out herself, you know, Mistress. You write to her for aid, and then you throw her goodwill in her face?"

Mistress Monbrith turned pale and clutched Diarmit to her. "I did not write to her," she said. She closed her eyes and took a deep breath. "Satya wrote to you for help finding my son, and this is what has become of us. This is the temptation that alchemy has wrought in our lives."

"Don't say that," Satya snapped.

"It isn't fair," Ahksell said. "Your son didn't learn how to cheat his neighbors from anyone in the sect."

"But where do we learn temptation from if not our betters?" Mistress Monbrith asked. "Sticking your noses into realms you have no—"

"Well, at least you admit Ahksell's better than you," Ibram intervened.

She gasped audibly, whether from being diverted from however she was about to insult Ahksell next or from the implication, Ibram couldn't say. Satya heaved breath from her body so quickly her spine bowed with its escape. She covered her eyes with one hand, and rested her elbow on the table; she slumped. Ibram inspected the crown of her head.

"Don't suppose you want to tell me why you contacted me in the first place," Ibram said. "I mean to say, all cards on the table, it feels like a poor choice."

Satya pressed her hand against her eyes and then pinched the bridge of her nose. She sat up with a snort of air, and rubbed over her collarbones as if she was cold. She shook her head and resumed her previous position.

"All right, let me put out an idea, if you don't mind, Amota Lakum," Ibram said.

Amota Lakum glanced about the table. "If you insist, I'll give you a moment."

Ibram gave himself a moment to picture how Ama might go about telling someone they'd done wrong. It wasn't difficult, he'd had a great many years of getting into scrapes as a child that she had had to pull him out of. She was one of history's greatest yellers, and well known for her stamina and eloquence. But Father...Father's disappointment had often felt more painful to Ibram, and when he'd been kind about it, it had been worse.

"I think you did—you do—want to find Rustam," he said, and set his elbow on the table and rested his chin on his hand. Diarmit's knee jabbed his thigh as he resituated himself. "And you called upon me to help..." He hated it, but it was true. "Because I didn't ask too many questions the last time."

Slowly, she raised her eyes to him. It was cold in the room, and Ibram could see her shivering a bit. There was a blanket in her lap that she drew up to her shoulders like a shawl. She put her hands in her lap, and shrugged.

"Oh come now, Satya," he said. "You're too smart not to see an opportunity when it approaches, and I admit, I handed you a great big dazzling chance at finding Rustam without having to answer uncomfortable questions concerning why he ran away to begin with. That's my fault for trusting what looked like decent folk, and I take the blame for it."

"We are decent folk," Satya said. Her eyes gleamed wetly; she brushed her hand beneath them.

Ibram shrugged. "Every family needs a plan for where to go in an emergency, and you wrote to me. That's what I told Ladyship, you know. I told her you were wasting your intellect out here in Fontis, making correct change for folk and never stirring a step outside your front door."

Mistress Monbrith made a warning noise in her throat; Ibram ignored her. He focused instead on how Satya's eyes fell on every article in the room that they could see, except for him. Her mouth, lush though it was, took a decidedly downward tilt. He shifted his head and sighed.

"You know, I think it was because I saw a bit of myself in you? When it came time for my Ama to teach me how to read, she sent me along to the preceptory school, but when she wanted me to learn something important, she gave me lessons straight from *A Seasonable Time* because I'm Yilka the Green's sworn adherent, and needed to learn her way home. Have you ever read it?"

"We have not," Mistress Monbrith said, and pressed her lips together. "But it is better to learn the important facets of life from your deity."

"You know what I'm talking about, don't you, young mistress?" Ibram asked. "Actions from the world, intent from the heavens. You still have your copy of Bedris' *Guide to The Natural World.*"

Satya breathed in sharply; she always had been quick. "I'm not an alchemaster!" she exclaimed. "And neither is Rustam—and by oblivion, Harken Tolk wasn't either."

"Then why did Diarmit ask my friend Attendant Solari here at dinner if he could turn something into gold?"

"Because he listens to fools like that Imriska Suugan," Mistress Monbrith said. Ibram glanced to her. "The girl has her head turned by that Attendant at the Bedris school."

She was clutching her falcon pendant in her right hand and Diarmit in her left. "That Serisan is always filling their heads with seditious talk, teaching them about the Sundered Legion and how the Valley of the Lakes was lost. It's—"

"Mistress," Ahksell interrupted so gently Ibram could have imagined he'd practiced it. "Attendant Serisan does not lie about history and fact. The Advisor forbids the teaching of unlawful history, not the truth."

"And either way, no village miss can learn how to spin gold from a Bedris schoolroom," Ibram said. "That takes special classes, I'm sure."

"Rustam wouldn't know how," Mistress Monbrith said quickly, "and he would never—none of my children would ever—"

She broke off and tucked her face into her shoulder. Her body shook for a moment as if she was taking some kind of blow, and then she raised her head. She glared at Ibram, stiff-mouthed, and with hard eyes.

"No one in this room is responsible for these counterfeits coins, nor for allowing my oldest son to escape."

She said it with finality and nodded. Probably, a firm jaw and a sharp tongue had gotten Mistress Monbrith her way more often than not. To be sure, this time her stubborn nature had led her to a cell, but Ibram couldn't fault her for the attempt. He didn't think he'd bear up half so well.

"Am I to understand, Mistress," Amota Lakum said, "that you never knew where the money in your coffers came from?"

"Of course, I did," Mistress Monbrith said. There was a sort of grim satisfaction to the frame of her face. "It came from our customers, who then went on to sell their wares up the living mountain."

"And all those small villages just like Fontis in between," Ahksell said.

"Not to mention the freeholders," Ibram pointed at him. "The farmers and herders, the Imperial Bureau in Lityen, her gracious majesty's scribes here and in Itol and Lillia, and probably north to Sigisbrite, even. You can catch the river there, I remember."

"In truth, we can be certain that after three years, Master Rustam's fakes have made their way all across the countryside," Amota Lakum said. "This is a serious offense, as you well know."

"Might be some of these warders have been paid in worthless coin," Ibram said.

"But we didn't do it!" Diarmit squirmed free of his mother's arm and looked around the table. He crinkled his paper in his hands. "We didn't!"

"Quiet now," Mistress Monbrith said. She took the scroll from Diarmit's hands and rolled it up correctly. "This doesn't concern you."

"Then why can't we go home?" he asked. "I don't like it here, and Imriska—"

Mistress Monbrith slapped the scroll on the table; it rolled to the left slightly. Ibram saw it was a practice page from the bright reader's handbook.

"If you speak to me about that child one more time!" she exclaimed.

Diarmit sat back and crossed his arms. He ducked his head.

"Well then, what's to be done?" Ibram asked. "I want Diarmit to go home, too." Diarmit peeked at him; Ibram winked. "I want you all to go," he continued. "Cangsa, I even want me to go home, because the only person I can reasonably say will be sleeping in their own bed currently is myself and I'd like to be right for once. So how do we fix that?"

"You being right?" Satya asked.

Ibram snorted a laugh, and she grinned weakly at him. "See, I'm on your side, actually."

"Oh?" Satya asked. She sniffed and cleared her throat, and then wiped her eyes on her sleeve.

"I want this all resolved as happily as possible," Ibram said. "I think you brought me down in all faith to find your brother. But we all here know that window is closing fast."

Satya took a deep breath. Ibram waved his hand. "So when did you learn about Harken Tolk and Rustam's personal mint?" he asked.

"About a year into Rustam's apprenticeship," Satya said. She glanced at her mother, and down to her lap. "They weren't very subtle. Rustam suddenly had pocket money I couldn't account for in our books."

"And you didn't say anything?" Ibram asked.

Satya sighed and rubbed her forehead. "The money was welcome," she said. "Folks would stop to drink, but they wouldn't stay. Some of the wood in our walls had boreholes in it; whole sections needed repairing. Mother wanted improvements made."

"Don't you put this on me," her mother interrupted. "We would have managed."

When Master Harken died," Satya spoked over her with a grim, fixed look to her face. "Rustam panicked and came running to the draughtshop. He was screaming for a healer, and I left Emil in the common room while Mother went into the village to get Mistress Immel. He said Master Harken had lost his breath and couldn't get it back."

She shook her head; her face collapsed into itself for a brief moment, but she recovered herself. Ibram bobbed his head up and down. "So much you told me before," he said. "What did you leave out?"

"When we returned to the forge—it really doesn't take long when you run—Master Harken wasn't in there. He'd gone out the back and collapsed." She paused and rubbed her palm across her collarbones. She gripped the front of her bodice. "They'd been in the middle of making coins, the blanks before the designs are struck."

"And what did you do, Mistress Satya?" Amota Lakum asked carefully.

Satya dropped her hand into her lap. "Well, I knew we couldn't explain it away. It wasn't farm repair for the Alths! He showed me the dies in a box and I made him promise to stop. I made him swear not to do it anymore. He'd only begun because custom was slow, but we didn't need the coin! At least, we didn't by then. Not really, anyway, but then our cellar got damp and spoiled the stores."

"And what happens when you go against your goddess and break the laws of your empire?" Mistress Monbrith snapped. "Lost custom! Food that spoils! Guests who prefer the open road!"

"All of which meant we needed that coin to survive!" Satya bit back. "So the Sovereign Twins can add that to their divine consciences as well."

"Don't you dare say that in my company again," her mother hissed.

Ibram watched them both carefully. "Have you told this to the warders?"

The two of them broke off their angry staring match. Her mother angled her gaze to a corner of the little cell. Satya merely shrugged. "Is there a point to that now?" she asked. "I figured this...whole ordeal couldn't be worse."

"It's dangerous," Ahksell said. "To lie before and tell the truth now casts everything said in a very weak light."

"What did you say to the warders whose money you possibly have stolen?" Amota Lakum asked.

"I didn't steal anything from the warders," Satya exclaimed.

"Mentor Tikari is checking every purse and chest in the village," Ahksell said. "Including those belonging to the Cohort of Peace. She's keeping a tally of false coin so the victims can apply to the court for remuneration, but Runner aid your feet if it's Commander Osthanes' pocket you've picked."

Satya's entire body flinched at the thought of additional punishment. The Monbriths' situation was only getting worse, and cooperation could only slightly mitigate events. Ibram felt the back of his head tighten; his neck crackled when he stretched it. He picked up the paper scroll and turned it over in his hands.

"His brother is a Lecturer in Kandrilat, you know," Amota Lakum said.

The time to discover how he knew that or why it mattered was later, but Ibram was almost entirely derailed. The vision flashed before his eyes of two Commander Osthanes, glaring at him in tandem, and it was not a happy one. He shook his head.

"And you will like our answers better than that warder he sent to collect us did?" Mistress Monbrith asked, as Ibram refocused. "What business is it of the Sect of Seven Fires?"

"Like it or not, Mistress, the Sect of Seven Fires administers to this corner of the province," Ahksell said. "We are its representatives. And if that doesn't convince you, then I'll just mention that we are the only persons still interested in keeping you from a very slow death."

A short silence fell. Then, Satya cleared her throat and, with a quick look in her mother's direction, nodded decisively. "What else do you want to know?"

"What changes did you make to the litany to the Speaker?" Ibram asked. "He ran after that bad night, correct?"

"None," Mistress Monbrith said.

"So perhaps Rustam did," Amota Lakum said. "Was he in the habit? I've known dualists to add a name or two when they're calling on their goddesses."

"We are not dualists," Mistress Monbrith said. "The Empress is not divine."

"Just the most beloved of all mortals," Ibram said, and nodded. "So he goes to pray, just like you've been telling him to, and then one night he runs out, upset, because his candles never lit?"

Satya and her mother shared another glance. "It didn't seem like anything."

"Yet it's the only thing anyone ever talks bout," Ibram said. "Sounds bad to me. You're not Isconian spies, are you?"

"No!" Mistress Monbrith exclaimed, and looked very alarmed.

"Well, scratch that from the list."

Amota Lakum frowned. "Ibram."

Ibram sighed. "I just don't understand the problem."

"We don't know where he is," Satya insisted. "He was distressed.

He said…he asked if he was doing the right thing.”

Ibram blinked and then paused. “Well,” he said finally. “Did he talk to you about what Madji Anlines told him?”

Mistress Monbrith looked at him as if he were insane. “What would Rustam have to talk about with the dramseller?” she asked.

Satya looked down at her hands in her lap. Her soft brown hair was caught up around her head and caught the light from the glowbulb well. Ibram glanced at Ahksell, who raised his eyebrows back.

“She says you had a longstanding contract with her,” he said. “And that she spoke with Rustam before he ran away.”

“Madji Anlines drinks half her product before it gets to you and then charges for ‘damages’,” Mistress Monbrith said. “I’d put up with it for too long, and when her contract came up, we chose not to renew. There’s always shops in Delbrite willing to send goods up to us.”

“So we add a third charge to the middleman rather than solely the brewery,” Satya muttered.

“What was that?” Mistress Monbrith snapped.

“You see know why we needed the money?” Satya said. “It’s half the cost to pay the overland travel tax as it is for the river—”

“At the cost of months between shipments,” Mistress Monbrith said.

“We don’t require that much in the way of spirits at all,” Satya said. “Our beer’s just as good as any wine or ryer Madji could deliver.”

“So why keep the contract at all?” Amota Lakum asked.

Ibram sat back in the straw pallet and resisted the urge to scratch his legs. Perhaps it didn’t matter why Rustam had run away beyond the fact that he had. To be sure, he’d probably no notion in his head that the town would be facing anything but a heavy fine—which would doubtless have been somewhat paid with his own specially made coinage. Given his family’s general trend of thought, Rustam probably felt some small measure of satisfaction about that. Ibram felt the urge to rub his eyebrow and tucked his thumb into his fist.

“In memory of our father.” Satya shook her head; her face was flushed. “If that Madji did say something to him…it wouldn’t surprise me. They used to spend time together, moving the cases into the draughtshop.”

"Was she friends with Master Tolk?" Ahksell asked.

Satya shrugged. "Who can say?"

"Madji might," Ibram said. "Since the warders have her in custody. Think she'll wind up in here with you?"

Mistress Monbrith made a noise like air escaping a kettle. She shook her head and pushed loose hair off of her face. "That old misery is not welcome," she snapped.

"Unfortunate thing with cells," Ibram said. "You don't get to pick who's inside with you."

Satya pounded her fist on the table, and then covered her face with both hands. She groaned and then dropped them back into her lap. "He only had to say nothing but the truth. He was helping Master Harken in the forge, when he fell down dead, and that was an end to it, but he wouldn't—he kept turning it over in his mind." She scoffed. "As if heart attacks were some kind of divine punishment."

Ibram poked the paper scroll into his left palm, and then set it back down on the table. "Hasi Terin said he was holding a vigil the night before the trial?"

Satya's eyebrows furrowed; she frowned. "No, he didn't. He never went back in to visit the altar after the candles didn't light."

Ibram nodded, and then looked about the table. Ahksell shook his head slightly and shrugged. Amota Lakum appeared placid as a stream. The Monbriths all acted like another strong blow of wind would scatter them into pieces, and for all Ibram knew they were right.

Someone knocked on the cell door. They all looked over as keys clicked down a succession of locks, and then a tray-bearing servant appeared in the doorway next to a warder. She was clearly nervous, or perhaps shaking with anger at serving prisoners, Ibram couldn't tell. Ahksell obligingly got to his feet and backed up in order to accommodate the new arrival.

Ibram sighed. The servant banged her tray down on the middle of the table, stood up and walked away without a word. The stack of cups tumbled off the tray, and Amota Lakum gathered them up. He placed all three correctly upright in front of Satya. Ibram smelled salt and potatoes and very little else in the communal pot of quash before him. The pitcher was probably water. It was a far cry from the dinner Mistress Monbrith had laid out for them before. Had the warders left Emil back at the draughtshop to see to the place? Someone would have to; they couldn't stay in the anteroom of Mistress Denrind's manor forever. The warder holding the door open made a face in Ibram's direction. She jerked her head sideways.

Ibram smacked his hands together, and the Monbriths all startled. Such a small family. "Well, I don't know where he is, and you don't, and Commander Osthanes is rounding up the Alths," he said. "We should leave you to your meal."

"They were truly just the first name that came to mind," Satya said. "I don't know...I mean, either way."

Mistress Monbrith blinked rapidly at the meager tray in front of her. "Yes," she said.

Amota Lakum struggled to his feet and made a credible bow. The cell was of a sufficient size, but six people inside of it made for cramped quarters. Ibram wriggled away from the table and off the straw pallet before he was able to rock to his feet. Diarmit reached out and took back his paper scroll, out of the way of his mother passing out the spoons. She placed an extra back onto the tray, some harried kitchen servant had made a mistake in their counting.

Ibram paused. Four spoons for four Monbriths, except there were only three now...but, actually, they were *five*. He tilted his head and thought for a moment while Amota Lakum exited the cell. Ahksell paused at the door.

"Ibram?" he prompted.

Ibram crouched back down. "Mistress Monbrith, what happened to your brother?"

Mistress Monbrith frowned, though more in surprise than anger. "Vlasti?" she asked. "How did you hear about him?"

"Oh," Ibram waved his hand. "Mistress Suugan mentioned she was in school with you both for a time. I just wondered where he was. Seems like a hard thing to just leave Emil to look after your property while you're, um, away. We might get a message to him."

Mistress Monbrith turned a spoon over in her fingers. "My brother decided he wanted no part of the draughtshop or his family when the

Speaker refused him at twenty. I thank you for the thought, but I doubt he could induced to return."

"He's a lay cleric now," Satya said. "We visit him in Thelis occasionally, but haven't for some time."

A thrumming string like a gittern began vibrating in Ibram's chest. He stood up and bowed. "Thank you all," he said. "I hope you have a good meal."

He pointed at the door, and let Ahksell leave first before stepping over the threshold himself. The warder closed the door behind them, and locked it. Outside, Amota Lakum glanced up and frowned immediately upon seeing Ibram's face.

He said something to the warder he had been speaking with, clapped him on the shoulder, and then gestured in Ibram's direction. Ibram quick-stepped it to his side and then waited, shifting from left foot to right until Ahksell caught up to him in the middle of the reception hall.

"Where's Lady Azadiya?" he whispered furiously, conscious of how sound echoed off the walls. "He's a lay cleric in Thelis!"

"What?" Amota Lakum said. "Who is?"

Ibram prodded Ahksell's arm. "Well? Where is she? You're her Attendant!"

"Ibram, I've been with you!" Ahksell exclaimed. He'd also retrieved his gar. "I don't know where she is!"

"Well then, come on!" Ibram said, and strode to the front entrance. "I've finally remembered something useful!"

They caught up to him in the market square, which was just as tense as it had been before Mentor Tikari took a swing at anyone. Ibram looked about himself. A crowd of villagers carrying bundles and a smaller group of traders carrying nothing spewed out from the alleyway that led to the shay shop. He caught sight of Mistress Suugan walking down the side of the road with a bag in each hand.

Ibram raised one hand in the air as he hurried towards her. "Mistress Suugan!"

She paused and waited for Ibram to catch up. "Good evening," she said.

"Good evening," he replied. "I don't suppose you've seen Lady

Azadiya anywhere about? She said she was going shopping."

Which, now he was thinking about it, was an astonishingly inane thought. She had to be doing something else, something to do with Mentor Perhara... Ibram shook his head to clear it and focused on Mistress Suugan. She nodded quickly.

"Well, she's not in the shay shop," Mistress Suugan hefted her bags. "Zosi's closed up. Says all he'll be doing now is making hardtack."

"Hardtack?" Ahksell asked.

She nodded. "Says it will last longer than real bread."

Ibram paused, briefly set aback. If they didn't hurry, there'd be no grain sold to Fontis. Strange to think of something so common becoming scarce.

Ladyship. He needed to speak with Lady Azadiya. He raised his arm and hit Ahksell in the chest. A crowd of alchemists were directing a pallet of completed wall sections out of Mistress Denrind's house. A tall stack had already been gathered.

"I see," he said. "Mistress? Has Vlasti Monbrith ever come home for a visit?"

"When the children were born," she said, puzzled. "But he always left again. I think they visit him now that everyone's old enough to travel."

"She'll be by Salacia's carriages," Ahksell said. "Let's allow Mistress Suugan to go back to her business."

"I will!" Ibram said, already on his way. "Thank you!"

"You're welcome!" she called after them.

"Ibram will you slow down and tell us what is going on?" Amota Lakum did not sound approving as he loped alongside Ahksell behind Ibram.

"I will not!" Ibram kept his head up and moving. The alchemists from Salacia hadn't fit into the livery yard, the stables could barely keep up the demand for feed what with the warders and the merchants. So they had set them down in a row nearest the front gate to the village. It blocked some of the houses there, of course, but with all the events in the market square, Ibram thought the villagers were used to it by now.

The carriages were, in fact, swarming with Attendants. Glowbulbs in sailing lights hung in the air, anchored by thin chains. All the back doors were flung wide and boxes were being carried in and out in a flurry of movement. A growing wall of crates was taking shape by the first carriage. The Attendants looked up as Ibram passed.

"Lady Azadiya!" he yelled.

Amota Lakum grabbed him by the shoulder and pulled him to a stop. "Do not shout for Ladyship like a fish trader in a market," he hissed.

"We are in a market, though," Ahksell said.

"Don't you start," Amota Lakum said, and Ahksell cleared his throat. "Now, Ibram, you will tell me what's so important that you have to go jumping around like a goat on fire."

"I have always found that an incredibly disturbing image, you know," Lady Azadiya said.

Ibram twisted around in Amota Lakum's grasp. Ladyship stood by the opposite end of the crates with a tiny Attendant hovering at her elbow. She was just in her gown and mitts with her hair still up. The Attendant had two thin yellow braids of hair wrapped around her head and a worried expression on her face. Lady Azadiya's net of gemstones hung around her neck glinted in the last of the evening light.

"Ladyship, I apologize for the disturbance," Amota Lakum said.

"I don't," Ibram said. "I have brought back knowledge."

She tilted her head. "Have you? Well then, you better come inside."

Ibram bounced on the balls of his feet and grinned in Ahksell's direction. He followed Lady Azadiya into the nearest carriage, and Amota Lakum closed the door behind them. The curved painted ceiling was high enough that they could stand, if a bit awkwardly. The carriage was big enough that it held three benches instead of two, one against the front wall and then the rest folded up against the walls on either side. Lady Azadiya settled herself on the smaller bench along the wall.

"Ladyship, Mistress Monbrith's brother—you remember, Mistress Suugan mentioned him? Satya just told me he's a lay cleric at the shrine at Thelis."

"There isn't a cleric in Thelis," Amota Lakum said. "Just a groundskeeper."

Ibram whirled behind him, pointed, and then swerved back around. "There isn't a *Lecturer* in Thelis," he said. "Vlasti Monbrith was refused by the Speaker—just like his nephew was—and he left the draughtshop. Mistress Monbrith said he hasn't been back in years."

Lady Azadiya hummed in thought. "Interesting. So you believe the groundskeeper in Thelis is this Vlasti?"

Ibram nodded. "I do, and what's more I think that's where Rustam went when he ran away. Who else would understand being rejected by his own goddess?"

"Thelis is a day's travel from Fontis and that is by horse," Ladyship said. "He would have had to travel very quickly on foot. Besides which the warders have already searched the premises, the groundskeeper let them in, in fact."

Ibram's chest sunk for a breath; he'd forgotten that. Still, he pressed on. "But who is to say Rustam wasn't secreted in some...hideaway, a root cellar beneath the groundskeeper's hut! He might not even have reached the shrine when they searched."

"And they merely passed him on the road?" Ahksell said. "Ibram, I don't think the warders would make that mistake. Rustam's not some kind of expert woodsman. He wouldn't be able to stay concealed for so long."

"Yet he has so far. It's all the more reason why someone must be helping him!" Ibram lifted both hands and then swatted his sides. "I know Commander Osthanes thinks Rustam's...I don't even know what you would call it. Being passed in a relay down the entire Alth clan, but why would he depend on strangers when there's a perfect good estranged family member on hand?"

"It's a good point," Lady Azadiya said with a slow nod. "But it doesn't say much for the warders if you're correct."

Ibram tucked both of his thumbs in his fists; his forehead itched. "Folk around here remember Mistress Monbrith's brother, but," he said, "whoever they sent out to the shrine obviously didn't know Vlasti Monbrith was in Thelis, or they would have mentioned in him by name, rather than simply calling him 'the groundskeeper'."

"You want to go to Thelis and prove your theory?" Lady Azadiya asked. Her mouth had taken a decidedly upward curve.

"Ladyship, I do."

She nodded. Amota Lakum cleared his throat, and her eyes flashed towards him. She leaned back against the carriage wall.

"Take Ahksell with you," Lady Azadiya said. "You sound like you're developing a cold, Lakum. Stay in Fontis and gather my shopping."

"And as well," Ibram said, jabbing a finger in the air. "What do you mean by that? There's nothing in Fontis to shop for!"

Lady Azadiya breathed slowly through her nose, and cleared her throat. Ibram rocked back on his heels and dropped his hand back down again.

"Or I could think on it some more, and return with conjectures all by myself," Ibram said.

Ladyship nodded. Her expression had become prickly. It must have been the amount of time she had been having to devote to actually using her Vissilian accent. Ibram turned to go, and then reversed himself. "We have no horses," he said.

"Take Antio and your carriage in the morning," she said. "We won't be needing them yet."

"In the morning?" Ibram repeated.

She nodded. "You wish to drive through the night, and then fall asleep in the middle of the day? I have never understood how that is supposed to save time. No, there is no point in running off into the forest half-mad or risking being too tired to capture Rustam if he is found."

"Half-mad," Ibram muttered. "I am not!"

"We have little time and less to go on," she reminded him. "In such cases as these I am willing to indulge your intuitive leaps, but you have responsibilities in Fontis as well."

Ibram bowed. His heartbeat doubled in his chest. "Thank you, Ladyship," he said.

She picked a thread in her left mitt. "And don't forget to tell Commander Osthanes you will be leaving. I want to make certain you can get back inside Fontis upon your return."

"Of course, we'll go now." Ibram turned to the back of the carriage. He pushed at Ahksell to get him closer to the door. It was best to leave before she changed her mind. "Move, move come on!"

Ahksell let himself be hurried out of the carriage and down its steps. On the ground, he whirled and held up his hand in front of Ibram's chest.

"Wait!" he blurted out.

Ibram wavered, but clung to the doorframe and regained his balance. "What for?"

Ahksell opened his mouth by no words came out. "I forgot—you should tell Ladyship about—"

Ibram put up his hand and Ahksell stopped speaking. Over his shoulder, Ibram could see a woman lurking by the next carriage, on the side away from most folks' view. She crossed her arms, but this time there was no fiddling with her hood.

"Good evening, Attendant Serisan," he said. "I think it's marvelous how quickly you get around this village."

"Is that Sotiria?" Lady Azadiya asked from inside the carriage. "Better let her in. To be sure, it's grown cold."

Ibram's breath stuttered out in a laugh. He shook his head. Ahksell rubbed his hand down his face; he pinched the bridge of his nose, and furrowed his eyebrows for a moment.

"Yes, Mentor," he said, and dropped his hand.

Ahksell walked down the last steps backwards and swung to his left, making way for Ibram to be let down from the carriage. He went right and Attendant Serisan walked forward. Ibram put his hands on his stomach and bowed deeply as she climbed into the carriage. Ahksell tsked sharply.

Ibram rose, and put on his best polite smile while between them the steps were raised and the door closed. Ahksell pointed at him.

"Don't say a word, Ibram."

He shook his head. "Whatever do you mean, Attendant Solari?"

"Not! A single word!"

Ibram considered the closed door above him. He couldn't hear anything, but that was no matter. He walked past Ahksell towards the market, and patted him on the arm as he brushed by. Ahksell squinted and frowned at him. He reached for his gar, which he had left outside, and they walked together back towards Mistress Denrind's manor.

"It's not that I don't want to tell you," Ahksell said.

"Except you don't, and you haven't," Ibram said. "And, also, to be sure, you said you don't want me in trouble."

"As well I don't!"

Ibram briefly consulted the sky, but it returned no answers. He supposed this ferreting out of secrets sort of work was Yilka the Green's doing in recompense for the luck of finding the debased coins in the first place. Second place?

"Anyway," Ibram said. "I have resigned myself to it."

"You have?" Ahksell asked.

"Of course," Ibram said. He dodged around the lingering remains of the crowd being funneled to Mentor Tikari. Torches clamped to tripods had been taken out to lighten the square, the ones the burned green and typically were used to smoke out insects. They cast an incredibly eerie light over the proceedings.

"Whose decision was that?" he asked as they passed by that old Mistress Madji, who was staring into the crowd from its side. She had a bandage around her hand, and her hair slicked back. Her head looked like a skull in the half-light.

"I think it's what was available," Ahksell said. "Mentor Tikari needs light, and she doesn't care where it comes from."

"But Salacia has sailing lights," Ibram said. "Even you have yours."

Ahksell's shoulders rose and fell in time with his ground-eating pace. "I expect she said something nasty to Mentor Perhara, and negotiations sputtered."

Ibram snorted and smacked Ahksell on the back. Ahksell grinned. Ibram caught up to him and they lapsed into silence. Ibram considered his options. It seemed clear to him now that Attendant Serisan wasn't here for Ahksell, but on some mission for Lady Azadiya, which meant she was poaching an Attendant from Bedris. Perhaps she was the compiler Lady Azadiya had spoken of to Mentor Perhara. Though, apparently, Ladyship was using his attendants with permission. In turn, this suggested they were up to something nefarious, or at least...something that might be officially frowned upon. Of course, concerning Judge E'grard, there was no telling what punishment anything but the strictest submission to imperial law might bring about.

17

Ibram pondered the facts as he knew them. Ahksell had gone to Serisan first. They had been... Ibram frowned. They'd been talking about village students—about Diarmit! But Ahksell had said it wasn't a productive conversation, and then he had walled himself up with Ladyship while Ibram relearned horses with Amota Lakum and Attendant Serisan had shown up in Fontis. He grinned to himself. With her hood up, as if it would hide her from all sight.

What if it hadn't—what if her goal hadn't been hiding? Or, at least, not to truly hide. She doubtless knew it couldn't be possible to conceal herself for long in Fontis. After all, she taught their children, so—

Ibram stopped walking, right beneath the front gate of Mistress Denrind's house. Ahksell continued on a few paces, realized he'd been abandoned, and then turned around. Ibram's eyes widened; he tasted cold air in his mouth. Ahksell's entire body tensed in alarm. He walked back and hunched his shoulders, tucking his gar into his elbow.

"Ibram?" he asked.

The back of Ibram's head vibrated to life in a storm of prickled skin and pounding nerves. He clamped his jaw shut, and poked Ahksell hard in the chest. Ahksell barely moved, but he frowned. Ibram poked him again.

"I cannot believe you!" Ibram said, and poked him a third time. "You complete—a shopping list! An actual—mmph!"

Ahksell clamped his left hand over Ibram's mouth and then crowded him. "Would you be quiet?" he whispered furiously. "You don't know what you're talking about!"

Ibram reached over his arm and shook his finger in Ahksell's face. "I knew Ladyship wouldn't stop meddling!" he exclaimed, but since it was through Ahksell's hand, he wasn't certain it translated.

"Shh!" Ahksell hushed him.

Ibram rolled his eyes and batted at Ahksell's arm. Ahksell frowned at him, but let go, and Ibram wiggled his jaw. He wiped the back of his hand over his mouth.

"You're such a good soul," Ibram said.

If he could be seen to blush, Ahksell would have been red as a ripe cinnak by now, Ibram was sure of it. He recovered his dignity well enough, but the damage was done. Ibram waggled his eyebrows.

"Where is Ladyship putting them? In with her new furs? Safe in her new boxes? Did you come up with the scheme, or did she? I wager she was impressed."

"We're not talking about this now," Ahksell said.

"Right under the judge's nose." Ibram laughed, but kept his voice low. "Is there a signal prepared for gathering all of Serisan's little ones up? You know I'll help."

"Of course there is," Ahksell said and then hushed him when Ibram opened his mouth. "We're not talking about this, I said. I said it very clearly."

"Later tonight suits me fine," Ibram said.

"Tomorrow," Ahksell said.

"Tonight."

Ahksell narrowed his eyes. "Tomorrow."

Ibram sighed. "Fine," he said, "Never let it be said I'm a poor winner."

"You haven't won anything!" Ahksell insisted as they walked through the front gate. The little front courtyard was barely enough to be called by its name, but once in the reception hall the air felt even colder than outside. He glanced to his left at the Monbriths' cell. The warders leant on its walls, and looked to be asleep on their feet.

"Hmm," Ibram nodded. He gestured to the right and then the left. "Where do you think we'll find Commander Osthanes?"

"Oh." Ahksell looked about and then waved his hand at a passing servant.

They left before the sun rose, when everyone else in the draughtshop —and no doubt, the village—still slept. It was cold and dark outside, lit only by Ahksell's sailing light, which he had clamped to the carriage in the frame usually reserved for a lamp. They ate as they traveled, silently, keeping their refilled flask of shay between them to share the warmth. Ibram stretched himself as best he could in the driver's bench, wrapped in one of the blankets discovered under a bench in the carriage from last night, and licked oil off his palm.

A trio of warders camped on the side of the road looked up as they passed. Osthanes had staggered encampments all along the imperial road up to the imperial boundary. They were more plentiful when they were closer to Fontis, of course, but each improvised blockade had three to a campfire, all very correct and prepared to turn away or keep within as was called for. Antio ducked her head up and down, jingling her harness as they waited for two of the warders to move aside their improvised log barrier so the carriage could pass. Ibram made sure the wax seal Commander Osthanes had given them as an official license was still affixed to the wagon above their heads. One of the warders raised her hand; Ibram raised his back.

"How do you keep forgetting your cloak?" Ahksell picked up their argument again while he guided Antio down the road.

"I didn't forget it," Ibram said. "You didn't return it to me."

"Because you forgot it."

"I have a blanket! I'm perfectly comfortable."

"You look like my sickly grandfather," Ahksell said.

Ibram reached down to the foot well and brought up his shay cup in both hands. "Well youngster," he said, in his best wavering old man voice. "In my day, we respected our elders."

Ahksell snorted. Ibram grinned and drank down the last of his shay. He made sure the half-empty flask between them was capped shut, and then dropped the cup into the sack at his feet. He'd managed to negotiate a full basket of food for the journey from Emil in the morning, in recompense for being the only paid customers. They had a sack of dried cinnaks, a rope of sausage, goat cheese and bread, and even two small flasks of oil and black vinegar along with a dark clay jug of ale for when the shay ran out. Traveling with Ahksell apparently meant Ibram got to eat from the high table no matter where he was.

"You're in a better mood," Ahksell said.

Ibram glanced at him and then shrugged. He held his blanket closed with his right hand. "Am I?"

Ahksell nodded, and gave the reins a little flick. Antio was moving faster in a four-beat amble rather than her usual trot, with her neck up and braced in the reins. She went far more smoothly than Gilma ever had.

Ibram leaned his head left and then right. "I suppose I am," he said. "Feels good to be doing something."

He watched the thick tree cover fly above their heads in all its shades of green; the wind had picked up as the morning continued. He hoped it was a good sign. The road was empty of travelers but a few grey spotted fenek jumped out of sight as their carriage clattered past. Ibram put his boots up on the ledge of the foot well, and laced his fingers over his stomach.

"Well, we are watered and fed," Ibram turned his head against the carriage wall. "What's Ladyship going to do with all the children she's stealing from under Judge E'grard's nose?"

Ahksell had grown into a firm, upright sort of a man, so he didn't protest or drop the reins or pull Antio to a stop to loudly protest the slur against Ladyship's honor. Instead, he gripped the reins tightly, and cleared his throat. The carriage rattled along the road.

"I don't know what you're referring to," Ahksell said.

Ibram grinned. "On account of how right I am?" he laughed. "Ahksell, you didn't really think I wouldn't put it together, did you?"

Ahksell groaned.

"I'm hurt! I'm astounded." Ibram sat up higher on the driving bench. "But I am also entirely correct, yes? That's what is going on, and you tried to keep me out of it."

Ahksell frowned at him. "That is not a laughing matter you're discussing."

"Well, you have only Amota Lakum to blame," he said. "He told me to take care and pay attention, or I'd never get the saddle on the horse."

"What?" Ahksell added a confused wrinkle to his frown.

"I don't know, if I'm quite honest, but I've been hearing the same advice since I was thirteen and it had to be good for something at least once."

Ibram let his blanket fall down his shoulders to his waist. He leaned his elbows on his knees and grinned expectantly. Ahksell took a deep and calming breath.

"If you wish, I can just tell you all the ways you made an utter hash of your secret," Ibram offered.

"I don't want to talk about this at all," Ahksell said.

"Ah, but what else is there to do?" Ibram asked. "We're in the middle of the forest. You want to count needles on the trees?"

Ahksell jerked his chin in the direction of the forest. "Certainly!" he said brightly. "Start with that droopy, crooked one."

"Aww," Ibram said with a grin. "Now then, you did very good! Had me fooled for a good...oh, half day at least."

"Half a day?" Ahksell sat up straight in outrage. "You were wandering about like a drunken squirrel, hunting about for—for—" He gestured aimlessly.

"Clues?" Ibram offered.

"Oh, be quiet."

"I'm only paid for silence when Ladyship commands it," Ibram shrugged. "Unless you'd like to toss me a flick's worth of picaio or two."

Ahksell groaned, and dropped his head down for a moment. He lifted it on his next inhalation and glared at him. Ibram raised his right hand in front of himself and picked at a hangnail.

"First of all," he said, bringing his hand in for closer inspection. "If you didn't want my attention, then you shouldn't have asked for a private talk with Ladyship so publicly."

"I can talk with Mentor any time I like!"

"To be sure, but doing it in such an ostentatious way? And then going on and on about how it wasn't my business because I'm merely your lowly agent?"

"Ibram, I didn't mean it like that—"

Ibram waved his hand in the air. "Mist in the mountains, my humongous friend. But really, all you had to do was wait until she was alone, or I was off on an errand, and then talk with her. I wouldn't have noticed a thing for at least a few minutes."

Ahksell very obviously rolled his eyes. "So speaks the human bloodhound."

"And then Attendant Serisan appeared in the market," Ibram continued. "She has a figure, I'm happy to say, that is very hard to dismiss from the mind." Ahksell elbowed him; Ibram rocked with the blow, but continued. "And she's running around with a hood over her face! As if a new person in a town closed off from the rest of the world isn't going to draw attention? How did she get in anyway?"

Ahksell shrugged. "Maybe she didn't."

"Ah, so you admit there's a chance she's there?"

"Ibram."

Ibram waved the question away. Above them, the sun was beginning to finally burn away the haze. He ran his hand through his hair and squeezed the back of his head.

"Anyway," he said. "To make a detailed story short, my young Learner."

"I'm not afraid to thump you," Ahksell said. "I'm taller this time, so there'll be no climbing trees to escape me."

Ibram snorted, and cleared his throat. "If Attendant Serisan is in the market square, talking to all the young mothers, while Lady Azadiya raises the hopes of Mistress and Master Suugan by extolling the virtues of their little girl still being able to take a test of aptitude up the living mountain, then the two cannot be unrelated. Couple that with Mentor Perhara's willingness to provide room in his carriages for Ladyship's shopping and..." Ibram clapped his hands together and then turned his palms upward to the sun. "Whisht goes the arrow shaft to the target."

Ibram waited. Ahksell said nothing. Antio clopped along.

Ah well, some people couldn't stand a revelation they couldn't take part in. He leaned a bit closer, and Ahksell leaned away. It wasn't comfortable, most probably for either of them, so Ibram regained his previous seat. He could be magnanimous.

"So?" he asked. "How will Ladyship do it? Are we packing them in those crates the Attendants were lifting out last night?"

"I don't know what you're talking about," Ahksell said. "But you spin a very pretty story."

Ibram groaned.

Ahksell raised his voice. "And if it happened to be true, in any part of it, I would be very proud of you."

"Oh well, if you're proud of me," Ibram muttered.

"But of course every action taken against an imperial judge's rulings itself constitutes an act of law-breaking, and as such, I am duty-bound to refute all your entirely fantastical claims."

"This is good," Ibram said. "Are you practicing? I can help. I'll find some ashes for my hair and pretend to be E'grard."

"And while I admit that you may have seen Attendant Serisan last night," Ahksell continued with a fixed stare in front of him. "I can only say that she has nothing to do with any ideas you might have of Mentor Hobon's goals in Fontis."

"Oh?" Ibram said. "Why was she there? Is she writing down the village's last day's for posterity?"

"She...came to drop off a few educational texts," Ahksell said. "So that the children might continue their learning."

"While they're invisible half-ghosts trying to avoid being run over by late summer caravans?" Ibram interlaced his fingers over his belly and tsked.

"There is nothing in the law that says you can't speak to your neighbors," Ahksell said. "Especially in times of trouble."

Ibram shook his head. "A risky business, hard to coordinate. Ladyship must have the soul of a smuggler."

"Whatever you're talking about," Ahksell said, "it won't matter if we find Rustam, will it?"

Ibram laughed, a bark of air and noise and shook his head. He crossed his arms and grinned at the trees. "No," he said. "It won't."

Ahksell frowned at him again, or perhaps still was more accurate. Ibram widened his eyes. He hummed and Ahksell whipped his head back around to face the front. Ibram settled back against the carriage in triumph.

⚜

They crossed the imperial boundary by midday. The sun was actually out for a wonder, pouring a veritable deluge of light across the road and dappling the trees. The air smelled sweetly of grass and earth. They stopped to let Antio rest and drink in a clearing a little ways beside the road.

Ibram took a walk around the carriage to stretch his legs and then unhitched Antio from the carriage to let Ahksell have a chance to return feeling to his limbs as well. Antio immediately began to nose at the ground, but didn't feed. Ibram ran his hand through her tangled coarse mane.

"No biting, please," he said.

"She doesn't bite," Ahksell called from the spot on the opposite side of the carriage where he was stretching his legs.

"I think that's the first words I've heard out of you in the last hour," Ibram replied, while working a knot out of Antio's mane.

"There's only so much conversation a man can have on the road before the amount of bugs he swallows renders talking unpalatable."

Ibram laughed, and Antio shuffled her hooves. He pet down her back and stepped out of the way. Horses were all right, as beasts went, but he much preferred conversing with his own kind.

"Well, do we eat here?" He asked. "Or do we press onwards?"

Ahksell walked forward from the carriage. He ran his hand over his face; he looked tired. "You really think he's in Thelis?"

Ibram crossed his arms and nodded. "I do," he said. "Or his uncle knows where he is. I think it's too much of a coincidence. The warders obviously didn't know they were related."

"So he gave them a false name."

"Or they never asked," Ibram sighed. "I've never counted, but I'm laying odds that Osthanes' force is stretched thin over these parts. Even with the addition of the local warders from the waystations, they're usually just called to service for Delbrite after all."

"And Judge E'grard is pulling them all back to Fontis," Ahksell said, and nodded. "Probably with all the villagers with them."

"Those freeholders are running out of time to hide," Ibram said.

Ahksell hushed him; Ibram shrugged. Ahksell frowned.

"Now, don't look at me like that! I'm not making light of it," Ibram said.

Ahksell went back to the carriage to retrieve food for Antio. Ibram took a moment to consider the green tree tops surrounding them. The needles from a floppy-limbed blic tree wavered in the breeze. He could smell plants and fresh air. It was almost too nice a day to be thinking about capturing a fugitive. He indulged himself in a lungful of forest air, and then breathed out through his mouth.

"Do you think they'll have searched Madji Anlines' herder's hut by now?" Ibram asked.

"Must have," Ahksell said as he came back with the nose bag. He shook his head. "They'll have questioned her at the very least."

"Satya didn't seem to think she had anything to do with Rustam."

"Satya has lied before," Ahksell pointed out.

Well," Ibram said, and then shrugged. Out of his hands now, and as much as he wished to be in the room putting Madji to the test, he was equally glad to be out of that village. He hadn't noticed how tense he'd become until they were a mile away and his back unknotted like someone had cut a string. "If she did spread that rumor about the sect stealing money, I don't think she really thought Mentor Tikari would attack someone."

"She doesn't know Tikari very well, then." Ahksell snorted. "She's got a temper. Usually spends her days holed up in her laboratory. Hilbert says he only sees her at meal times or when she needs someone to hold a flask."

Ibram stepped back so Ahksell could attach the bag to Antio's bridle. "Well, Attendant Zorion would know."

Ahksell chuckled. "He's not so bad," he said with a pat to Antio's neck. "They both get very wrapped up in their work, and Tikari's set her mind on a universal solvent. They have schedules and everything."

Ibram felt his mouth curl up at one end. "Do you know her?"

Ahksell made a face. "Well enough," he said. "I know of her, mostly. You know how Afsoun is. They make most of the money, and they never let anyone else forget it."

"It's hard not to stand tall when your founder created the imperial drainage system," Ibram said.

Ahksell laughed. "It bought the land, didn't it? We wouldn't be here if he hadn't."

Ibram's laughter skittered out between his teeth. He stretched out his back and looked about the clearing. The spot looked nice enough, with a few old pits covered in dirt that he suspected were the remains of old campfires. It was a logical place to stop, after all.

"Still, it's not a rumor I thought would come up," Ibram said. "They're all getting those little receipts after all."

"They only *might* get their money back, though," Ahksell pointed out. "The Bureau of Currency keeps its own time."

"But she doesn't profit from telling people lies, does she?" Ibram rolled his shoulders and stretched his back. "It's not like getting Tikari angry means she'd go away. She and Zorion have to test all the coinage in Fontis."

Yilka's megrims, that sounded like a terrible job, now Ibram thought of it. Thankless and tedious, and if the smell was anything to go on, a dangerous health risk. He rubbed his eyebrow with his thumb, and then dropped his hand.

The burbling of the stream and the smell of the forest surrounded them. Ibram frowned back at the old campfires. The clearing wasn't large, but it was big enough for a small farm. A sudden chill ran down his back, but he shook himself. He was being foolish, not every open space was a sanctioned village in bucolic disguise. He glanced back towards the road.

"I don't know if anyone has to profit from it, really," Ahksell said.

"I mean, she could be trying to...what's the word? She could be just stirring up trouble because it amuses her. She said she told Rustam that the court would make him drink truth serum, correct? And he believed her."

Ibram nodded. "Because everyone knows alchemists drink strange brews and hear color."

Ahksell glared at him. "That's just a side effect of the first round of agility tests and it goes away quickly," he said.

Ibram spread his hands. "I'm merely saying it's known that alchemists have many different sorts of infusions for a variety of occasions, and the courts benefit from their trade. I bet Rustam's seen Mistress Denrind down a cup or two when settling a dispute."

"It makes as much sense as it doesn't," Ahksell said, and Ibram laughed. Ahksell went to the front of the carriage; he pulled out the sack of food Emil had sent them off with and handed it to Ibram. Ahksell took the jug of ale by the neck and held it at his side, tilting his head up to the overhanging branches. The wind made them sway into each other, a few with early leaves fluttered like fans.

"We'll have to find a place to leave the carriage once we reach Thelis," Ahksell said. "Antio will need stabling, and I doubt the shrine will be able to accommodate us."

"No, I suppose not," Ibram said.

They both fell silent.

"We'll get to Thelis and back in time, won't we?" he asked. "We have days."

"Absolutely we will," Ahksell said.

"Unless Judge E'grard gets impatient," Ibram said.

"Mentor can hold him off."

"Unless she can't."

Ahksell put his hands on his hips and turned to gaze back at the road. He looked back at Ibram and pressed his lips together. Ibram considered the sky and then the old campsites again.

"The horse needs to eat, doesn't she?" he asked.

"And then she'll need to rest a bit," Ahksell said.

Ibram nodded. He bounced on the balls of his feet. The carriage rocked behind him. Ibram readjusted his grip on the food sack; he could smell cheese very strongly, like an old stocking. He sneezed.

Ahksell stood up. "That's it, I think."

From a little ways off, Antio whickered. Ibram towed the earth with his boot; it felt solid but mud sucked at his sole. He juggled the packages into the crook of his right arm.

"Let's eat in the carriage," he called out. "Ground's too wet."

"All right with me," Ahksell said, and walked around the back to unlock the door.

Ibram frowned down at the food and he, too, walked to the opposite end of the carriage. There would be people in Thelis who would provide the groundskeeper with food; Ibram doubted there was room at the shrine to farm his own. They might notice if the order had increased enough for two people. If they had a shay shop—or even simply a provisioner—then they could make discrete inquiries under the guise of eating breakfast.

Ahksell climbed in first with the jug of ale, and then Ibram stepped up after him. Their carriage was much plainer than Lady Azadiya's conveyance. Their roof was plain pale wood and the two thinly padded benches were folded against the walls. Ahksell had to bend over to release their latches, and when he sat down his head was a mere five inches from the ceiling. Ibram sat down opposite him, and dumped most of the food parcels on top of his bench. Ahksell kept hold of the ale and popped its stopper with his thumb.

He leaned forward and unpinned the leather cover of the one window, and then attached it to the hook in the top part of the frame. With the door open as well, they had a good cross-breeze, but the old campsites were out of view. Ibram cleared his throat and began to unwrap the food parcels.

"Rustam must have traveled on foot," he said as he picked up the bread. He sniffed it, and then tore the round in half. It felt stale and a little crumbly. He set down one half for himself, and then handed the rest to Ahksell.

"Strangers to a shrine aren't uncommon," Ahksell said.

"Doesn't mean no one paid them any mind," Ibram said. "Strangers to a village mean two things: money or trouble."

Ahksell drank directly from the jug of ale. "Or both."

Ibram tore off a bite of bread and wiggled it between his fingers. "Osthanes said he'd sent out missives to surrounding villages," he said. "But he sent a search party here, why do you think he did that?"

Ahksell reached over and cut a sliver of cheese off the hunk they'd been given. He balanced it on a wedge of bread and carefully ate it, wiping crumbs from the corner of his mouth with his thumb. Ibram did the same with his piece of bread.

"Thelis is certainly reachable," Ahksell said as he chewed. "It's the nearest village outside the border."

"But as you pointed out, Rustam is no woodsman."

"A raw walker, like Hasi said."

"I should have asked why the commander sent two warders to Thelis so soon," Ibram said.

"It was hard enough to get the wax seal," Ahksell said. "He didn't look in the mood for questions as well."

Ibram frowned. "He's never just accepted 'it's for sect business' before."

"He's frazzled," Ahksell said. "We all are."

And if Osthanes didn't ask, then he could not tell the Judge if E'grard inquired about where Ibram and Ahksell had gone. It was such a neat bit of flimflam, it was a pity it couldn't work with all the rest of them in the village. Ibram looked down at his meal, a sudden acrid taste in the back of his throat. There were so many folk in Fontis, utterly unconnected with the Monbriths at all, and yet they were all of them now intimately attached by fate. Ibram coughed around a bite of bread and shook his head. Ahksell was staring up at the ceiling, chewing absently.

Conversation quieted down as they attended to their meals. Emil made a good sausage with some kind of peppery kick that made Ahksell cough and Ibram's eyes watered. They ate their fill, and then packed the rest of it up for later. If Rustam was in Thelis, then Ibram didn't want to stop for anything but making sure Antio didn't die in harness. He took the reins this time, so that Ahksell could take a bit of ease. They had to get back before Judge E'grard declared his patience at an end.

He found as the drive went on that his left heel wouldn't stop jiggling against the floor of the foot well, and he lost a goodly amount of time to concentrating on making sure his limbs didn't betray his nerves. It wouldn't do for Ahksell to think he was losing his grip on himself, after all. Antio pulled the carriage like a champion, eating ground with every step. As they grew closer to Thelis, other travelers appeared on the smaller roads that crossed the main imperial pathway, farmers and even a few drovers which forced them to stop until their herds had passed. He misliked the delay; it felt all a little unreal. The daily lives of so many folk were continuing peaceably while not a day's ride away, an entire village literally teetered at the edge of the abyss.

While Ibram drove Ahksell sat up tall in the seat next to him. There was a figure, man or woman he couldn't tell, leading two oxen on a plow in the field to the left of the carriage. The land outside the imperial boundary wasn't that much different from the land within it, the same trees and grasses, but there was a more of a rolling feel to it.

"This is where it happened, you know," Ahksell remarked casually.

Ibram startled a bit. Neither of them had spoken much after lunch. "Where what happened?" he asked, and looked out of the rolling farmlands.

"In the year 17 Junya," he said and waved his hand at a burst of feathery grass in a ditch. The stalks rippled and bent backwards. "This is where the Suuvan Mountain Riders made their last stand."

"How can you tell?"

"There's still a hum in the air," Ahksell said. "The earth's not forgotten its reshaping."

Ibram paid closer attention to his surroundings. "Now that you mention it," he said, "It does look like the ground's been flattened."

In fact, the whole area was rather like a gigantic hand might smooth wrinkles from a blanket. Junya had been the last middle kingdom to fall to the empire, an alchemist's principality at the base of a great mountain. Ibram swallowed. The great wars of conquest had been vast cataclysms, and not even the landscape had been safe from the empire's battalions, soldiers and alchemists alike. Events like that weren't supposed to happen anymore, not since the last conquest to the east, and yet, here they all were again.

Cattle lowed from a field up ahead; he could see the farmer unlocking their pen. Ibram slowed. While waiting for the herd to make their way across the road into the field on the other side, Ibram walked a circuit around Antio and the carriage to stretch his legs. Ahksell did the same from the opposite side, and they met across the foot well. The sun had never become more than a pale imitation of summer, but it hadn't rained, and Ibram faced east to thank Yilka the Green and ring a single soundless bell for a quick return trip.

18

In the dark, with nothing but the stars above them, the empty spaces to either side of the road seemed altogether too close. The air was sharp and the wind held a chill in it as it brushed across Ibram's body. The noise of Antio's hooves and the carriage wheels as they jounced down the road grew louder as the night insects began chirping. Ahksell offered to take the reins again, but Ibram refused. He needed to be doing something, and if it was only driving the carriage, it was at least a task to focus on rather than untangling his own thoughts.

Lights flickered ahead of them about an hour after Ahksell had closed his eyes for a nap. Ibram blinked, squeezed his eyelids further shut, and then opened them. He could almost make out the outline of the pile of wooden buildings that made up Thelis in the distance. He shivered; the night had grown colder without trees to defray the wind.

Ibram glanced about them. They were surrounded by what was most probably farmland, and the ditches on either side of the road seemed well maintained. Rustam wouldn't have been able to hide in the brush around here, but then he might not have needed to if it was late enough. Had he hidden in a ditch while the warders rode past him after all? Ibram had to admit that it seemed possible now, when there was no light but his own to travel by. And further, if the warders hadn't traveled by night for fear of their horses failing, then he could have slipped into Thelis and been with his uncle before morning, after the shrine had been searched.

He put his right rein into his left hand for a moment, and rubbed the back of his neck. The village grew closer and closer still, until they were past its border and driving down the main road towards the flicker of torchlight. Only the draughtshop or an inn would be open this late. Ibram tapped his companion on the shoulder.

"Ahksell," he whispered. He coughed, and then cleared his throat. "Ahksell!"

Ahksell snorted awake. "Yes! What? It's not bubbling yet."

Ibram scrubbed his arm over his forehead. Ahead of them, Antio walked with a tired step. It was no good for a horse. They'd have to make sure she had the good fodder in whatever passed for a stable in the village. The walls of the houses seemed to loom.

"All right," he said. The back of his head began to pound in time with his heartbeat. "Rouse yourself, or people will think all alchemists droll as badly as you do."

Ahksell laughed through his yawn, and Ibram felt his lips stretch into a brief grin. He rotated his shoulders to relax the muscles. His stomach jittered.

"Whereabouts is this shrine, do you think?"

Ahksell resettled himself on the bench; his hands clenched and unclenched in front of him. "I don't know," he said. "We'll have to ask when we get there."

"In Nyarribrite, the temple is a separate building in the middle of town," Ibram said. "Big and painted blue. But the shrine in Honfri was in the forest by itself."

Ahksell nodded. "It will probably be painted the same, I should think," he said.

"Well, I know that," Ibram snapped. The torches were closer, but all of a sudden he couldn't drive another foot. He pulled Antio to a stop in the middle of the road, and tossed the reins down before half-falling out of the carriage. His feet hit the road with dull thuds. His head dropped low as he sucked air down deep into his lungs and blew it out again.

"Yilka's megrims and broken *dice*," Ibram groaned as he stretched his aching body backwards, arms over his head. The sound echoed around the buildings, but no one stirred. He could hear the dim sounds of folk far off, probably the draughtshop's patrons.

"Ibram?" Ahksell turned to him.

Ibram shook his head. The cold night air hurt his eyes, and so he closed them. He dropped his arms and stood there, listening to Ahksell jump down and then his great clomping footsteps as Ahksell approached. Ladyship never made a sound when she moved, perhaps it was a skill that came with age. The air ruffled his hair back from his face. Ibram breathed in and then out again; his heart turned over and then throbbed as if it hurt.

"Ahksell, what if he's not there?" Ibram asked as his throat tightened on every word. "What if we go to the shrine and he isn't there?"

It was a thought he'd been unable to dislodge the whole of the trip. He'd been wrong about so many things, overlooked important details. What if this was merely another wrong move? He opened his eyes and stared at the shuttered windows across the street. Ahksell stood beside him, so still he didn't seem to be breathing, which was fine because Ibram couldn't seem to find the correct amount of air to fill his lungs. He waited until Ahksell shook himself, and clasped Ibram on the shoulder.

"No, now, no," Ahksell said, and shook him a little. "Ibram, we can't think like that."

Ibram covered his face with both palms and dragged them down his cheeks. He groaned. "Are you certain? Because that is all I am thinking right now."

He stared at the village buildings around them. It was much like Fontis, really. Houses built to share a wall, honey-combed together with larger roofs showing from further away, a few shared chimneys in the bigger homes. Thelis was only on one side of the road, however, which Ibram counted as good. After all, if Rustam was there then it meant he really only had one direction to run in and, if Rustam wasn't to be found, Ibram could confidently say he could merely walk into the fields surrounding the village and let the plants use him as fodder.

"Ibram, breathe," Ahksell commanded.

Ibram inhaled; his chest shuddered.

"And now out," Ahksell said.

Ibram exhaled. The back of his head throbbed in time with his blinking.

"Do you think I'm going to enjoy life in the archives?" he asked. "Are there windows?"

"Well, it's underground," Ahksell said.

"The entirety of Fontis," Ibram said. He made a fist and then blew his fingers outwards. "Poof!"

"This is not your fault!" Ahksell said. "It is all Rustam, if he had not run—"

"We would never have uncovered the counterfeiting because of my incompetence."

"No, I don't think that's true," Ahksell said, quite firmly.

Ibram turned on the bench to face him. "It isn't?"

Ahksell's jaw tightened. He sighed and gave Ibram a little shake. "I'm not saying it wasn't a mistake," he said, and Ibram rolled his eyes. He took another deep breath; it pained him, but seemed to help the flickering dark edges of his vision.

"But you had an entire family covering up Rustam's crime and a man who died of completely natural causes," Ahksell said. "And you've done nothing but try and fix it, haven't you? That's why we're here, isn't it?"

"We have to do something, to be sure," Ibram said.

"So we are," Ahksell said, and squeezed his shoulder again. "We're... we're rolling the dice!"

Laughter escaped Ibram in a gasp. He bobbed his head and clapped his hand on top of Ahksell's. He shook himself free, and then turned back to the carriage. Antio whickered tiredly.

"Oh don't let the Runner hear that," he said.

Ahksell laughed and bumped him aside to grab the reins from the carriage. He took hold of them, and then moved to stand at Antio's head. He turned to Ibram, outlined vaguely by the light up ahead of them.

"Come on," he said, "let's walk her the rest of the way. It will do us good to stretch a bit."

Ibram's backside ached from sitting so long; he stretched his arms out and cracked his knuckles. Ahksell made a gagging sound as Ibram resettled his clothes and calmed himself. No point in looking like a fool, even if it was dark out. He walked to stand by his friend, and they began leading Antio forward.

"I'm not joking," Ibram said, and pitched his voice lightly. "You start talking about my dice and then your candles won't light."

Ahksell laughed again and knocked their shoulders together. "Let's go find a stable," he said. "I think we've got a fugitive to catch."

It took a moment, but Thelis had a sign of a horse posted just beyond the draughtshop. They rousted out a sleepy groom when they walked into the livery yard, and left Antio getting a much deserved pampering, before returning a few doors downward to the draughtshop. Helpfully, its front door was open, bracketed by lit torches, and Ibram could hear loud conversations through it.

The draughtshop was half-full when Ibram walked through the door, a mixed crowd, and none so richly dressed as Ahksell who spread quiet and cautious looks as he stepped inside. The place was more commonly constructed than the Monbriths' spot, the kitchen was a roaring fire below a large metal hood in the middle of the room. Cauldrons of food stuck on trivets bubbled behind the low fence set about to entice customers into eating, but deny them the ability to steal. The smoke in the air was reasonable for that sort of place, large enough to tint the air a rather dingy grey, but most of it was swept up to the bell-shaped hood. A man dressed in a leather apron looked up from wiping cups behind the bar, but set his rag aside when he saw that Ibram walked directly to him.

"Good evening," Ibram said. "I don't suppose you have rooms for the night? Anything to eat?"

The man nodded, but his eyes were still on Ahksell the entire time. Ibram glanced between them. He leaned his elbow on the bar. They probably should have tried to hide Ahksell's uniform. What if someone ran around telling folk they'd seen a real alchemist wandering about? Still, too late now.

Ibram sighed. "The Attendant has traveled far," he said, a bit more officiously. "And we'll have further still to go. Do you have any place available for him to sleep?"

That got a response. The man dragged his eyes in Ibram's direction. He quickly looked back to Ahksell, as if he were a richly dressed ghost, but the spell was broken.

"We don't see much travel here," he said. "We keep the common room for sleeping, but that's all."

Ibram took a slow glance around. The place was clean enough, but dark, and it reeked of a sharp but damp unidentifiable funk. He raised his eyebrows at Ahksell, who shrugged, but also shook his head slightly.

"I think I'm more in need of a meal than a place to sleep tonight," Ahksell said. "I apologize for the hour, but I don't suppose there's anything available to eat?"

The barkeeper grunted. "We've got quash left," he said. "Quarter of the wife's best cheese and some potato and leek stew."

They were in the midst of good farmland, so it couldn't be all bad. Ibram noticed the conversations around them remained at an ebb. Clearly, they were the greatest entertainment Thelis had seen in sometime.

"A bowl of quash will do for me," he said. "Attendant?"

"I'll take the stew and any bread left," Ahksell said.

The barkeep grunted again, but to Ibram the prospect of coin made it sound a little more approving. He raised his hand above his head, and gave a short wave. Then he dropped his arm and grabbed the cup he'd just been wiping.

"Drink?" the man asked.

"Beer will do," Ibram said.

"I'm going to find a place to sit," Ahksell said. "You'll wait for the food?"

"Yes, Attendant," Ibram said.

A woman in a white tunic and brown trousers wrapped in a smock walked away from the far corner of the room. She touched both hands to the back of her low bun and hair stick, and then hurried to the gate and slipped through it to the cauldron hanging over the kitchen fire in the middle of the room. Ibram leaned on the bar.

"How much?" he asked.

A light flickered in the man's eyes. "Fifteen faunts for the meal, five for the deposit on our serviceware," he said.

Ibram supposed the price included a tax for being a stranger, but considering what Amota Lakum had paid in Fontis, he handed over the coins without a murmur. The man counted them in the palm and then turned away to dump them into his strongbox. Ibram stayed.

It was an even chance that the barkeeper would be able to answer Ibram's questions about the shrine and its occupant. Vlasti Monbrith might prefer to drink in his own home, but Ibram doubted it. Ibram had never met a lay cleric, but to be sure, they probably needed a drink every now and again. Still, no one thought well of a nosy stranger, and it might make the barkeeper hold his tongue, or worse, spit in the beer.

Ibram wrinkled his nose, and then sneezed into his arm. "Beg your pardon," he said.

The barkeeper glanced over his shoulder. "Not at all," he said automatically.

Ibram could hear the sounds of pouring. He frowned. It was never a good sign when they hid the pitcher. He turned around and saw Ahksell had taken up a spot at the end of an empty trestle table, but near enough to the other patrons to hear their conversations. Ibram hummed to himself; he turned back around.

"Is there any place dedicated to the pantheon around these parts?" he asked, just a touch too loudly. "The Attendant wants to pray before we push on."

The barkeeper turned around with two wooden cups in either hand. He plunked them on the bar and then leaned on it. He looked over the top of Ibram's head to Ahksell and then back again.

"You staying for long?" he asked.

Ibram shook his head. "Leaving in the morning," he said. "The horse needed to rest, and my eyes were about to fall out of my head from driving at night."

The barkeeper nodded. He had a rough face, pale, with a short grey beard. He considered Ahksell again. "Not many of his kind come out here," he said. "And those that do, never stop."

Ibram shrugged. "Do you get many travelers?"

"More during the harvests," the barkeeper said. "We do all right."

"And a lively crowd it is, as well, Master Barkeeper." Ibram began gathering up the cups.

"Had a bit of a ruckus," the man said. "Excitement makes folk hungry."

"A ruckus?" Ibram asked. "Thieves?"

The barkeeper shook his head. "Nothing like," he said. "The opposite, even."

"Ah," Ibram said. "I had heard of that occurring as well. We had a bit of reversed trouble on the road ourselves. Warders stopped us on the round out of the boundary."

"Is that so?" the barkeeper asked. He picked up his rag again. "We had a squad show up here not too long ago. Searched high and low, and even took a trip up to shrine."

"What were they looking for?" Ibram asked, and widened his eyes. He was still young-looking enough to pull it off, after all.

The barkeeper's face barely moved, but Ibram got the distinct sense the man wanted him to leave. Ibram tilted his head, and took a drink from his mug. It tasted like soured wheat dipped in water, but he smiled as he swallowed.

"Fugitive out of Fontis," the barkeeper said grudgingly. "Sounds like a nasty situation, really. Whole town's paying for it, they say."

Ibram whistled lowly. "That so," he said. "Hope they catch the scoundrel, then."

"Isn't Fontis behind your master's line?" the barkeeper asked, and nodded to Ahksell.

Ibram shrugged. "I know the village, but it's a big province," he said. "Not for me to say why, but the Attendant's on his way to Nyarribrite on sect business. Something to do with a lady's writing automaton. But there is a shrine?" Ibram leaned in. He wanted the man to think him only interested in finding a place for Ahksell to pray, after all, rather than warders or Fontis. "Is it dedicated or is it the complete pantheon?"

"It's to the Speaker," the barkeep said. "Are you for her?"

"No, but the Attendant is," Ibram lied. "Where is it again?"

The barkeeper twisted his rag and let the water fall behind the counter, hopefully into a bucket. He sucked his teeth. "Up behind the headman's manor," he said. "About a ten minutes' walk into the trees. If the gate's locked, just shout for Old Vlasti, and he'll let you in."

Ibram nodded. "Old Vlasti," he repeated. "He's the Lecturer?"

The barkeeper snorted. "He's as close as you'll get out here. He's a bit of a cracked egg, but he keeps the place clean enough. Comes in for a hot meal every now and again."

"Oh," Ibram said, and made a show of looking around the common room. "Is he here now? Maybe he can arrange a time for the Attendant to visit."

The barkeeper shook his head. "Hasn't been seen for a seven day. If you go up and find him dead, you'll let us know?"

Ibram blinked and paused. "I will," he said at last. "That—yes, thank you."

The barkeeper nodded, and Ibram brought the beer over to Ahksell. The food had already arrived, and he was in the process of stirring his stew. Ibram sat down. He set the cup in his left hand in front of Ahksell and kept the right.

"It's sour," he warned in a low voice.

Ahksell took a sip, and winced. "It is," he said. "What were you two talking about so secretly?"

"No secret," Ibram said as he picked up his spoon. He stuck it in the quash, which was a little too watery for Ibram's taste. "Old Vlasti runs the shrine here."

"He didn't even change his name?" Ahksell asked. His eyes widened.

"Or the warders didn't care to take it down in full," Ibram said and shrugged. "Also, he hasn't been seen around lately, and if he's dead we're to come back and tell someone."

Ahksell coughed around his mouthful of food. "Runner's corns," he gasped.

"And you're for the Speaker now," Ibram said. "Please adjust your oaths."

"May your throat dry up," Ahksell snapped.

Ibram raised his cup of beer to lips, swallowed, and restrained himself from gagging. He twisted his neck left and right to relax the muscles, but it didn't really help. He set down the cup and pressed his right hand fully to the scratched tabletop.

Ahksell rolled his eyes, and dug into his food. He slurped his stew. Ibram stirred his own meal.

"How long does Antio need to rest, do you think?" Ibram asked very quietly.

"We have to give her the rest of the night—what there is left of it—and probably a good amount in the morning as well," Ahksell said.

"Can we risk trying to buy a change of horse?"

Ahksell shook his head. "Mentor Tikari swore what I had left was proper, but I don't have enough for a new horse."

Ibram looked around and shoved quash in his mouth. "And I doubt we could get a good one here."

"I vote for getting a solid night's rest," Ahksell said. "We can visit the shrine in the morning and catch whoever is up there unawares."

Ibram yawned. "If Vlasti hasn't been in town and no one's gone up, then it's safe enough. I can go along with that," he said.

⁂

The carriage's folding beds made an excellent approximation of a bed, but Ibram found himself awake the rest of the night. In lieu of dreaming, he spent the time staring up at the carriage ceiling, and listening to Ahksell's feet thud against the wall every time the man so much as twitched in his sleep. He ran through every possible tactic that might aid them on the morning. He dreamed up scenarios where Rustam ran, where he attacked them, where Old Vlasti turned out to be seven days dead and his nephew had taken his place as a holy cleric. Well, not a true holy cleric. As long as either of them had been refused the actual taking of orders, Ibram could still drag them back for questioning. It was a dark night, and nothing could turn his thoughts from the threat of failure.

He opened his eyes when dawn's light limped in through their open window. Ahksell awoke with his customary snort, and Ibram pretended to be bright-eyed with renewed energy. After stretching and taking stock of their provisions, they took a walk. It was early enough that only the water-gathering crowd was up and about Thelis' well in the center of the market square. A few matronly folk were arranged in a loose line, carrying buckets. Ibram stretched his arms over his head until his back cracked, and then relaxed.

"Do you see some place like a headman's house?" he asked.

"I don't know," Ahksell yawned. "That one seems the largest."

He pointed off to the right. One building had a roof that loomed over its neighbors, and a little gate. Like most of its neighbors, it was made of dark wood and was rather more sturdy than elegant. It was separated from the other buildings by alleyways small enough that two people could not have walked side by side.

"Well," Ibram said. He bounced on the balls of his feet and tucked his thumbs into his belt. He swallowed, strangely conscious of how his throat moved.

Ahksell coughed and breathed out loudly. Ibram looked at him, and Ahksell nodded back. "Where's the shrine again?"

"He said it was behind the headman's house about a ten minutes' walk away," Ibram said, nodding. He felt his blood begin to speed up in his veins, like he'd been in Ama's caffa stash. "Let's go and see."

They crossed the market square directly. Ibram nodded politely to the matronly folk at the well as they passed, and then he led the way up one of the alleys around the headman's house. Ibram's stomach tightened. The alley was cold and the wood was grey; the nails had turned green with damp. He glanced up at the walls looming above his head.

"This just seems unhealthy," he muttered.

"Try it from my perspective," Ahksell said behind him.

Ibram peeked over his shoulder. Ahksell was sidling through the alley, forced sideways by the bulk of his shoulders. Ibram chuckled as he turned back around, and felt the knot in his gut loosen a bit. Ahksell pushed him forward a few steps.

"Well, that's ridiculous," he said as they emerged. "There has to be an easier way than what we just did."

Ibram looked down at the packed earth road and then to the right. He pointed. Ahksell sighed.

"That rather large and open pathway leads past the stables, I imagine," he said.

Ibram nodded. "Where we slept, yes."

"Let's not speak of this part of the journey when we get back to Fontis." Ahksell snorted, and Ibram covered his mouth to hide a sudden, wild giggle. He cleared his throat, and turned to walk in the opposite direction, where a clear path led up a small hill to a one level building, painted blue, with a faceted wooden roof. 'Old Vlasti' and possibly his fugitive nephew were in there, and there was no doubt that they would be able to spy him and Ahksell coming.

Ibram took a deep and solid breath. He put his hand around the hilt of his sica, and then nodded. "Well, time to find out."

They walked up together at an easy pace, so that if anyone did see them, it wouldn't be alarming. Strangers, to be sure, and one was an alchemist, but if the boy could hide with a squad of warders on his tail, he wouldn't run at the sight of a green gambeson. Besides, it was a place of worship, they could hardly keep visitors out.

"You talk first," he muttered with his eyes sweeping left and right for any kind of movement. If Rustam was here, he still might run, and if he wasn't here... Well, that was a different matter. Ibram turned his head and his neck cracked alarmingly.

"I will," Ahksell said. His hands clenched and unclenched; he was probably wishing for his gar back in the carriage. "He might recognize your voice."

As they neared the end of the trail leading up to the shrine, an old man dressed in a long blue woolen robe came out of the entryway. It was done in the southern style, gathered up at the arms to show the tunic underneath it, and long enough to brush the tops of the man's boots, with slits at the sides for movement. The man's hair was mostly grey, with a few stubbornly brown bits clinging on to the sides of his head. His face was severe and his jaw was quite sharp. Master Monbrith looked a lot like his sister.

Ibram paused and bowed politely. Ahksell moved ahead of him. He also bowed and, this time, it was returned.

"Good day, Master Monbrith," Ahksell said and smiled politely. "I'm sorry to disturb you so early."

The old man paused. "I'm afraid you have the better of me," he said in a gruff but polished voice.

"Oh, my man here asked in the village where I might visit for a moment of worship before continuing on to Nyarribrite," Ahksell said. "The folk at the draughtshop pointed me to you."

He hadn't denied the name, which made Ibram's entire body break into prickles and bumps. He strained his ears for the sounds of someone else in the vicinity, but all he heard was birdsong. He wriggled his toes in his boots, and pretended to be nothing more than a bored servant, waiting on his betters.

Master Monbrith's eyes were quite sharp. He took Ahksell's measure and then moved quickly on to Ibram. He crossed his arms.

"The shrine is open to all who come here," he said finally, and a little bit as if it pained him. "If you would like to follow me?"

"I would," Ahksell said. He glanced over his shoulder and gestured at Ibram. "Come along."

"Ah, your servant is also a believer?" Master Monbrith asked. He held one hand out, flattened, as if he were about to push Ibram back over his threshold.

"He is," Ahksell said a little quickly. "He's remarkably devout actually."

Ibram smiled, and bowed again. He tried to project the air of a man with an eager need to say something nice to his goddess. The air smelled like fresh whitewash; perhaps a repair had just been completed. Master Monbrith narrowed his eyes at him, but his hand dropped. He turned to face front once more and led them inside the shrine.

The blue building creaked loudly as they entered, as if in a stiff wind. It was no larger than a peasant's home, really, and completely enclosed. The roof was held up by a circle of wooden pillars around what would have been an exposed courtyard. The walls had been painted white with large shuttered windows flung open to catch the sun.

It was remarkably cold inside; Ibram breathed out and could see his breath. He frowned. The air had been much warmer on the walk up. He surveyed the area as Master Monbrith led Ahksell towards the altar. There were two small rooms connected to the larger main space, big enough for ten people to worship. One of the curtained doorways was narrow enough that it was most probably for storage, but the other, with the curtain swept aside, looked like a sleeping room. Neither had doors, but both had blind spots so that Ibram couldn't say they were completely empty.

Paint flaked off the nearest pillar as he passed. Ibram stopped and peered at the wood. It looked cracked, like the shell of an egg, as if the merest push would splinter the support and bang would go the roof. He bent down to pick up one of the flakes on the floor; it dripped like it had been freshly painted. He looked over the floor and saw more flakes splattered thickly upon the ground around each of the supports.

Ahksell cleared his throat, and Ibram stood up quickly. He took a step back to maintain his balance and brushed his hands clean, though paint smeared his palms. He hurried forward—back to Ahksell's side.

"We are in the middle of remodeling," Master Monbrith said stiffly. "I apologize for the mess."

Something wooden cracked loudly, and he flinched. Ibram's heart pounded. No building sounded like that when it was in good working order. Master Monbrith was either an exceedingly poor groundskeeper, or he was a bad lay cleric. A very bad lay cleric harboring a criminal in his shrine, and lying to the warders in a holy place. They said the Speaker was slow to anger, but quick to action. Ahksell smiled and nodded.

"We?" he repeated. "Is there another Lecturer here?"

Master Monbrith went pale; something snapped above their heads. "I am not a Lecturer!" he said quickly, and raised both hands in front of himself. "I merely look after the shrine until the Speaker sees fit to provide it with a cleric again. I am only the groundskeeper."

"Oh," Ahksell said. "I apologize, I didn't hear your title in the village. It was really quite late when we arrived."

His eyes flickered towards Ibram as he placed a slight emphasis on 'we.' Ibram nodded back; he'd caught it too.

"I do minister in a small way to my fellow villagers," Monbrith said and relaxed when nothing else in the building made a noise. "When we speak truth we bring honor to the goddess."

He clasped his hands in front of him, and then turned and bowed towards the altar in the center of the room. It was dressed in long white linen fabric, one huge solid piece that draped to the floor and smaller pieces edged in a black border that formed a row of triangles pointing down, and a final bolt of fabric layered like gauze on top of that. Ibram considered it; Ahksell had said the Monbriths' altar in Fontis had also been decorated in expensive white linen. It was entirely possible that the money to pay the milliner had come from Harken Tolk and Rustam.

A golden mosaic icon of the Speaker arguing her case for Vissilia in the court of the Advisor lay in the center held in place by a dark wooden frame and bracketed by braids of fresh blue and purple lillia flowers. Apart from that, the entire building was plain, and moreover, falling apart. Why spend the money on the altar when what was needed was a carpenter and possibly the construction of an entirely new building? A small bell rang out behind Ibram; he turned and saw through the front door to the lane down to Thelis.

"I shall leave you to your prayers," Monbrith said. "The candles are in the box on the floor. They are free, but a donation of a faunt or two is always accepted."

Ibram ducked his chin to his chest and bit his lips together. He wanted to bounce on his feet. He could just see a good third of the small room which Master Monbrith was walking into. Rustam could be in there, listening. He could be hiding in a—a crate or an airing cupboard.

He looked up and met Ahksell's eyes. Ibram jerked his head towards the altar, and then pointed at Monbrith's back. He followed Monbrith and then paused at the empty threshold. The man walked into the room and turned back around with his hand upraised. He stepped back, startled.

"What are you doing sneaking up on me?" he asked.

"Do you have some water?" Ibram lifted his hands to show his paint-smeared palms.

'How did you do that?" Monbrith asked.

Ibram shrugged. "I touched some of those paint flakes you've got on the floor." He leaned into the room; Monbrith fell back. "What kind of treatment goes on your wood around here that it refuses to take a fresh coat?"

There was an old blanket hung by string that Monbrith doubtless used to trap the warmth in winter. A low table in the center of the room held a wooden plate with the remains of breakfast upon it and a cup next to a pitcher. There was a frame for hanging clothes and an open window which threw sharp sunlight into every corner. A small pallet lay in one corner and a pile of blankets were folded neatly on top of it.

"I'm but a poor groundskeeper," Monbrith said, sharply. "I can't always afford the best materials."

Ibram shook his head, and glanced at the table again. There was something funny about the plate. "It's a bad man to take advantage of a lay cleric, don't you agree?"

"Lay cleric? I have not the honor," Master Monbrith said. He swallowed. "I've got a basin for washing here, you're welcome to it."

He turned and walked to a bucket in the corner. Ibram stepped closer to the table, and tilted his head. He heard a splash of something being dipped in water, and bent down. He glanced up at Monbrith's back and then squinted down at the breakfast setting. One cup, a spoon, one pitcher, one...no, there was two plates on the table; they were stacked. Ibram straightened quickly, just as Master Monbrith returned with a dripping rag. He handed it to Ibram, and then crossed his arms over his chest.

"Really?" Ibram asked, while his mind raced ahead. "Don't think I've ever seen a groundskeeper in a blue robe like that, before. And you did say you helped the villagers down there."

Two plates didn't mean anything, necessarily. Lots of folk had more than one plate, and Monbrith wasn't impoverished. It was easy enough to carve a good pair of wooden plates if you had the skill, and any passing merchant might have a set or two for sale. But who ate their breakfast on a stack of such things? He wished he could duck down and get a look to see if a second cup and spoon lay underneath the table. Rustam wouldn't fit under such a low thing, though, and it was best not to be hasty.

Ibram bowed shortly, and wiped the damp rag on his hands. It didn't help much, to be sure, but it was nice to try. He took a casual look about him in the bright light; there didn't seem anywhere to hide.

"One need not be a cleric to help their fellow worshippers," Monbrith said stiffly.

Ibram nodded while he rubbed his hands together. The floor where he walked was solid packed earth. No doubt the warders had come away believing there was no secret cellar to withdraw to. A gambeson in dull brown hung from the airing frame, but Master Monbrith was a slight fellow. If he tried to wear that great article he'd be swimming in fabric, but a big strapping blacksmith's apprentice like Rustam might fill it out nicely. Ibram ignored the increasing clamor of his heartbeat and gave his hands a good final scrub. He handed the rag back and smiled.

"Thank you," he said.

He left the room at a careful pace and the man swished his curtain closed behind him. Ahksell was standing by the only other room, the little closet. Ibram spread his hands; Ahksell shook his head.

Ibram's heart sank, too full to be anything by a distraction. Had Rustam seen their approach and ducked into the forest? He put his hands on his hips, turned to stare out the nearest window, and then twisted back to stare at Ahksell.

Ahksell shrugged. Ibram waved his hands silently to indicate the empty room. Ahksell raised his hands and shrugged again. Ibram's breath left his body in a rush. He bent his head and rubbed his eyebrow with his thumb. Hang it, if they'd arrived while Rustam was out gathering mushrooms or something, they were sunk.

Wind blew through the windows and the entire shrine lurched alarmingly. He whipped his face up towards the roof, shoulders already hunching against imaginary falling beams, but the wood above them held firm. Ahksell rubbed his hand over his jaw and walked into the center of the room; Ibram met him there, in front of the altar.

"What are we going to do?" Ahksell whispered furiously.

"I have no idea," Ibram said, and matched him in both tone and volume. "We have a little time. He thinks you're praying, so get to it."

"What?"

"Go pray!" Ibram pointed in the direction of the altar. "I'll—I'll think of something."

Ahksell frowned at him, but went over to the small box of sticks of fragrant wood on the floor. He picked two up, and then bowed with a stick in either hand. Then he raised his hands from his stomach and held the sticks over his bowed head.

Ibram had no idea why they called them candles instead of torches, but that was Vissilians for you, ordering the universe as they saw fit. He turned in a slow complete circle, taking in his surroundings. The entire room was of a piece, and what had looked like fresh paint when they entered was beginning to turn grey in the increasingly bright light. It was all too strange, and very much the sort of developments he might expect in a peeved goddess' shrine.

Yet the warders had been in the exact same location as Ibram, and they hadn't seen it. He frowned. Maybe he was reading too much into it. Light changed in the morning, and though the place did look like it was in need of a good remodeling that didn't mean it wasn't normal decay. He huffed, and his breath billowed out in a cloud of steam; it really was freezing and not a little damp. Ibram paused. He walked outside the shrine, and the heat of the sun touched him. The cold felt solid at his back. He walked further away, and felt himself grow warmer.

All right, that was not at all natural. He walked back inside the shrine and shivered as he crossed the threshold. Before him, he saw Ahksell murmuring his prayers. He looked past him to the fancy altar, and stared at the aquiline lines of the Speaker's face in the icon. It always boggled him how a lady famous for arguing looked so serene in her official portraits. He supposed it was what Ladyship called 'artistic license.'

Ibram's chest felt heavy, weighing on his lungs. Rustam wasn't in the small living area, nor in the storage closet. He very much was not in the big wide empty room Ibram was drowning in at the moment. He eyed the front door. He hadn't heard anything like a man jumping out a window to hide outside. He jiggled his left heel. Just as Monbrith must have seen them walking up the road, they would have seen a man running around outside the property. He was sure of it, mostly. There was no cover, nor even a shed by the shrine.

He moved up across the center of the room, and kept his eyes on the icon of the Speaker again from the left. Yilka the Green didn't like portraits. At best, she allowed images of dice and bells and sometimes, confusingly, a woman's hand wrapped entirely in green ribbons, which Ibram had never quite understood, but allowed it made for a nicer picture than a person with three faces. A hard tap landed on the back of his head; Ibram whirled around, fists up, and blinked into nothingness. Ahksell continued to mutter by the altar.

Slowly, Ibram uncurled his fists and held his hands up. A bell sound where there were no bells, and now a smack on the head. A room that was too cold for the season.

"Ahksell," he said.

Ahksell paused in his mutterings to shush him. Ibram rubbed the back of his head; he looked quickly about himself. It was bitterly cold. A crack was developing on the wall right before his eyes. He bowed, just to be on the safe side. "My apologies, Oh Great Lady," he muttered. "Out in a minute."

That was probably most improper, but Ibram wasn't a cleric and he also was very unsure which deity had just smacked him like a naughty pet. Did they work together? What kind of division of labor had the Merrilian deities created with the Vissilian pantheon when the empire took over? He eyed Ahksell's back, and slowly began walking towards him. He'd said something. Ibram frowned.

"It takes a great deal of power to touch the real world, does it not, Ahksell?" he said. "Divine to real and real to divine, yeah?"

Ahksell glanced over his shoulder. "It does," he said slowly. "It takes effort."

"A shrine is a place of collected power," Ibram said.

Ahksell turned to face him, still holding his sticks in both hands. "Yes," he said. "But you're not going to be able to speak to your goddess here. A shrine that's been allowed to fall into a condition such as this? You might even be able to roll your dice without a murmur of trouble."

"The warders didn't say anything about the condition of the shrine, just that Rustam wasn't there," Ibram said. "Is it possible that all this —" he gestured to the failing paint and cracking walls. "—is the result of Rustam's arrival?"

Ibram stepped up beside Ahksell. He opened his mouth and then closed it. He stared at the altar; it was the one place in the shrine no one would touch. Not even the warders. But no. No, surely not. They were devout people. Master Monbrith had run away to be a lay cleric, even. The long white linen covering the altar with its icon and flowers swayed in the wind. The flowers were withering.

Ibram felt a flutter in his chest. Rustam was a fugitive from Her Gracious Majesty's justice, and an offense against Soliya IV was an offense against the pantheon, to be sure. And that altar was the only thing in the entire place a good Vissilian subject would never dare disturb.

Ibram leaned over to Ahksell. He patted Ahksell's arm for his attention, and when Ahksell raised his head, Ibram held up one finger.

He cleared his throat. "Rustam, you should come out now," he said loudly.

Ahksell dropped his sticks. "What?" he asked.

Master Monbrith appeared in his little room's doorway. "Did you call me, young master?" he asked.

Ibram sighed. "It's not a good thing you're doing, to be sure, Rustam," he said. "You remember me? Ibram Ucalegon? I came down when your Master Harken died, and you lied to me."

Master Monbrith came bursting into the room in a swirl of fabric. Around him the shrine creaked and he flinched back a step. "There is no one but myself here!" he snapped. "And my name is Vlasti!"

"Oh, I know, it's very old fashioned," Ibram said. "You all are, really. Diarmit and Satya and Rustam and Jorie and Vlasti. Royals and clerics to the heavens every last one of you." He stared hard at the altar and put his hands on his hips. "Which is why it is particularly bad to be hiding under the Speaker's altar, Rustam!"

"Ibram!" Ahksell grasped him by the arm.

"Oh, I'm not saying he touched it," Ibram said and pulled free. "You wouldn't allow that, would you, Master Vlasti?"

Old Vlasti opened his mouth, but Ibram continued. "But first, you have to tell me, if no one can touch the altar, who adds those lovely flowers? Do you just toss them on, and hope for the best? Can you give all that linen a good shake for dust once in a good while? Because who would dare check beneath a holy altar. That's *blasphemy*."

Vlasti's face turned maroon; he shook for a moment and then his entire body went tense. "How dare you come into this shrine and defile it with your—"

A support cracked in half. They all whirled to look at it, and then Ibram heard the scuffle of guilty feet. He swerved back around and there was Rustam Monbrith, covered in dust and running full tilt towards the nearest open window.

"Ahksell!" Ibram yelled. He ran forward but Vlasti ploughed into him, sending them both to the floor. They rolled, and Ibram landed on top. He struggled free and kicked out, catching Vlasti in the knee as he stumbled backwards.

He heard the rip of fabric and saw a piece of tunic dangling in the air. Ibram groaned and lurched forward onto his feet already at a run. The window pane hit his stomach, but he could see Rustam's broad back, torn shirt flapping in his wake as he ran for it.

"Oh for—go around!" Ibram yelled and pulled himself out the window and down to the ground.

He kicked off, the wind at his back, and ran for Catha the Grey's fickle favor after his target. The ground was hard packed and the sun was out, so Ibram had a fantastic view of the man easily pounding his way to freedom. He hunched his shoulders and leaned into his speed. He felt propelled, like his stride was wider, his footing more secure; his lungs pumped for air.

"You utter—" Ibram shouted, "utter coward! You'd let your sister die starving to save yourself!"

Rustam faltered, like he'd hit a dip in the ground, but kept going.

Ibram jumped a ditch and tried to come at him from an angle. The land was flat until a man actually needed to travel across it and then suddenly every hill and dale and pebble was under his feet. He stumbled and bent double, arms pinwheeling for balance. He grabbed a rock and stood up; Rustam was still in range.

"Luck as work in my arm," he muttered as he reared back and flung the stone forward. It soared high, faster than Ibram had ever thrown anything. He sucked in air and then ran after its arc. They had reached the stables. Folk with their horses turned to stare. The rock tore through the air and struck Rustam directly between the shoulder blades. He stumbled and fell to one knee, and then Ibram was on him. He lunged and before Rustam could regain his feet, Ibram kicked him in the back of the thigh hard enough to make him bellow. Rustam fell on his back; Ibram drew his sica and stepped on the boy's right hand.

Rustam roared in pain and punched out at Ibram's hip with his left. Ibram swept his arm down, knocking Rustam's blow aside, and then jabbed his blade at Rustam's panting face. The boy flinched back. His arm dropped behind himself for balance. He was a broad one, heavy in the shoulders and across the chest, with a strong forehead and a soft chin. He curled his trapped fingers around Ibram's boot and Ibram leaned his weight down. Rustam kicked the ground and moaned. He fell back, mouth trembling, and stared up at the sky, gulping in air.

"Get off me!"

"Rustam Monbrith," Ibram said. He heard running behind him. "There's a judge in Fontis who'd dearly love to make your acquaintance."

Someone moved to Ibram's right; he swerved his upper body and raised his sica in front of him. The sun glinted off the curved blade. The stable boy from last night stopped his approach and let his hands hang from his sides, obviously empty.

"Now, we're peaceful folk here, Master Westerner," the stable boy said. "There's no need for violence."

Ahksell ran up to them, holding Vlasti Monbrith by the scruff of the neck, and looking decidedly worse for wear. He'd lost a button on his gambeson and something that looked like metal rope was wrapped around Vlasti's hands.

"Go and find your headman," Ahksell snapped.

The stable boy gawked at him, and then took a wavering step backwards.

"This village is a shambles!" Ahksell declared. "Lying to warders! Harboring fugitives! You get me your headman, boy, or I'll be taking you with me back up the living mountain!"

He shook Vlasti Monbrith like a sullen ragdoll for emphasis. Rustam moaned again. The stable boy ran for it.

"And someone get me a rope!" Ibram yelled at his back.

He stepped off of Rustam and returned the point of his sica to a spot vaguely in the center of his chest. Rustam panted up at him; he had dark circles under his eyes and stress lines at his mouth. Ibram shook his head.

"Penance does not have to occur behind the bars of a cell," his uncle said behind Ibram. "He admitted responsibility!"

Ibram stared Rustam down, until the boy's big brown eyes skittered towards the stable and remained focused there. "He may inform his village so," Ibram said. "Since it's their lives he's risking."

That made Rustam look back to him. He pouted. "What are you talking about?" he asked. "It's just a fine, that's all. That's what they said in the common room!"

Ibram dragged air into his lungs, fresh and sharp. He blew it outwards again and shook his head. "Plenty of time to set you straight on the road back."

❧

Once Ahksell had explained exactly what manner of folk had been hiding away in Thelis' shrine, and by whose authority they had tied up a longtime resident, the headman of Thelis was all too happy to see them on their way. Ibram's credentials were unneeded.

Ibram and the stable boy removed blankets, crates, gar, and anything else the Monbriths might find useful in an escape from inside the carriage. Some of it, he arranged to have returned to the Sect of Seven Fires, payment upon delivery, but the food he put in the foot well beneath the driving bench and they strapped Ahksell's gar to the side of the carriage. Antio was restive. She took some coaxing to get back in harness, but once Ahksell had her pointed down the road she settled into her best ground-eating pace.

Ibram shook his gambeson out on the side of the carriage and then dropped it into his lap. Sweat made the back of his tunic stick from his neck to the small of his spine. "I cannot believe you grabbed his tunic and it tore."

Ahksell squirmed in his seat. "It was a moving target! Those are hard to capture."

"You caught Madji well enough."

"She was further away."

That made no sense, but Ibram allowed it to slide. "So it's a problem of *control*. You'll have to tell Ladyship," he said instead.

Ahksell groaned. "I know."

"She'll make you practice with the learners."

"Ibram."

"They'll probably throw things at you."

"Yeah, well, you were tackled by an old man," Ahksell said, and Ibram laughed aloud. He crossed his feet at the ankles and stretched his arms out over his head. Someone hit the back of the carriage from inside, but he ignored it. There were two lightning locks on the window and the door; neither Rustam nor his uncle was escaping any time soon. He turned his face into the wind.

"Yes, I was," Ibram said. "But he was a wily old man, so I don't count it against myself."

Ahksell tried not to, but laughter overtook him. He took a deep breath, grinned at the sky, and then let it out. "I spent the entire time in that shrine apologizing for the lies you told, you know," he said.

Ibram watched the scenery for a moment. "What lies?" he asked. "I told nothing but the truth. I told you Rustam would be there, didn't I?"

He eyed Ahksell as he drove. It was probably best not to tell him about being tapped upside the head. He could mention it to Lady Azadiya and let her sort it out when he made his full report. At the very least, actually capturing Rustam had to grant him a little leniency. He'd fixed his mistake and he'd been smart enough to catch something others had missed. Amota Evren's underground dungeon full of papers was further and further away all the time.

They lapsed into silence as they drove onward. The farmlands around Thelis bloomed with green plants under a light grey sky. Ibram tossed both feet up on the top of the foot well. He angled his head towards the sky and hummed to himself.

They'd gotten a late start—they had expected to, of course—but that meant they'd have to push on through nightfall. Judge E'grard's final verdict would most definitely have to be changed if they brought back Rustam. He reached up and touched the heavy wax seal affixed to the front of the carriage. He let his hand drop. Ibram licked his lips and frowned up at the sky. He sat up.

"We'll have to feed them, won't we?" he asked. "When we have to rest Antio?"

Ahksell nodded. "I suppose so."

"I've never had prisoners before," Ibram said. "I'm not certain how to do that."

Ahksell held the reins in both hands, but briefly took his eyes off the road. "Neither do I, really."

"When I was in the North, they never actually got around to feeding me," Ibram said. "I don't even have a good example."

"What about the other times you've been locked up?"

"You can't count those," Ibram said. "I was hardly inside the cell for a day."

"Well," Ahksell sighed. "I suppose there's time enough to come up with a plan."

✦

Perhaps it was merely Ibram's imagination, but they seemed to reach the edge of the forest that much more quickly than they'd left it. It was well past midday and the sky was just beginning to darken, but Ibram could not have possibly felt less tired. Ahksell pulled Antio to a stop for a rest and a drink, and then divided the remaining food into thirds. Then, Ahksell apportioned it into fourths.

"They can have all the cheese," Ibram said. "It's smelling worse than yesterday."

Ahksell sighed, and gathered it all up into a piece of fabric. He tied it up and then held the food out. "At least there's enough for two."

Ibram took the parcel out of his hands, and nodded. Ahksell went over to the windowpane. He blew on his first two fingers and thumb, and then rubbed them together. A thin blue crackle of energy sparked off his fingernails. He reached out and pinched open the lock on the window. The leather flap rolled up with a snap, and Rustam stuck his head out.

"Are we to be let out?" he demanded. "I...need to seek nature."

Ibram held out the parcel of food. "Hungry?"

Rustam frowned at him like a thundercloud, but stuck his arm out of the small window, and grabbed the food. He disappeared from the window, and Ibram heard thunking. He waited with Ahksell but the uncle didn't appear. Ibram craned his neck. He could hear talking, but not what was being said.

Vlasti Monbrith's dour face popped up in the open window. "Who is attending to the shrine while I am away?" he asked brusquely.

Ibram shrugged. He rubbed the back of his neck and fought back a yawn. The excitement of earlier had gradually sunk into an unquiet idleness as the journey continued. He'd spent most of it composing his notes for Lady Azadiya in his mind; this time it would not merely be orderly, but thorough as well.

"Probably someone who won't hide a criminal in it," Ibram said. "I think it needs a good scrubbing with soap and water myself."

Vlasti frowned heavily. "A penitent in fear of oblivion is always welcome to hear the Speaker's voice."

"Even when she says no? Consider your best interests, Master Monbrith. Rustam's counterfeited a lot of Her Gracious Majesty's coinage, and questions have been asked. *Imperial* questions."

Vlasti's eyes popped wide; he turned pale and then a ruddy color that bled down his neck. He disappeared from the window, and Rustam reappeared. His mouth trembled.

"I still need to go out," he said.

Ibram looked at Ahksell, eyebrows raised; Ahksell nodded back.

He opened his mouth, and Rustam reappeared. He was too big for the window and only managed to stick his head out.

"My uncle has to as well," Rustam announced.

Ibram nodded. "Well," he said. "I'm sorry, young master, but you'll have to control yourself."

"Oh you must be joking," Rustam said. "We've been in here for hours!"

"Well, if you hadn't committed a serious offense and lost your head we none of us would be here, would we?" Ibram said. "So you've brought this on yourselves."

"It's not right," Rustam protested.

"Are you going to run again?"

Rustam frowned deeply and with his whole face. His hair had turned stringy and he brushed it out of his face. He scrubbed over his eyes with the heel of his palm.

"I won't run," he said.

"You ran from the court," Ibram said. "Your entire village was sanctioned because of it."

Rustam dropped his hand; it hit the windowpane hard enough that Ibram winced. "Sanctioned?" he repeated. "What does that mean?"

Ibram sighed. He looked down at his boots and waved at Ahksell. He spit to the side as Ahksell began to explain, and walked away to stare at the trees. Ibram moved further away, where they'd tied Antio to a handy tree with a bit of forage and some clear water from the stream. There wasn't much forage left, but the water was still high in the bucket. She whickered and bobbed her head at his approach.

He reached out and drew his hand down her back, shushing her. He breathed in; the air smelled like trees and sweaty horse, but Ibram didn't mind it. He heard a crackle, and turned. Ahksell walked closer.

"How'd they take it?" he asked.

Ahksell shook his head. "Not very well," he said. "I don't think the extent of the punishment had quite reached Thelis. His uncle would have dragged Rustam back by his hair, if he knew."

Ibram shook his head. "I don't suppose you can keep hold of one, while I take the other behind one of these trees for a moment?"

Ahksell's whole face puckered for the space of a breath. "I'm liking this prisoner transport duty less and less."

Ibram laughed, but nodded. They turned back. Ahksell opened the lock on the door, and Ibram drew his sica.

"You can come out for a bit of privacy," Ibram announced. "One at a time, though. We'll start with Rustam."

Rustam appeared in the doorway of the carriage, and blinked down at them. He climbed down the steps and stood on the forest floor, rubbing his hands together. Ahksell locked the door behind the boy, and Ibram escorted him into the woods.

⁜

They traded off and then let the Monbriths stretch their backs for a moment in fast fading light. Ibram kept his dagger drawn, but neither seemed like they were about to run. Ahksell had placed their food in the carriage; they weren't going to stop again.

"I need to go home," Rustam said as he walked back up inside the carriage.

"That's the spirit," Ibram clapped him on the back. "You just settle right back into the carriage and we'll be off by moonlight."

Rustam stopped and turned to him. He was taller than Ibram by an inch or so, and his face loomed above him. He swallowed three times.

"I'm not a liar," he said. "Not really, and I didn't kill him."

"Oh we know," Ibram said. He waved his hand not carrying his weapon back in the correct direction. "Now, back in the carriage."

"I would never have gone if I'd known!"

"Good, good, you work on that statement for the judge," Ibram said.

It took far too long, in Ibram's opinion, to get everyone fed, watered, and on the road again, but somehow they managed it. Ahksell hooked Antio back into her harness and snuck her something Ibram pretended not to see as he took up the reins for his turn at driving. They heard the occasional mutter from inside the carriage, but otherwise nothing. In the darkness the trees seemed to blur together and blocked the moonlight. Ahksell got out his little sailing light and chained it to the top of the carriage, but it didn't help much.

Ibram slowed the rig, and peered through the gloom. "Worst thought?" he muttered.

"A tree has fallen across the road and we're going to break our necks," Ahksell said.

"Commander Osthanes has rescinded all his past permissions and we're going to be stopped by the first warders we come across," Ibram said.

"Forcing us to overpower them."

"Culminating in a race."

"They'd fire on us."

Ibram risked looking away from the road. "They have arrows?"

"They'll hit Antio."

"Hey now!" Ibram said, and Antio neighed. He lowered his voice. "She'll hear you."

"You asked for my worst thought!"

"Well, think of a different one!"

Ahksell shifted next to him, and knocked their knees together. "Just keep driving," he said.

Ibram clicked his tongue and steadied Antio's head with the reins in both hands. He pulled back softly and she sped up immediately. Ibram rocked back in the driving bench. She was a good little thing; she could keep her speed up for a while, but Antio was seeing hard use now. He'd speak to Ladyship about it when they got back, after they dropped Rustam and his uncle into Osthanes' lap.

The wind began to rush around them as Ibram drove further down the imperial road. They splashed into small pools of water, and around them the night grew longer as the darkness deepened. Antio's gait never stumbled, but he could hear the horse breathing a bit louder than he liked. At one point, Ibram closed his eyes for a mere breath, and snorted awake when Ahksell started loudly praying to the Runner for guidance as well as speed, and Ibram realized he'd grabbed the reins right from Ibram's hands. Ibram tried to appreciate the respite, but fidgeted so much Ahksell passed them back again after a mile or so.

Irritating noises aside, driving or merely sitting, Ibram strained his eyes through the journey, trying to see beyond the flick of Antio's ears ahead of him. The sound of the hoofs boomed on the roadway. His back ached from staying in one position for so long.

"I don't suppose it's you making that light up ahead?" he asked without moving his head. His entire body felt clenched in place.

"No, but—"

"Halt! Stop in the name of the Empress!" A voice shouted by the side of the road, and Ibram pulled the rig to a stop. He lowered the reins carefully and stretched his back out. He felt like a fist just beginning to move freely. His spine popped.

19

Three figures stepped out from the brush in the side of the road. One of them held up a torch, and another detached themselves to hold Antio's head. Ibram squinted at them. The woman with the torch wore a pointy helmet. They'd reached the first cordon.

"You'll have to turn around," the warder without a job said. "This portion of the imperial road is closed."

Ibram groaned and leaned his upper body over into a stretch. "We have permission to travel," he said. "Commander Osthanes gave us the entry seal himself."

"Oh, is that so?" the warder by Antio asked. He gave her ears a pat. "Did he give you a hug as well?"

"You may check the seal yourself," Ahksell said loudly and severely. He knocked his hand on the carriage. "As directed by Warder Kamos, we affixed it to our carriage up here."

The three warders grew less amused. They looked amongst each other, and then the one carrying the torch swung up to the side of the carriage that Ahksell was on. Her eyes widened as she got a good close look at Attendant Solari, lack of sleep and comfort notwithstanding, but she raised the torch and took a serious, careful, appraisal of the wax seal. Ibram watched the flame. He couldn't shake the sudden fear that the fire would melt the wax and then they wouldn't be allowed onward.

"It looks real enough," the warder finally said, and swung down.

Ibram slumped against the back of the bench and closed his eyes. He shifted the right rein into his left hand and rubbed his forehead. His skin was clammy with cold.

"Why do you need to get into Fontis so much?" the warder holding Antio asked. "If you know Commander Osthanes, you know there's not much to be done now."

Ibram swallowed and opened his eyes. He nodded, though he wasn't certain anyone could see it. "We've got the fugitive," he said. "He's in the back here with his uncle."

Someone gasped while shock spread like a pool around the rig. Warden Horse-Grabber stopped his petting. The one with the torch swung it towards the body of the carriage like Rustam was going to pop out. The torch came back to frame Ahksell in its light.

"You know the Judge called an end to the search, didn't you?" she asked. "They've got half those walls up, I think."

Ibram's entire heart dropped into his stomach and drowned in it. He clenched the reins too tightly and forced his hands to relax. He leaned forward.

"He's made his decision?" Ibram asked. "I thought we still had a day!"

"How? Why?" Ahksell asked sharply.

"They sent the word down," the warder said. "They didn't tell us why."

"But we've got him," Ibram said; his chest felt hollow. "Is it official? What did the messenger say?"

The torch wavered in her hand. "Just said we were to focus on containment."

"I thought it was supposed to be finished yesterday," the one standing by himself said. "Only one of the alchemists came over funny and demanded a full fathom examination of the abyssal positioning on account of the flooding last year. She halted the works for a good seven hours."

Ibram looked over at Ahksell. His heartbeat picked up like a bellows. Something, or someone. He sensed Lady Azadiya's hand in that reprieve.

"It's not official until E'grard's got the writ in hand," Ibram said.

"You can't tell me Mentor Perhara isn't dragging his heels," Ahksell said.

"They're due to start again this morning," the warder said. "I wouldn't be surprised if the judge has got a work crew out already."

Ibram turned around on the bench. "I thank you for letting us know, Warder…"

"Kulis."

"Warder Kulis," Ibram took hold of the reins again and forced himself to sit up straight. "We still have a bit of a road ahead of us, so if you'll just tell your friend to let go of my horse's head we'll be on our way."

The warders shared a quick look at each other. Warder Kulis made a hand sign at Warden Horse-Grabber, who shook his head. Ibram's heel jiggled on the floor.

"Warder Kulis?" Ahksell prompted.

"Don't be foolish," Kulis said. "That horse is near done. She needs a good wipe down and a feed."

Ibram's skin flared in alarm. He swallowed hard and glanced at Ahksell, who looked grim as death in the torchlight. Antio's head was hanging a bit low.

"We'll see to her," Warder Kulis continued. "Tannev, your Dash is trained for a rig, isn't she? Hitch her to their carriage. We'll take care of this one." She looked up at Ahksell and then over at Ibram, dark eyed and stern-faced in the torchlight. She nodded brusquely. "We'll send Dayo ahead of you on Flyer with the word, you won't have to stop."

Ibram's throat clenched tightly; he nodded his thanks convulsively, and the warders stepped back to divide up the work. He set the reins back down and slid sideways into Ahksell.

"What do you think of that?" Ahksell murmured.

"Finally," Ibram said and rubbed the back of his head. "A horse with a proper name."

Warder Dayo's horse ran purely like lightning. After they hitched Dash, Ibram charged up the road without pause, three blasts from Kulis' horn still ringing in their ears, and still that horse was barely in sight. The wind whipped past them as the sky lightened. At the second cordon, Warder Dayo split off and they gained a different front rider. As they rattled past the camp, Dayo raised his horn and three sharp blasts rang out. Ahead, the front rider picked up the signal until it rang out all around them.

The new outrider kept the pace punishing. At the last hurdle, the three warders let them all careen past, and blew their horn in the same pattern. Ibram drove poised above the driving bench, balancing on the balls of his feet, as if that would make the carriage inch out a lick more speed. They were in the outskirts of Fontis now, the Monbrith property lay just ahead. In the distance, he could see the lone rider galloping onward; the horn blew again. Someone in the distance picked it up.

"Think that'll wake up the judge?" Ibram yelled over the noise of the carriage.

"If that doesn't, we will!" Ahksell shouted back with a grin.

They crested the small rise that marked the final leg of the journey. Dash snorted as Ibram pulled back on the reins to slow her down. There was a wall around Fontis, or at least in the back half of it, high with untreated wood and roughly nailed together. It covered almost the entire road with only a foot clear. Ahksell saw the planks and shivered.

"We aren't going to fit!" Ibram yelled.

Ahead, Ibram saw their front rider pull her horse to the side and keep going into the village. He could hear dim shouting. The horns blasted again.

"If I go into the ditch, this is going to be a very short return trip," Ibram said as he guided Dash as far to the right as he thought safe. The road narrowed; one of the wheels began to shake.

"You won't go into the ditch," Ahksell said. He stood abruptly and grabbed the carriage roof behind him. "Hold on!"

Ibram tightened his grip once more on the reins. Ahksell breathed in through his mouth, and Ibram felt the air swerve to the left across his face. He glanced over and then back to the road and then returned to Ahksell. Ahksell drew his hand back to his chest, palm out and fingers curled at the first knuckle. The air shook around him; the hairs on the back of Ibram's neck stood up and vibrated. He cracked his neck to the side; his ears rang. Dash neighed in alarm.

Ahksell thrust out his arm at the same time as his breath, and held his hand out, steady. The entire world seemed to blur and lean forward before them. Ibram whooped in shock and delight. A cracking groan erupted in front of them as the wooden wall dragged itself backwards, curling like butter under a hot spoon as the carriage rattled closer. Ibram glanced up, sweat a cold river down his back.

"Well done!" he shouted.

"Keep going!" Ahksell shouted back. He dared a look down to beam wildly. His hand began to shake, the wall groaned beneath its unnatural bend. Ibram heard thumps from inside the carriage as he took them past the wall, but no one screamed, so he counted it as a victory. Ahksell yelled and whipped his arm around and back. He collapsed into his seat. A great shattering wave of noise splintered the air.

Ibram grinned. "They don't make lumber like they used to!"

Ahksell wiped his sleeve over his forehead. "Momentum is a wonderful thing!"

He waved his hand at the road as it sprouted people like weeds ahead of them, shouting for them to get out of the way. They thundered into Fontis on the warder's heels and pulled to a stop in front of Mistress Denrind's manor house just as the sun truly shone over the clouds. The front gate was a hive of warders, some not even in uniform yet. Their front rider's horse was standing, breathing like a bellows, while two folk ran up from the stables.

"What's going on?" Warder Kamos shouted from within the crowd. "Who sounded the horns?"

Ibram tossed the reins aside and stood up on the driver's bench. "Warder Kamos!"

"I'm going to find Mentor Hobon!" Ahksell yelled as he jumped down from the carriage. He pushed his way through the crowd to get in the front gate. Ibram stayed where he was. He waved until he had Warder Kamos' attention.

"We've got him! Them!" he shouted above the racket of two dozen warders attempting to discipline themselves into silence.

"What?" Kamos yelled back. He started pushing his way forward.

Ibram jumped down to stand by the carriage. He grabbed the first sleepy-eyed servant he found carrying a bucket, most probably for use in the house.

"I need water for this horse!"

The servant reared back in Ibram's grasp. "Yes, yes of course," he said.

"Ucalegon, what is all this noise?" Kamos asked.

Ibram turned his head, and grinned widely. His eyes ached, his head throbbed, and his hands were made of cramps held together by wire. He felt ready to drop dead and dance a jig all at the same time.

"I've got Rustam Monbrith and his incredibly strange uncle tucked up in my carriage here," Ibram said. He dropped the smile, since Kamos appeared to be growing concerned. He tried for staid and responsible, instead. "Could you take charge of them while I make my report?"

Ibram paused for air, it seemed strangely difficult to take the stuff in. Warder Kamos stared at him. Ibram breathed out and stared back. The servant whimpered, and Ibram realized he still had the man by the arms. He released him at once.

"My apologies. Water for the horse, understand?"

"Yes, yes," the servant said and wriggled through the crowd to freedom.

Ibram turned back around. Warder Kamos had almost recovered himself. He stared at the carriage and then back to Ibram. Ibram laughed and if it was a little wild, he felt he'd earned it.

"I've got to go and make my report," Ibram said.

He raced off to the strains of Kamos yelling for prisoners' chains, charged through the reception hall, and into the public courtyard. Wooden planks were still piled in the middle. He dashed through the construction area, rather than around it, and then up and into Mistress Denrind's family courtyard.

A flock of servants ran back and forth on the terrace, some of them appeared to actually have morning duties, while a good third looked merely to be enjoying the show. The garden area was awash in guests and servants and a roaring Commander Osthanes, fully dressed and shouting at one of his warders. Ibram paused on the terrace to orient himself. Judge E'grard had awoken and his servant along with him, both of them in robes thrown over their chemises. Lady Azadiya stood near Commander Osthanes in a long light green robe belted by a wide piece of cloth with her hair down, while Amota Lakum and Attendant Serisan bracketed her on either side. Ibram couldn't think where she had gotten the change of clothes. Ahksell stood before her, talking almost as fast as his hands could move. Mentors Tikari and Perhara stood in their own little pairing, but appeared to be ignoring each other, while Attendant Zorion and the two Uxios made up another party. Mistresses Denrind and Islozia flitted around the outskirts of the garden, going from group to group and speaking with increasingly flushed cheeks.

"Ladyship!" Ibram yelled from the steps.

Lady Azadiya looked up at him. She patted the air at Ahksell's side, breaking him off mid-word, and then pointed in Ibram's direction. Ahksell turned and waved his entire arm in an arc back and forth. Ibram quickly stepped down into Mistress Denrind's family garden, careful to avoid the overturned sod, and made his way over to him. He bobbed into a bow.

"He was there, I take it," Lady Azadiya said. "Get up, will you?"

Ibram bounced on the balls of his feet. "He was, Ladyship," he said. "Are we back in time? Has the judge signed the writ? Oblivion's too good for him, I swear it."

She crossed her arms and the wide sleeves of her robe fell to her elbows. She took a moment to regard him, and Ibram felt his entire face heat. He beamed at her, and her mouth curled upwards. She nodded, glanced about at the mess they were all making of the garden, and laughed.

"*Riant*, Ibram," she said. "Very well done."

He clasped his hands behind his back, and stood next to Ahksell. His blood skittered underneath his flesh and set it shivering. Ibram elbowed him; he elbowed back. Then, Ahksell caught him when Ibram listed a little too far off center. Amota Lakum sighed.

"Good morning, Amota," Ibram said. "Am I supposed to recognize Attendant Serisan, or not?"

Lady Azadiya cocked her head and nodded slowly. "I think perhaps a night's rest would do you some good," she said.

Ibram blinked the dots out of his eyes. "Yes, Ladyship," he said.

"What in the Speaker's Charge is happening here?" Commander Osthanes roared. He stamped his way over to Ibram, waving his warder away irritably, and slammed his helmet on his head. "Was it you who got them to blow the mustering horns?"

Ibram shook his head. "Commander, I tell you truly, it was their own idea! I don't think we paused for breath after Warder Kulis stopped us at the cordon."

"They were a little rude," Ahksell said, "but very professional."

Commander Osthanes' nostrils flared when he grunted. Ibram supposed he wasn't much of a morning person; it had been the same in Delbrite. Ibram set his weight on his heels, the ground was a bit uneven.

"The trick is really not to go to bed, Commander," he said.

Osthanes frowned suspiciously. "What?"

"He was under the altar, did you know?"

"*What?*"

Ahksell waved his hand at about chest height. "No, he means Rustam was under the altar," he said. "And then we chased him."

Ibram nodded. "He's faster than you think."

Lady Azadiya raised her hand, just as Osthanes opened his mouth. "I think this is a conversation best held back for the judge," she said. She stood to one side of the group. "Mistress Denrind!"

The headwoman popped out from behind Mentor Tikari. "Yes, Mentor Hobon?"

"I believe breakfast and a moment to compose ourselves is in order," Ladyship said in a loud voice that cut easily through the others' excited conversations. "If Judge E'grard has no objection, we shall adjourn and my agent will compose his report to appear before him in your office, perhaps in an hour?"

"I would be amenable to that, Mentor." Judge E'grard very clearly disliked being managed so obviously, but he was also half-dressed in the early morning. He nodded, sour-faced, and roughly gestured for his assistant to accompany him. He returned to the terrace in a decidedly legal huff, most probably to remain in his bedroom.

"I'm afraid my office would be too small to accommodate everyone necessary," Mistress Denrind said. "Perhaps the sitting room you used previously, Mentor?"

"Mistress, you think of everything," Lady Azadiya said.

Mistress Denrind bobbed up and down in a deep bow, and then ran after the judge, clapping her hands for her servants. Lady Azadiya smiled politely at her back and turned to Commander Osthanes.

"And you wish to look over your fugitive as well, I am sure. My agent here—" She waved her hand to Amota Lakum. "—will provide a written transcription of his capture for you to measure against Rustam's interrogation. Will that be sufficient for your purposes? Or should you like to speak further with Ibram."

Commander Osthanes ground his teeth and glared at Ibram directly. Ibram stood away from Ahksell and squared his shoulders. Osthanes' face smoothed into a barely restrained neutrality when he bowed to Ladyship, but she merely waved him back up. Her belt had little pink flowers on it. He wavered on his feet like a bloodhound on the leash.

"It had better be a thorough report," he said to the air between Ladyship and Ibram.

"My best handwriting," Amota Lakum said.

Osthanes sucked his teeth sharply, and then turned on his heel. He stalked up the stairs with his fellow warder. Ibram startled, and then took a step after him. He'd forgotten an important part. Had he? He might have.

"They're behind a lightning lock!" he called out to Osthanes' back. "We kept them in the back the whole way!"

"A lightning lock?" Mentor Tikari said behind him. "Oh hang.

Hilbert, go out and supervise the warders before someone bills us for losing a finger."

Attendant Zorion took off running and met up with the Commander at the entrance. They disappeared down the steps to the public courtyard together and Ibram turned back to Lady Azadiya.

"I think today deserves caffa," she said. "You two come with me, I'm sure Lakum and Sotiria wouldn't mind giving up their bedroom while you make your report."

"Are we allowed to know the ending of this matter, Azadiya?" Mentor Perhara asked. "Or must I breakfast with Tikari alone?"

Lady Azadiya sighed and held her hair away from her neck with both hands. She shook the entire dark mass out and then let it fall free. "You might as well both come along, Ziv," she said. "Though, I warn you now, some of you will have to share the kissing couch."

⁂

Breakfast was brought in on two large trays carried by a harried pair of women, who laid the feast out on top of a large flat-topped trunk that Ibram vaguely remembered from Lady Azadiya's carriage. Ladyship had been given a bedroom connected by an open wall to a small sitting room, which clearly had seen service as both workroom and sleeping area. There was a stack of papers and a pile of well-used pens next to a pot of ink, and several empty oil lamps next to clumps of blankets. Mistress Denrind sent in a canister of shay and a pot of hot water bubbling over a short fat candle next to a clay pitcher, but Lady Azadiya had a personal store of caffa which she ground with her own hands, set into a small contraption, and then poured out for everyone.

Even with the caffa, just the act of sitting down and eating made Ibram's eyelids threaten to shut entirely. He perched on the edge of the kissing couch and pinched Ahksell when he looked like he was about to sleep; Ahksell returned the favor. In between bites of quash, and quite a few distracting moments when Tikari or Perhara asked a question, Lady Azadiya drew the story out in a coherent format for Commander Osthanes and the judge. Then, she sent Ibram and

Ahksell to bed as if they were children again, and forced them awake in time for a wash.

"You've got clean faces and hands," Amota Lakum said, as he inspected Ibram with a critical eye. "But you smell like the open road."

"It'll bring a touch of realism to our explanations, then," Ibram said.

Amota Lakum sighed heavily, and swatted Ibram's shoulders with both hands. "Straighten your gambeson, and let us go. We don't want to be late for the judge's decision."

When he turned his back, Ibram raised his arm and sniffed. He frowned. Well, it had only aired for a bit, and every bit helped, he supposed. He fixed his clothes and retied his belt. When he stepped out of the sitting room, Mentor Perhara looked up and nodded.

"Ready for your final performance?" he asked.

Ibram looked about the room. The rest of the party seemed ready to go. Lady Azadiya had changed into yet another dress, moss green with diagonal closures at the bodice; the trunk formerly used as a table was open to reveal the back of her previous robe. All the alchemists except for Ahksell had their gars in hand.

"I would guess so," Ibram said and ran his finger underneath his collar.

Mistress Islozia met them at the door, and bowed. There was a looseness to the line of her jaw now. She stepped back and gestured to her left. Lady Azadiya left first and they all followed behind. Ibram wound up walking next to Mentor Perhara, which made no sense since, by all rights, he should have exited first. The right side of Ibram's body tingled for a moment. In the corner of Ibram's sight, Perhara seemed calm enough. He walked with purpose and had no trouble keeping pace with the group.

He noticed Ibram watching him sooner than anticipated, and inclined his head. "I'm told you picked a fight with one of my agents," he said. A light shone briefly in his eye, and then went out.

Ah yes, the Uxios worked for Mentor Perhara. Would it make this conversation better or worse if he admitted he didn't know which Uxio was which? Ibram swallowed. "I did, Mentor," he said. "But only for professional reasons."

"Oh?"

"Well..." Ibram turned his head to walk in silence a little ways down the hall before they emerged onto the terrace. "Warders like it when you behave in ways they expect. It reassures them somehow."

"And they expect you to pick fights?"

Ibram opened his mouth, and then closed it. "They expect arms-for-hire to behave inappropriately when bored," he said. Not that he'd thought about his explanations before doing it, but it was true enough. "And it gave Warder Kamos something to do with a result. It's never fun to run around and find nothing, makes a man snappish."

Mentor Perhara nodded. He considered the back of Amota Lakum's head in front of him for a moment, and then returned his gaze to Ibram. Ibram became intensely focused on crossing the threshold into the public courtyard.

"And so you relaxed him by fighting with my agent," Perhara noted.

"It was really nothing more than a scuffle," Ibram said.

"Perhaps the next time, you can arrange the matter beforehand," Perhara said. "You will find agents attached to Salacia are very amenable to striking bargains."

The hairs on the nape of Ibram's neck all stood up at once. The words 'very amenable to striking bargains' ran about his head for a very ugly moment. They were at the door to the sitting room, and so Ibram stopped walking to allow Mentor Perhara over the threshold first. Then he entered and closed the door behind him.

The furniture had been rearranged far back against the walls in the sitting room so that Judge E'grard sat behind a table in the middle, while Lady Azadiya sat near to him on the low couch with Mistress Denrind. Amota Lakum and Attendant Serisan stood behind her, while his assistant stood at the judge's shoulder with her writing tablet at the ready. Commander Osthanes and Warder Kamos held up the wall to their immediate left. Mentors Tikari and Perhara had taken the remaining chairs, leaving only Ahksell and Ibram standing in the middle of the room. To their right, Rustam Monbrith, his uncle, and the rest of the Monbrith family knelt on the floor. Rustam was in chains and his family were roped together at the wrists.

Ibram saw Diarmit sitting near his sister. He stared up at him as

Ibram walked by, and hid his face when Ibram smiled. Satya smiled back, but the worry lines bracketing her mouth dragged down her lips quickly. Ibram nodded and then faced front.

Judge E'grard sat forward in his chair and interlaced his fingers. "I am informed, Attendant Solari," he began, "that you and Master Ucalegon have returned to Fontis with our fugitive."

Ibram glanced at Ahksell, and stepped up to his right shoulder. He clasped his arms behind his back and stood up straight. Ahksell cleared his throat and nodded.

"That is correct, your honor," he said. "Ibram correctly deduced that Rustam was hiding with his uncle, Vlasti Monbrith, in the shrine at Thelis."

Judge E'grard nodded; his lips twisted as he cast a severe look at Commander Osthanes. "Yes, the groundskeeper," he said. "I was given to understand the shrine had already been searched?"

Commander Osthanes' face was a study in professionalism. "I sent two men ahead of the regular search parties," he said, "to Thelis, Frumill, and Hardi in case the boy had had more time to escape than his sister had previously thought. The warders I sent to Thelis found no evidence of Rustam."

"I don't know about back then, but when we arrived he was hiding under the altar," Ibram said. "No one would think to touch that, would they?"

Mistress Denrind gasped, and even the judge looked a bit perturbed. Mistress Monbrith bowed her head; her shoulders wavered. Ibram paused to let the information take full effect.

"How did you know about the shrine?" Judge E'grard asked after a moment to recover himself.

"It was after speaking with the Monbriths—the Mistresses Monbriths, I mean, your honor," Ibram said and spread out his right hand. "They've been nothing but helpful." A flash of thought, a memory of dinner, and Ibram blinked rapidly as he finally clicked the puzzle together in the front of his mind. "When we were at dinner after the young mistress Monbrith had requested aid, we asked if there were places in the area Rustam would know how to reach. She told us part of the family's religious duties. They visited two places: the shrine at Thelis and the temple in Delbrite.

I discounted it at first, of course. Delbrite's too far away, and when Commander Osthanes said they'd cleared Thelis, I forgot about it completely. But then in conversation with Lady Azadiya, Mistress Suugan mentioned that Jorie Monbrith had a brother—"

"A fool and a failure," Mistress Monbrith snapped. "And he never understood that the Speaker hears lies in the heart as well as those spoken."

"I have never lied!" Vlasti Monbrith exclaimed. He rose up on his knees, and Warder Kamos put his hand to his sword hilt; Vlasti ignored it. "Rustam was not present in my shrine when the warders arrived, and they merely asked my occupation! They called me 'Old Vlasti' as does every man and woman in Thelis. Am I to be humbled for not supplying answers to questions never spoken? Am I to be censured for providing aid to a penitent man? My own blood?"

"Sit down, Monbrith," Warder Kamos snapped. "You're not in your shrine now, and you'll speak when you're commanded to."

"It's falling apart now," Ibram said. He nodded at Alia, the judge's assistant. She had that fixed look about her that said she was committing all of this to memory. "Walls developed cracks while Attendant Solari and I searched the place. I'd say the Speaker's making her opinion of you pretty clear, Master Monbrith." He leaned to his right. "That was before you tackled me while Rustam ran away, you remember?"

Rustam's head sank low on his shoulders. His uncle sat back on his heels. He looked at his sister, but Mistress Monbrith turned her face away.

Judge E'grard nodded gravely. "You sheltered a man who committed crimes against the Speaker's most favored child," he said. "Harboring fugitives from Her Gracious Majesty's justice is also a serious offense."

Vlasti shook his head and would not meet the judge's eyes. E'grard turned back to Ibram. He tapped the table where a short stack of papers lay. Ibram felt his heart shudder in his chest. This man still held every soul in Fontis between the palms of his hands. He could pour balm or poison on them as he pleased. He glanced at Lady Azadiya, who watched the judge with a calm face and narrowed eyes.

"From these reports," Judge E'grard said. "I am to understand that you, Rustam Monbrith, and the deceased Master Harken Tolk were the sole purveyors of these counterfeit coins, both the clipped items and the plugged?"

Rustam's head came up; he seemed puzzled. He glanced around the room, and then up to the judge.

"Well, is this true?" the judge asked.

Panic drained Rustam's face of color. "I..."

"He means did you make them all yourself, or did someone help you?" Commander Osthanes asked.

"Oh," Rustam said. His bulky body relaxed a fraction; his hands clinked in their chains. "Yes, your honor. I know there were other people, because Master Harken sometimes talked about them when he was telling me about his travels, but here in Fontis, it was just us two."

"What role did the dramseller Madji Anlines play?" the judge asked.

Rustam swallowed. He looked a bit green, to be sure. "She helped."

Commander Osthanes coughed. "Your honor," he said. "Upon interrogation, Mistress Anlines was discovered to be in possession of four medium-sized sacks of coins, in addition to a locked money chest. We've confiscated the contents of her converted herder's hut, and are awaiting the results of Mentor Tikari's report."

"Does she still remain in your custody, Commander?" Mentor Perhara asked.

"Of course she does," Mentor Tikari said. "I haven't completed my assessment yet. Hilbert wants to try out a new infusion."

In any normal day, Ibram would have grown alarmed and cautious at that thought. Now, though, his mind was on more immediate concerns. "She had a longstanding contract at the Monbrith's draught-shop," he said. "Just to remind you. And she likes telling folk horrible stories for her own entertainment."

Judge E'grard's nodded and eyed the Monbriths over his steepled hands. Rustam squirmed beneath his gaze, but Satya met the Judge's look and held her chin high. Ibram couldn't help but admire her for it.

"Your family knew nothing?" the judge asked them. "Even though they had access to the forge both during the time Master Tolk stayed in their draughtshop and when he was not present, and the area reverted solely back to their use?"

Rustam shook his head. "I didn't tell anyone! I promised I wouldn't, and it didn't…Well, I know Mother wouldn't approve."

"She doesn't," his mother said behind him. "I would have turned Tolk into Mistress Denrind's guards the moment I knew, your honor."

"But not your son?" Judge E'grard raised his eyebrows, and Mistress Monbrith lapsed into silence.

"I," Satya began with her chin raised.

"Madji," Rustam said suddenly over her. "Mistress Madji and Master Harken were friends from the road; they covered the same route, and that was how Master Harken knew to come to the draughtshop. She told him about us. She…" he trailed away and breathed hard, shoving air in his lungs as fast as it left his mouth. "She came up to me in the common room because she was worried about the arrangement. She wanted to know whether I was going to continue Master Harken's work and I… Well, I had not decided. But, you see," he stopped and looked wildly about the room, "she would need to know. She said if we made too many coins to use in the village, she would take them in her wagon to spread around."

Many things suddenly came together in Ibram's mind. He looked over to Lady Azadiya and saw the grim set of her face. She caught his eye and shook her head. Ibram looked down. Satya rocked Diarmit slightly in her grip. She looked up at Ibram; they both winced at each other. Ibram sighed.

"We all are possessed of one life," Lady Azadiya said, "and what a vinegared soul like Madji Anlines might do to keep hers seems entirely plausible considering recent events."

Rustam's head bobbed up and down. "She told me the court has an alchemist that makes you drink a foul shay and it makes you tell the truth, no matter what. She said it makes you talk and talk and you can't help yourself but spill everything—and—and I couldn't! I couldn't let on what we'd been doing, so I waited a night in the Tyal's—"

"I knew," Satya said loudly, and Ibram turned his head to look at her. Her face was set in hard lines, she had never more closely resembled her mother. "I knew what he was doing, and I helped him hide it. I found out when I was sent out with a meal for them, and Rustam was making blanks. I helped them both hide their activities from Mother and Diarmit. Mother spends all her time complaining about the cost of everything, even our education, but she does nothing about it!"

She stood up from her seat on the floor; Diarmit slipped down to stand. Satya tossed her head and wisps of hair flew out of her face and then back again. Her cheeks flushed and then paled, making her freckles stand out even more.

"I'm the one," she said fiercely, "who has to come up with new suppliers when she fires them, or figure out where the money's coming from when she decides we need another door added to the draughtshop. She won't even let me hire another servant to help Emil! The money kept the household in peace for once. It bought Diarmit's scrolls when she took him out of school—and the Speaker knows he's got a bright mind, he needs something more than his letters. But Rustam's always been clumsy and—"

"Now, that's not fair!" Rustam protested. "Satya—"

"Be quiet!" she snapped, and her brother shut his mouth. "Judge E'grard, you know I came to you immediately when I realized my brother had run. I'm not one of those folk who shirk their duties and I'll not forgo my punishment if it means someone else is harmed by it. We're caught, Rustam. We're all of us caught."

Diarmit squirmed at her side, and she pressed her lips to his hair. She raised her head, and met Ibram's eyes squarely. Ibram swallowed. He didn't like it, and neither did she. He nodded and turned back to the front of the room.

"I didn't know about that," Ibram said. "To be sure, your honor, it was Satya who called me down to help and it was through her that I found him. I think that counts for something."

"Regret, Master Ucalegon," Judge E'grard said, "is not a mitigating circumstance."

Lady Azadiya waved her head from left to right. "True, your honor," she said. "But new evidence is certainly cause for reevaluation. After all, you were brought here to preside over a trial to send Harken Tolk on to his final destination. He is still in your cold box, is he not, Mistress Denrind?"

"He is, Mentor," Mistress Denrind said. "It's becoming difficult to maintain."

"I'm sure it is," she said. "Isn't that something which must be dealt with before any further proceedings as to Master Monbrith's guilt—or indeed his family's complicity?"

"You are correct, Mentor Hobon," Judge E'grard said, and his face was as stiff as his tone was sour. "But no matter why I was first called to Fontis, the result of Rustam's flight is still a criminal offense, and that is what must be dealt with. I have already levied my opinion in that regard."

Ibram stepped forward. "We arrived back to the village well within the time you set for Rustam's return!" he protested. "What is the point of bringing him back if you're only going to impose the same decision?"

Judge E'grard turned to him. If he'd been a smiling man, Ibram felt sure he'd be beaming now. He tapped his first two fingers on the table and nodded. "Because it is the right thing to do," he said. "A fugitive must always be brought to justice."

Ibram looked about the room. Commander Osthanes and Warder Kamos stood silently. Everyone did. Even Lady Azadiya was silent and grim, and Ibram's lungs twisted into knots. He shook his head.

"I've never heard of a case where the return of a vanished First Finder merited as harsh of a sentence as their desertion," Ahksell said. "What justice is there without any mercy?"

Judge E'grard looked taken aback. "I beg your pardon, young man?"

"Now, to be sure," Lady Azadiya said. She stood and held out her hand; Amota Lakum lay a handful of papers on it. "Adherence to the law is the empire's greatest asset, is it not, your honor?"

"It is, Mentor Hobon," he replied. "And I caution your Attendant to remember that respect for my office is respect for the crown."

"Oh, we are all aware of that," Ladyship replied. "Which is why we've been so very helpful in this endeavor. Haven't we, Ibram?"

"Yes, Ladyship," he said and swallowed. He saw Attendant Serisan grin at him and switched his attention to the papers in Lady Azadiya's hand.

She tilted her head; her long braid was capped at the end with an enameled grey bird. "It was my agent who uncovered your counterfeiters, and my Attendant who confirmed Harken Tolk wasn't murdered."

"I'm the one who made sure there were no alchemasters running amok," Mentor Tikari said. "Which there are none."

"And I am most assuredly the only one in this room who could actually carry out the probable sentence you put forth *if* young Master Monbrith was not returned," Mentor Perhara said. He smiled. "That was the understanding you had with Mistress Denrind, was it not?"

"It was," Judge E'grard said. He seemed displeased, like he'd smelled something rotten.

"Not really a deal at all," Mentor Perhara said. "Not as I understand Vissilian law, anyway. In fact, is it not true that the resolution of one legal problem—the absence of a central witness—calls for the legal resumption of a trial?"

Judge E'grard's hand clenched into a fist on his desk. "Just as the punishment of Rustam Monbrith's absence was left to my discretion, so is Master Monbrith's punishment on his return. Alia? The relevant section."

The judge's assistant cleared her throat delicately, and looked into the middle distance as Ibram had seen folk do when reciting from memory. "Upon discovery of an unclaimed or unknown deceased body—"

"Please," Lady Azadiya interrupted. She raised her hand. "No one here would dare dispute your authority, your honor, nor your right to dispense justice within the law. I am merely bringing to your attention certain facts which might add nuance to your resolve."

"Indeed, Mentor Hobon," Judge E'grard asked severely. "And what is that?"

Lady Azadiya walked to the table, and laid her papers upon it. "We are blessed with one of the Advisor's most intelligent creatures," she announced. "By which I mean, Attendant Serisan of the Preceptory of Bedris, who is tasked with teaching the children of Fontis. As I relayed to you last night, the circumstances of Fontis' punishment are by their very rarity under the careful eye of our betters in the Court of Chancery, who will need to be rigorously informed of every detail of our conduct. Don't you agree, Mentor Perhara?"

"That has been my experience," Perhara said and lazily perused his fingernails. "Lord Aker's very particular."

"Now, to the point. I have here," Lady Azadiya tapped the papers, "a full list of every child in Fontis from the newly born to the age of ten, all of whom are below the Age of Reason."

Judge E'grard looked at her sharply and opened his mouth, but Lady Azadiya smiled in his face and continued. "As the world knows, the Vissilian Empire is guided not merely by physical law but by divine justice. Which, I am assured by the signed writ of Lecturer Osthanes here—" She tapped the papers. "—states clearly that no child below the Age of Reason is subject to civil or criminal law excepting in cases of custody or inheritance. Is this true, Judge E'grard?"

The judge's broad face began to be tinged with red. "It is," he said.

"And thus, no broad overarching punishment, such as a sanctioning, can be undertaken without first removing those persons the law cannot touch?" Lady Azadiya asked.

"That is also true," Judge E'grard allowed.

"How did you get a message to my brother?" Commander Osthanes demanded. "Why contact him at all?"

She looked at him. "Messenger bird, of course," she said. "He's a lovely man, by the way. You must be so proud. Family keeps us honest, to be sure."

She turned away and Commander Osthanes stared holes into the side of her head. Slowly, he brought his patience strip out of his pocket, and rubbed its buttons. Lady Azadiya had already transferred her gaze to the judge, staring directly into his cold eyes.

"Seeing as this is the case," she said. "Ibram will now cut Diarmit Monbrith free from his bonds."

Ibram jumped. He looked down at the Monbriths, and then wrapped his hand around the hilt of his sica. Satya looked up at him. She whispered something to her little brother, and he stuck out his arm. The rope had been loosely tied around his wrist. Ibram bent, drew his blade, and cut the boy free. Diarmit wrapped both arms around his sister and Ibram stood up.

"All done, Ladyship," he said.

"Now," she said with all evident satisfaction. "As to the case itself, on what grounds do you levy a punishment for one crime and ignore the other?"

"I beg your pardon," Judge E'grard raised his voice sharply.

"Rustam Monbrith is by his own admission guilty of counterfeiting," she said. "An outrage of justice calls for a trial. In fact, does not a returned First Finder demand a retrial of the interrupted occasion that preceded it? Alia, the relevant section."

Alia opened her mouth, and then jerked her head towards Ladyship, shock in every part of her face. She looked to her own employer and then back up to Lady Azadiya. Lady Azadiya clicked her fingers at her.

"In the event," Alia began in a shaking voice, "that the First Finder is returned or returns of his own accord—"

"We did roust him out," Ibram said, glancing at Ahksell.

"But when he found out the punishment the judge handed down, he swore he would have come back," Ahksell said, and nodded.

Alia cleared her throat very loudly. "Then a trial will reconvene," she continued severely, "wherein the facts of the original case will be presented and judgement upon the merits of the case will proceed accordingly. If the actions of the First Finder are discovered to require further investigation, a separate trial will be begun upon the closure of the first trial and all representatives of the court and the Bureau of Justice are charged to perform their duties in all due diligence."

"A second trial," Lady Azadiya said. "Commander Osthanes, forgive me, can another trial in Fontis be carried out if all the witnesses and even the accused have been locked away from reality for fifty years?"

"It cannot, Mentor Hobon," he said.

"Can it occur outside of Fontis?" she asked, staring down at the judge in his seat. "Can Rustam Monbrith's sacred right to be taken to account by the Court Civil be accomplished without any persons there involved able to provide witness or give testimony?"

Commander Osthanes shook his head. "No," he said again.

Ibram's throat clenched, and he swallowed deeply. He looked down to Rustam's head, still bowed, and then back up to Lady Azadiya. She turned her head and regarded the entire Monbrith clan fondly.

Yilka's megrims, had Rustam's crime actually saved his entire village? Ibram stared at Judge E'grard's slowly reddening face. He clenched his hand on his hilt, and saw Ahksell shift his weight from the corner of his eye. The entire room was silent.

"And, do you know, I also think it would be very difficult to figure out who Master Tolk's other associates were," Lady Azadiya dug the knife in that last little bit, and smiled while she did it. "I mean to say, if Rustam—"

"Yes, Lady Hobon, I think we all understand what you are saying," Judge E'grard interrupted her. His face had turned piebald, splotched an intemperate red under the eyes and at his temples.

Lady Azadiya settled back and overlaid her hands, one over the other. "I'm sure as astute a magistrate as you are, Master E'grard, will come to a just and expedient conclusion."

Ibram forced himself to breath normally, and looked nowhere but at Judge E'grard. The judge was not a man to be pushed, but there Lady Azadiya stood before him, her head tilted at a precise and polite angle of inquiry. Rustam must be tried twice, once for running and again for counterfeiting. Beside him, Ahksell shifted his weight from his right to his left. Ibram stuck his elbow out and caught Ahksell on the return; they both froze.

Judge E'grard breathed in and out sharply. His shoulders slumped and then straightened as if someone had pulled his strings taut. "In light," he growled, and then cleared his throat to speak more clearly. "In light of the reappearance of the First Finder, and in due deference to the requirements of Commander Osthanes' new investigation, I rescind the order of sanction against the village of Fontis. Alia, write out a new directive rescheduling the inquest of Harken Tolk and then speak with Commander Osthanes' man on the time he might need for a new trial concerning the accused's...newly discovered crimes."

She'd done it. Yilka the Green's bells rang out and all the dice pointed upwards; Lady Azadiya had the judge *cold*. Ibram dug his elbow into Ahksell's side, but stuffed the urge to jump for joy deep down inside him where it belonged. He clenched both hands into fists. Lady Azadiya inclined her head to the judge.

"You are ever wise, your honor," she said, and resumed her seat.

Mistress Denrind turned pale and then red, and then settled into a blooming pink as she bounded to her feet. "What happens to the Monbriths?" she demanded. "Are they to remain with the warders?"

Judge E'grard dragged Lady Azadiya's list in front of himself, picked the pages up, and then smacked them down on the table. "Of course they are," he snapped. "The child below the Age of Reason shall be given into Mistress Denrind's care, but for the course of the investigation the lot of them shall be remanded in the available cell."

"That anteroom will never fit all of them," Ibram said.

"Then Mistress Denrind will figure it out," the judge barked, and Ibram shut his mouth.

"I will, of course," Mistress Denrind said firmly. She looked to Commander Osthanes. "In coordination with the Cohort of Peace."

"Then that settles it," Mentor Perhara said. He stood and stretched his arms out in front of himself. His gar, which had formerly rested against the wall, came to his hand. "I will have to inform my Attendants, and the walls will need to be burned."

"Oh, I can help you there," Mentor Tikari said. She stood. "Zorion's off somewhere again, but once we find him, he'll have enough Torsion's Embrocation to purify the entire stack."

"I...might have made a mess of one panel, Mentor Perhara," Ahksell admitted meekly. "It's rather out of shape."

"Did you?" Mentor Perhara asked. He seemed pleasantly amused. "Ah well, we'll burn the pieces too."

Ibram dearly wanted to ask what Torsion's Embrocation consisted of, but he refrained. Alchemists had gotten touchy about their concoctions ever since some Learner had let slip the recipe for the luminescent sand in the glowbulbs. He stepped aside with Ahksell as the two mentors went past. Mistress Islozia opened and then closed the door behind them.

"If that's your final decision, your honor?" Commander Osthanes asked. He walked to the Judge's desk. Judge E'grard nodded brusquely, and the Commander turned to Warder Kamos and then the Monbriths. His arm flew between them.

"All right, get them up! Get them up," he ordered. "Time to start sorting this out for good."

The Monbriths all stood as best they were able, being either bound together or merely chained. Rustam's head sunk lower even as he rose, and his uncle was not much better, but his mother and sister stood with their chins leading. Satya held Diarmit's hand and smiled at him.

"May he be placed with the Suugans, Commander?" she asked and looked up quickly. "They already have a girl his age."

Commander Osthanes rubbed his patience strip, but nodded. "We'll see, Mistress," he said, as Mistress Islozia opened the door again. "Now, can we be on our way?"

The accused were led from the room with their escorts, and none of them looked back; Ibram checked. His eyebrow itched; he tucked his thumbs against his palms instead. He breathed in and out, and then turned back around. He saw Ahksell looking at him, and shook his head.

"Well," Lady Azadiya said, and stood. She called her gar to her side, and then gestured at her left and right. "Shall we leave you to your reports, your honor? I know events have happened rather quickly."

Attendant Serisan and Amota Lakum came out from behind the couch. Ibram moved aside to accommodate them.

"Yes, Mentor Hobon," Judge E'grard said in a strained voice. "I believe I have a lot of work to do."

"Then, I thank you for your service," Lady Azadiya said and bowed shortly. "And wish you well."

Mistress Denrind caught her hand as Ladyship turned to leave and pressed it between her palms. She shook for a moment, overcome, and then bowed. Lady Azadiya laid her free hand close to Mistress Denrind's biceps and urged her upright again.

"How good to meet you," she said and delicately removed her trapped fingers. "Ibram told me only good things, you know. I think perhaps you have much to discuss with the judge?"

Mistress Denrind nodded jerkily, but stood tall. "Yes, yes, we do."

"Then I bid you good day." Lady Azadiya turned gracefully. She was already out the door before Ibram fully realized she had moved, and then it was a scramble to catch up to her in the hallway. He beat a path behind Amota Lakum and Attendant Serisan, a froth of excitement boiling beneath his skin. Ibram's hands clenched and unclenched.

"Is that it?" Ahksell whispered at his side. "We won?"

"I—I think?" Ibram whispered back. "I think so."

He laughed, and then clapped a hand over his mouth. It was awful, of course. It was awful for the Monbriths, who were still in the thick of two investigations. The village was never going to forget what they'd done and, even if no one else was charged, then they still had to face the utter terror they'd created. Ahksell and he were going to have to write out much more complete reports, and Ibram would probably have to tell someone he thought a goddess hit him upside the head. His father might have to testify at Rustam's next trial, and he broke out in hives every time he traveled even one mile from Lityen.

Ibram took a deep breath to steady himself as they came out from the sitting room and out into the packed earth courtyard. But Fontis was going to be around long enough to be angry at the Monbriths. He had fixed his mistake in time to save the Suugans and the Terins and the Kolesars' shay shop. All those children on the list Attendant Serisan had gathered were to be tucked up in their beds that night, rather than in the sect's carriages.

He grinned to himself, and caught Lady Azadiya's calculating eye. He ducked his chin and rubbed the back of his neck. Doubtless, he remained one step outside of Lady Azadiya's good graces; he'd find out just how far he stood when they returned home to Lityen. He glanced towards Ahksell, who rocked on his heels and heaved an immense sigh of relief. Ibram laughed, and let himself feel a little glow of contentment. Ladyship couldn't argue with their results—not even Amota Lakum's disapproval could turn aside that fact. In front of them, Mentor Perhara had his hands outstretched with a pendant on a long string between them. Slowly, he raised the remaining building materials and sent them directly into Mentor Tikari's pyre. The flames burned green.

"We had better go and help him," Ladyship said. "Lakum, go find an Attendant and see about organizing another pyre in the village square. Ahksell, make sure Attendant Perhara doesn't embarrass himself when that Pendant of Ascension loses its charge."

Ibram laughed again. Ahksell poked him. He poked back. He turned his head and Ahksell beamed. In the center of the courtyard, a large timber cracked in two on the pyre, sending purple sparks flying out into the air. Amota Lakum bowed to Ladyship and retreated towards the entrance with Attendant Serisan. Ahksell clapped Ibram on the shoulder and jumped over the railing to land in the courtyard with an ostentatious roll.

Lady Azadiya walked to Ibram's side. She sighed deeply as the flames rose higher and leaned her gar against the railing. Ibram inclined himself in Ladyship's direction, and she raised her eyebrows at him indulgently. Ibram grinned.

"Yes, yes, well done as I said," Lady Azadiya said as she raised her chin to observe the pyre.

"You said I was wonderful, actually," Ibram said. "I remember it distinctly."

"That's not a direct translation of riant," she said wryly.

"Close enough."

She chuckled. "Ibram, go and make sure the carriages are prepared for our trip home."

He stepped away and then paused, and returned to her side. "So you aren't going to let me go?" he asked. "Or send me underground to Amota Evren's archive?"

"Let you go?" she repeated. "Why would I do that? Oh no, Ibram, I like an agent who recognizes when he is at fault just as much as when others are in the wrong."

"But Amota Lakum—"

She clapped when Ahksell pulled an entire section into the flame without dispersing the coals. "Your amota works for me," Lady Azadiya said. "And if I am satisfied than he may considered himself to be so as well. This is not to say I will be ignoring you from now on." She smiled and Ibram thought he saw a golden glow, surely reflected from the fire, in her eyes. "We shall have to see what happens next."

AUTHOR'S NOTE

Thank you for reading my novel! I hope you enjoyed reading *The Gilty Party* as much as I enjoyed writing it.

If you've left a review for my work, thank you again! Reviews help others find my book.

Look out for the next adventure in The Alchemist's Agent series: The Elixir of Inheritance *coming soon!*

ABOUT THE AUTHOR

E. M. Burnham likes fantasies, mysteries, and stories of all shapes and sizes, which is why she's decided to write them all at once. She's been a Jedi, a Fellow of The Ring, a Trekker, and even a Newsie, raised on Agatha Christie with a shot of Dorothy L. Sayers and a chaser of Margery Allingham.

She has lived and worked on three continents (and somehow earned two masters degrees in the midst of all that moving!) but settled down to be near her family in the United States. Check out her other work at emburnham.com

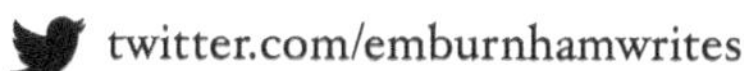 twitter.com/emburnhamwrites

ALSO BY E. M. BURNHAM

THE ALCHEMIST'S AGENT SERIES

Cursebird On A Wire

The Gilty Party

STANDALONE WORKS

You Fight You Get Back uP